DARK ECSTASY

"Jean," Nicole whispered, "come here. Remember what I said last night—that every woman who looked at you would wonder . . ."

"How it is to bed with Satan?" Jean mocked.

"Yes. And now I know—God help me, I know!"

"You think me evil, then?" he murmured.

"No—no. I think you wild and terrible and wonderful beyond belief, and I am now truly afraid. You are burned in with fire upon the very tissue of my soul. What will become of me when you have fled?"

"I shall come back to you," he whispered, *"though it be from hell itself. . . ."*

"DAZZLING!"
—*The New York Times*

FRANK YERBY

THE DEVIL'S LAUGHTER

A DELL BOOK

Published by
DELL PUBLISHING CO., INC.
1 Dag Hammarskjold Plaza
New York, N.Y. 10017
Copyright © 1953 by Frank Yerby
All rights reserved. For information
contact The Dial Press, New York, N.Y. 10017.
Dell ® TM 681510, Dell Publishing Co., Inc.

ISBN: 0-440-11917-0

Reprinted by arrangement with The Dial Press
Printed in the United States of America
Previous Dell Edition #1917
New Dell Edition
First printing—October 1977

1

"It's been a long time," Lucienne Talbot said.

Jean Paul looked at her.

"Sorry?" he said.

"Yes!" Lucienne said. "Yes, yes, yes! I'm sick of this. . . ."

Jean looked around the room. All the light came from the fireplace though it was still late afternoon outside. The fireglow flickered on the brown walls, washed the copperware with warmth. He saw the cookpot on the fire, smelled the little fish bubbling in the stew. The copper pots gleamed. He could see his own face in them, a little distorted, all planes and angles. His black eyes looked huge.

Lucienne stood up, the motion abrupt but not ungraceful. He could see her tawny hair reflected in the copper pans. Nothing she ever does is ungraceful, he thought. And she should always be washed in firelight—like now. . . .

The firelight made a painting: the crusty loaves on the table with the wine and the cheese; the bellows, the tongs, the andirons in their places; the sudden, yellow-white glow of the pillowcase on the little bed, half hidden behind the screen.

"I like it," Jean Paul said.

"You like anything! I—I didn't start out with you for this, Jean Paul Marin! Not to hide in an attic. Not to live in fear of the police. Not to become your mistress. No, something more shameful than even a mistress, because men are sometimes proud of their mistresses. . . ."

"I'm proud of you," Jean Paul said.

"I doubt it!" Lucienne spat. "You'd think I was old and ugly. You never take me anywhere. You hide me here in this filthy hole. Name of a name! I don't know why I ever took up with you, Jean!"

"Why did you?" Jean Paul said.

"I don't know! God knows you're nothing to look at. And as for brains—a millstone couldn't be any thicker than whatever that is you have between your ears. Talents? None. Prospects? Many. I'll name them for you. . . ."

"Don't bother," Jean Paul said.

"You don't want to hear them, do you, Jean Marin? Not very pleasant—your prospects, since they start with being hanged for high treason and end with being drawn and quartered! I still don't see why I ever . . ."

Jean smiled again. His smile was something. It did things to his face, making it almost handsome.

"You said it was because you loved me," he said.

"I lied! Or I was a fool. Or both. Yes, both. When I think of my career . . ."

"What career?" Jean Paul said cruelly.

"Oh, you! I would have had a career, but for you. Men looked at me. Noblemen. I didn't dance badly, and I was improving. . . ."

"Then I came along. Jean Paul Marin, son of Henri Marin, the shipowner. Richest man on the whole Côte d'Azur. Sure that had nothing to do with it, *Chérie?*"

She stared at him. The firelight was in the hazel eyes that changed color with the weather, or the dress she was wearing, making them yellow. Like a tigress, Jean thought.

"Yes," she said, "that had something to do with it. That had everything to do with it. I thought I'd wear velvet and be covered with diamonds. Why else would I have accepted you?"

"Sorry I disappointed you," Jean Paul said.

"I knew your father was a straitlaced old vulture. But you said he'd get used to the idea of your being married to an actress. . . ."

"A dancer," Jean corrected.

"What's the difference? Anyhow I didn't think that two years later, I still wouldn't be married to you, that I'd still be risking disgrace—and for what?"

"My father is—difficult," Jean sighed.

"Difficult? He's impossible! But you're worse. You with your revolutionary cant. You fool! Can't you see that the world you're trying to destroy is the only one I can make my way in? Or you—for that matter. Destroy privilege and you rid France of all the men rich enough and grand enough to offer patronage. . . ."

"I don't need patronage," Jean Paul said. "All I want is justice. . . ."

"Hang justice! And you're still depending upon patronage. If it weren't for your father, you couldn't even afford this miserable hole. . . ."

Jean Paul stared at her. After two years he still had that feeling, looking at her. He hurt. This tall, tawny one. This untamed one with the grace of a great cat. And the claws.

"I've had enough," she said. "I should be dancing at l'Opéra by now—acting at the Comédie Française. And I will, too! In spite of you, Jean Paul!"

"By whose patronage?" Jean said. "The Comte de Gravereau's? But such men as he demand a price. What are you prepared to pay?"

"That's my business," she said flatly. "But as far as the price is concerned, I'll tell you that. The same price, my Jeannot, I bought you with—good enough?"

"Too good," Jean Paul said.

He looked at her, seeing her cheeks flushed in the firelight, the good bones of her face, her cheekbones high, angular, causing her hazel eyes to slant a little, the mouth full, pouting, so that almost he could feel it, the long, slim, good legs, molding the peasant's dress she wore, and suddenly he wanted her. Or rather he wanted her more acutely than usual, because he wanted her all the time.

He came over to her.

"Don't touch me!" she snarled at him.

But he put up his big hands and caught her, hurting her arms, and she threw herself backward away from him, turning her face from side to side so that he had to bring one of his hands up and catch her chin, holding it so hard that he bruised her a little.

Her mouth was ice. But it didn't stay like that. It never did. That was the one thing that was left between them after all the quarreling.

He could feel it moving under his, forming words that came out muffled, but not fighting any more, not drawing away, whispering: "You beast! Damn your eyes, Jeannot, my Jeannot, I hate you, you know me too well, too well, my Jeannot, oh, damn you, let me go!"

But he didn't let her go and her mouth wasn't making

sounds any more, but it was still moving, softening upon his, moving, clinging, opening under the steady pressure, and the whole of her made one long caress, scalding through the layers of clothing.

She was aware suddenly, that he was laughing. He thrust her away from him, hard, holding her at arm's length, by the shoulders, and his clear baritone laughter rang among the rafters. It was one of the many things he could do that were absolutely fiendish.

"You dog!" she whispered. "Dog and son of a dog! How could you. . . ."

He looked at her and his black eyes were alight with laughter and with malice.

"This way," he said, "I know you shall always be waiting for my return. . . ."

Then he picked up a bundle of manuscripts from the table, and started for the door.

Lucienne stared at him.

"But, Jeannot, your supper?" she said, and her voice was almost tender.

"I'm not hungry," he laughed. "Except, perhaps, for love. . . ."

Then he went out of the door and closed it softly behind him.

Lucienne stood there a long time, staring at the door. Then, very slowly, she smiled.

"There has always been more than one purveyor of that commodity, my Jeannot," she said softly. Then she turned back to the fire.

Jean Paul Marin stopped at the edge of the road leading up to the village and looked at the sky. He stood there only a few minutes, but while he watched, the clouds that had been piling up all afternoon over the Mediterranean ran together so that there wasn't any blue left and the little talking wind got a noise into it like crying. The colors went out of everything, leaving the world etched in grays, and the wind went searching along the land with a moaning sound until the trees were bending over before it and Jean knew what it was.

The mistral. He hated the mistral with that curious kind of hatred he had for all the things he couldn't understand. He wasn't superstitious, but he knew that the mistral did things to people. It was an ugly, nervous wind and it went on day and night without stopping sometimes for weeks and things happened because of that wind. There would be tavern brawls in the village and peasant wives would be beaten, and if, as usually happened this time of year, the supply of white bread failed—there might even be a few minor *Jacqueries* . . . even—murders. For the mistral always whispered things into a man's heart that shouldn't be there. . . .

He stood there a moment, listening to the wind. It tugged at his cloak, and whipped his hair about his face and little prickly things crawled up and down his spine. Every fear he had spoke to him out of it. Every hate. He could hear Lucienne's voice in it, saying the things she had said to him that night a week ago, when he had come into the Inn and found her seated across the table from the Comte de Gravereau, both her small hands imprisoned in his noble clasp. . . .

Jean had started toward them. But at the last moment, Gervais la Moyte, Comte de Gravereau, had stood up, laughing. Lucienne got up more slowly. She was smiling. Then the Comte bowed over her hand and was gone.

Jean came up to her and stood beside her. It was a long time before she noticed he was there. When she did, she saw the pain in his eyes.

She had smiled at him then. Wound her fingers through his hair.

"Don't be silly, Jean," she said; "I'm quite accustomed to pleasantries from that sort of gallant. You mustn't mind. It's one of the risks of my art. . . ."

"Lucienne," he had said, thickly.

"I prefer," she murmured, "someone solid and—and real—like you, my Jeannot. . . ."

But all the time, her eyes had kept straying toward that door.

Hearing the sound of her voice, remembered now in the mistral, the pain Jean Paul felt was physical, real.

"*Merde!*" he screamed aloud into the teeth of the wind, and plodded on, up the hill.

He was twenty years old that November day of 1784, and, physically, he wasn't very imposing. He was well above average height, but he was very thin. His hands and feet didn't fit the rest of him. His mouth was too big,

too; but he wasn't ugly. His mouth saved him from that—
his big, wide, mobile mouth that always looked like it was
going to laugh—and usually did. But his laughter was
strange. It was filled with mockery for all things under
earth and heaven, even for himself. His sister, Thérèse,
called it devil's laughter, and hated the sound of it. . . .

He had a good nose, straight and thin and a little arched,
and his eyes were very fine. They were big and black and
laughing, and they had lights in them—mocking lights.
His hair hadn't any lights. It was black, too, and hung
down uncombed and unpowdered to his shoulders. The
whole of him made a discordant ensemble that people
found vaguely disturbing. Lucienne, for instance, said he
was an *enragé*, a madman, and that he had fierce eyes.

That wasn't true. They were wild sometimes—with pain,
with passion, but most of the time they were filled with
malicious glee at the follies of mankind. Sometimes, when
he was alone, they were deep and dark and brooding—a
little haunted. His walk, his way of carrying himself was
just like the rest of his family's, so that anyone could
recognize the Marins even at a distance; but his face was
different. Only those men born strangers into their world
have faces like that.

He was. He couldn't accept it.

"Jean Paul," the Abbé Grégoire said, "will either be
destroyed by life—or he'll change it. . . . There won't be
any compromises. . . ."

As usual, the Abbé Grégoire was right.

He walked on, now, into the teeth of the mistral. He
hated that wind, but like all the things he hated, it had
for him a perverse fascination. He was like that. Everything he disliked had in it some quality which excited his
admiration.

Even Gervais la Moyte, Comte de Gravereau.

I'll kill him, he thought, bending over against the wind.
I'll stick an épée into his guts and twist it. . . . But at
the same time that wickedly honest part of his mind he
had no control over whispered: You'd give your soul to
be like him, wouldn't you, Jean Paul Marin? To be tall as
he is and fair with laughing blue eyes—to be witty and
gay—to ride like him, to dance, to whisper words like
little pearls into a woman's ear. . . . Wouldn't you Jean
Paul? Wouldn't you?

And straightening up, he loosed his laughter. The wind took it, snatching it away from his lips, leaving them moving soundlessly, his whole body jerking with laughter.

"Jean Paul Marin," he laughed, "you're a fool!"

He went on then, up the steep path toward the village perched like a crow's nest on the mountain top, bending over once more before the wind, holding his tricorne on his head with one hand, and gathering his cloak together with the other.

Before he was halfway there, it started to rain. The rain came down in sheets, slanting before the wind, and in two minutes he was soaked to the skin. But he didn't increase his pace. He took a queer, dark pleasure in his discomfort. The rain was like needles of ice, and the mistral talked through it. Here, higher up, the trees were different from the ones on the shores of the Mediterranean. They had leaves that could change color, could fall.

The leaves went whipping before the wind, and collected in the roadside ditches, become torrents now, and hurtled down the mountainside with the water. The road was paved with cobblestones, glistening with the rain, and it was hard to keep his footing. He slipped time and again, but he went on doggedly.

Then he was walking the crooked streets of the little village. Even in that rain, there were a few people about, wrapped in their rags, and when they turned at the sound of his good boots on the stones, he could see the hunger in their eyes. Saint Jule, the village, was like many another village in France, rather better off, in fact, than most, but every time Jean Paul saw it, he wanted to curse. Or cry. It was the domain of the Comte de Gravereau, usually busy at the elaborate idleness of Versailles.

Except now, Jean thought bitterly, when he has more important things to do!

But the Comte's bailiffs and the local farmer-general of taxes were not idle. Jean Paul saw an old woman, stooping in the rain, carefully picking up one by one the chicken feathers that the rain had washed from someone else's yard and left before her door.

It was, he knew, a matter of life and death with her. The feathers meant to the collectors that she could afford to eat fowl, and therefore her assessment could be increased. What she paid now, left her on the edge of starvation. Any increase would be a death sentence. A slow death, but very certain.

He stopped beside her and helped her at the task. His fingers were young and nimble. He made short work of it.

She smiled at him out of her lined face, and part of the wetness on her cheeks was tears.

"My thanks, M'sieur," she said.

Jean looked at her. He wondered, idly, how old she was. He knew she was probably many years short of the sixty she looked, but when he asked her, her answer shocked him.

"Twenty-eight, M'sieur," the old woman said.

He fumbled in his pocket and came out with a louis d'or. But the woman shook her head.

"Haven't you any little money, M'sieur?" she said. "Where could I change a louis? At the grocer's, the butcher's? You know better, M'sieur. With my lord's spies about, were I to come in with such a fortune, the bailiffs would be waiting at my door before I reached home again. . . ."

Jean Paul put the louis back and came out with a handful of écus and sous—all the small change he had. It was much less than the louis d'or he had offered her, but she was better off with less. At least, by using extreme caution, she could spend the smaller coins. They would last her weeks—even months.

She dropped the money into a big pocket in her skirt. Then she seized both his hands and covered them with kisses. Jean stood there and took it, the pain moving inside his heart.

"It won't always be like this," he growled.

"I know, M'sieur," she whispered, "but I won't live to see it. . . ."

Jean walked on, slowly. He was going to the house of Pierre du Pain, his partner in crime. Pierre was perfect for the task. No one would ever dream that this droll fellow, commonly supposed to be mad, was a printer, and an expert one at that. Nor was there anything strange in the association of Jean Paul Marin and the man he himself had hired as night watchman for certain of the Marin warehouses. That these warehouses contained a printing press, paper, ink and other supplies, nobody knew —not even Henri Marin. All the authorities and the in-

furiated nobility did know was that someone was flooding
the whole Côte d'Azur with quite treasonable pamphlets,
written with diabolical skill. For their telling style, Jean
Paul was responsible. For the printing, Pierre. . . .

But he never got to Pierre's house. For as he turned the
last corner, he saw Raoul, his manservant, running toward
him.

"M'sieur Jean!" Raoul called, breathlessly. "By all the
Saints, I have searched the whole world over for you!"

Jean mocked him with his eyes.

"That is grave," he smiled. "This is something of importance, doubtless?"

"Of the gravest importance," Raoul panted. "Your
respected sister, Mademoiselle Thérèse, demands to see
you. She·warned me not to return without you. . . ."

"*Enfer!*" Jean swore. Then he smiled again. His little
sister was very dear to him. "Very well, Raoul," he said,
"I'll come. . . ."

Thérèse was waiting for him at the big iron gate of the
Villa Marin. She was wrapped in a cloak, but her head
was bare. Down here, on the Côte itself, the rain had
stopped, and even the mistral was only a murmur.

At the sight of him, she stamped her tiny foot.

"Jean, Jean," she cried, "how you do try my patience!
We have been waiting for you for hours. . . ."

Jean looked at his sister. Thérèse Marin was small, like
all the Marins. But unlike Henri Marin, her father, and
Bertrand, her eldest brother, she had a kind of delicate
beauty, inherited from the mother who had died in giving her birth. Of them all, only Jean Paul was like her; for
in him, too, the basic coarseness of the Marins had been
refined.

But now his gift for mockery got the better of him. He
made her a sweeping bow.

"I am at your command, Mademoiselle," he said drily,
"or is it—" he paused, splitting the word deliberately into
two syllables, "Ma Dame Thérèse, Comtesse de Gravereau?"

Thérèse looked at him. Her eyes were the exact dupli-
cates of his own—except that they had no mockery in
them, but only tenderness.

"Jean," she said gently, "why must you be this way?
So—so prickly. Why can't you accept life as it is?"

"Because," Jean said, "I'm me. Because, my little sister,

I happen to love you. And because I don't like to see pearls cast before swine."

"Jean Paul!" Thérèse said.

"That hurts, doesn't it, little sister? The truth always does. Gervais la Moyte, Comte de Gravereau—very fine, eh? But strip away those titles, those pretty, meaningless words, and what have you left? Gervais la Moyte, blackguard. Gervais la Moyte, roué, drunkard, gamester. And we're supposed to make a leg before such a man. I read for the law; I finished the Lycée, and afterwards the University. I've forgotten more than that man has ever known. For what then, do I owe him homage? Because some ancestor of his was a brigand who built a castle near a bridge or at a crossroad and made himself rich and powerful by thievery? They are still all thieves, your fine nobles! And I, for one, would make an end to them!"

Thérèse put her hands over her ears.

"I won't listen to you," she said.

"Ah, but you will," Jean laughed. "You, and ultimately all the world. You know, don't you, why he is here? No, don't tell me that, not the simple answer. To ask our father for your hand—that, of course. But why, Thérèse? Name of heaven, why?"

"Because," Thérèse said, "because I am pretty and good and he loves me. . . ."

"Name of a name! Thérèse, how can you be so stupid? There are any number of noblewomen who are pretty. There may even be a few among them who are good, though that I doubt. You've seen this man. You know how proud he is. Why then would he sully his ancient line with the blood of commoners? The answer is simple, my poor Thérèse. Because he is poor and we are rich. Like all his arrogant breed, he thought his lands, his feudal dues: rents, *corvées, traites, lods et ventes, plaits-à-marcis, banvins* and a thousand others would last him forever. He dreamed of spending more than his income for the rest of his life without going into bankruptcy. . . ."

Thérèse stood there, looking at her brother. But she didn't interrupt him.

"All over France, now, the lines are crumbling. And always for this same reason. We bourgeois are intelligent, patient, industrious. And the nobles are too proud, too indolent to engage in trade. All France is sunk in ruin because of them. The King, without knowing it, is as ruined as the rest. They try expedients now—anything to save themselves. The King makes great offices with rich stipends and no duties, but even that cannot save them all. . . .

"So now, if you are Gervais la Moyte, what must you do? How can you keep up your châteaux, your stables, your gaming, wenching, your assorted mistresses from l'Opéra and the Comédie? Simple, my boy, why didn't I think of it before? That Simone de Beauvieux, old Marquis de Beauvieux' eldest daughter—didn't she save the old man by marrying into a maritime family? Rich canaille, fat, stupid oxen—with, I grant you, a certain head for trade. . . . Let's see now, what was their name? Martine —Marin, that's it! Now, wasn't there something about a daughter? Probably bovine and dull; but still, my old one, the sacrifice must be made. . . ."

"Stop it!" Thérèse screamed at him. "You stop it this instant, Jean!"

He looked at her. She was crying.

"I'm sorry, Thérèse," he said, "I didn't mean to make you cry. . . ."

He bent and kissed her, gently. She stopped crying after a few minutes—smiled at him.

"Come," she said, "Father sent for you. . . ."

Jean Paul stiffened.

"Why?" he growled.

"M'sieur le Comte is leaving us. Father wants you there so that we might all say good-bye properly."

"Leaving us?" Jean said.

"Yes. He has asked for my hand—and—and has been accepted. Father feels that the whole family should show him every courtesy—now. . . ."

"I'll see him turning on a spit above a bed of coals in hell first!" Jean roared. "Thérèse, how could you?"

"Because I am a woman," Thérèse whispered. "And Gervais is very fair; you must admit that, Jean. . . ."

Jean Paul stared at his sister.

"You're trying to tell me that you love this *cochon?*" he got out. "That's it, Thérèse?"

Thérèse bowed her head.

"That's it, Jean," she whispered. "I love him—I do, oh, I do!"

"The sweet blue eyes of God!" Jean swore.

"You mustn't swear, Jean," Thérèse said gently. "He's going to try to do better. He promised me that. I had heard of his evil ways—I—I taxed him with them. He admitted quite freely he has been no saint. He swore he'd never grieve me. And he could have lied, Jean. It was fine of him not to. . . ."

"His kind are too proud to lie," Jean said. "But they do worse. . . ."

"There is nothing worse," Thérèse said.

"Dear God!" Jean Paul whispered.

"Besides, you're being unfair, Jean. Gervais is a nobleman and a man of honor. Yet you scream at me if I so much as mention his name. Odd, isn't it? Let me or anyone else say aught of that common little theatre girl, Lucienne Talbot . . ."

"Thérèse!"

"You see? She dances half naked at the Comédie—and God alone knows what she does afterwards. But to your mind, that painted little minx is both fair and good. . . ."

"She is! I'd stake my life on that."

"Pray God you never have to," Thérèse said. "Come Jean, Father will grow impatient—and you still have to change your clothes. Instead of staying in out of the rain like a sensible person . . ."

"Hang Father's impatience," Jean said; "and I won't change my clothes. La Moyte can see me like this, and be damned! I tell you . . ."

"Oh, don't be childish!" Thérèse said. "Gervais won't care in the slightest how bedraggled you are. You will only shame me. Is that what you want?"

Jean smiled at her, quite suddenly.

"No, little sister," he said, "that's not what I want. Come along, I'll change . . ."

They went up to the villa through the icily perfect formal garden. Everything in it had been tortured into geometric forms. Even the shrubs themselves.

"I hate it!" Jean Paul burst out. "Why—"

"I know," Thérèse said patiently. "Why didn't they leave nature alone—à la Jean-Jacques Rousseau? You won't draw me into that argument again. Here we are. Now you go and get dressed!"

"Your obedient servant, Madame la Comtesse!" Jean

mocked, and ran up the stairs to his room. When he came down again, he looked very little better than before, except that his clothes were dry.

In the doorway of the grand salon, Jean Paul paused, gazing at the guests. He saw the Abbé Grégoire's wise old face, seamed and lined above his brown robe. There was the meager form of Simone, Jean's sister-in-law. She was trying to be gracious to the Abbé, condescending to her dull clod of a husband, and to ignore her father-in-law. She was failing in all three attempts. It was in the nature of things that she should fail.

Only Gervais la Moyte, Comte de Gravereau, was entirely at ease. And that, too, was in the nature of things.

He towered by a full head over everyone else in the salon except Jean. And he was taller than Jean by a full two inches. He was incredibly handsome. And in his court dress, a pale blue habit à la française of heavily embroidered silk, with the rich, creamy lace of his lingerie shirt and cravat spilling out at throat and bosom and wrist, his lace handkerchief trailing with negligent arrogance between the fingers of his left hand, his blond hair powdered into exquisite whiteness, his smallsword with the jeweled hilt flaring the tails of his coat, he was a peacock among barnyard fowl.

He looked at Jean, and his blue eyes were cold. This one, he thought suddenly, is dangerous. Don't know when I've seen a more intelligent face. And intelligence among the lower orders is dangerous, especially now. . . .

He took out a golden snuffbox ornamented with the crest of the house of Gravereau, and took snuff delicately, touching the lace handkerchief lightly to his nostrils.

Jean Paul stood there. Sweated. All his laughter had left him now. His hatred for this man was sickness, physical pain.

Gervais smiled at him.

"Ah," he said, "the young philosopher condescends to join our mundane gathering? So good of you, Jean. . . ."

Jean Paul didn't answer. Don't bait me, he thought. By God's love, don't bait me. I am but inches away from murder now. . . .

But Gervais was bowing over Thérèse's small hand.

"Mademoiselle will forgive me," he murmured, "that I must depart with such haste from so happy a scene. My departure is indeed painful to me, more painful than she can possibly imagine. . . ."

"Then," Thérèse breathed, her eyes dark stars, "why do you go, M'sieur?"

"The pressure of court affairs," he whispered. "A mission for His Majesty. More than that I cannot say—even to you, Mademoiselle. I trust that you will forgive me?"

"You are forgiven," Thérèse smiled, "if you will come again—soon. . . ."

"My feet will be winged," Gervais laughed. Then he turned to the others.

"Your blessing, good Abbé," he said, and knelt upon one knee before the old priest. The Abbé Grégoire murmured the Latin words, and made the sign of the cross above the Comte's head. Gervais rose, and taking the Abbé's hand, kissed his ring as though he were the Pope.

"And now my good father-in-law-to-be," he said, and embraced Henri Marin, kissing him upon both cheeks. Jean saw his father's dark face go mahogany red with embarrassed pleasure, and in spite of himself, he contrasted his father's squat ugliness, born of his dark Sicilian blood, with Gervais la Moyte's striking good looks. Father, Jean thought, looks like Punch—and Bertrand is even uglier. . . .

Bertrand, being himself a member of the Noblesse, by virtue of having purchased an office that carried with it a title—to such desperate straits had the King of France come—and having married Simone de Beauvieux, daughter of an authentic, if extremely decayed noble house, received much the same sort of embrace. But there was a difference. Slight, but still a difference.

Jean Paul saw at once what it was. Gervais was capable of a real affection for his father-in-law-to-be. Henri Marin was simple and without pretense. He was still, actually, Enrico Marino, a sturdy Sicilian brigand-pirate, catapulted by a trick of fate into great fortune, because alone of his numerous brothers, he had seen that more could be gained on the side of the law than fighting against it. Gervais could admire this bluff old rogue.

But the true nobility, the Noblesse de l'épée, the nobles of the sword, had nothing but contempt for the new Noblesse de la Robe, the men who had bought their way out of the ranks of commoners by trading upon the financial distress of the realm. That the old nobility was itself responsible for this distress did not in any way mitigate their ferocious contempt for these presumptuous upstarts preening themselves in borrowed feathers. Gervais, Jean realized, would never forgive Bertrand for his effrontery in having married a noblewoman, even so sad a specimen of nobility as Simone. His embrace then, was tinged with the most graceful display of contempt imaginable.

And, bending over Simone's hand, he scarcely troubled to conceal his mockery. He would have had more respect for a daughter of joy than he had for a noblewoman who married a commoner.

"So, my dear Simone," he murmured, so that none but she could hear him, "we become birds of a feather, eh?"

But Jean saw her stiffen, and guessed at his words.

Then it was Jean Paul's turn. Gervais was approaching him, his right hand outstretched. The social distinctions were to be drawn to the hair. A simple handshake—and even this was condescension—was to suffice for Jean Paul Marin.

Jean stood there, his hands at his side. I will be damned and in hell he thought, before I will take his hand.

Gervais stopped, his hand still outstretched. His blue eyes became splinters of ice.

"I offered you my hand, Marin," he said.

"I am aware of that, M'sieur le Comte," Jean said.

"Jean!" Thérèse cried.

Jean could feel the eyes of the others upon him, hot as coals in embarrassed rage. Only Simone, for an instant, permitted a tiny light of admiration to show, then it was gone, and he was left alone to face the pack.

"I am still offering you my hand," Gervais said, and his smile was deadly.

"And I," Jean said, furious that his voice shook a little, "am still within my rights when I refuse to take the hand of one of the despoilers of France. Or would M'sieur prefer that I shake hands with him and then send for servants with water and towels and wash my hands in his presence?"

Gervais let his hand fall. The smile on his face never wavered. In spite of himself, Jean had to admire his bearing.

"You are courageous, *M. le Philosophe*," Gervais said.

"But then, perhaps, you are merely sure of yourself. I should scarcely risk jeopardizing the affections of Mademoiselle, your sister, by sending my lackeys to cane you within an inch of your life as you so richly deserve for your bad manners. Upon that you rely, is it not so?"

"I rely upon nothing," Jean said, "but my good right arm—with an épée, or a saber, or even a pistol—as M'sieur prefers. . . ."

Gervais stared at him. Then he threw back his head and laughed, merrily.

"Now really, Marin," he said, "but you are fantastic!"

Then he turned and bowed grandly to the others.

"I choose to forget this display," he smiled. "Youth—and too much wine, perhaps. Mayhap the boy should be bled. I should be glad to place my personal physician at your disposal, M'sieur Marin. . . ."

"He'll be bled all right," Henri Marin roared, "but with a horsewhip, not a scalpel! Jean, go to your room, and await my pleasure! This instant, boy!"

Jean looked at his father. Then very slowly, he smiled.

"Fantastic," he murmured. "I thank you for that word, M. le Comte. But I can think of a better. You are not fantastic, Father—you are merely grotesque. And not everything is for sale, as you will learn one day. . . ."

"Go to your room!" Henri Marin thundered.

"No," Jean said, easily, pleasantly; "I do only what I please. And if ever again you lay hands upon me, I shall forget you are my father, a fact that I have always regretted infinitely. . . . Ah, yes, I shall forget it quite easily. . . ."

Then, looking at the others, he started to laugh.

"Why do you laugh?" Bertrand demanded.

"I am seeing visions," Jean said, the laughter bubbling through his voice. "I see the comic dance that M. le Comte will soon do upon thin air, supported only by the noose about his neck; how odd the good Abbé will look defrocked of his robe of vain superstitions; Bertrand de-titled, plundered of his riches; Simone, and you, my poor sister, trying to boil your patents of nobility to make a stew to ease your hunger. . . ."

Henri Marin stared at his son.

"And me?" he growled uneasily.

Jean stopped laughing.

"You, my poor father," he said gently, "will be spared all pain. Because you won't be here to see any of these things. . . ."

"Mad!" Gervais la Moyte spat.

"Ah, yes," Jean smiled; "or, perhaps sane, and living in a mad world. Who knows?"

Then he marched out the door, leaving the sound of his laughter trailing behind him.

The others stood there, staring at one another. There was something eerie about that laughter. Something, the Abbé Grégoire thought suddenly, demonic. . . .

"*Ma foi!*" he said aloud, "the boy's possessed!"

At the sound of his voice, they all turned toward him. Then one by one by one they bowed their heads, hearing the chant of exorcism falling from the old man's lips.

And even the Comte de Gravereau quailed before the acceptance in their eyes.

2

When Jean Paul came out of the villa, it was raining again. But he smiled into the rain, lifting his lean face so that trickles of water ran down his cheeks. The weather suited his mood.

Again he went up the road, winding up from the seashore into the foothills of the Alpes Maritimes, going by Lucienne's house without even pausing. It took him the better part of an hour to reach Saint Jule, for the village was high up in the lower Alpes. He wound through the crooked cobblestone streets of the village and stopped at last before a house.

It was made of stone like all the houses in Saint Jule, and the tiles of the roof poured torrents into the streets. He knocked. The door opened the barest crack. Then it was flung wide, and Pierre du Pain stood there, grinning.

"Come in, come in!" he laughed. "Marianne! Regard our fine friend of a philosopher! He looks like a Gallic cock refused by all the hens and drooping in his plumage, the poor old one!"

Pierre had red hair and eyes that were a mixture of green and blue. A peasant, lacking the usual dead, beaten animal's face of a peasant. His face, Jean thought, for the thousandth time, is half saint's, half satyr's. A brave face, though, and intelligent. But mad, like my own. We live in a world suited only to madmen; so perhaps we shall both survive. . . .

He smiled at his friend. Pierre's father had been a well-to-do peasant, a thing that had been possible in Pierre's boyhood, and was possible even now in scattered sections of France, usually those whose kindly, rustic nobility attached themselves to the land and refused to waste their substance at Versailles. He had sent the boy to study for the priesthood, with the result that Pierre could read and write not only French, but Latin and Greek. And his intelligence and skill had proved Pierre's downfall. For among the authors he had read had been Rousseau, Voltaire, and Montesquieu. . . .

So Pierre had quit the cloister, deciding that a God who permitted the bulk of the people to starve in the midst of the richest agricultural country in all Europe had scant need of his services. Shortly thereafter he had met Marianne, which clinched matters. . . .

After that, he had worked at a dozen trades, apprenticing himself at last to the printers of Marseille. And it was there that Jean Paul Marin, sent down by his father to have some bills of lading printed, had found him.

"Come in, Jean," Marianne was saying, "let me dry your things. Some wine, perhaps?"

It was one of Jean Paul's triumphs that he had at last induced the wife of his friend to call him Jean instead of M'sieur, or even Patron. He was proud of that. One day, there would be no more Seigneurs, my lords, patrons . . . some day. . . .

"Wine?" Pierre roared. "But of course! On such a day, a man has need of wine. Especially a philosopher—for what happens when one's philosophy has been drenched by the rains and whipped by the lash of the mistral?"

"Shut up!" Jean snapped at him in mock wrath.

"Ah, *M. le Philosophe* is in an ill humor! That's grave. But everything is always grave with our philosopher, and it always makes nothing, hein? Have you reserved for me my silken bed at le Petit Trianon, with *l'Autrichienne* in it, perhaps?"

"You," Jean grinned, "offend my nostrils. Yes, Marianne, I'll have wine."

"We'll work tonight?" Pierre said. "It's good to work. I will set up in print all the fine, brave, glorious words of my philosopher who seeks to destroy a system in which he, himself, is rich and powerful, for the benefit of the poor, stupid canaille. When the revolution comes, I shall be a prince. I shall condescend to let *M. le Philosophe* keep my stables. I shall make him spade up the dung of horses, and banish him from my presence because he will then offend *my* nostrils. *Ça ira!*"

"You're drunk," Marianne snapped.

"Ah, yes! 'Tis good to be drunk, my dear. Better to be

drunk with wine than with words. For I am not one of the
illusioned ones like my philosophic friend, here. He cannot
see that when one up-ends the whole world, one merely
sets up a new nobility, which, lacking the years of practice of the old, cannot help but be more brutish in its
oppressions. . . ."

"You believe that?" Jean said, looking at him.

"I know it. Equality is an idea foreign to the mind of
man. Level every man overnight, and what will you have,
my Jean? The clever, the ruthless will claw their way to
the top, and again you will have Nobles, Bourgeois, and
Canaille—called by different names perhaps—but always
the same things. The more it changes—don't look at me
like that, *mon vieux!* It is true. I am desolate that it is
true. I regret infinitely that it is true. But man is the
most obscene of all animals, always greedy, brutish, and
vile. . . ."

"But man produces philosophers," Jean smiled, "and
poets. . . ."

"And painters, and whores—which are the noblest of
his works. For they ease the sickness at the heart of man
more than any poet, or any philosopher!"

"Pierre!" Marianne said.

"Forgive me," Pierre laughed, and pinched her round
cheek. "A good wife is even better—for she combines
within herself courtesan, cook, and companion. . . ."

"Liar," Jean laughed.

"I don't lie. If I have any sickness, it is the sickness of
truth. It makes a difference, then, that the grandson of
M. le Comte de Gravereau shall be a peasant and sweat
in the sun? Will he be any less a peasant? Will his hunger
be less, or his stripes less painful? Jean, my Jean, brother
of my heart—the thing you do is madness, and is better
left undone. . . ."

"What should I do, then?" Jean said.

"Sit in the sun and drink your wine. Make love. Laugh
—but not as you usually laugh, with a demented devil.
Laugh from your belly, your good, full belly with good
laughter. Beget sons, many sons and always refuse to
think. For that is the final sickness for which there is no
cure. . . ."

"You're mad," Jean chuckled and stretched out his legs
toward the fire, so that the smoke curled from his sodden
boots.

Marianne was busying herself before the fire, and Jean smelled the savory odor of the rabbit stew, cooked in wine, that came from the black pot hanging over the fire. If he had been a stranger, Pierre's supper would have disappeared in an instant into a specially prepared hiding place. In the first place, a peasant had always to give the appearance of starvation to escape the greedy fingers of his Seigneur's bailiffs; in the second, that Pierre had rabbit at all meant that he had been poaching upon the Comte's game preserves, and that was by law still a hanging offense, though the law was seldom so rigorously enforced nowadays.

He was, Jean discovered at the first taste of the stew, amazingly hungry. He had been cursed by nature with a miserably poor appetite, but tonight he equaled Pierre's ability as a trencherman. It would have been good to sit before the fire and continue their half-bantering, half-serious talk; but half a night's work lay before them.

Pierre kissed Marianne good-bye, and they went down the road until it met the fork that led down and away to Marseille. There, in the shadow of the trees, Jean had horses tethered; for the distance was too great to be covered on foot.

Two hours later, they were inside the largest of the Marin warehouses, busily engaging in moving packing boxes and bolts of silk. When they had moved all these things, a little door came into sight. Jean Paul had found this door quite by accident a year ago, when his father had made such a heavy shipment of goods to the colonies that it had been temporarily revealed. It led to a small room that Henri Marin had used early in his career as an office; but continuing prosperity had caused him to move his records to a separate office building, and the little room had been all but forgotten. Now, it housed a screw press, brought in piece by piece by Pierre and assembled in the little room, bales of paper, a cutting board, and racks of fine, expensive type.

By the light of a single candle, Pierre set to work, reading from the bundle of manuscripts that Jean Paul had brought with him.

"Name of a name!" he swore. "When are you going to learn to write simple French? Your style is an abomination. Who the devil can spell such words?"

"You can," Jean Paul told him.

"And your hand grows worse daily. Here, read this to me. . . ."

Jean read to him from the manuscript. He had to admit that Pierre's criticism of his handwriting was justified. He had some difficulty making out what he himself had written.

There was no sound, after that, but the creak of the screw, as they turned it, bringing down the press upon the sheets of paper. They took turns at the screw, one of them feeding the sheets onto the bed as the other brought the press down by walking around it holding on to the two-handed lever, thus causing its threaded shaft to descend through the gigantic bolt that held it up. It was hard work, so they changed places often in order that each of them might have a chance to rest.

It was after midnight when they had finished. They gathered up the printed broadsides, and tied them into bundles. Then they left the little room, and placed all the goods they had removed once more in front of the door.

They moved through the streets of the city on foot, as the ring of the horses' hoofs on the stones might have attracted the Guard. They stopped, always before a boulangerie, a baker's shop, and hid the bundles nearby where the baker could find them. The next morning, at daylight, each woman who bought a loaf, would find it wrapped in what appeared to be castoff printed matter. But in the houses of the poor, twenty or more people would be gathered around the lawyer, or scribe, or even, often, the parish priest, who, miserably underpaid and overworked, was nearly always on the side of the people, listening to Jean Paul Marin's burning words.

Some days later, a torn and greasy sheet would find its way into the hands of the authorities. There would be a mighty scurrying about, and titled heads would bend worriedly over their wine, but nothing ever came of it, because the police were unable to even discover the mechanics of distribution, since Pierre and Jean Paul seldom repeated the same tactics. This week, the bakers of Marseille; the next, the grocers; the following, the sellers of wine. And always the murmuring of the people grew. . . .

They rode back into Saint Jule at four in the morning, and stabled the horses. Then Jean took his leave, and started back on foot toward the villa.

But he never reached it. He had gone scarcely an hundred yards from Pierre's door, when he heard a man's voice thundering oaths, and the crack of a whip, followed by screams.

He started running toward the sound. When he was close, he saw what it was. A woodcutter's cart had blocked the path of a great coach. In his haste to avoid the onrushing horses, since the nobles always drove like the wind, the woodcutter had turned too sharply, and his load had shifted, thus tilting his two-wheel cart half over, and jamming it firmly between the walls of the houses that lined the narrow street.

Jean saw this at a glance. He knew without even thinking about it, what the woodcutter had been doing to cause him to drive through the streets of Saint Jule at four o'clock in the morning. He, quite simply, had been stealing timber from his Seigneur's woods, since all the forest where the peasant woodmen were allowed to chop firewood had long since been cut or burned over.

But what caused Jean Paul Marin to go sick all over with pure rage was the coachman's method of dealing with the emergency. He had gotten down from his high seat, and was encouraging the woodcutter in his frenzied efforts to right his cart, by the simple expedients of roaring curses at him, and beating him with the coaching whip.

Jean put his hand into the pocket of his coat and came out with one of the pair of pistols he always carried. He moved forward quickly, walking soundlessly on the balls of his feet, and when he was close enough, he swung the pistol sidewise, catching the coachman on the side of his face, so hard that the flesh broke under the blow and the man went over backward into the mud. He came up roaring, only to face the yawning muzzle of the pistol.

Jean held it on him, steadily, and backed away until he came to the door of the coach. He jerked it open, and without looking inside, said mockingly:

"My Lord will please have the goodness to descend?"

There was no answer. Jean glanced quickly into the coach. It was empty.

He whirled, just in time to avoid a blow from one of the footmen who rode behind the coach. He jerked out the other pistol and pointed it upward.

"Come down," he said, "all of you . . ."

Sullenly, the Comte de Gravereau's lackeys descended.

If, Jean thought wryly, I am to be cheated of the major pleasure of making my Lord of Gravereau load wood, I shall at least have the lesser, of having it done by these pampered lackeys of his. . . .

"Now, gentlemen," he said pleasantly, "you will now have the goodness to right the cart of our esteemed friend, the woodcutter. . . ."

They stared at him.

"The alternative," Jean laughed, "would scarcely be so pleasant. For, if you refuse, you leave me no other course but to regretfully have to burn your brains. . . ."

The two pistols were persuasion enough. Clad in all their finery, silken breeches, and broidered frockcoats, plumed tricornes, and lace cravats, they put their shoulders against the high wheel of the cart and pushed mightily. Slowly it righted. But a number of logs lay scattered about.

"And now," Jean said airily, "the wood!"

They picked up the logs and put them back on the cart. The woodcutter drove off, his face ashen with terror.

I will have to make another diversion for them, Jean thought. Can't let them drive away so handily to report this matter. . . .

He walked quietly up to the coachman, who was standing there trembling, his finery ruined with mud and bark and resin, and one side of his face covered with blood from Jean's blow.

"The horses," Jean barked; "loose them!"

"But—" the coachman quavered; "it's worth my life, Sir Highwayman! My Lord awaits me, and I am already half an hour late. If I delay longer . . ."

Jean studied him, but he wasn't seeing the man at all. Something black and formless came alive inside his chest. It sat upon his lungs, stopping his breath. It wrapped slimy tentacles around his heart.

"Where," he whispered, "does my Lord await you?"

"At—at the house of that maid with the reddish hair. . . . Please, M'sieur Highwayman. . . ."

"Loose them!" Jean thundered.

Slowly the coachman loosed the yoke that coupled the shaft to the coach. Jean picked up the whip with his left hand, still keeping one pistol pointed at the lackeys. Then, straightening up, he brought the whip down across the backs of the four horses. They were off at once, galloping down the narrow street.

"You are not to follow me," Jean said slowly. "At this moment to kill anyone connected with the Comte de Gravereau would be a pleasure. . . ."

He backed away from them, down the street. When he was far enough away, he turned and ran. It was downhill all the way. When he got to the house, he wasn't even breathing hard.

The door was neither locked nor bolted. Lucienne knew that he never returned from his forays into Marseille before the afternoon of the next day. . . .

There were still live coals among the ashes of the burned out fire. It took him a long time to get the candles lit, his hands trembled so.

He stood there, looking at them. They were both sleeping, peacefully. He took a step toward the bed. Another. He stopped, hanging there, his eyes blinded by a scalding rush of tears.

When he straightened at last, the tears were gone. What had come to take their place was rage at his own weakness. Then—murder. He took out both the pistols and aimed them very carefully.

But he didn't pull the triggers. He couldn't.

She was too lovely, lying there in the flickering glow of the candlelight, cushioned upon the wild tangle of her own tawny hair. Too lithe-lovely, sweetcurving, washed in candle glow. He watched, lost, the play of light and shadow upon her face; the lips moist, warm, a little parted; the rest of her incredibly perfect, softrising flame-tipped, falling away into waist hollow, hip curve, thigh sweep, long flow of calf and gemlike ankles above her tiny, ivory and alabaster feet. . . .

He turned, and without knowing why he did so, hurled a log upon the almost dead fire. The crash brought them upright at once.

"I thought you might have need of warmth," he said quietly, "if only to accustom you to where you're going. I'm told it's very warm in hell. . . ."

"Jean!" Lucienne screamed.

He smiled at her.

"You're nice to look at," he whispered. "Even now when the sight of you should sicken me. . . . 'Tis a pity to spoil all that loveliness."

"Marin," Gervais got out, "let her go. Surely you wouldn't—"

"I am not a gentleman, my lord," Jean laughed. "I have no honor, remember? Yesterday, my lord refused to meet me—Strange, you have that power, M'sieur le Comte. You can refuse to meet your inferiors, with no reflection upon your honor. . . ."

He paused, still smiling.

"But strip away your finery, and you become just another man. Not a bad specimen, either, for a noble. . . . Don't be troubled, my Lord of Gravereau. My honor is not due to an accident of birth. It is branded upon my soul. Here, catch!"

He threw the second pistol upon the bed.

Gervais picked it up. Then he looked at himself ruefully. "Like this?" he said.

"It troubles my lord to go out of the world in the same dress he came into it?" Jean Paul mocked. "It is rather less imposing than a habit à la française, isn't it? Very well, I shall wait until Monseigneur is suitably attired. . . ."

"Jeannot, for God's love!" Lucienne said.

"The Opéra, the Comédie Française," Jean Paul whispered. "But you have no head for business, my love, or you would have known better than to make your payment in advance. . . ."

"Now, I'm ready," Gervais said. "Though, at this range . . ."

"Both of us shall very likely die," Jean smiled. "That troubles you, my lord? A pity. Yesterday, you could have made the arrangements to suit yourself. . . . Ready, my lord?"

He saw Lucienne's eyes widening. But she was staring past him.

"Seize him!" the Comte de Gravereau roared.

Jean whirled. The coachman and the other three lackeys came hurtling through the door.

Jean sighed, and lifted his pistol.

"It appears," he said regretfully, "that I shall have to kill some of you, after all. . . ."

The click of the flintlock in Gervais la Moyte's hand broke through into Lucienne's consciousness. She saw, in the instant before she hurled herself upon him, that he had cocked the pistol. She was too late. But not too late to deflect his aim and thereby save Jean's life.

The noise of the shot was deafening in the little room.

Lucienne saw the mushroom of smoke, and the stab of

orange flame. Then Jean Paul Marin shook a little and bent over backward, becoming suddenly boneless. As he struck the floor, his own pistol spun out from his hand.

"You—you shot him!" Lucienne whispered. "You shot him in the back. . . ."

Gervais smiled.

"Where else would you have me shoot—a dog?" he said.

Lucienne's hands came up, curving into talons, her nails raking at his eyes.

And Gervais la Moyte, Comte de Gravereau, whose training included all the useful arts, including how to handle the women of the inferior orders, drew back his hand and slapped her to the hearth.

"Come," he said to his servants, "we'd best leave them here—both of them. . . ."

But in the doorway he turned and saw Lucienne. She had come up on one knee, and the light of the awakened fire washed her all over with flickering gold. She was something to see.

I, Gervais la Moyte reflected, shall never forget this sight as long as I live. . . .

Then he went out the door, closing it softly behind him.

3

The woodsman's cart wound down the steep road toward the seashore. Lucienne had piled it high with feather mattresses and comforters, but every time one of the big wheels struck a stone, Jean Paul had to bite his lip to keep from groaning. He had emerged from the half-world of dreams and delirium only a week ago, but in that week he had found out how tenderly Lucienne had nursed him. After the first day when the local *chirurgien* had probed for the flattened ball, and set the splintered rib which had prevented its reaching a vital organ, she had guarded him with tender fierceness, forbidding the doctor to again set foot inside the door. She had scant respect for doctors, and her disrespect was more than justified; it is doubtful whether Jean Paul would have survived the tender mercies of a French physician of the seventeen eighties. It could scarcely do a man good to be bled, Lucienne reasoned, when he had already lost more blood than anybody could rightly afford to lose; or to be purged when he was too weak to lift a spoon of *potage* to his own lips. . . .

Does one hand truly wash the other? Jean Paul thought, as he lay there in the jolting cart, watching her tawny hair blowing backward in the breeze. She saved my life—after having put it in jeopardy in the first place with her faithlessness. . . . The one thing should wipe out the other, but does it? Strange. . . . All my friends call me a philosopher, but I am nearly dead of trying to become a man of action. I am but badly fitted for the role. . . .

Pierre calls me illusioned, says I am drunk with words; but no drunkenness under high heaven can equal the intoxication of acting strongly, boldly, when the time to act has come. . . .

Lucienne half turned on the high seat where she sat

beside the woodcutter. From where he lay Jean could see
the sunlight like a halo in her hair, the white clouds
sweeping by but inches above her head, across a sky bluer
than any sky has been since time began or would ever be
again. Wisps of pine needles broke it, dancing in the
wind, bare branches of oak and sycamore, the crying
white of birch. Everything was oddly broken, foreshort-
ened, viewed from that position from which a man rarely
sees his world. . . .

But it's good for thinking, Jean mused; it lends itself
to long, slow thoughts. What measure do ye measure,
that ye be not measured by? Lucienne has loved and
cherished me; and that love to me was a thing above all
price. But—and he smiled a little gazing up at her—'tis
you who put the valuation upon it, my sweet; it was you
made of it a thing that could be bought and sold, and
at thieves' market prices. Ah, Lucienne, Lucienne—the
thing you want can never be bought, always and forever
it must be earned. And the sweat and tears you put into
it are the measure of its value. . . . For were the King,
himself, to set you upon the stage, before the footlights
that have for you more luster than diamonds, only your
own skill, your own talent could keep you there—and
these you have or have not beyond the hope of purchas-
ing. . . .

She turned again, and tucked the blankets firmly up
around his neck, for it was December now, and cold,
despite the clarity of the sky. Her fingers strayed, lingeringly across his cheek, and at their touch he knew with
aching bitterness how little right he had to be called philosopher.

For the pain was back again; not the bad, the crippling
pain from his wound, but the other, the very bad, the
unthinkable, the unbearable hurt that was inside him. It
had no definite location, but filled up the whole of him. It
was inside him and outside him, around him expanding
until the sky was alive with it, contracting to a single
white-hot blade of anguish that probed and twisted,
and tore until all his blood ran screaming through his
veins.

He wondered why she couldn't hear that screaming. To
him it was real and definite and echoed in his ears. It
died to the whimpering of a frightened child, and rose to

the sick, insufferable screeching of a criminal dying under torture. It was bad, very bad, almost the worst thing in the whole world. Almost, but not quite.

He knew what the worst thing was, and every time she touched him, it came back to him and lived inside his mind. The worst thing, the thing he tried to shut from his mind was memory. And he could not. He could not at all.

It was alive. More alive than he was. More living than the poor, bruised and broken thing he called his body. It was visual and tactile; it had warmth, softness, texture, even odor. And it had been perfect. Darkly, beautifully perfect.

And because it had been so, her act of betrayal became for him a double profanation, both of herself, her body which was the very fount and temple of his idolatry, and of the integrity of love itself. He would go on; he would live, eat food, breathe air; but his death, when finally it came, would be but the culmination of the act of dying that began the night he had lit the candles with trembling hands and found her sleeping beside the Lord of Gravereau. . . .

I will not even leave her, he realized bitterly; because I cannot. Except by the door of death, itself, I am powerless to leave her side. But what we will have from now on will be like a priceless vase that has been smashed upon the floor, and skillfully mended—all of a piece, perhaps, but, God, how ugly the cracks show in the light!

She turned and saw his face, and what was in it troubled her.

"Jeannot," she whispered, "do not think of that. . . . It's all gone—finished. Don't you understand that, my Jeannot? I—I was dazzled. A noble, a great noble—and so wondrously fair, too; you comprehend. . . . I was weak and foolish. But when the two of you were put to the test, 'twas you who behaved nobly, nay, gallantly even, giving him an honorable chance to defend himself, and he . . ."

"For God's love, shut up!" Jean screamed at her.

She looked at him, and her mouth quivered. Then very slowly and with great dignity, she started to cry.

The woodcutter stared at him curiously.

"We'd best hurry," he croaked; "he's in fever again. . . ."

Lucienne stopped crying, accepting this easy explanation.

Jean smiled at her, thinking: It's not so simple, Lucienne. Nothing in life is ever that simple—or exactly what we expect, or what we want it to be. Perhaps that's why our language is full of labels: nobles, priest, bourgeois, peasant, madman, saint. We have to simplify, don't we? Say a noble, and at once we think of Gervais la Moyte, Comte de Gravereau; forgetting at that instant, Robert Roget Marie la Moyte, his father, a man as different from him as day is from night. I remember how all the peasants wept the night he died. . . . Say peasant and the picture is of a dumb, beaten animal, earthstained, smelling of the stable; but Pierre du Pain is a peasant, just as I am a bourgeois—and a madman. . . .

Ah, yes, we'll go on inventing our labels that never fit anything, manufacturing our oversimplifications because we weary of the ceaseless pain of thinking, of having to weigh and measure every man on the face of earth, having to sort out the subtle differences that mark him off from every other man. . . .

But so much thinking tired him. He dozed off and on, aware even in his sleep of the jolting of the cart, the creaking of the harness, and the fitful gusts of the wind. . . .

What awakened him finally was the fact that the cart had stopped. Voices came over to him. They were familiar voices; he knew that he had heard them before.

"Nom de Dieu! It's the young master! M'sieur Marin has had an army of police searching for him! He lives? Thank God for that, or else I would not have had the heart to bear the news. . . ."

He lay there with his eyes closed, in a blissful lassitude of surrender to his weakness, in the unexpected luxury of complete absence of pain. Perhaps he slept again, for surely Thérèse could not have appeared instantly over the mile-long distance that separated the villa from the iron gate.

"Jean!" she got out, her voice high, but taut, strangling. "Merciful God, what have they done to you?"

He tried to find his voice, to tell them it was nothing, an accident—but he was tired, so tired, and no sound came out of his throat, though his lips moved, shaping the words.

"You!" Thérèse whispered, her voice hoarse with un-utterable loathing; "you've killed him! You unspeakable streetwalker! Oh, God, God, how many times have I begged him to stay away from you—I knew in my heart . . ."

"What did you know, little sister?" Jean croaked, but the laughter moved through his voice, shaking it like dry reeds in the wind. "That Lucienne would one day kill me? But not so quickly, sweet sister, and surely not by so wild and barbaric a means. She is more subtle than that, and there are pleasanter ways. . . ."

"He raves," Thérèse said. "Oh, Jean, Jean . . ."

"I didn't do this," Lucienne said. "Ask him, he will tell you."

Thérèse stared at her, fury in her black eyes.

"He would lie," she said. "For you, he would lie—as he has so many times before. . . ."

"There's no use talking to you," Lucienne said bitterly. "Take him, Mademoiselle, take your precious brother who has cost me a thousand times more than he is worth!"

Jean Paul raised himself up on one elbow, and hung there long enough to see his sister's face contorted with rage; but the effort was too much for him, and again he had the now familiar sensation of being borne out upon a tide of darkness, sinking fathoms deep into utter night.

When he fought his way upward into light and air again, he was in his own room, and his whole family was standing around his bed.

"Lucienne?" he whispered.

"She is in prison," his brother snapped, "where she be-longs. We need only a statement from you before we can press the charges. . . ."

Jean Paul looked at his brother, and his mouth made the shape of laughter; but he was too weak to let it out.

"You are fantastic, Bertrand," he got out, "really fan-tastic. Go and have her released this instant!"

"Son," Henri Marin rumbled, "we've forgiven you your folly. You're young, and of my blood, so this wildness of yours is natural. But this misplaced gallantry becomes you but ill. That vixen must have the punishment she de-serves!"

Jean smiled.

"For what, Father?" he murmured. "For saving my life?"

"She saved your life?" Simone snapped. "Now really, Jean . . ."

"I assure you, my revered and honored sister-in-law, that she did. She saw the assassin take aim and struck his arm so that the shot that would have surely killed me was deflected. Afterwards she had me placed in her own bed and nursed me night and day until the life came back into me. . . ."

"It was not the first time you've been in her bed, I'll warrant," Simone said.

Jean looked at her.

"You're a great lady, aren't you?" he chuckled. "Simone de Sainte Juste, Marquise de Beauvieux—but still, how much of a petite bourgeoise you have become!"

"Jean," Thérèse said, "look at me. Now tell me that again—that she saved your life. . . ."

Jean Paul looked at his sister gravely.

"Yes, little sister," he said gently. "She saved my life— and at great cost to herself, perhaps even at the risk of her own. . . ."

Thérèse straightened up, and met Simone's eyes.

"He's telling the truth," she said quietly.

"I know," Simone snapped. "God, what fools we women are!"

"Bertrand—" Thérèse said.

"All right, all right!" Bertrand growled. "I'll go and have her freed, though the authorities will think me a precious fool, and wonder what hold she has on us!"

Jean Paul gazed at Bertrand, and his eyes were filled with dark mockery.

"Your reasons become you, my brother," he murmured; "but, then, your reasons always do, don't they?"

"Hush, Jean," Thérèse said, "you mustn't tire yourself. . . ."

He felt better now, very much better and stronger, but very sleepy. It was good to drift off into sleep, knowing it to be sleep, not unconsciousness, hearing their voices become bee-drone, breeze murmur. . . . He slept a long time, and very deeply. When he woke up, he was terribly hungry. And that, too, was good; for it was the first time

he had felt any real desire for food since Gervais la
Moyte had shot him.

Thérèse was sitting by the bed, feeding him the scalding
soup. He could feel the life flowing back into his body
with every spoonful. It was good to be alive, to have
feelings again, even though his wound ached damnably.

Then Bertrand Marin strode into the room.

"She's free," he announced without any preamble whatever.

"Good!" Jean Paul said, and the strength of his own
voice startled him. "Thank you infinitely, my brother. . . ."

"Don't thank me," Bertrand said. "I didn't do it. She
was already gone when I got there. I stopped at her house
—I—I felt honor bound to convey our apologies. She
was gone. They said she had quit the village. . . ."

"But," Thérèse said, "if you did not have her freed,
Bertrand, then how—?"

Bertrand's face changed. A deep red appeared low on
his jaw, and climbed upward until it reached his ears.
Then they reddened, too. Jean could almost see them
burn.

"A—a certain great lord," he spluttered, "ordered it.
. . . It seems he had a certain interest in the wench. . . ."

Jean Paul stared at his brother. He stared at him a long
time. Then he started to laugh. It was a faint ghost of his
usual rich baritone mirth. It was husk dry, rasping, so low
that they saw that he was laughing more than they heard
the sound. But it was terrible, nonetheless. Bertrand
couldn't stand it. He turned on his heel and marched out
of the room with as much dignity as he could muster.

Thérèse's face was white.

"Jean," she whispered, "he thinks—you think. . . . But it
couldn't be! Gervais left Saint Jule over a week ago. . . ."

Jean subsided. He reached over and patted her hand.

"I never think, little sister," he said gently; "'tis a
dangerous business, thinking—very apt to drive a man
mad."

But after she had gone to her own chaste chamber, to
worry the matter over in her mind, Jean lay very still
and stared at the ceiling.

And so, my Lord of Gravereau, he thought bitterly,
again you show your hand. And always, with that fiendish
luck of yours, you strike at the right time—just after my

precious kindred have given another display of the unparalleled Marin stupidity. Dear God, how much of life is encompassed round about by the two small letters of that word "if". . . . If Thérèse had greeted her kindly. If Bertrand and my father had not chosen to display their power and authority. If that ball had missed me entirely, or had been aimed more truly. . . .

In the next room, Thérèse thought she heard him laughing. But it was not laughter that she heard.

Thereafter, strangely enough, his recovery was rapid. The Abbé Grégoire called it a miracle.

"I have seen men die," he said, "of wounds less grave. God has laid His mark upon you, my son. He has destined you for great works. . . ."

"God?" Jean mocked; "or Satan? Which, good Father? I don't believe in miracles. The devil, they say, takes care of his own. . . ."

But it was a miracle, nonetheless—of a kind that neither Abbé Grégoire nor Jean Paul Marin understood. The miraculous lay in how far the human will can dominate the weakness of the flesh; and in this the strength of a man's purpose counts far more than whether it be good or ill.

Jean Paul's purpose was very strong. He meant simply to kill the Comte de Gravereau.

He waited a fortnight to be sure of his strength. It was not long enough, but his hatred was stronger than his judgment. He dressed himself in the middle of the night, and went down to the stables, armed with pistols, a dagger, and a saber. He had no plan, but the various weapons he bore would fit almost any contingency. For provisions he took along a loaf, a flagon of wine, and a cheese. Then he mounted Roland, his black stallion, and rode away from the Villa Marin.

He reached the Château de Gravereau late in the afternoon of the next day. Although it was long before night, the great hall was loud with revelry. Chevaliers and their ladies passed in and out with little more than a salute from the Comte's guard.

At nightfall, Jean Paul knew, it would be much more difficult to gain access to the château than it was now. He glanced at his clothes. Were he to wear a banner of scarlet about his neck, it would not have drawn the attention of

the guards more quickly than the way he was dressed.
Among the proud and wealthy mercantile classes of the
third estate, nothing was more galling than the laws which
forced them to dress in sober browns, blacks, and grays,
while the nobility could and did attire itself in all the
colors of the rainbow. Jean Paul's lean, aristocratic looks
would have passed muster, but not his good suit of black
broadcloth. His hair was out of the question. He wore it
loose, hanging down about his shoulders. To mingle with
that throng, it should have been clubbed into a Cadogan,
with a pigtail tied with velvet ribbons, or even the back hair
gathered into a small velvet bag. He didn't need a wig,
for after Rousseau and the other philosophers had set
the vogue for simplicity, most of the younger nobles
wore their own hair; even powder was beginning to go
out of fashion.

Still, to have to climb the high wall, topped with spikes
and broken glass, in the dead of night without making a
sound was quite a proposition. And once inside the wall,
how was he to get into the château itself?

He sat there on his horse, frowning.

If I were dressed right, he mused, if I could match their
foppery, I could stroll in without being noticed and hide
myself until night comes. Maybe I could buy a cast-off
suit in the village?

But he dismissed that idea as soon as it came. The
Noblesse always passed their cast-off clothing to their servants. He had the money to buy a suit, but that involved
a week's wait at best while the tailor made it to his measure, if, indeed, he could find a tailor daring enough to
make him a kind of clothes he had no legal right to wear.
A bribe—of course. But there still remained the element
of time. . . .

Your man of action, he told himself, is always basically
an *improviseur* . . . there must be yet another way. . . .

There was. He saw it as soon as he heard a group of
noble young roisterers singing. All of them were far gone
with wine.

Now, Jean breathed, all I have to do is to wait until
one of them passes this way alone. Pray God it's one near
my size. . . .

He didn't have long to wait. A tall youth broke away
from the others and made his way towards a thicket

about twenty yards from where Jean sat on his horse. His face was greenish, his purpose evident.

"Enfer!" Jean swore; "I hope he doesn't soil that suit!"

He touched Roland with his heels, and that well-trained beast moved silently forward. When they came up behind the young noble, he was bending over retching with wine-sickness. Jean Paul waited until he straightened up, then brought the barrel of his pistol down with considerable force upon the young noble's head.

The man crumpled soundlessly to earth. Jean dismounted, thanking his stars for the infernal racket the rest of them were making, and stripped the young nobleman to the skin, taking away even his smallclothes, for which he had no use.

I rather think he'll give some consideration to the matter, he mused gleefully, before reappearing before the ladies in his authentically noble hide. . . .

But to make the matter doubly sure, he bound the young nobleman's wrists and ankles together with some tough vine, and gagged him with his own simple cravat, reserving the noble's elaborate lacy one for his coming disguise.

A few minutes later, the transformation was complete, except for the nobleman's red-heeled shoes, which were much too tight for Jean Paul's somewhat plebeian feet, and the lank black horse's mane that grew upon his head.

His own good boots would have to serve. As for hair, there was doubtless a good hairdresser in any village attached to a noble house. He remounted and rode toward the village thinking:

As a man of action, Jean Paul, you haven't done too badly—so far.

He was right about the hairdresser. The man, with one glance at his rich attire, was at once all cringing servility.

"My lordship's hair? But of course! 'Twill not be an easy task, my lord. If you will pardon my boldness, may I ask how long it has been since my lord has had it done?"

"Not in years," Jean said airily. " 'Twas a vow I made. And the lady has but today released me from it. Come, man! Your scissors, curling tongs—your powder! Be quick about it— My Lord of Gravereau expects me at the Château within the hour. . . ."

"Ah youth!" the hairdresser sighed; "ah love! Even in

my humble station I understand these things. When I have
done, my lord may rest assured that the lady's stony heart
will melt like snow before the noonday sun. My lord
will please be seated?"

The man's fingers were deft. In a shade under an hour,
Jean Paul had been clipped, curled, bagged, and tied.
The hairdresser next led him to another seat before an
apparatus that looked for all the world like a pillory.

It was. After one questioning glance, Jean Paul allowed
his head to be placed through the semicircular opening in
the lower board, and the upper was lowered, thus firmly
imprisoning his head. Then the hairdresser appeared on
the other side with a pistol in his hand.

Hell's bells! Jean swore silently; what gave me away?

Then he saw that the pistol was no ordinary weapon,
and guessed it was some special implement of the hairdresser's trade. He aimed it at Jean's head. There was a
click, and all the world was filled with a cloud of fine
white powder. Jean lost his breath, coughed and sneezed
violently.

"A thousand pardons, my lord!" the hairdresser gasped;
"I should have warned my lord to hold his breath!"

"Damn, man, you've strangled me!" Jean Paul roared.
"Have a care, won't you?"

"Yes, my lord, forgive me, my lord," the hairdresser
whispered. "I'm afraid, my lord, that with hair as black as
my lord's, it will require several additional shots. . . ."

"Go ahead, then," Jean commanded; "I must be at my
best tonight."

This time he was prepared, and held his breath. When,
at last, the hairdresser held a mirror up before him, Jean
Paul was amazed. A stranger stared back at him. A young
prince. The transformation was startling. He would have
to apologize to no man for his looks, now; not even to
the Lord of Gravereau.

As he rode once more toward the château, after having
paid and tipped the hairdresser extravagantly, he felt like
singing. He was neither frightened nor nervous. For he
was one of those people, who, without knowing it, are
born actors. Their flair for dramatizing themselves is so
instinctive that they become the role they are currently
playing. It is to be doubted that any more arrogant young
lordling ever entered the Château de Gravereau than
this bourgeois son of a Marseille merchant. . . .

It was ludicrously easy. The guards at the gate paid no attention to him at all. He strode in, mingled with the throng, took wine from the bowing servants, laughed at the sallies of the Duc de Gramont, and even ventured a few of his own. . . .

To test his disguise, he walked to within one scant yard of the Comte de Gravereau, and made him an elaborate bow. Gervais la Moyte stared, and for a moment his eyes were troubled. Then he smiled and bowed in his turn.

"Glad to see you've arrived, Julien," he said: "You've had wine?"

"Of course, Gervais," Jean Paul laughed; "but I'll be delighted to repeat the offense. . . ."

Gervais languidly indicated a sideboard covered with bottles and glasses with an imposing servant in attendance.

"Help yourself," he said; "meanwhile, there are other pleasures. . . ."

Then he put his arm back around the waist of the painted little minx at his side.

Jean Paul walked away on pure air.

Julien! He laughed inside himself; I wonder who the devil Julien is! What frightfully precious luck! If only the beggar doesn't appear in person!

But he never reached the wine. He had that odd, prickly sensation that warns the over-sensitive that they are being watched. He turned, and came face to face with a girl of some twenty years or perhaps even less. He forgot his courtly manners. He stopped quite frankly and stared.

She was a small girl, and very beautiful. Even looking at her he couldn't believe it. Her hair, he decided, when unpowdered, must be the exact shade of the Comte de Gravereau's, because her brows and lashes were pure blonde. Her eyes were the color of the Mediterranean, far out, on a summer day. Her lips were shell pink, moist, and a little parted. She was staring at him with undisguised wonder.

"You," she said firmly, "are not Julien!"

"Of course I'm not," Jean Paul laughed, "though I have been accused of it. Who the devil is this Julien anyhow?"

"Julien Lamont, Marquis de Saint Gravert," the small girl said matter of factly. "He's a distant cousin; we don't see him often. But my brother has had more to drink

than I have, or he would have been able to see that you
aren't Julien. . . ."

"Your—your brother?" Jean whispered.

"Gervais. You were talking to him just now. You do
know Gervais, don't you?"

"Very well," Jean laughed. "May I ask what you call
yourself, Mademoiselle?"

"Nicole," she said.

"An enchanting name, Mademoiselle," Jean Paul said,
and bent and kissed her hand.

"And your name, M'sieur?" Nicole said.

Jean thought fast; then he smiled.

"Giovanni Paolo Marino," he laughed, "Conte di Roccasecca. . . ."

"Italian, eh?" Nicole said gravely, "no wonder you're
so handsome."

Jean's eyebrows crawled upward.

"I am honored that you think so, Mademoiselle," he
said.

"But you are. You're ever so much handsomer than
Julien. That's how I knew you weren't he. But you speak
French so perfectly. Know what I think? I think you're
an impostor. I don't think you're Italian at all. Speak
some for me."

"Some what?" Jean Paul demanded.

"Italian, silly! What on earth did you think I meant?"

"I didn't know," Jean laughed. Then he obliged, praying
that she didn't know enough of that tongue to distin-
guish the rough Sicilian dialect he had learned at his
father's knee from the lovely, rippling Tuscan that he
couldn't speak at all.

Nicole closed her eyes as she listened to him.

"Beautiful!" she sighed and opened them again when
he had finished. "Still, it is strange—that you speak both
languages so well, I mean. . . ."

"My mother was French," Jean explained. That was
the beauty of his lie—that most of it was true. His father
had come from a tiny Sicilian town called Roccasecca,
Dry Rock, in French; Giovanni Paolo Marino was not too
bad a translation of Jean Paul Marin; and as for the title,
Roccasecca had never had a lord, so little harm could
result from remedying the omission.

His success intoxicated him. He grew bold.

"I'll tell you another secret," he whispered; "I wasn't invited to this fête. . . ."

"Weren't you?" she said serenely; "neither were most of the others. They just came. . . ."

He threw back his head and laughed aloud, joyously.

"Still," she said, gravely, cocking her little head to one side as she considered the matter, "I'd better keep you out of Gervais' way. He knows the others; and he might find out that you aren't Julien. Let me see, where can I take you?"

"To Mademoiselle's bedroom, of course," Jean suggested smoothly. He had long since been aware how much of her oddity of manner was the product of wine.

She considered this idea, too, with the same appealing gravity.

"Good," she said at last; "they would never think of looking for you there. But I shall have to come down after a time and be seen about, or Gervais might come looking for me." She took his hand and gave it a little squeeze. "But I'll come back," she whispered, putting her lips close to his face. "You see—I like you!"

Jean stared at her. Then he started to laugh. There was something irresistibly comic about the idea of paying Gervais la Moyte back in his own coin.

"Wait," Nicole whispered. "We mustn't go up the stairway together. Everybody would see us. I'll go up first, and you have another cup or two. Then you come up . . . no! That won't do. The longer you stay down here, the greater the risk that Gervais will find you out. . . . You go first. It's the second door to the left on the first floor. . . ."

Jean kissed her hand again, and mounted the stairs. Inside her bedroom, a fire was burning in the fireplace, and Jean realized suddenly how cold it had grown. He thought about the poor devil he had robbed and left naked and bound in the woods.

Can't leave him like that, he thought; the poor fool will catch his death . . . I don't relish killing a man who never harmed me, even indirectly. . . .

He glanced quickly about the room. It was lovely. Everything was done in pale blue, heavily ornamented with gilt work. There was a huge mirror with a great frame of carved and gilded wood, in which he could see his face with the firelight flickering on it. In that light he looked more Mephistophelian than ever. The firescreen of blue Chinese silk had gold figures worked into it, and the marble mantel and cornices around the fireplace were heavily incised with gold. The chairs were in the mode of the present reign, Louis XVI, delicate and fine, with their giltwork showing through the pale blue paint. The fine crystal chandelier was not lit, but its myriads of crystal beads and bangles caught the firelight and brightened the whole room. Even the blue and giltwork bed, fit for the Queen herself, was canopied with delicate blue silk, and the pillows and coverlets were the same color. . . .

Jean could picture how Nicole la Moyte would look in this room, and the picture warmed him. But first he had a task to do. He opened all the closets until he found the linens, and selected a heavy blanket from among them. Then he came out into the hall. As he suspected, there was a back stairway leading down to the rez-de-chausée, or ground floor.

He went down it, found himself in a hall pantry; paused long enough to purloin a bottle of wine. His new-found talent for thievery delighted him; all his new-found talents did. He was extraordinarily pleased with himself, which, had he been entirely sober, he would have regarded as a warning of impending trouble. But he was not entirely sober.

He went straight to the place where he had left his victim. The poor young nobleman was thrashing about, trying to make enough noise to attract someone's attention. But everyone had gone inside now, and he was too far away to be heard by the guards. Jean bent down and touched his shoulder. The young nobleman turned over, and stared into the muzzle of Jean's pistol, and was still.

Jean wrapped him carefully in the blanket. Then he straightened up, and looked at him.

"Make one sound," he warned, "and I will burn your brains."

He took the gag out of the young nobleman's mouth. Then he uncorked the wine and poured a stiff drink down his victim's throat. The nobleman spluttered, and Jean took the wine away.

"More!" the young man croaked; "I'm freezing!"

Jean stood by patiently until the young man had drunk three quarters of the wine. Ordinarily he would have been consumed with impatience to get back to the fair Nicole, but the good wine in his own belly robbed him of a sense of time, and made him strangely calm. He bent down to replace the gag, but saw, to his amusement, that his victim was already asleep.

He marched grandly back toward the house. But coming up the drive, the cold sweep of the wind sobered him a bit, and he remembered, oddly, the cool generalship with which Nicole had arranged their first rendezvous.

Displays a practiced hand, he thought; she's walked the primrose path many a time before. . . .

Then he stopped short, amazed at how unpleasant he found that thought.

"You, Jean Paul Marin," he told himself sternly, "are a sentimental ass!" But the thought displeased him all the same. He walked through the hall until he came once more to the back stairway. As he passed the grand salon, the noise of revelry seemed to have doubled in volume.

Good! he thought; we won't be disturbed. . . .

But, when he was once more inside the room, he could not find Nicole. He had expected that she would have joined him by this time, but the room was empty. Moodily, he sat down by the fire to wait. Then he heard it—the unmistakable sound of someone crying. It came from the big bed.

He went over to it, and pushed aside the canopy. Nicole was lying face down on the bed, with utter disregard of the ruin she was doing to her sacque, or robe à la française, of the heaviest, finest white silk, with broad panniers and stitched back pleats, ornamented all over with seed pearls.

"He's gone," she whispered to herself; "he's gone and I'll never see him again, and I think I'd rather die! *Nom de Dieu,* why did he ever have to come here at all? It wasn't fair to let me meet him and talk with him and then. . . ." She subsided into a long trail of wordless sobbing.

Jean stood there, looking at her, a smile of pure self-mockery twisting his mouth.

Consider well, he taunted himself, how much of this is sentiment and how much wine, before you become intoxicated with flattery. . . .

Then very gently he bent down and touched her bare shoulder.

She whirled, stared at him, her eyes in the firelight, like star sapphires from her tears.

"Oh!" she said furiously; "how long have you been standing there listening to me?"

"This long," he murmured, and bending down again, he kissed her mouth very slowly and gently and well, cherishing it with his own so that when finally he drew away, she remained like that in the same position, her head elevated, arched backward on the slim column of her throat, her mouth, soft, parted, sweet sighing as though she were still suspended by his kiss, and from under each of her closed lids the great tears made a track like diamonds down her cheeks.

"Too long," she whispered; "far too long!"

He sat down beside her on the great bed, and drew her to him. She came to him without any protest at all, and her slim arms stole upward and locked themselves about his neck.

"I'm sorry that you heard me, Gio—Gio—oh, God, I cannot even say your name!"

"Call me Jean," he whispered; "it is the same . . ."

"Jean—I love that name. . . ." She put her cheek against his, and stared off into the firelight. "Tell me, Jean," she murmured; "can a woman love a man she has seen but once, and then only for a few clockticks? Either I love you, or I am mad; and either way it is the same. . . ."

"Wine helps," Jean mocked.

"I—I thought that, too," Nicole said sadly. "So after you had gone upstairs, I went back into the kitchen and had the servants make me a whole pot of *café noir*. I drank it all. That's what took me so long. And when I had finished it, your face was clearer in my mind than ever before, and I knew it was not wine. Then I came up here, and found you gone. . . ." She shuddered suddenly, thinking of it.

He turned her toward him, seeing her head tilting back, waiting, her eyes closing, her mouth—and suddenly it was all wrong. This was not the vengeance that he had planned. This had gone wrong, and the other, the killing was going wrong too, for in a few more minutes he was not going to be able to do it.

He kissed her savagely, twisting his mouth into hers, hurting her with the pain that was inside him now, so that she started in surprise, drawing back, but he ground

her to him, furiously, feeling cheated, loathing himself
with a bottomless loathing, until she did not draw away,
but kissed him back wildly, digging her fingertips into the
rich brocade of his stolen coat, until, more from fury at
this trick fate had played upon him than from passion,
he sent his hand searching amid all the silks and laces
until he found her body and caressed it roughly, as though
she were a peasant.

He heard the sharp intake of her breath; but she did
not try to stop him. She drew away her mouth, and
brought it up beside his ear.

"Jean," she whispered, "my Jean, my dearest, oh my
dearest, please, Jean, oh my darling please—at least listen
to me: I will not stop you I cannot stop you I—I—God
help me, I want you so! But listen, dearest—please, Jean
—Jeannot, hear me. . . ."

It was that word that halted him, that tender diminu-
tive, Jeannot—that Lucienne had always called him. He
straightened up and sat there looking at her, disheveled,
bare-limbed, her mouth a little swollen, her face tear-
streaked. She came up from the bed wildly, and locked her
arms about him once more crying:

"Hold me! Don't ever let me go—oh, Jeannot, Jeannot,
I am mad, sick with love for you! I didn't want it like this
. . . I thought that when finally I came to love a man it
would be for always; that there would be vows said before
God's priest, and in the sight of men . . . I never wanted
a guilty, shameful love; but Jean, my love, Jeannot, my
heart, my soul—if this is all I can be to you—then take
me!"

He sat there without moving, looking at her; and what
was inside his heart was death itself and hell.

"You mean," he said harshly, "that you have never
known a man?"

Her glance was startled, but when she spoke, her voice
was very gentle.

"Of course not, Jean," she said. Then: "Is that what
you thought of me?"

"Yes," he mocked her; "I thought just that. . . ."

"Oh!" she whispered, and the tears were there again,
bright and sudden in her eyes. "I—I deserved that, I
guess. The way I acted downstairs. I was trying to be
bold. 'Tis the fashion now to be bold. . . ."

She wasn't lying, and he knew it. He stood up, suddenly, paused a moment, looking at her.

It's gone, all gone, he thought bitterly, all the things I came here to accomplish. I cannot make of her an instrument of my vengeance; I cannot strike Gervais la Moyte through her, and leave her broken. And now, God in His Infinite Mercy, pity me, I cannot kill him who came from the same womb as she!

"Good-bye," he said.

"Good-bye?" she echoed; "not—not au revoir?"

"No, little Nicole," he murmured, "good-bye—adieu. Because this cannot be. . . ."

She sprang up from the bed and caught him by his shoulders, clinging to him, kissing his mouth, his throat, his eyes, whispering:

"Why? Oh Jean, why? Tell me—tell me—tell me, by God's love, Jeannot, why?"

"I lied to you," he told her, his voice flat, controlled, almost calm. "I am neither Italian, nor a noble. I am a bourgeois, and an enemy of your brother, nay, indeed, of your whole class, which I have worked ceaselessly to destroy. So—sweet Nicole, dear Nicole, you must forget me —since neither Church nor State, nor least of all your brother, would ever sanction a marriage between us two. . . ."

"Forget you?" she breathed; "never! Take me with you. We can go far away where no one ever heard of Gravereau and—"

Slowly he shook his head.

"The world is not that wide," he whispered.

She stood back from him, and the twin sapphires that were her eyes were enormous in her pale face. Her hands came up, the jewels on her fingers catching the light, and her fingers dug into the brocade of his coat, working convulsively.

"No!" she got out, her voice hoarse, shuddering; "I cannot, will not let you go! If we must hide by day, and flee by night, live upon crusts and wear rags, I am going with you, Jeannot! This you cannot deny me!"

"You little fool!" Jean murmured; "you sweet, romantic little fool!"

Then he bent down once more and found her mouth, the two of them clinging together, so lost in that kiss, that neither heard until it was too late, the crash of the door swinging open.

Gervais la Moyte stood there, épée in hand, with a blanket-wrapped figure at his side and behind him a mob of young nobles all with naked rapiers in their hands.

"That's him," Jean Paul's victim cried, "that's—dear God!"

Gervais pushed him backward through the door, and stepped back himself, slamming it after him. They heard his voice, trembling, deathsickness in every note saying:

"My Lords and Gentlemen, I cannot deny what your eyes have seen. But I issue here and now a blanket challenge to every manjack of you that dares remember it!"

There was a silence, then another voice drawled:

"Oh, confound your theatrics, Gervais, none of us will breathe a word; and not because of your swordsmanship, either. I, for one, hold myself a deadlier blade than you any day in the week. But the honor of our entire class is at stake. Now stand aside and let us deal with the fellow. . . ."

"No," Gervais said quietly; "it's my affair, and mine alone. I shall resent any interference. . . ."

Inside the room, Nicole came alive first.

"Go!" she got out, her voice hoarse with terror; "through that window—you can climb down—there's a trellis—and —by God's love, Jeannot, go!"

"No," Jean laughed; "I will not run from him, Nicole. This time my Lord of Gravereau and I must settle scores once and for all. . . ."

The door opened quietly, and Gervais stepped in, closing it behind him.

"So, Marin," he whispered; "you have at last forced me to kill you, eh?"

"Marin?" Nicole said; "not—not her brother?"

"You didn't even know the name, you filthy little baggage?" Gervais growled; "I shall deal with you next—and to your life's end, you'll dare not recall this day!"

"My lord had better consider well his words," Jean Paul mocked. "With all the excuses I have to kill you now, 'tis vain to add another. . . ." Then very quietly he drew a pistol from his pocket and aimed it at the Comte de Gravereau's heart.

"Jean!" Nicole wept. "Please, Jean, do not fire! He—he is my brother; you must not—you can't. . . ."

Very slowly Jean brought his weapon down.

"It appears, M'sieur le Comte," he mocked, "that we must be again cheated of the pleasure of killing each other. I bid you au revoir, and beg you not to follow me, or else I shall be forced to slightly maim you, to say the least. . . ."

Then he turned his back deliberately and walked with superb control toward the window. He put one leg through it, then he paused, looking at Nicole.

"Adieu, little dove," he murmured; " 'tis better like this. . . ."

"No!" Nicole said, and came forward in a wild rush. She threw both arms about his neck, embracing him in anguish and terror and bitter grief, kissing his face, his eyes. . . . She was between him and Gervais, of course, and her heavy silk ball dress hid Jean's lean form almost entirely; but from Gervais' face, Jean could see how she must have looked to her brother at that moment.

Pure madness flamed in Gervais' eyes. He put out his hand and jerked her cruelly away from Jean, spinning her about to face him with the same hard motion.

"Nicole!" he grated. "By God's own love, I—"

"You see how it is, my brother?" Nicole interrupted him quietly. "I would die for him with great joy. So now you must let him go. For if you kill him, whatever you do with me afterwards—whether you send me into a nunnery, or procure a *lettre de cachet* from the King and imprison me, or lock me in a chamber here, I shall be dead within the hour that I learn of his death. . . ."

They heard, all of them, the nobles in the hall impatient at long delay, muttering to themselves.

Gervais stared at Jean Paul. He was trembling.

"Go, you baseborn bastard!" he snarled. "Damn you, go!"

Going through that window, Jean Paul Marin loosed his mocking laughter. He laughed too soon. For as he released his hold upon the trellis, and jumped the last ten feet to the ground, he fell into the waiting arms of a horde of grooms, pages, footmen, led by that same coachman whose face he had broken open with a pistol blow. . . .

4

How long had it been? Jean Paul didn't know. He hung there by the manacles which encircled his wrists and ankles. But for them he would have pitched forward on his face. His eyes were closed, but he was conscious. Trickles of the filthy water they had flung into his face to revive him dripped from the rags of his clothing to the floor. He had learned, finally, to take the cold dousing of water in his face without showing signs of consciousness. For every time he opened his eyes, they started beating him again.

The rags they had left of his clothing were sticking to him in two dozen places. But even half dead as he was, his thoughts continued on their old, ironic bent.

His suit they've ruined; he thought wryly; mine's as good as new. . . . Precious lot of good that'll do me. I shall never need a suit again. . . .

"He's shamming," the head coachman growled. "Here, let me at him! I'll bring him around. . . ."

Jean heard his footsteps nearing. Then there was another sound, a clanking, as of chains.

Jean opened his eyes the barest slit. In the coachman's hairy fist there were two short lengths of chain.

"Scar me up, will you?" the coachman roared. "Spoiled my looks so that the maids shudder when they look at me! Let's see what you'll look like when I'm done with you, M'sieur Bourgeois-Prince!"

He swung the chains with all his strength, full into Jean Paul's face. They bit into his forehead between his eyes, broke his nose, and opened his face from forehead to upper lip, in one long diagonal swipe.

"Oh!" Jean choked, hoarsely; "oh, my God!"

"Not so pretty, now—eh, boys?" the coachman chuckled. "Let's see if I can improve matters a bit. . . ."

He swung the bloody chains far back, held them back. But before he could bring them whistling down again, a voice stopped him. A very clear, soprano voice, speaking quietly so that only the tiniest edge in the upper registers revealed the hysteria lurking beneath its calm.

"Stop it!" Nicole said. "If you do that again, Augustin, I shall have you whipped until there isn't an inch of flesh left on your back. . . ."

"My lady!" the coachman croaked, "how on earth . . ."

" 'Tis no concern of yours, Augustin. But I am here with my brother's full permission. Release him!"

"But—but—my lady!"

"You heard me! I have here a note from your lord, since I was aware that you would not believe me. M'sieur Marin is not to be tortured. Not any—more. . . . In return for that, I've promised my brother not to help him escape, which is hardly possible now, seeing what you've done. . . ."

Augustin took the note, and looked at it. He could not read it; but he had a peasant's awe of the written word.

" 'Tis my lord's hand," he muttered. "Don't understand this—still we've no real choice . . . give me the keys, Jules. . . ."

Jean felt, rather heard, the keys turning in the locks of the manacles. Then his support was gone, and he pitched forward; but two of the grooms caught him, and lowered him gently to the floor.

"Take him up," Nicole commanded, "and carry him to the little chamber. Thereafter you will take the key to my brother, as I promised. . . ."

They picked Jean Paul up and bore him to the little room in another part of the cave, or cellar, which had been built by Gervais' father for the sole purpose of detaining members of his own family who were in need of discipline. Therefore, though it was very plain, it was comfortable. It had a good bed, a washstand, and even a chair. In this room, Gervais la Moyte had often sat in his youth, and meditated upon his sins. . . .

They laid him down upon the bed, and stood there uneasily, watching Nicole.

"Now bring water—hot water, and cloths for bandages. You, Jules, go tell the cook to make some broth. And bring a bottle of wine. The best. Be off with you, you villains!"

When they had gone, Jean opened his eyes, and even managed a smile, though it hurt his broken face damnably to do so.

"How," he whispered, "did you manage all this?"

"Don't talk!" she got out, "please don't try to talk! Oh, Jeannot, Jeannot, my darling—what have they done to you?"

"Enough," Jean grinned, but the effort cracked his broken mouth so that he could taste the hot, salt wetness of his blood.

She collapsed upon him, shuddering, despite all the blood, and sweat and filthy sewage water he was covered with.

"You'll ruin your clothes," he croaked.

"My clothes!" she spat. "You lie there like that with your poor face all broken and ruined, and talk about my clothes! Oh, Jean, my Jean—you were so handsome—and now, and now . . ."

She couldn't finish. Her own sobs choked her.

"I'm a sight, eh?" he muttered, and brought up his hand to stroke her shining hair, now innocent of powder. "Good—now you shall get over this folly of loving me. . . ."

She sat there, looking at him a long time before she spoke again.

"Yes, Jeannot," she whispered, "I shall be one day freed of loving you—that day when I am laid beside you in the earth. Perhaps, not even then; for if there is any truth in the teachings of the Church, I shall go on loving you through all eternity. . . ."

Jean caught both her small hands in his own and gripped them, hard.

"Don't talk like that," he groaned. "You know not what you say!"

"I know all right. The scar upon your face will be unto me a badge of honor, since you got it for my sake; I think you will always be beautiful in my sight—with that proud, manly beauty of yours like one of God's own angels come down to earth. I even think that beast of a coachman failed, for no scar could really destroy your beauty, which comes from within you, and is of your soul. . . ."

"Speak no more of beauty," Jean half wept, "while

you sit there with yours blinding me, and I have no strength to take you in my arms!"

"Oh, Jeannot I—" she began, but the footman appeared with the water and the cloths. She dismissed the man with a curt nod. She was very busy for an hour after that. She had to soak his rags away from his broken flesh, and even so, often they stuck fast, and she had to pull them free, bringing blood.

But she kept at it grimly, her face whiter than death, while Jean fainted from the pain of it. He was aware at last, of a certain coolness, and it was this that revived him. He glanced down and saw that he was naked. He made futile motions with his arms and legs in an effort to cover himself. But she smiled at him tenderly, and went on bathing him.

"Don't be troubled, my Jean," she said gently; "now you are mine, and your body is like my own. Besides, it is very fine—or it was, and it will be fine again, when I have healed you. . . ."

A little later, swathed in bandages and healing salves, he lay there and for the second time in the space of weeks, allowed himself to be fed, like a child. Then he went to sleep with her arms about his neck, his head pillowed on her bosom.

When he awoke, she was still there. All her care had done its work, and he felt better, though painfully weak.

"How is it," he said, "that you can do all this? If your brother were to come . . ."

"He won't," she smiled. "By now, he is nearly to your house, to pay a call upon your sister. . . ."

"God!" Jean Paul swore.

"Don't swear, my Jeannot—I shall always call you that, for I see you like that name. I—I had to do something. I could not let you die of torture. . . . This morning, there was a new swarm of creditors. I pointed out to Gervais, that if he had you killed, he could scarcely hope to recoup by marrying your Thérèse; I also suggested that he might speed up matters, if he appeared before her and offered clemency for you as the price of an immediate marriage. . . ."

"Clemency!" Jean groaned, "at such a price!"

"She loves him, Jean—as I love you. I—I've seen her letters. They made me weep. My brother is not worthy of such love. So now, you are to be imprisoned for a short space of time—a year or two perhaps, so that Gervais can comply with the law, which he dare not disregard, considering how many witnesses there were to our folly. . . . He hopes that by the time you're freed, he'll have me safely wed; but he does not really know me, Jeannot. I shall wait for you until the end of time and beyond that if need be. . . . Then we shall go away together you and I, to His Majesty's colonies in America, and live beside that great river with the unpronounceable name . . ."

"The Mississippi," Jean whispered; "how full of dreams you are, my sweet. . . ."

"Tell me about Thérèse," Nicole said. "What is she like?"

"She," Jean groped for words, "is like a little bird. She is very small—smaller even than you are, and dark like me. I think that she's very pretty, but then, perhaps I am prejudiced in her favor. . . ."

"No," Nicole said, "you are always very clear, my Jeannot. I know I shall love her, dearly. She is the reason for the quarrel between you and Gervais, is she not?"

"Yes," Jean said, glad that this was only half a lie.

"Why, Jean? My brother is of a great house, and he is very handsome. Besides, she loves him. Why are you so set against this match?"

"Because," Jean said, "he is noble, and I hate all nobles —except you, Nicole—who have despoiled our country and brought it to the brink of ruin. Besides, as you know well, your brother is wild and thoughtless in his ways. Worst of all, he wants my sister only for the dowry she will bring, for he has never loved her. . . ."

"And I love you; perhaps you love me a little—I hope you do . . . and yet we cannot wed because of this foolishness of the classes; oh, Jeannot, I don't care what you do! Destroy the world as we know it if you will, as long as I can be yours!"

"It's a very unjust world," Jean said gravely.

"I know it," Nicole said; "but then I'm not sure that justice really exists in the heart of man. Go to sleep, now, my Jeannot; you have much need of rest. . . ."

And Jean Paul Marin closed his eyes and slept the whole night long, innocently as a child, cradled in her arms.

She came to see him every day thereafter. And, when finally, she did not come, Jean Paul knew Gervais had returned. He could walk about now; all his stripes had healed, except the really bad one—the one across his face. He begged Nicole for a mirror, but she refused to bring him one.

"Wait until it is well, my sweet," she whispered; "it will be less bad to look at then. . . ."

But he got an inkling of how he looked, when, on the morning after his return, Gervais la Moyte stopped in to visit him.

Jean Paul saw him blanch. Then a low, almost soundless whistle escaped his lips.

"Well, Marin," he said at last, "I think now we are quits. On Sunday next, your sister and I will be wed. And with that face of yours, you'll seduce no more high-born maids—nor low-born either, I'll wager. I pity you—you were rather a handsome devil, at that. . . ."

"What is to be done with me?" Jean demanded.

"You will be remanded before His Majesty's Lieutenant, tomorrow—on the lesser charges of breaking and entering, and malicious mischief—none of which carry the death penalty, as your assault upon Gaston le Chaplier would have surely done. The usual sentence is from five to ten years in the galleys. I will try to get you off as lightly as possible, as I promised your sister—and mine. *Nom de Dieu*, how you have bewitched her! But then, you have your graces, haven't you? I congratulate you upon the perfect way you carried off that masquerade. I actually thought my cousin Julien's manners were improving. . . ."

Jean's smile hurt his broken face.

"Thank you, my lord," he said.

"Ah," Gervais said, "that's better. You begin to see, I think, the folly of your ways. Come to me when you have finished your sentence and I will ask His Majesty to give you a post befitting your indisputable talents—in the colonies of course. Such firebrands as you are better out of France. . . ."

Jean smiled again.

"You flatter me, my lord," he said.

For the life of him, when he left that chamber, the Comte de Gravereau could not be sure whether Jean

Paul had seen the light, or whether he himself, had been subjected to the subtlest of mockery. He dismissed the thought, as he did all thoughts that troubled him. It was a habit of his class. A habit that would one day prove fatal to them all. . . .

The Comte was closeted with the King's Lieutenant for half an hour before Jean's trial. Whatever he said to that Royal Magistrate must have been quite effective, for Jean Paul escaped the preparatory questioning, which included mutilation by iron or by fire, the perforation of the tongue or the lips, whipping until blood flowed and a few other such niceties still included in the penal law of France in 1784, and regularly employed in cases such as his.

Trained to the law as he was, Jean Paul realized just how great his debt to the Comte de Gravereau was. He tried to tell himself that he would rather have suffered all these things than to be indebted to Gervais la Moyte at the expense of both Thérèse and Nicole. But his brief experience with torture at the hands of experts had shown him the limits of his strength, and he was quite honestly glad to escape any more suffering.

Half an hour later, he had been sentenced to five years in the galleys. Had he not been a lawyer, Jean Paul would have despaired utterly; for few men survived even one year at the oars of the galleys under the lash of the slave drivers. But Jean knew that though the law remained on the statute books, the galleys, themselves, no longer existed; the worst he could expect was a *bagne,* a convict camp, which, though it was as close an approximation of hell as the penal authorities could make it, was still a thousand times better than the galleys which it had superseded. Men often served out their sentences in the *bagnes* and emerged alive; but from the galleys—never.

He was led under guard to a rude stockade a few leagues from the village and thrust inside. M. Gerade, the Intendant, looked up with a groan.

"My God," he groaned, "not another one!"

"I'm afraid so, M. l'Intendant," Jean Paul said mockingly.

M. Gerade stared at him.

"And this one speaks French," he said, "not peasant gabble! Your name?"

"Jean Paul Marin," Jean said, "late Advocate at Law

from Saint Jule and Bas Alpines, Supervisor of Stocks and Supplies for Marin et Fils, and now—common criminal."

M. Gerade studied him for a long moment. Then he threw back his head and roared with laughter.

"Damn my eyes, boy!" he laughed. "I like you! what the devil happened to your face?"

"Compliments of the retainers of His Lordship, Gervais la Moyte, Comte de Gravereau," Jean told him.

"That bastard!" The Intendant spat, then turning to Jean's guards: "What are the charges against this man?"

"Breaking and entering, malicious mischief," they chorused.

M. Gerade wrote on the record book before him.

"All right," he growled, "be off with you. He's under my jurisdiction, now. . . ."

He looked around until his gaze fell upon a filthy wretch.

"You!" he bellowed, "bring up a log!"

The wretch came up with a log and placed it before the Intendant.

"Have a seat, *M'sieur l'Avocat*," M. Gerade said.

Jean sat down, staring at this strange official with frank curiosity. M. Renoir Gerade was a tall, thin man with a lean, kindly face. He was, Jean realized, the last man on earth one would expect to find in such a position.

"Now, my boy," he said pleasantly, "tell me what really happened. Your name's Marin. You mentioned being of Marin et Fils—which means you are one of the sons. As a Marin, you could buy that bastard Gravereau ten times over and demand change. Obviously you didn't enter Château Gravereau to steal something. What the devil were you doing there?"

I have already been sentenced, Jean reflected. And damn my soul if this isn't a human being!

"I went there," he laughed, "to put a foot of cold steel or an ounce of lead through M. le Comte's guts."

"Too bad you didn't succeed," Gerade said calmly. "But this becomes astonishing! You went there to murder la Moyte, and you're remanded to me with these childish charges; name of heaven, Marin, why?"

"Gervais la Moyte is all but bankrupt," Jean said. "To recoup, he engages himself to my sister. Obviously he couldn't have me put to death, or there would have been no wedding. . . ."

"I see," Gerade sighed. "Poor girl! Motive enough for killing him, I'd say. . . . Had you any other?"

Jean's face was bleak, suddenly.

"He—he debauched the girl I was to have married," he whispered.

"And my only daughter," the Intendant said bitterly. "She—killed herself, my poor Marie. . . ."

"My sympathies, *M'sieur l'Intendant*," Jean Paul said.

"And mine to you," M. Gerade replied, and put out his hand. Jean gripped it, hard. And both of them knew that a lifelong friendship had begun.

Jean looked around the stockade. It was filled with men, women, and children, all of them filthy, in rags, and half starved. An astonishing number of the women were great with child.

"All of them will be," the Intendant said, seeing his look, "by the time we reach Toulon. It's the system of herding them all together indiscriminately. . . . If a man is not criminal when we get our hands on him, he always is, by the time we let him go. . . ."

"But," Jean said, "why are they here? Surely all these women and children are not . . ."

"Criminals? Most assuredly not. You know the law of 1764?"

"Three years in the galleys for begging," Jean said slowly, "if you're able bodied. Nine for a second offense. A third—life. . . . Dear God, but we live in a barbaric country!"

"And they have to beg," the Intendant said sadly. "It's that or starve. The land's allowed to lie fallow for years, because it can't produce enough to pay the taxes to keep creatures like la Moyte in sensual idleness at Versailles. Let a peasant look the least bit fat or prosperous, and they double the impost—and then they clap a man in the *bagne* for begging a crust of bread to feed his starving babies with. . . ."

"I know," Jean Paul whispered.

"I do what I can," the Intendant said, "but they don't allow me enough to feed one-third the prisoners they send me. And the really vicious thing is that a man need not really be a beggar. All he has to do is be accused, by an enemy or someone who stands to profit by his imprisonment. . . ."

"But who the devil could profit by jailing these poor devils?" Jean demanded.

M. Gerade pointed.

"See those women? Most of them were pregnant when they came here. Their seducers—nobles, mostly, as these women are of the servant class—accused them of vagabondage and thus removed a possible embarrassment from their path. The children? Accused by stepmothers, second wives, to clear the way for their own progeny. The men, by their brothers, by their children, by their wives, to gain some trifling inheritance. . . . And I have to try to feed them on five sous a day apiece— Name of God, it's enough to drive a man mad!"

"Couldn't you free them?" Jean said. "As I remember the law, you have that power. . . ."

"You're the lawyer," Gerade growled. "Think again. Remember that long list of conditions under which they can be freed?"

"A solvent person," Jean thought aloud, frowning in his effort to reduce the fog of legal terminology into plain words, "must guarantee the mendicant—give him a job, or promise to support him—that is it, isn't it, M. Gerade?"

"That's it, all right," Renoir Gerade said angrily. "You know how many they arrested the first year this law was put into effect? Fifty thousand. Damn my eyes, Marin— you find fifty thousand solvent persons in France! Just find them. Then try to persuade them to guarantee a like number of beggars!"

He looked at Jean Paul quizzically.

"Now," he said, "I'll have to find you some straw to sleep on, and a few rags to cover you so that you won't freeze. But it'll only be for one night. Tomorrow we start the march to Toulon. . . ."

Jean got up from the log, but he stood there, waiting. Something in Renoir Gerade's tone told him to wait.

"We move from one stockade to another," the Intendant went on. "At each one we pick up additional prisoners. But with their confounded economizing on everything but folly, they don't increase my guards. . . ."

Jean Paul's eyes searched his face. But M. Gerade talked in the same bland manner.

"If we followed the coast, it wouldn't be so bad. But we have to go up to Avignon, and come back by way of Arles and Aix, picking up prisoners at each stop. By the time we leave Aix, I always have more prisoners than I could handle with twice the guards I have . . . and in those mountains . . ."

Jean made him a magnificent bow.

"May I say, *M'sieur l'Intendant*," he laughed, "that you are a prince?"

"And you," Renoir Gerade smiled drily, "are one damned fine lawyer. Shame to keep a brain like yours locked up. . . . Off with you, now, or you'll miss your supper. . . ."

Jean Paul missed his supper anyway. It consisted of water, ancient, moldy bread, and two ounces of salted grease. But, when, in the morning, he learned that all their meals were always the same, he resolved to eat it if it killed him, for he was going to need all his strength.

They bypassed Marseille, and went up the mountain passes toward Avignon, the prisoners being herded along like so many sheep. On the first day's march, one of the women died of a miscarriage. Out of pity, M. Gerade slowed the pace until they were barely crawling, but the women and children suffered horribly just the same. When they made camp the first night, and were shivering around the campfires, Jean Paul came up to the Intendant with a request.

"Would it," he smiled, "be stretching matters too far if I wrote a letter? I don't know what the precise regulations are on that point. . . ."

"As far as I know, there aren't any," Gerade said. "The men who drafted the law didn't believe, I think, that they'd ever have a criminal who could read or write. So write anyway, my learned footpad. You'll find paper, pens, and ink in that portfolio of mine over by the tree. . . ."

Jean Paul sat down near the campfire and began to write. As he did so, a little knot of filthy beggars gathered silently around him and stared in open-mouthed awe at his flying pen. Jean wrote on, serenely, for he was certain that none of them could read his words.

"I'll post it for you by diligence the first large town we pass through," M. Gerade told him. Then, looking at the address, the Intendant stared at him.

"Mademoiselle Nicole la Moyte, Comtesse de Gravereau, Château Gravereau," he whispered; "mon Dieu, boy,
—are you mad!"

"Yes," Jean laughed, "quite. But I hope you'll post it
for me all the same. . . ."

Thereafter, Jean Paul Marin became the most sought
after man among the prisoners. They came to him one by
one, those of them who had loved ones from whom they
had been snatched away, and begged him to write letters
for them. The kindly Intendant permitted him to do so,
and even lent him his own folding table for the work. Jean
wrote letters for his guards, who, being themselves of the
people, were no better trained.

But, if before he had thought that he knew much of the
misery of the peasantry of France, he now plumbed it to
its bitter depths. The letters that he penned nightly were
enough to wring tears from a marble statue. Before, Jean
Paul had had some misgivings about his belief that the
richest country in all Europe was being misgoverned into
poverty; but after one week as unofficial scribe for the
prisoners, he had none; more—his belief had deepened
into certainty. . . .

Nicole la Moyte was having her long blonde hair
brushed by her maid when a footman brought her Jean
Paul's letter. She took it listlessly and laid it unopened on
the glass top of her dressing table. Her eyes were red
and swollen from crying, and the last thing in the world
that she felt like doing was reading letters.

I wonder where he is now? she thought. He's probably
hungry and cold—and his poor face. . . . But at the
thought of Jean Paul's broken face she couldn't keep back
her tears. She jerked forward away from Marie's brush
strokes, and leaned her face against her arms.

"There, there, child," Marie said, "you mustn't take on.
He's better out of your life. . . . And all, he isn't your
kind, and—"

"Oh, shut up!" Nicole screamed at her. "If Jeannot
isn't my kind, why then I haven't any kind! I don't care
what his mother and father were! He was so good and
gentle, and so beautiful, too—until they ruined his face!
Oh, Marie, can't you understand?"

"I do understand," Marie said, "only . . ."

Nicole silenced her with an abrupt motion. She had picked up the letter, mainly to wipe away the blots her own tears had made upon it. But once she had it in her hand, something about it caught her attention. After a moment, she saw what it was. The handwriting was utterly strange to her. She had received many letters, but always from young people of her own set, and from relatives, so that she could always tell at a glance whom the letter was from. But she had never seen this hand before in her life.

Her fingers trembled as she opened it, for some obscure instinct told her long before she began to read, what it was.

Marie stood behind her, and read the letter over her shoulder. Marie was very proud of the fact that her young mistress had taught her to read, and seldom missed an opportunity to practice, since her knowledge, almost unheard of in a servant, made her a power, much sought after by the whole domestic staff.

She had almost finished it by the time Nicole pressed it to her bosom, hiding the words. Marie stood there, watching the reflection of her young mistress' eyes in the mirror. They were blue stars, widening with joy. They were twin sapphires, brighter than any diamond.

Then Nicole was out of the chair and skipping about the room. She caught Marie to her in a fierce hug.

"Oh, Marie!" she cried. "He's alive and all right! Besides, I'm going to—I can't tell you that. Run down and tell Augustin to saddle my mare. And Beau Prince also, put my brother's best saddle on him! Then come back and help me into my riding dress! I'm going away—for a whole week, maybe longer. . . ."

"Where?" Marie demanded sternly.

"That, Marie, is none of your affair! Go now—hurry. . . ."

"But when my lord, your brother . . ."

"Comes back from his honeymoon? Don't trouble yourself, Marie. By then, I shall either be safely back here, or so far away he'll never find me. Now stop your chatter, and do as I say!"

When, half an hour later, Nicole la Moyte came down the stairs and mounted Vite Belle, her mare, taking the reins of her brother's stallion from the hands of Augustin, and leading that proud beast after her, she made one of the classic mistakes that real aristocrats in all times and places fall into so readily. With the exception of her maidservant, with whom she was in close daily contact, it was quite impossible for her to think of the horde of servants about the Château Gravereau as people.

Therefore it never entered her mind what great folly it was to command the head coachman, who hated Jean Paul Marin with all his heart, and who was, additionally, Marie's husband, to make the early arrangements for her flight. She was scarcely beyond the first bend of the road before Augustin stormed into her bedchamber.

"What is she up to?" he roared at his wife. "Taking Beau Prince—sending Jules and Reneau to prepare the hunting lodge up at Carpentras . . . a rendezvous? Don't lie to me, wench! And with him, no doubt . . . God's eyes! Has he escaped then?"

"I—I don't know," Marie whispered.

"You don't know! Perhaps a touch of this crop would improve your memory. Ah! You don't like that, do you? Perhaps still another would ease the pain of the first . . ."

"Stop it!" Marie screeched; "for God's love, Augustin, please!"

"But I like beating you," Augustin smiled, flexing the riding crop between his two hands. "I think perhaps you would like to be as reckless as your mistress, riding off alone to the scandal of all the world. But this stops you, doesn't it? And this, and this and this!"

"Augustin!"

"Only if you'll tell me what she's doing, and where he is! Tell me, Marie! Or, rather, don't tell me. I'm beginning to really enjoy this!"

"I'll tell you," Marie wept. "He—he plans to escape in the mountains . . . the guards are too few and the commandant is sympathetic. He's going to go north over the trail through Gap and Briançon into Italy. She is to meet him and supply him with money and clothes—"

"And her own fair person, no doubt!" Augustin mocked. "My lord will reward me hugely for this. . . ."

"And you, of course, my hero," Marie sneered, "will overtake him with a horde of lackeys, and bring him back in chains!"

"So," Augustin snapped, "what's to prevent me?"

"The police. The mountain gendarmerie. 'Twill be your words against hers, and since when in France have the words of a baseborn coachman stood against a gentle lady's?"

She was right. Augustin saw that at once. He stood there, scowling at her.

"Oh, Augustin," Marie went on, pressing her advantage, "stay out of this! The less we have to do with the affairs of the Noblesse, the better. . . ."

"But when my lord comes back and finds I saddled the horses," Augustin groaned.

"You knew not where she was going. She explained the second mount as being for a friend—'My Lord,' you'll say, ' 'twas not my place to disobey my lady. . . .' "

Augustin's face brightened suddenly, and Marie knew the sinking feeling that she had talked too long.

"My lord's cousin, the Duc de Gramont!" Augustin exulted. "He has a lodge not far from Carpentras—and in this snowy weather, he'll surely be hunting there! Thank you, wench, for that caution. I'll ride alone, bearing this news to the Duc. He'll lead his lackeys. Then let the mountain gendarmes gainsay him!"

"But," Marie half wept, "to so expose this shameful thing. . . . Think you my lord would not rather . . ."

"I expose nothing!" Augustin laughed. "The Duc was among the first of the noblemen who broke into this very chamber and found your lady, whose nobility does not extend to her morals, in the arms of that peasant swine!"

"You speak of swine!" Marie snapped. "That boy has the looks and manners of a prince. . . ."

"Not any more," Augustin grinned; "you should see him now!"

Then he was gone, making a great clatter on the stairs.

I shall freeze within the hour, Jean thought. But he pushed on through the snow. If Nicole did not get my letter, I'll find a quick death in these mountains. Stupid to keep to the trail. But Gerade has no guards to spare to send after me. Besides, I think he meant me to flee. He put the idea into my head, himself. . . .

He stumbled on. It was January now, and here in the Basses-Alpes, the snow had begun to fall in November. His boots were good enough, but the rest of his clothing had long since been reduced to rags. He was blue with cold, and his breath made a cloud of vapor in the frosty air.

Where he was going, on the trail through Carpentras, Gap and Briançon, the road climbed all the way to Gap, its highest point, which was more than three thousand feet high. Below Carpentras it wasn't very high, and even there it was bitterly cold. He didn't like to think what it was going to be like at that pass through Gap—if he ever lived to reach it. . . .

By night, he was already beginning to fall from weakness and fatigue. Each time he found it harder and harder to get up. Death by freezing is a seductive thing; the victim has little sensation of discomfort. He hadn't had time to steal a tinderbox, so he had no means of making a fire. Even if I had got one, he thought wryly, I'd have scant chance of getting this ice-coated timber burning. . . .

His only chance lay in his ability to keep moving, to keep the blood circulating through his body. He pounded his body with his arms, but even this effort weakened him. The freshly healed stripe across his face ached damnably.

He fell, got up, stumbled on, fell again, clawed his way to his hands and knees, fought his way upright, and swayed there, knowing in his heart he hadn't the strength to make one more quarter mile. He stood there swaying on his feet thinking:

There is only one certainty in this world and that is that life always cheats you. Whatever it gives with one hand it takes away with the other, and always more than it gives. And I was overjoyed at the prospect of escape, never dreaming that it was into death that I was escaping . . . well, Jean Paul Marin, once again you've proved yourself a fool! And with that he threw back his head and laughed aloud, sending the boom of his mocking laughter echoing against the snowy hills. . . .

And it was his laughter that saved him, for, but for the sound of it, Nicole never would have found him in that gathering dark. Two minutes later, she had pulled up her mare beside him, sending up clods of snow all over him, hurled herself down from the saddle and was locked in his arms.

She kissed his dirty, bearded, half-frozen face all over, clinging to him, crying:

"Jeannot, my Jeannot, oh my own, I have found you, I've found you, and now you'll never go away from me again—never!"

Jean Paul pushed her away with the last of his fading strength, and standing there holding her by the shoulders he smiled at her, seeing her as beautiful as an angel with the snow crystals powdering her fur cap, dusting her lashes with white, and the big tears freezing on her cheeks.

"If," he laughed weakly, "you don't give me something to wrap myself in, and a spot of brandy, I shall go away from you—permanently. . . ."

"Oh," she gasped, "you're freezing—my poor darling, and I was chattering on. . . ."

"You're still chattering on," Jean mocked, "and I'm still freezing. . . ."

She whirled back to her mare, and loosed the straps of her saddle-roll. From it she took a magnificent greatcoat with a fur collar, and a fur cap, and helped Jean into them. Then she brought a bottle of brandy from the saddle bags. Jean had some difficulty opening it with his half-frozen fingers, but he got it open at last and poured a good three fingers of it down his throat, feeling it like fire going down, then curling warmly in his belly, sending the good warmth out through his limbs, and the strength coming back to him amazingly.

He mounted Beau Prince, while she stood by anxiously, fearing that he would fall, but though he swayed a bit in the saddle, he displayed a practiced horsemanship that calmed her fears.

"Where to, my lady?" he laughed.

"Up the road in the direction you were going," Nicole said. "But we turn off just before we get to Carpentras—because my brother has a hunting lodge there in the hills. You—we," and her face flamed bright scarlet as she corrected herself, "will stay there tonight. . . ." She stopped, and the plume of her breath enveloped her face. She rode over close to him. "I hope," she whispered, "that God will forgive me for my thoughts; but Jeannot, Jeannot —let us ride fast—for, love, I cannot wait!"

They pounded up the snowy trail. This is madness, Jean Paul thought. To be safe, I should put a night's ride between me and all pursuers. But God in Heaven, she is worth risking death for!

She seemed to have guessed his thought, for she turned in the saddle and called out:

"My brother will be away for weeks! There won't be any pursuit, my Jean!"

He saw, to his vast astonishment, as they rode up to that lodge, the flicker of firelight showing through the windows.

"I sent servants to make a fire," Nicole said calmly, "and to leave food, and other supplies. But don't trouble yourself, my Jeannot, they should be gone by now. I told them to . . ."

"You," Jean said incredulously, "entrusted your plans to servants? Oh, Nicole—don't you see that you've condemned us both?"

She stared at him.

"You mean that they'll fly to my brother with the news?" she laughed. "But how could they, Jeannot mine, when my brother is away upon his honeymoon—and they know not where he is?"

"His honeymoon," Jean whispered. "Dear God!"

"Don't just sit there!" Nicole said. "Get down and help me down—oh, Jean—hurry!"

They stood beside each other before the roaring fire, with Nicole's small head nestled upon his shoulder. She straightened up at last and looked at him.

"It's a good thing I love you so," she laughed, "for I fear I couldn't stand you now. Truly, Jeannot, you are a sight!"

Jean ran his hand ruefully through his thick, black beard.

"My brother has razors here," Nicole said, "and we can melt some snow for hot water. You get the snow, and I'll bring in the clothes I brought you. Then we'll have supper—" She leaned forward, pure deviltry in her blue eyes. "Yes, yes, we'll have supper, and much wine; for you, my Jeannot, are half starved and very weak—" She swayed there before him, her eyes filled with laughter and with tenderness. "That must be remedied," she whispered, "for by all the Saints, this night you'll have need of strength!"

Then she whirled away from him, and went out into the swirling snow.

Seeing his face in the mirror as he shaved, Jean Paul was very troubled. It was the first time he had seen his reflection since the coachman had broken his face. With his wild black beard, he looked like a devil out of Hell. His broken nose had healed crookedly, and as more and more of his face came into view as he removed the beard, he liked less what he saw. The ragged, white scar, paler than the rest of his skin, zigzagged down his face like a bolt of lightning; starting between his eyes, and crossing his broken nose, it drew one corner of his mouth upward into a permanent half smile.

And yet, strangely, all this devastation did not destroy his good looks. It merely changed them. With his own deep sensitivity, Jean Paul hated his new face, but it was Nicole who defined it.

"Oh!" she gasped, as he emerged from the little room, washed and shaved, and wearing her brother's good suit, "Oh, Jean—how changed you are!"

"I know," he said bitterly, "I look like a beast!"

But she came up to him and ran her fingertips lightly down that scar, and going up on tiptoe she kissed his strangely smiling mouth.

"No, my love," she whispered, "not like a beast—like a devil, rather. Like a strangely beautiful devil. . . ."

"Beautiful?" Jean snorted.

"Yes, yes! You were always the handsomest thing in the world, and they couldn't destroy that. But they changed it. They've made Lucifer of you—Mephistopheles—I—I think I'm a little afraid of you now. Jeannot, promise me one thing. . . ."

"Yes, love?"

"Don't try to live up to this face—or else I shall lose you. There isn't a woman alive who won't be intrigued by it. They—they'll all think—"

"What will they think, little Nicole?"

"They'll wonder how it would be to bed with Satan," Nicole whispered. "They'll dream of terrible, unimaginable delights they could not even put in words, for there aren't any words— Oh, Jeannot, Jeannot—you see? Look now at what that face of yours has already made me say!"

It was time now, Jean saw, to relieve the tension.

"If," he mocked, "you don't get me my supper, you'll see what a devil I am!"

"Yes, my lord," she murmured. "My lord and master—and you are, you know—for always. . . ."

There was good wine, and bread and cheese, and a

huge roast, slices of which they toasted over the fire. An hour later, Jean had half forgotten his imprisonment, his suffering, all the things that had happened to him. He stretched out in his chair before the fire, filled with contentment.

Then Nicole came up behind his chair and put her arms around his neck.

"Come," she whispered. "There is so little time, my Jean—so precious little time. . . ."

The other room had a fire in it too, because Jean had made one there to dress and shave by. It had burned low, but there was light enough for him to see her by. Her body was like snow with the glow of sunset on it. But she ran away from him quickly, and dived among the icy covers, and lay there shivering.

"I'm freezing!" she whispered; "oh Jeannot, Jeannot, hurry before I die of cold—

"And of wanting you," she murmured, when he took her in his arms. "Oh Jean, my Jean, be gentle with me—for I'm afraid! Be the angel that you are, not like that devil-mask you wear now. For you aren't a devil, are you Jean? You aren't, you aren't, you ar—"

First in the morning, before it was light, Jean Paul got up very quietly without awakening her, and made a fire in the fireplace. But the noise he made brought her upright in the little bed, then she lay back again, staring at him. He turned toward her with a smile, gathering the greatcoat he was wearing like a *robe de chambre* about his naked body.

"It will be warm soon," he said gently, "then we can get up. . . ."

"Jean," she whispered, "come here. . . ."

He went over and sat down on the edge of the bed. She put up her bare arm and touched his face again.

"Yes," she said, and her voice had something in it like—like awe, Jean decided. "Yes, yes—this is your face! Remember what I said last night—that every woman who looked at you would wonder . . ."

"How it is to bed with Satan?" Jean mocked.

"Yes. And now I know—God help me, I know!"

Jean's black eyes were troubled.

"You think me evil, then?" he murmured.

"No—no. I think you wild and terrible and wonderful beyond belief, and I am now truly afraid. . . ."

"Don't be, little Nicole," Jean said tenderly. "I would never harm you. . . ."

"But you have harmed me, Jean! You—you've destroyed me, so that I am no more me, but a woman I don't know, a creature I never dreamed existed. I took you in my arms and into my body and that should have been a simple thing. But it was not, for nothing with you is ever simple, or what anyone would expect it to be. . . . Oh, Jeannot, Jeannot, I am branded with your love! You are a part of me now, burned in with fire upon the very tissue of my soul, so that never again shall I be free of you. . . ."

"Hush," Jean whispered, holding her, stroking her bright hair.

"What will become of me, now, Jeannot?" she sobbed. "What will happen when you have fled, and I am left to watch the night fall without you beside me in the dark? I—I can stand the days—but when it is night, I think I shall go mad—mad of wanting you, needing you, my body starving for you, my arms aching to hold you, Jeannot—so close, so close!—my eyes blind, not seeing anyone else not wanting to— Oh, Jeannot, Jeannot—I shall die!"

"I shall come back to you, Nicole," Jean whispered, "though it be from hell itself!"

He had no way of knowing, when he spoke, how much truth there was in his words.

She lay there looking at him and some of the grief went out of her eyes. It was warmer in the room now, for the fire had blazed up. Then Jean Paul caught the coverlet she was holding against her throat and drew it down until it lay about her feet.

She made no effort to cover herself, but lay there, watching his face.

"Am I that beautiful?" she whispered. "Tell me, Jeannot —am I?"

"Yes," he said; "oh, God, yes!"

She stretched out her arms to him, like slender wands of snow in the firelight.

"Come to me, my Jean," she said.

And thereby, she condemned him, for else they would have been up and away by the time the Duc de Gramont and his armed retainers surrounded the lodge.

Jean Paul had no arms with which to fight, and it would have been useless anyway, because by so doing, he would only have endangered Nicole.

The Duc de Gramont had the decency to give them time to dress; then he took Nicole la Moyte back to his own château. But the worst of it was, he sent Jean Paul Marin directly to Toulon in a locked coach, surrounded by armed guards, so that he had no chance to escape again.

It was four full years before Jean Paul saw the light of day again, unbroken by prison bars or unshadowed by the high wall of a work camp. Four full years—in hell.

5

The prisoners were strung out along the unfinished roadbed like ants in the sun. There were no clouds, no trees, no shade. The sky was yellow-white with sun, the blue washed out with sunglare, and from the rocks the convicts were crushing with hammers, a white dust rose shimmering into the air unstirred by any breeze.

Prisoner number Thirteen Thousand Two Hundred Eleven, called by the other convicts and the guards alike, Nez Cassé, Broken Nose, lifted his heavy sledge, the muscles of his biceps coiling and knotting like great pythons, and brought it whistling downward. The rock exploded under the impact, pieces of it flying out in every direction. And Nez Cassé laughed aloud.

"Damn it, Nez!" one of the others growled, "stop that crazy laughing! Fair sets a man's teeth on edge, it does . . . What in the name of all the Saints do you find to laugh at anyhow?"

"Something I thought about," Nez Cassé said quietly.

He had remembered then, at that moment, how an old convict had spat on the ground at the sight of the thin provincial lawyer with the battered face the first day they had brought him into Toulon.

"He," the old villain rasped, "won't last the year . . ."

And he hadn't. For Jean Paul Marin changed in that year into something else—something new, different. He no longer stooped; he had gained eight inches about his chest, and two about each arm; he could stand a blow from the fist of a powerful man in the pit of his stomach without giving a breath. He was bronzed all over from the sun, except the white lightning of the scar tissue that zigzagged down his face, and the red, livid letters, T. F., for *Temps Forçat*, or time prisoner, branded upon his forearm.

He flexed his arms, feeling the play of the great ropes of

muscle under the satiny bronze of his skin. It was a thing he
often did, because it pleased him.

Proud of yourself, aren't you? he mocked himself; it's
an accomplishment of some magnitude to have become a
great animal like the rest. . . .

He saw the boys coming up the road, carrying the big
kettles of food for the prisoners. Then the whistle blew
and they all dropped their picks and hammers, and shuf-
fled forward awkwardly, with the curious, musclebound
motions of men who are being slowly worked to death
under a tropical sun.

One of the boys passed out the filthy, forever unwashed
wooden bowls, and the others ladled up the unspeakably
vile mess that served the *forçats* as food.

Jean Paul wiped the rockdust and sweat from his face
with one grimy hand. Then he began to eat very slowly,
without actually tasting the abomination they had given
him, his eyes squinting against the sunglare. He could
feel the heat against the tender stripes on his back where
they had lashed him bloody after the last of his many
attempts to escape. That had been nearly a year ago—but
his back was still tender in the sun.

It's nearly time now, he mused. August, 1788—the
people have had time enough to ponder this business of
the States-General, and the listing of complaints. . . .
Yes, yes—'tis time! Exit the man of action, and reenter
the philosopher! For certainly to fight a man with his own
weapons is a species of folly that has cost me dearly.
Not brawn—brains! Now to try a blade the like of which
they have not in their scabbards. . . . These guards
are but tools of the Noblesse, but what happens when
they become aware that they exist only to serve another's
pleasures?

Out of the corner of his eye, he saw Sergeant Lampe,
one of their guards, approaching. He raised his head and
grinned at the sergeant.

"When I am freed," he said pleasantly, "and you, Sergeant, have become Marshal of France—will you give
me a place as your orderly?"

Lampe stopped, his face becoming beet red in the sun.

"Don't bait me, Nez Cassé," he growled, "or I'll take a
gunbutt to you!"

Jean smiled steadily at the Sergeant. They both knew

how much chance Lampe had of becoming even a Captain. All the offices in the army from that rank on up were reserved for the Noblesse. Lampe would be a sergeant until he died.

"Forgive me, *mon Sergent*," Jean laughed; "I did not mean to put you into a temper. 'Tis far too hot to fly into a temper. The brain boils, and sunstroke comes easily enough without that. Come, sit, and join our magnificent repast. Some red wine, and breast of pheasant, perhaps? Or does *mon Sergent* prefer *côte de veau, sauté en Madère?*"

Sly grins showed on the faces of the other convicts. The food the guards ate was distinguished only in quantity from the abomination the *forçats* were wolfing noisily down at the moment.

"Damn your eyes, Nez Cassé," Lampe roared, "I'll—"

"Wait," Jean Paul said pleasantly; "I was about to tell these lords and gentlemen of His Majesty's most justly celebrated summer resort—"

The roar of the convicts' laughter drowned his words. Jean held up his hands for silence. "A story. Or rather a parable. You, *mon Sergent,* would do well to listen. 'Tis a most instructive parable—beneficial even to mighty warriors. . . ."

And before the bemused sergeant could stop him, he began:

"In a far country," he said slowly, watching Lampe's eyes, "there were two tribes of asses. And one of these tribes had blue coats—" a warning gesture stopped the convicts' snickers, "and the other had gray coats, brown coats, black coats, any kind of coats except blue. But the peculiarity of the second tribe's coats was that whatever color they were, they looked like rags. . . ."

"What damnable tomfoolery is this?" Lampe began; but Jean smiled at him.

"Wisdom, Sergeant," he laughed, "horse-sense, or rather ass-sense. Listen! Now in all other things, but color, the asses were alike. They brayed like asses, they ate like asses, they even smelt like asses. . . ."

No gesture of his could stop the convicts' laughter now. Lampe, himself, smiled grimly.

"Go on," he said; "we'll see if this earns you a taste of the cat. . . ."

Jean Paul bowed.

"I think not," he said. "Later, when the sergeant has had time to think about these things, he may even thank me. But the strangest thing about these long-eared ones was that, being asses, they didn't know that they were asses. But the lords of the land set grievous burdens upon the ragged asses, and with great cleverness, set the blue asses to guarding them while they worked. . . ."

A light of comprehension showed in Lampe's eyes.

"Naturally, this pleased the blue asses, because it made them feel important. But they were fed no better than the ragged ones, and guarding their less fortunate brothers kept them prisoners, too; though they did not realize this. Of course, the lords of the land, showed them some kindnesses; for instance, instead of beating them with whips, their masters only used the flat of the sword. . . ."

Despite himself, Sergeant Lampe gave a bitter nod.

I have him now! Jean exulted, then he went on: "Into this land there came a philosopher. He saw the fate of the asses, the blue, and the ragged, how their lords loaded them with burdens, beat them, starved them, took away even their bread and their salt. . . ."

Nothing could stop the roar of the prisoners at the word "salt." Nothing in France was more hated than the tax on salt. Even Lampe shared their grim pleasure, for he was a peasant, too.

"So he resolved to help the asses, and being Physiocrat, and having all knowledge at his fingertips, he began by opening their eyes. And all the asses saw that they were asses, and great was their consternation. The blue asses remembered how they were recruited into service: 'Come boys, soup, fish, meat and salad is what you get to eat in the regiment,' " and Jean's voice took on the false heartiness of the recruiting agent, " 'I don't deceive you—pie and Arbois wine are the extras.' And the ragged ones remembered their colts, dying of swollen bellies from eating mashed whole bran and water, there being nothing else. . . ."

Jean smiled full into the sergeant's eyes.

"Then," he said quietly, "all the asses took counsel together. And each ass brayed out his *cahier des plaintes et doléances*—" He paused deliberately, waiting for the bitter laughter, for the King had already promised to summon the States-General for the first time since 1614, and had asked all three Estates, Clergy, Nobles, and Commons, to submit a list of their grievances under the high-sounding title that Jean Paul had just pronounced. The laughter, when it came, was a thunderclap. Sergeant Lampe joined in it.

"As," Jean repeated smiling, "each ass brayed out his list of complaints and grievances, their anger mounted like the whirlwind. They remembered that their hoofs were hard and sharp, their muscles strong. Then—" again he stopped.

"Go on," Lampe prodded, "what happened then?"

"I don't know," Jean said simply. "How can I, or any of us here know, *mon Sergent*—since it is agreed that we are not asses, but men?"

Lampe stared at him, his heavy face working.

"Get back to work, you devils!" he roared; "and you, Nez Cassé, I'll deal with you!"

But as he walked away, he heard, clear above the clatter of the sledge hammers against the rocks, the soaring boom of Jean's laughter.

But three days later, he called Jean aside.

"Listen, Nez," he growled; "I've done some thinking about the things you said. And damn my eyes, if they ain't true! Told that story of yours the other night at mess—and you should have heard the boys roar. . . ."

Jean waited, smiling his perpetual, satanic smile.

"There was some talk," the sergeant went on, eyeing Jean narrowly, "of exchanging views with other regiments with an eye to getting our just deserts. But, damn it, man! we're from the same stock as these poor devils inside the walls, and learning is the thing we lack. . . . Of course, some of the corporals, and most of the sergeants can read a bit, and even write a fairish hand . . . but we ain't got the words, Nez—not the fine and proper words like you were using the other day; 'tis known that you're an educated man, a lawyer, some say, so I thought about you. Said to myself, It's been a long time since Nez Cassé gave us any trouble. Settled down a bit, kind of found himself—"

"Thank you, *mon Sergent*," Jean smiled; "that's very true. . . ."

" 'S all right. Wondered if you wouldn't listen to some of the boys' ideas, and set them down in good style . . .

might be able to do you a favor, ease up on your work a bit, say—not too much, though, because that would cause complaints from the others. . . ."

Jean Paul made a deep bow.

"Sergeant," he laughed, "I'd be only too honored!"

"Good! Tonight I'm going to smuggle you into the barracks. There'll be a table set up, and writing materials . . . then the boys will have their say. You set it all down, proper like. We'll see that it gets into the right hands. . . ."

Into the right hands—or into the wrong hands; I have no way of knowing, Jean Paul thought often enough in the next six months. It's like dueling in the dark against a foe I cannot see—who evades me with marvelous agility, but gives me back no blows, knowing that in the end I must exhaust myself. . . .

But he kept trying, from the last days of the August heat until the mistral went crying along the land and the nights took on a chill like iron.

"How's it going, Nez?" the convicts asked. They understood what he was doing.

"Well enough, I think," Jean said; but he didn't really know. Not all of it at least. Not entirely.

"Three more of the guards went over the hill last night —" the words moved along from bearded mouth to crusted ear down the long line until they reached him. "Keep it up, Nez—you're getting to them. Stick 'em where it hurts!"

"I'll keep it up, all right," Jean said. "But you're giving me too much credit. These pig slops they have to eat along with us are enough to make a man desert, not to mention the beatings they get from their officers. . . ."

A warning shove from the next man in line stopped him. Looking up, he saw Sergeant Lampe coming toward him. With the sergeant was a small man in a spotless, flawlessly pressed uniform, resplendent with gold braid.

"The King's Lieutenant!" the convict next to him hissed. "Now what the devil—?"

Jean studied the face of M. Joseph Gaspard, Marquis de Coteau, Lieutenant Criminel to His Most Puissant Majesty, and Superintendent in charge of the prison.

Sergeant Lampe pointed Jean Paul out.

"That's him," he said. "That's the one, there. . . ."

Lieutenant Gaspard stared at Jean with frank curiosity.

"This villainous brute?" he said.

"He's the one, all right," Sergeant Lampe said.

"The name is Marin, I believe?"

Sergeant Lampe nodded.

"Marin," the Lieutenant said, "come here!"

Jean Paul put his pick down slowly, and walked over to the King's Lieutenant. There was an unholy joy in his black eyes, and the crooked smile on his face was more pronounced than ever.

M. Gaspard found himself at a disadvantage. The pomp and circumstance of his high office weren't helped by the fact that he had to look upward to see into Jean Paul's eyes. It wasn't a pleasant sensation, especially since this muscular young brute with the broken face persisted in smiling at him.

"What the devil are you grinning at?" he snapped.

Jean's smile widened.

"A thousand pardons, my lord," he said; "but the smile I cannot help. 'Tis a fixture of my face, enscribed there by the loving hands of those who captured me. . . ."

"I see," M. Gaspard said. But he was conscious that unaccountably his dignity had suffered. He twisted his face into his sternest, most official frown.

"You're wondering, doubtless," he said, "about the purpose of this visit. . . ."

"I never wonder," Jean smiled. " 'Tis a bootless business. But if his Lordship cares to divulge the reasons for this unexpected honor . . ."

"Damn it, man—stop talking like a book!" M. Gaspard roared. "Use the speech natural to you. Such airs don't impress me!"

"That," Lampe said, "is the way he always talks, my lord."

"Who," M. Gaspard demanded, "taught a baseborn villain like you to talk like a gentleman?"

"My mother," Jean said, "who was gently bred. And after her, the professors of the Lycée at Lyon, then, subsequently, those at the University of Paris where I read for the law. I fear his Lordship must bear with the pedantry of my speech, since I know no other way of expressing myself. . . ."

M. Gaspard glanced at Sergeant Lampe.

"Explains a lot, doesn't it?" he growled. "Those villagers at Saint Jule were not quite the fools I thought them—"

"Hardly, my lord," Sergeant Lampe said.

The Lieutenant eyed Jean Paul for some moments.

"I had this morning," he said, "a long letter signed by a literary rascal who calls himself Pierre du Pain. . . ."

Jean's eyes kindled.

"I see that you know him," M. Gaspard said.

"Yes, my lord," Jean murmured.

"It seems that the villagers of Saint Jule have paid you the singular honor of electing you as their representative to the States-General. I see now that you're not ill fitted for the post. But whatever intent His Majesty has in calling up that archaic body, he certainly didn't dream that peasant fools would try to send up a branded *forçat* to sit in deliberation over matters of state. . . ."

"Why not, my lord?" Jean said easily; "if, as you, yourself have admitted, the branded convict is not ill fitted for the post?"

"Damn my eyes!" the Lieutenant swore. "I didn't come here to engage in legal debates, Marin! I came out of curiosity to see what manner of man could command so much attention from behind the bars of a jail. But I'd better warn you, I think. You're going to be more closely watched than any other man in this prison. Any attempt to escape will be dealt with promptly and severely. *Mon Dieu!* What has France come to?"

"Shall I attempt to tell you, my lord?" Jean Paul smiled.

M. Gaspard stared at him. Then a glint appeared in his little blue eyes.

"Why yes, Marin," he said drily, "do. 'Twould be most instructive to learn what's wrong with France—from *your* lips."

Jean Paul ignored the perceptible sneer in the Lieutenant's voice. He looked past M. Gaspard—through him.

"The mistral," he said softly, "that strange wind that talks darkly inside a man's heart, my lord. It's been blowing over France a long time, and it's growing. 'Twill be a whirlwind soon. . . ."

"You're mad!" M. Gaspard spat.

"There are voices in it," Jean went on; "the voices of the men who gather together all over France now, using words they would have been hanged for two short years ago. The voices of the peasants meeting in their little towns—like Saint Jule, my lord, while provincial lawyers like myself listen and write down the endless lists of their bitter griefs. And being thus set down in words, the words take fire, and the wind of discontent snatches them up and sends them like sparks throughout the land—"

He paused, smiling at the King's Lieutenant. But M. Gaspard made no move to stop him.

"The wind grows, my lord—becomes a gale. Provincial Assemblies, unheard of in most places for centuries, sit. The people hear the facts, see the mountains of their burdens added up in cold figures. They learn now that they, living in actual starvation, pay the taxes of the whole nation while noble and priest escape—they, who in every bad winter these past sixty years have come to eat the bark of trees, the fodder painfully scraped together for their animals, who accept in dumb misery that one child out of every three will die in his tender years of a multitude of ills—all of which, my lord, can be lumped under a single heading: hunger. . . ."

Within the range of his voice, the picks and shovels had come to a halt; but neither Sergeant Lampe nor M. Gaspard noticed it. They were staring at Jean Paul Marin, listening to the torrent of words that poured from his broken mouth.

"There is muttering in that wind now," he went on, "anger in that gale. The King, poor, foolish statesman, has breached his own defenses by his very invitation to complain. The *cahiers des doléances* make mountains of paper, and the rising wind of the people's anger catches them now, my lord, so that they cover all of France like snow. . . .

"Paris is full of deserters from the army—I'm told that my lord's own Corps de Garde has contributed to that number. There are riots in Marseille; *Jacqueries* in scattered places. And here and there a lordly château burns. This is France today, M'sieur le Marquis. And all that is wrong with her is that the people have had their fill of wrongs, and will bear them no longer. . . ."

He smiled crookedly at the King's Lieutenant.

"Even among my lord's own class, this is so," he said; "for certainly brave men like my lord must be tired of having their just rewards for the honorable scars they suffered in the King's behalf intercepted by some perfumed idler at Versailles. . . ."

M. Gaspard whirled to face Sergeant Lampe.

"Put this madman in solitary!" he roared; then he turned upon his heel and strode away.

It was night. Jean Paul could tell that. Now he could no longer see his fingers no matter how close he held them before his eyes. During the day, he could see the outlines of things. A little light filtered around the edges of the cover of the "hole." He thought that he had been in solitary for two days and part of a third. This was certainly the beginning of the third night. But it was hard to count the passage of time. Men kept in the hole long enough always lost count. And those kept there too long, lost their minds.

That wasn't going to happen to him if he could help it. He had spent many hours the first day thinking about his past: about Lucienne; about Nicole. Then it came to him that thinking about Nicole, remembering her, was scarcely the best way to keep a grip upon his sanity. So he proceeded to make elaborate plans for his political future.

A newspaper—that was the idea. Once in Paris, with Pierre with him, he would be able to mold the minds of the masses—sway them as easily as he had swayed Sergeant Lampe and the guard. An easy bootstrap to power. And once he was established, then—

Nicole. God in Heaven! La Moyte may have married her off by now—or shut her up in a convent. She may have forgotten me. Women do forget. Their minds and hearts are essentially fickle. Take Lucienne, for instance.
. . .

Devil take Lucienne! he thought. Then he threw back his head and laughed aloud.

It was the sound of his laughter that made him notice the difference. It soared upward, freely, no longer echoing against the iron cover in the top that was the only way into or out of the hole. A minute later he felt the cold night air on his face.

He stood up, sweating. He heard the scrape of the iron cover moving. Then, far off and faint, he saw the blessed twinkle of a star.

"Nez!"

"Here!" he laughed. "Did you think I'd gone for a walk?"

"Rope," the voice from above whispered. "Sending it down, now. Feel for it!"

He groped endlessly in the pitch blackness. Then, suddenly, startlingly, it brushed against his face. He caught it, gave it a tug. Then he was being hauled upward. Rough hands seized him, pulled him over the edge.

"Here's a sack," they told him. "There's bread in it, and cheese. A bottle of wine, too. Present from Sergeant Lampe. . . ."

"Lampe!" Jean gasped.

"Yes. How do you think we got the rope and the food? The guards left them where we could find them. Sack's half full of papers they want you to put before the States. . . ."

"You mean they're turning me loose?" Jean breathed.

"Not all of them. Just three guards who happen to come from Saint Jule. Said where we could hear 'em, speaking extra loud: 'If Marin's good enough for my folks, he's good enough for me!' Swore that they didn't know anybody any better at getting a point across without getting a body's back up. . . . And Lampe was in on it too. Didn't say a word to us, direct . . . just made things convenient like. Cell door unlocked. Outside door, too. This sack and rope and this stick where we could find them. Padlock stuck through the hole cover bolts like it was locked, but it wasn't. . . ."

"Bless them!" Jean said.

"Bless yourself, Nez—you talked 'em into it. Better get moving now. You'd best be a long ways from here by daylight. Don't think they're going to hunt for you—leastways not where they think they'll find you. . . ."

"Thanks, boys," Jean said. "You don't know how much—"

"Shut your trap, Nez, and get a move on! We don't need thanks. Just put in a word for us when you get up to Paris. . . ."

They moved off in a group to the wall. Jean stopped there, and gripped each of their horny paws hard. Then they boosted him up, and passed the sack and the stout stick up to him. Jean let them fall to the ground outside the wall.

"Au 'voir, boys!" he whispered, and dropped after them.

He crouched there, listening. He had no idea what

time it was, and that was the one thing he needed to know. Like all the convicts, he had a rough idea of what times the guards made their rounds. On each of the other attempts he had made to escape, he had figured the intervals correctly, so that he had been far away from the *bagne* when they finally recaptured him. But his sojourn in the hole had distorted his sense of time. He didn't know where the guards were at the moment.

The worst of it was he was on the wrong side of the prison. He meant to make his way along the seashore toward Marseille and Villa Marin. That was the shortest route, and under ordinary conditions the most dangerous. But from what the *forçats* who had helped him escape had told him, conditions were now anything but ordinary.

I'll have to chance it, he decided, and moved off through the darkness. This business of having to circle the walls to get to the sea instead of striking out for the hills at once at least doubles the danger of running into the guards. And damn my eyes if there's even a rock or a bush I can hide behind. I'll have to run and pray God they miss. . . .

He walked very quietly, stepping on the balls of his feet like a cat. It was a nerve-racking thing. To move quietly, he had to move slowly, and every instinct he had urged him to run. He was shaking, and the sound of his heart was like a drumroll in the darkness.

As it was, he had no time. The two guards came upon him suddenly, from around a corner, so that he didn't even have the advantage of being able to see the light of their lantern before they reached him. The muscles of his thighs tightened. He dropped his sack, dug in his heels hard— Then he stopped. To run was suicide. Here, on this flat stretch, the worst shot in the world could put a ball through his back before he had gone five yards. He stood there, waiting. When they were close, he spoke to them.

"*Bon soir, Messieurs,*" he said very quietly.

The muskets came level, pointing at his chest. One of them lifted a lantern so that it shone full into Jean's face. He stood there, sweating.

They didn't say anything. One of them looked at the other. In the light of the lantern, Jean could see his slow grin.

"Could have sworn I heard a noise," he said loudly. "Didn't you, Raoul?"

The other guard looked at Jean. His left eye drooped into a wink.

"Not me," he said stoutly; "all this political talk has got you jumpy, Hébert. Come on—we've got our rounds to make. Some of those devils might think that tonight's a good time—to escape. . . ."

Then they brought their muskets back up to their shoulders, and walked around Jean Paul, leaving him standing there.

He was, for a long moment, literally too weak to move. But when he did move, he struck out boldly in a fast, loping trot that ate up the distance between the *bagne* and the shore. Only when he was a good league away from the prison did he pause long enough to loose his laughter.

Early in the morning, he sat on the seashore eating a crust of bread. Five days walking, he thought, perhaps six. And I haven't a sou to pay my passage on a diligence or a Turgotine. Even if I had some money—the way I'm dressed, I'd have to go by *carrosse,* and damn my eyes if I couldn't get there faster, walking. . . . If I were to bypass Marseille, I could get to Château Gravereau in another two-three days. . . .

He brought his hand up and felt his thick, black beard. Slowly he shook his head. That—no. Bearded, goat-smelling, looking like a fiend out of hell—no. This face of mine is hard enough to take clean shaven, above a good suit and a clean cravat. Before, Nicole was caught up in a romantic dream. No dream can last this long. The shock would be too much for her. . . .

He got up slowly and started walking, pacing himself, going neither too fast nor too slowly so that he could last the whole day. By noon, he was no longer alone. The road was choked with vagabonds, men, women, and children, all of them as dirty and ill favored as he. Before the end of the day, the supply of bread and cheese that was to have lasted him the whole journey was gone. He hadn't been able to stand the hunger in the children's eyes.

The second day, he left the road, and struck out across country.

If, he thought bitterly, I have no more food to give them, at least I don't have to watch them starve. . . .

But he became aware, as the day wore on, that he was in some danger of starving himself. Walking through

woodlands and over deserted *arpents* of land, left fallow
by their owners because at best they couldn't grow enough
upon them to pay the taxes, burned up his energy. If he
could have rested, remained still, his hunger and thirst
would have been less. But he was a man possessed, fury-
driven.

He had to get back, take up the broken threads of his
life. He had to find Nicole again, and afterwards to take
his place in the reshaping of the nation. He had the feeling
of coming into life again, of being resurrected out of
death.

So he drove himself, walking faster, faster, while his
empty belly growled its protest, and his tongue thickened
with lack of water.

Thirst did not trouble him long. There were streams to
cross, so he was able to drink. But by nightfall the gnawing
in his middle had become too fierce to deny. It pushed
him on although he was drunken with fatigue.

He was about to give up, to lie down and forget his
hunger in sleep, when he saw the first dim lights of a
village. He came first to the château of the lord whose
domain the village was, but he knew better than to try to
beg food there. At best, the Seigneur's guards would have
driven him from the door with staves; at worst, they might
even turn him over to the gendarmerie under the law
against vagrancy. And I, he grinned to himself, wryly,
have had my fill of jails. . . .

He was beginning to pass other houses now. From the
way they were built, he guessed that this was one of those
regions that had a well-off peasantry—or for some reason
even possessed a bourgeoisie. A highroad, perhaps, over
which goods could be shipped; or a canal, that would
account for a mercantile class. But the houses were of
stone, tight, and well built, and from the amount of light
that poured from the windows, the inhabitants could
afford to be lavish with their candles.

Still, he hesitated before knocking at any of the doors.
He was painfully aware of the effect his appearance might
have upon a startled householder.

If, he mused, a bearded, broken-faced fiend, clad in
filthy rags were to knock at my door, I'd go for a pistol
before he had a chance to state his errand. . . . Better
keep moving—look for a place a little more isolated, so if

they make an outcry, I'll at least have a chance to run. . . .

He found what he was looking for, after another few minutes: a house, set well back from the road, larger and more imposing than the rest. He started up the path to the door. He had almost reached it, when it flew open and three men burst out. They were running as soon as their feet touched the path, but they ran clumsily because they were burdened with many objects.

He moved forward at once, lifting his stout stick as he came.

Luck! he grinned; I'll have a meal from this work and money too—or I miss my guess. . . . They'll be grateful enough for almost anything when I return these goods these brigands have taken. . . .

Then he was upon them, swinging the cudgel up, smashing it down, hearing the sick, wooden sound it made, as it struck their thick skulls.

"Gendarmes!" one of them yelped; "run for it, boys!"

He fell back and let them go, for he had accomplished all he had set out to do. They dropped their burdens in their flight, throwing them away as they ran.

Jean stopped and picked up several of the articles. Among them was a moneybag. It was pleasantly heavy. He took it and as many of the other things as he could carry and went up to the door. There was no answer to his knocking.

Probably tied them up, he decided. Then he shouldered open the door, and moved into the house. The candles were still burning, but the house seemed empty. Jean Paul moved through it; but he didn't find them until he came to the dining room. The householder, a stout bourgeois, lay on the floor, in a pool of his own blood. One of the thieves had dashed out his brains with an andiron. His wife lay not far from him. She had died very quickly and cleanly from a single knife thrust. There wasn't even much blood.

It came to Jean Paul, then, how much his stay in prison had changed him. Before, he thought calmly, I would have been sick to my guts at the sight of this. And now . . . now I have work to do.

First, food. The bourgeois' larder was plentifully supplied. Jean sat in the kitchen, a few yards from the bodies of the murdered couple, and washed down cold fowl and bread and *petit pois* with good wine. Then he went back outside and gathered up the stolen articles. There were clothes among them. Jean tried on the dead man's coat. It fitted him well, because the bourgeois had been a stout man, but the sleeves were inches too short.

The only fire still burning was in the dining room with the bodies. It would take too long to make another. So he hung a kettle over it, stripping off his filthy rags while he waited. When the water was hot enough, he washed himself thoroughly, and made good use of the dead man's razor.

When he left the house, having accomplished all these things in the space of an hour, he had vastly bettered his chances. He was well dressed, if one did not notice that his sleeves were too short, and his pantaloons both too wide and too short. Fortunately, the dead man's feet had been even larger than his own, so his good boots were quite comfortable. In his pocket was enough gold to pay his passage on the fastest diligence, and for food and lodging on the journey. The dead man's hat was a little too small for him, but he perched it rakishly over one ear, knowing that to travel hatless would attract too much attention. He had taken no more of the money than he needed to reach home again.

Afterwards, he mused, I'll make discreet inquiries and return these things to the survivors, if any . . . for, whatever my sins, they haven't so far included thievery. . . .

The food and the wine had refreshed him, so he walked all night, striking back toward the main highway he had left. He came, just before dawn, to a large town on the highway itself.

He stopped outside of it, and wrapping himself in the murdered man's greatcloak, lay down in a field, and slept until after the sun was up. Even after he had awakened, he waited for two more hours, so that he could walk into the town at a reasonable time, and make his inquiries.

His changed luck held. By noon he was riding in great comfort on a fast diligence. A day and a half later, he was in Marseille. He rented a horse and rode out to the Villa Marin, reaching it two hours after nightfall.

The villa was dark. He lifted the bronze knocker and brought it down, hard. Again. But it took five minutes of thunderous knocking to arouse the household.

The servant who held up the candle quaked with fright at the sight of his face.

"Go get your master," Jean commanded. "Say to M. Henri Marin that a friend is here to see him. . . ."

"But—M'sieur—" the servant quavered; "M'sieur Marin has been dead these past two years, God rest his soul. . . ."

"Amen," Jean whispered; and a tight knot formed itself at the base of his throat. He had loved his noisy, bustling father, despite all the differences between them.

"M'sieur Bertrand, then?" he murmured.

The servant appeared reassured by his knowledge of the family's first names.

When Bertrand came at last, in his nightdress and cap, Jean was shocked. His brother looked tired, old.

He stared at his visitor with blank unrecognition.

"Who the devil are you?" he growled.

"Why, Bertie," Jean laughed; "is this any way to greet a brother?"

It was the sound of that laughter that brought the light of recognition into Bertrand's eyes.

"Jean!" he breathed. "My God! What have they done to your face?"

"Enough," Jean said drily. "But you might ask me in, Bertie. . . ."

"Oh, come in, come in by all means," Bertrand said nervously. "I—we had given you up . . . we tried hard to have you released, but . . ."

"I know," Jean said gravely; "the powers that be cannot be troubled with such trifles. . . ."

Then he walked past his brother into the hall, lighted now, since the old servant had been busy with the chandelier while they talked.

"*Mon Dieu!*" Bertrand breathed, "how you've changed. . . ."

"I know," Jean said. "Tell me about Father."

"He—he failed rapidly after you were taken," Bertrand said sadly. "I think he loved you more than he would admit even to himself. More, perhaps, than he did any of the rest of us. He kept saying how much you were like Mother . . . he spent a fortune in his efforts to get you freed. They took his money, and made excuses. Then with Thérèse gone, and all his efforts coming to naught, he lost heart. At the last, he even neglected the business. . . ."

Bertrand stared at his brother, and his little eyes were bleak and fierce.

"Damn your soul, Jean," he burst out passionately; "I wonder if you're worth it! Because whatever Latin nonsense those fools of doctors labeled it, 'twas a broken heart that Father died of. . . ."

Jean looked at Bertrand, and his eyes were very steady.

"You might have spared me that, Bertie," he said at last.

"Sorry," Bertrand whispered. "It's just that we've been through so much. . . . But then, you must have been too. You must be starving. I'll have Marie. . . ."

"No thank you," Jean whispered; "I have no taste for food now. Tomorrow, perhaps. All I need at the moment is a bed, though I doubt that I'll sleep. . . ."

Bertrand beckoned to the old servant.

"Show M'sieur Jean to his old room," he said. Then to Jean: "You'll find it unchanged. Father insisted upon that. . . ."

It was then that he saw the tears, bright and sudden in Jean's eyes.

Mon Dieu! he thought; he does have a heart, after all. . . .

But it was more than a week before Jean could begin his journey to the Château Gravereau. He was held back by the simple fact that not one of his old suits fitted him. His shoulders had broadened so that he could not get into the coats. And the work-built muscles of his arms and legs made his sleeves and pantaloons tight to the point of bursting. And no amount of driving could hasten the tailor in his work. The old man was a craftsman to the core, and refused to be hurried.

During that week of waiting, Jean Paul was exceedingly busy. He was closeted day and night with Pierre du Pain, and other representatives of the village. These sessions of the dressing gown, as he laughingly called them, were complicated by the great necessity of constantly doing the most difficult of all writing processes: condensing. The complaints submitted by the people of Saint Jule were so numerous they would have filled a shelf of folio volumes. Fortunately, they were quite repetitious, though often they were so worded that it could only be discovered by prolonged study that they dealt with the same things. But Jean was well fitted for this task. He was even more eloquent with his pen than with his tongue, and a natural sense of form enabled him to reduce the *cahier* of Saint Jule into a useful document, which, nevertheless, approached real brilliance in its style.

He soon saw, however, that it would be the work of weeks, perhaps even months to bring the document to completion. The King had not yet announced the date of the first meeting of the States-General, so Jean hoped that he would have enough time.

But not even the pressure of political affairs could hold him in check when his garments were at last done. He got up early in the morning and dressed himself with some care. He put on a rich brown frock coat with tassels, and pantaloons of the same color. Smart English jockey boots of dark leather came halfway up the calves of his legs. He wound and knotted his cravat of white silk, but his hair required the attention of a valet. Powder had gone completely out of fashion during his stay in prison; besides, Jean had always hated it. His own black hair, done up in Cadogan fashion, served well enough.

And, since it was quite cold, he put on an English redingote, a kind of greatcoat, decorated with four or five short capes over the shoulders and the back. His gloves, and his Pennsylvania hat, a low-crowned, flat-topped hat with a broad circular brim, made popular in France by the American Ambassador, Doctor Benjamin Franklin, completed his costume.

He surveyed himself in the mirror, and found the results good. His dress was both quiet and rich. It even softened the effect of his broken face. Actually, he was dimly aware that it did more. In rags, above his matted, filthy beard, his scars had merely made him look villainous. But in contrast to his rich, gentlemanly attire, under his carefully clubbed hair, his strange face became interesting, even provocative.

Nicole found it so once, he thought. Pray God she still does. . . .

At the Château Gravereau, he found, somewhat to his relief, that Gervais la Moyte was at Versailles. The fact should not have surprised him. Most of the nobles of any importance continued to ruin themselves to stay in the swim of the gay life of Louis XVI's artificial paradise. Nor was he surprised to find that Thérèse had been left behind. At Versailles, any wife was an inconvenience; a baseborn one doubly so. . . .

But seeing his sister coming toward him, her two thin hands outstretched, rage and grief rose in Jean Paul. Thérèse was shocking to look at. She was pitiful. Her black eyes were enormous in her thin face. The great blue circles of pain and grief that ringed them made them look even larger. Even from the end of the hall he could see her collarbones, the sinews of her neck. When she was close, something else in her face caught him. A moment later, he knew what it was. Death. This woman, this stranger who had been his beloved sister was dying.

And of the same malady, Jean thought grimly, that killed my father. Dear God! I'll make him pay for this!

Five feet away from him, Thérèse stopped. Jean could see her chin tremble.

"Your face!" she breathed; "oh, Jean, your face!"

Then she hurled herself forward, straight into his arms.

"Oh, Jean, Jean, Jean," she sobbed; "oh my poor darling, what have they done to you?"

"Beyond my face, nothing," he said gently; "and that is of no importance. The question, little sister, is: What has happened to you?"

Seated in the *petit salon,* she told him. Slowly—with a great many pauses and much searching for words.

"It is not that Gervais is cruel—not physically cruel at least. You must believe me, Jean. He—he has never struck me, or treated me with aught but great courtesy. That— that is perhaps it. Courtesy so great as to amount to ceremony. Oh, Jean, Jean—I'm a stranger to my own husband—not the wife of his bosom!"

Jean waited while she mastered her tears.

"I—I want children. Don't think me shameless, Jean, when I say these things. You are my brother and a man of the world. To—to have children—one—"

"Must do certain things," Jean supplied gently. "Things which between married lovers are right and wonderful and beautiful in the sight of God . . . and Gervais— doesn't?"

"Not—not with me, at least! I see him at intervals of three months, six, lately a year. When on rare occasions, out of lack of a more interesting partner, he deigns to consummate our marriage, I believe he practices certain arts to prevent the conception of a child. He is never unkind. He is simply and honestly astonished when I rail at him about his actresses, dancers—that Lucienne, Jean —he still sees her! After all these years she more than anyone else keeps a grip upon his heart. I think she must be very intelligent, really. No one else has lasted so long. . . ."

"She is," Jean said grimly. "Go on. . . ."

"The trouble is, I—I love him, Jean. He is still gay and charming and beautiful to me, Jean. I think that we have no child because he doesn't want an heir of half baseblood. Then there is the question of money . . . he ran through my dowry in a year, and after that all that he could borrow or squeeze out of father and Bertrand. . . .

"I put a stop to that finally. I went to them secretly and told them to let him have no more. That was after I found out that his promises to have you freed were just that—promises and no more. We are crushed under a mountain of debt, Jean. I can't go shopping any more because I can't bear the sullen looks and the occasional downright insolence I get from the tradespeople. If I didn't occasionally use the money that Bertrand sends me in secret to pay a few bills, I'd be both naked and starving. . . ."

"Leave him!" Jean growled. "Come home with us to the villa. This tale of yours would win an annulment from the Pope himself. Then you could marry some fine lad, who'd—"

"No, Jean," she whispered; "no, my brother. I shall never leave my husband, except upon my bier. . . ."

"The sweet blue eyes of God!" Jean swore.

"Don't swear, Jean," Thérèse said gently; "you know I don't like it. Besides, you haven't yet asked me—about Nicole. . . ."

Jean's breath caught somewhere down at the base of his throat.

"You—you knew about that?" he got out finally.

"She told me. I thought I knew you. That was obvious since you are my brother. But over and over again, listening to her, I found myself wondering: What manner of man or devil is this to inspire such love?"

"Where is she?" Jean whispered; "I'll go—"

"No, Jean. No, my darling. You mustn't go to her. You see, my poor brother, she is married. And to a good man, a fine man who respects and loves her. They—they have two children, Jean. A boy and a girl. . . . Jean! Don't look at me like that! Oh, Jean—Jean—"

But already he had put his head back and loosed peal after peal of demonic laughter.

She stared at him.

"You—can laugh—at this?"

"At this," he murmured. "At myself—at the world. 'What manner of man or devil is this,' he mimicked, 'to inspire such love?' "

"But she does love you," Thérèse said. "She is like me in that. She will go on loving you till the day she dies. That's why I ask you not to see her. Don't make it any harder for her than it is. . . ."

"Hard?" Jean mocked; "to be married to a good man, a fine man, who loves and respects her? To whom she has borne two children?"

"Oh, Jean, why are you men so dense! She was forced into that marriage. If Gervais had even given her the choice of marriage or the sisterhoods, I know she would have chosen the veil first. But he gave her no such choice. All he would allow her to do was to make the final choice between her various suitors. . . ."

"And whom did she choose?" Jean whispered.

"A distant cousin, Julien Lamont, Marquis de Saint Gravert."

"My God!" Jean breathed: "My double!"

"You knew that too? The first time I saw him I knew why she had chosen him. It's astonishing how much he looks like you. The children, the boy especially, could be yours. I—I like Julien immensely. I pray God he never learns why she insisted upon naming her firstborn—Jean. . . ."

Jean stood up.

"I must see her," he said. "I don't want to trouble her, or force her to renounce her vows—however they were made. But I love her, little sister—with all my heart. More than I love life itself. You should understand that. It may be that I'll never see her again after this. But I'm going to see her, Thérèse, I have to."

"I knew you'd say that," Thérèse sighed. "They don't live far from here. Nicole begged Julien to buy a house close by, so that she could visit me. She is the best, and the only real friend I have. We—we comfort each other. . . ."

She paused, looking at him.

"Go to her. Julien is away—at Versailles. He didn't want to go. I think she sends him away at intervals that she might have time to dream of you in peace. Jean, Jean, I wonder if you're worth it?"

"I wonder, too," Jean said. "Tell me how to get there. . . ."

An hour later, when he waited in that second hallway, he could not hear his thoughts for the beating of his heart. He heard the prattle of the children and died inside himself a thousand tortured deaths at the thought of their begetting, then her clear, sweet voice was saying:

"Sleep now, my loves. Maman will be back directly, as soon as she has seen the strange gentleman. . . .".

Then she stepped out into the hall. She stopped. One hand rose to her throat, froze there. All the color went out of her face. Even her lips were white.

Dear God, don't let her faint, Jean thought; then very slowly he smiled.

"Now that you have seen the strange gentleman," he mocked, "you may go back, Madame la Marquise, to your little loves. . . ."

"Jeannot!" she got out; "oh, Jeannot, Jeannot, Jeannot —they told me you were dead!"

Then she was flying through the hallway, into his arms.

In all my life, Jean realized, I have never been kissed like this. Nor will I ever be again though I live a thousand years. . . .

He stiffened his arms gently, pushing her away from him.

She hung there in his grip, her face whiter than death, the tears flooding her cheeks, so that her whole face was wet, and the great droplets spilled like diamonds in the light from her chin, making rivulets down her throat. He could feel her trembling. So great was his strength that he did not realize that he was holding her up. For when he released her, she crumpled soundlessly to the floor, and lay there, shaking all over with great, wracking sobs.

He picked her up, and walked with her up the stairs to her bedroom. He laid her down upon the bed and sat down beside her.

She put up her hand, slowly, and traced the outlines of his face as though to reassure herself, as if to make certain he was real. Her touch was as light as air, but it tore his heart apart.

In another moment, I shall weep, too, he groaned; and that would be bad, oh, very bad.

"I didn't tell Thérèse," she whispered; "I thought she had troubles enough. Gervais told me six months ago. That's why I sent Julien away, so that I could grieve my heart out in peace. If it weren't for the children, I should be mad by now—or dead, too—like Gervais said you were. . . ."

"Would God that I were!" Jean burst out.

"No, Jeannot—no, my love—my only love. 'Tis good even to be alive and in the same world with you. But to know I cannot go away with you the way I want to—and I do want to, Jeannot—so much, so much!—because of the children, you understand that, my Jean—that is the hard part—"

She stared at him, and her eyes were very bright.

"But once I was yours," she whispered; "and I can be again—now, tonight. Julien is away. . . ."

"No!" Jean said hoarsely; "by God's love, no!"

Her hands were very tender upon his face.

"Why not, my Jean?" she whispered.

"Thérèse says he's a good man, who loves you—that he's kind. I have had enough of betrayals in this life, little Nicole. I cannot explain it," he whispered; "but what there is between us cannot be dirtied—this way. . . ."

She smiled at him.

"But I love you," she said, "not him. I—I cannot rid myself of the feeling that my children are bastards—because they are not yours!"

He stood up suddenly. The motion was abrupt, jerky.

"That was a long time ago, Nicole," he said. "What happens if we refresh that memory? You want to send me away branded with you—aching with love of you every waking hour? The other is dim now—though unforgotten. But this now—Nicole, Nicole, would you have my mind, and heart blasted to match my face?"

She closed her eyes, and shook her head so that the tears under her shut lids were jetted out in a spray from the motion.

"I don't understand you!" she wept; "I only know that if you leave me now, I shall die. . . ."

He came to her then, cradling her in his great arms like a child. He kissed her very slowly and tenderly and without passion. He could feel her breathing quiet. She brought her hands up against his chest and pushed him away, gently.

"You're right, my Jeannot," she whispered; "now go—go quickly while I can still bear it!"

Four hours later, in Marseille, Jean Paul Marin was already as drunk as any noble lord. He downed formidable quantities of wine, trying to stun his senses, trying to ease what never in this life could be eased, the death in his heart. Finally, toward morning, he staggered away from the last *auberge* and made his way toward the livery stable.

He was meandering across the square, when a bedraggled daughter of joy accosted him. She touched him on the shoulder, whispering:

"A night of love, my lord? You seem lonely. . . ."

Lonely? Jean thought; I am dead of loneliness; I am slain by it. But not such loneliness as such as you could ease. . . . Mine, poor *poule,* is beyond price, and surcease from it cannot be bought by all the gold ever mined from the earth. . . .

Then he turned toward her with drunken kindliness, meaning to give her a franc or two, and she saw his face.

She stood there a long moment, staring at him. Her tired, bloodshot eyes softened.

"Come," she said gently. "With your poor, battered face, you must always have to purchase love—and this once it will be good to have it freely given. . . . Come, *mon pauvre*—dear Saints, how they must have hurt you!"

Jean swayed there, looking at her.

"Thank you," he said. "You are kind. But tonight, love is the very least of my needs. . . ."

"Another time, then," she murmured; "I am always here—and if . . ."

"No," Jean said, and turned away. He moved off, down the dim lighted street, thinking to himself: Behold your fate, Jean Paul Marin! To have lost the only girl on earth capable of loving you—and to be possessed of such a face that arouses the pity even of whores. . . .

He lurched on, in the direction of the stable. He was surprised at how blurred the street lamps had become all of a sudden. When he put his hands to his eyes to clear them, his fingers came away wet.

"Dear God!" he whispered. "Dear, kind, sweet God. . . ."

He leaned against the door of a house, and hung there, crying. And the morning crept in on the soft feet of a million small gray cats. . . .

6

He was free now. He could go. The trouble was he was so utterly weary. He could work all day under a broiling sun; but the work that he did between the fifteenth and the twenty-fifth of February, 1789 drained the last reserves of his strength. Sitting in the council chambers of *Monsieur l'Avocat du Roi* of the town of Saint Jule for eleven or twelve hours each day, listening to an endless stream of peasants telling their complaints was not too tiring, physically; but it had a way of getting inside of a man's heart and nerves that brought a stunning, stupefying fatigue one degree short of being insupportable.

When he got home at night, blind with weariness, his head splitting, he could not sleep. Lying on his bed, staring at the ceiling, he kept hearing their words:

"I pay my dues to the Seigneur. I pay to grind wheat at his mill. I pay to transport the produce across parish lines, across bridges, not once, but a hundred times! And the bailiffs come to search my house for salt. . . .

"Then the winter comes. After even a mild one, we go hungry. Last year, 'tis said the Seine was frozen from Paris to le Havre. My wife lost the new baby, and 'twas a mercy. One more child whimpering with hunger, and I would have gone mad!

"Killed the oxen for food. When spring came, my wife and my son had to draw the plough. The other children? Dead, your honor. In March, last, we had only soaked bran to give them. It swelled their little bellies until they passed blood. . . . Then they died, in convulsions, your worship, of eating roots and bark and bran. . . .

"I had a little gold put by. But the land swarms with hungry, desperate men—led by escaped convicts, by bandits from Italy. They came into the house. They held my wife's feet into the fire. When she started to scream, I gave them the gold. . . ."

"My daughter sells herself upon the streets of Marseille. My son has become a robber, hiding in the hills. He brought me a few ounces of refined salt, instead of that gray ordure which is all we can buy. Some one informed upon me. A friend, perhaps, whom I had let break bread with me. The bailiffs fined me all the money I had saved in five long years. I am too old, your worship to try again. . . .

"We left the house, the furniture, the land—everything and took to the road. Let them take it all! The taxes eat us up. With nothing, we can't be taxed. . . ."

"Dear God!" Jean Paul groaned, thinking of it.

But he had finished it at last: all the complaints and grievances of the Parish of Saint Jule. He had set down the demands of the people: that privilege be abolished, that all men be taxed equally, according to their wealth; that they be allowed to shoot the game which laid waste their fields, cut the wood in the forest without paying a Seigneur for it, themselves own the mills which ground their grain, press their own grapes for wine, without paying a *banvin,* assemble and make known their own desires to their elected representatives, have done forever with forced labor upon the roads, pay no tithe to the clergy, take back unto themselves the vast lands of the church, buy and use all the salt they pleased without paying a tax upon it, elect the officials, especially those having to do with taxation, and remove them, if need be, when they proved corrupt. . . .

These, and hundreds of others, Jean Paul Marin had set down in his cool forceful style, making a document that would stand out even among the thousands of *cahiers* presently to be brought before the States-General. There was nothing left now, but to take the coach for Paris; for on January twenty-fourth the King had announced that the first meetings would take place in May.

He had had made the neat black garments that had been prescribed for the members of the Third Estate. He had converted his entire inheritance into gold, for he meant never to return to the Côte d'Azur. But he lingered still. Weariness, he told himself; but it was more.

A few leagues away, beyond Marseille, a woman sat— crying perhaps, after she had put to sleep the children who should have been his, but were not. A woman he dreamed about, waking or asleep. A woman whom he wanted with a feeling that was close to actual, physical pain.

"Nicole, Nicole," he murmured into the darkness; "there are other starvations besides the lack of bread. And if a man dies of them more slowly, they kill him none the less. . . ."

I should ride to her and say good-bye, he thought, holding Pierre du Pain's letter in his hand. This removes my last excuse. . . .

He read it once more, by the light of the candles:

". . . No difficulty in finding lodgings within walking distance of each other, overcrowded though Paris is. Your money, of course, turned the trick. With enough money, anything is possible in Paris. Marianne is busy, cleaning both your lodgings and ours. They are both humble, but sufficient, I think. Yours is above a furniture-maker in the Faubourg Saint-Antoine—in sight of the Bastille, which in itself, is enough to sustain a man in his resolution to overcome all tyranny. . . ."

Except, Jean thought, the tyranny of a hopeless love. . . .

"Ours is but little further along," he read, "in the same district. Below it, on the rez-de-chaussée, is the press which I have already set up. I have hired journeymen printers, bought supplies; I await only your coming to begin. . . .

"One word of warning: look to your dress, that it be not too fine. The Paris mob grows hourly more restive. Good clothes alone now are enough to brand a man, as they attribute fine dress to nobles and exploiters, by which last they mean any rich bourgeois as well. I saw, only yesterday, a man of some seventy winters forced to kneel and kiss the ground before a bust of Necker, of whom he had been accused of speaking slightingly. . . .

"The mob has given me many a qualm about the rightness of our cause. I, for one, question the wisdom of disposing of even a Comte de Gravereau to place in his stead a herd of villainous, bearded, evil-smelling, murderous brutes, who, I swear God, have never been peasants or indeed aught else but the brigands they are now. . . . No woman is safe; I accompany Marianne to the baker's, armed with pistols. In which regard, I urge you to bring your own, and a plentiful supply of ammunition; for, by my lost faith, you will need it. . . ."

There was more; but Jean had ceased to read.

Tomorrow, he thought, to Gravereau, to bid adieu to

my poor sister. A letter, left in her hands for Nicole. For
I—I cannot. . . . If I saw her again, everything—her
marriage vows, every oath I've ever sworn would be like
snow in the noonday sun. . . .

Do you feel it, my love? This death inside your heart?
The silent screaming more terrible than that of any tortured wretch because it goes on and on forever and there
is no relief for it anywhere?

All my life, my family and my friends have complained
of my mockery, and my laughter. How long has it been
now since I laughed—or even smiled? Weeks—since I
last saw you. I must make an end to it—an end to—us.
. . . First, the letter. . . .

He got up from the bed, found ink, paper, quills, the
sandbox. He put them on his desk and sat before it. Two
hours later, he was still sitting there, staring at the almost
blank paper. All it had on it were the two words: "My
Own . . ."

He took out his penknife and put a new point on the
quills. They had been well pointed in the first place, and
his hand shook so he botched the job. He dipped the pen
into the inkwell, forgetting to wipe it on the edge as he
drew it out so that a string of drops sprayed across the
paper.

"Enfer!" he swore, and crumpled the sheet. He threw it
into the wastebasket, drew another toward him.

But he wrote nothing upon it, nothing at all.

I am facile with the pen, he thought bitterly; but where
is all my facility now?

He sat there, in the cold room, before his desk, sweating.
He was on the edge of something, and almost he knew
what it was. He remembered something that d'Hiver, an
actor who had frequented the Marin soirées had said once
in reply to the question of whether or not he felt the
emotions he depicted on the stage.

"Of course not!" the actor had laughed. "If you really
feel—it paralyzes you. . . ."

Real emotion—this dreadful excess of feeling I have, he
thought, stuns the senses. I see her face, even in the darkness of my mind, and there aren't any words left—nowhere in the world. Yet I must write it—I must!

But like many another less fluent man, all he wrote
was:

"I love you. I always shall. Forget, and forgive, one who adores you and who signs himself, forever, Jean. . . ."

He got up in the morning and rode toward the Château Gravereau. It took him a long time, because all the roads were choked with peasants and vagabonds. At the sight of his rich dress, they snarled at him:

"Aristocrat! Ere long we'll make an end to the likes of you!"

But they offered him no violence. That was yet to come.

The servant who opened the door, showed a white and frightened face that calmed a little with recognition.

"What ails you?" Jean growled at him; "you look like you've seen a ghost. . . ."

"The people, sir," the butler whispered; "they're growing ugly. There have been threats. . . . My lord's not too popular hereabouts. . . . Thank God, my lady's so kind. They adore her. I fear me we'd have been attacked before now, if it weren't for her . . . She's in the *petit salon*. . . . Go in, sir, she said I need never trouble to announce you, sir. . . ."

Jean Paul walked into the little sitting room. At the sound of his booted feet, two women rose from their chairs and turned to face him. Thérèse—and Nicole.

Dear God! Jean wept inside his heart; why must she be here now!

"Jean!" Thérèse said, "I'm so glad you came . . . We —we've been so frightened. . . ."

"Why?" Jean got out, unable to tear his gaze from Nicole's face.

"Augustin," Thérèse said; "the coachman—Nicole told me he was the one who—who hurt your face. He's run away, and joined the people. Now he's stirring them up against us. They haven't done anything but mutter threats at us, but . . ."

"And at your house?" Jean said quietly to Nicole.

"Nothing, yet," she whispered.

Jean felt himself trembling. Strange, he thought, anything she says, two words—"Nothing yet"—and my bones turn to water within me. . . .

"I think you exaggerate the danger," he smiled. "I know the people hereabouts. They're good folk, many of them are my friends—"

He stopped, watching Nicole's blue eyes widening, feeling as much as seeing how they searched his face. From where he stood, he could see her mouth softening, hear the quick, explosive outrush of her breath. And when he raised his eyes again, he saw the terrible hunger in her eyes.

With you, too, he thought bitterly, it's like that. God help us both. . . .

"Jeannot," she said, her voice high, taut, strangling, "why did you come?"

"To say good-bye," Jean said.

She didn't move or speak. But ten feet away across that room, Jean saw the anguish in her face, saw her eyes blurring, misting over with her tears, and she, hanging there, swaying a little, her gaze locked with his, unwavering, speaking through that purest communication that has no need for words, that is beyond words, above them. . . .

"Nicole," he rasped, "please, I—"

"Oh, for God's sake go and kiss him!" Thérèse sobbed. "Don't just stand there!"

An instant later, Nicole was in his arms, kissing his face, his throat, his eyes, with soft, wet lips that clung and broke, and clung again, tasting of salt and tears.

He found her mouth, and cherished it with his own, feeling it moving under his, forming words that came out muffled, broken, whimpering:

"To Paris—I know—Thérèse told me—to sit in the States—but Jeannot, Jeannot—I cannot—I will not—bear . . ."

But he stopped her words altogether, bruising her mouth with a savagery that was strangely all tenderness, spinning the world about their heads in terror and loss and rage and anguish, until Thérèse's sob-choked, "My God!" came over to him, and he released Nicole and stood back.

"It—it is better so, little Nicole," he murmured. "If I stayed here, near you . . ."

"I should destroy you," she said simply. "We would destroy each other. . . ."

She stood there, looking at him, and her eyes were very clear.

"You must go," she said slowly. "I understand that. The

country has to be saved, and only you and men like you can do that. But say you'll come back to me—say it— No, No! Don't talk of Julien to me! He is all Thérèse told you, good and kind and wise. . . . Too wise, I think, to hold on to a woman who doesn't want him. He'll set me free, if only you'll come back to me, Jeannot. . . . Tell me you will, tell me!"

"But how?" Jean said, "how can he, Nicole? You married him in good faith, in the church. You have children —and therefore no grounds for an annulment. You know how he can free you, Nicole? The only way? By dying. Do you want that, Nicole? Answer me! Do you?"

She stared at him.

"Yes!" she said fiercely. "For you, yes!"

"Nicole!" Thérèse gasped.

Nicole half turned toward her.

"I'm sorry," she said brokenly; "I wish I could say I didn't mean that, Thérèse. But I did—then, at that moment, I did. That was a wickedness—a very great wickedness, the worst. But you see, dear Thérèse, as far as Jean is concerned, I don't know right from wrong any more. I'm lost. I don't know day from night or what time it is or even what year. . . . I only know that I am dying of wanting him so, and that when he is gone, I shall truly die, not all at once, but by slow inches, over the space of months, perhaps—until I am all dead finally, and at peace. . . ."

She looked at Jean, and a slow smile broke the track of her tears.

"If I shall be at peace even then, my love. I think I shall become one of those ghostly women of the legends, searching the roads by moonlight, wringing my unsubstantial hands, wailing down the wind, calling your name. . . . Will you hear me, then, my Jean? Will you come to me finally in the dark realms and still my weeping?"

"Dear God!" Jean choked.

"Go," she murmured, "go, my Jeannot, and do your duty. Honor France by it, and yourself—and me. For this cannot be, and we know it. Now kiss me, quickly, Jeannot, and go. . . ."

She stood there a long time after he had gone. Then very slowly, she turned back to Thérèse. But it was not to her that she spoke.

"Yes," she whispered, "honor me, my Jean. For I think soon I shall have some right to be numbered among those who have died for France. For have I not given her the heart from out my body—all my breath, my hope— my life?"

There was no need for haste, but Jean rode back toward the villa at a thundering gallop. He drove his mount on furiously, with whip and spur, until the horse was covered with lather; he, who had always been kindness itself to his animals. Slowly his mood changed from fury to something very like acceptance—which was a good thing for the horse, else he would have broken its wind, or killed it.

A day later, he was on the diligence bound for the capital, with the absolute certainty that a chapter in his life was forever closed.

And a new one has opened, he thought with faint pleasure, as he sat with M. Reveillon, the prominent manufacturer of wallpapers, outside the Café Charpentier, at the foot of the Pont-Neuf. He had met Reveillon shortly after his arrival in Paris. The manufacturer had thought an order of wallpaper for the flat of a deputy to the States-General important enough to demand his personal attention.

Pierre and Marianne had already done wonders with the shabby flat in the Rue Saint-Antoine, near the Bastille; but two things had remained for Jean's own care: a broken balustrade, on the landing outside his door, five floors above the street, and hence exceedingly dangerous on a dark night, and the wallpaper.

Jean found that he liked the bustling manufacturer very much. M. Reveillon was the soul of kindness. He paid the very least of his workmen twenty-five sous a day, an unheard-of wage in Paris; he had kept his whole staff of three hundred and fifty on at full wages the whole of the terrible past winter, though in reality he had work for less than half of them. A liberal and a philanthropist, he had been chosen elector for the Sainte Marguerite district. In some ways, he reminded Jean of his own father. Yes, Jean mused, I like him very much. . . .

The wine at the Café Charpentier was good, and they soon found themselves surrounded. M. Reveillon was well

known and respected in the *quartier*, but it was Jean
Paul, himself, who was the center of attraction. The truth
of the matter was that the Parisians were starved for
news of the provinces. In its absence, all sorts of wild
rumors were flying about. Jean did his best to lay the
wildest of these at rest:

No, he knew of no châteaux burnt in Provence. Yes,
there had been rioting in Marseille; but that state of affairs had come happily to an end. Grain riots? Yes—
many, but small affairs. . . .

The talk rushed on in waves. If there is any one thing
your Parisian is master of, Jean thought wryly, it's talk.
I wonder how they'll acquit themselves when the time for
action has come?

He had time now, to listen, to fill in the details of the
picture. It was alarming, to say the least. All Paris was at
fever pitch. Every *quartier* had seen scattered rioting. . . .

He was on the point of asking Reveillon what measures were being taken to insure public safety, when he
saw a girl coming toward their table. She was a small
girl with inky-black hair, and enormous dark eyes. She
moved very slowly among the tables, offering the faded
flowers she had in her hand to first one then another of
the men. Something about the way she moved caught
Jean's attention. There was a curious hesitation to all her
movements. Then one of the habitués bought some of her
flowers, and she gave them to him. Though she was very
close to the man, she missed his outstretched hand by
several inches, and Jean Paul realized that she was blind.

He stared at her. He had seen blind beggars before, but
this one was different. When she was closer, he saw what
that difference was. She was lovely—utterly lovely. He
revised his thought consciously, aware as he did so, that
he was probably the only man in the sidewalk café who
was capable of thinking so. Because the blind flower girl's
beauty was entirely different from that of any other
woman he had ever known.

It lacks something, he mused, and it has something,
and both what it lacks and what it has are different. . . .

"That's Fleurette," Reveillon said, following his steady
gaze. "Everyone loves her, poor thing—her affliction has
made an angel of her. . . ."

"That's it!" Jean Paul said aloud. "She is like an angel,

isn't she—no, not an angel exactly, but certainly nothing of this world. Her beauty is ethereal. . . ."

"Ethereal?" Reveillon said. "Why, yes—you have something there. Strange I never thought of Fleurette as being beautiful. My taste runs to more fleshy women; and that poor child is mere skin and bones. . . ."

She was painfully thin, Jean saw, and her clothes were mere rags. But her face was saintly, and what she lacked was any hint of sensuality whatsoever. And what she has, he thought with a surge of deep pity, is the rarest thing in the world, patience, and real goodness. . . .

"Call her," he said to Reveillon.

The manufacturer stared at him. Then he shrugged.

"Each to his own taste," he muttered. "Fleurette, come over here!"

She came at once, using the sound of his voice to guide her.

When she was close, Jean Paul stared at her for several seconds before he spoke.

"Your flowers," he said gruffly, "give them to me—I'll take them all. . . ."

She passed them over, and he gave her a golden louis— a hundred times and more what they were worth.

"I—I have no small money, M'sieur," she said, "I cannot change this. . . ."

He had been fascinated by her fingertips' deft movement over the surface of the coin. Now he smiled at her, glad that she could not see his broken face.

"I didn't ask for change, little Fleurette," he said. "Take it, and buy yourself some warm clothes. . . ."

"Oh, I couldn't! It's too much and—"

"Take it," Jean Paul said.

"M'sieur is too kind," she murmured. Her voice, Jean noted, was high and clear and sweet, like certain notes of the violin, and again like little bells.

"It's a custom of mine," Jean laughed. "In every city, I always find a certain person who will bring me luck. You're my luck, here, Fleurette. You pass this way every day?"

"Yes, M'sieur," Fleurette said; "here, or wherever M'sieur wills. . . ."

"Then stand on the corner of the Rue Saint-Antoine and the Rue Saint Louis, every afternoon at fourteen hours," Jean said; "bring with you a nosegay—no a boutonnière—and I will buy one every day—for luck, little Fleurette—your luck, and mine. . . ."

"Thank you, M'sieur," Fleurette said. "You are very kind. . . ."

"And don't forget to buy warm clothes," Jean said. "You'll catch your death as you are."

"I'm used to the cold," Fleurette smiled. "I don't think I've really been warm in the wintertime in all my life."

"Dear God!" Jean whispered.

"But I shall buy a warm dress, and a cloak and shoes. It will be wonderful to be warmly dressed—" she stopped, and her child-like face was troubled, suddenly.

"What is it, Fleurette?" Jean said.

"I was thinking that I hoped you would approve of my choices, M'sieur. But then I remembered it could only be by accident if I happened to buy pretty things, for I cannot see how they will look . . ."

"Tomorrow morning at nine and a half hours," Jean said, "I will meet you at the same place. Then I will go with you and select your clothes."

"Would you?" Fleurette breathed. "Oh, thank you, M'sieur—thank you a thousand times!"

"Don't mention it," Jean smiled. "Till tomorrow, then . . ."

"Au 'voir, M'sieur," she whispered, "and thank you. . . ."

Jean was conscious that Reveillon was staring at him; and that the manufacturer's good, honest face was creased with frowning.

M. Reveillon was not one to hide his thoughts.

"Are you," he growled, "planning to seduce that poor waif?"

Jean stiffened in his seat, and his whole face darkened so that the scar became white lightning suddenly, zigzagging down his face. Then slowly he relaxed.

"Have you never heard of—pity, M. Reveillon?" he sighed.

"Forgive me," M. Reveillon said; "I have lived in Paris too long, I think. 'Tis unlikely that our effete corruptions should be widespread in the provinces. There is, you understand, a certain type of mind that would delight in her blindness—and her innocence—the better to lead her into practices of nameless vileness. I know a high police official with whom I'd leave my wife, but not a girl child under ten years. One great noble has twenty pages, all pretty boys of tender years. . . ."

"Please!" Jean said. He felt sick, just listening to it.

"Sorry. Perhaps there is a God, after all. It's no accident I think, that so many troubles should be visited upon this modern Sodom we have created. The wrath of God, M. Marin! Another cup, perhaps?"

"No thank you," Jean said; "I'd best be getting back now. I have a thousand things to do. . . ."

He had. All his days were filled, which was a good thing, for it left him no time for thinking. He bought the clothes for Fleurette—good, warm serviceable things, which were really not too pretty, but which delighted her good, simple heart. Marianne altered them for her, because she was so thin it was impossible to fit her. They were used clothes, castoffs of some great lady, for in those days, ready-made clothes did not exist. Jean had no objection to having clothes made for his protégée except the fact the times were out of joint. A dress that ordinarily would have been finished by the dressmaker in a week to ten days, now required three to five weeks, due to the difficulty in obtaining materials. In the meantime, poor Fleurette might die of the inclement March weather.

The ritual between them was now firmly established. Every day he bought a flower from her, paying her far more than it was worth. She stopped protesting about this after a while. She seemed to be more grateful for his company, for the few gentle words he exchanged with her each day than for the money. He learned many things about her: She was an orphan, living alone. She did not suffer too much, really; there were always kind ladies and gentlemen among the throngs of Paris. In the wintertime, when she could get no flowers, she made artificial ones of feathers, or of paper dipped in wax. The old woman who was concierge of the house where she lived mixed the colors for her. But she made more money when she had real flowers. . . .

Not that she needed very much money. She could live on five sous a day, as she had really very little appetite. Clothes were out of the question. These were the first she had ever had bought for her. All the rest of her rags were castoffs from the noble ladies. But since all the troubles, the noble ladies didn't come any more; and since she couldn't sew, her things had gradually been reduced to rags. . . .

Talking to her did things for Jean Paul Marin. He had suffered—more perhaps than the common run of men. But, what, actually, were his sufferings compared to this? He had lost the woman who loved him; but, some day, if the wound in his heart were healed, there might be another. This blind girl had never known love, a home, friends—or any of the thousands of things that he took as a matter of course.

It troubled him to discover how much he meant to her. She would begin smiling while he was still yards away from her, whether or not he were alone, or walking in the midst of a crowd. He asked her about that.

"I know your footsteps, M'sieur Jean," she said. "Everybody's footsteps sound different from everyone else's—didn't you know that? I think that we blind people hear better than people who have sight. Our sense of smell is keener, too. Nature, I think, tries to make up to us for our lack of eyes. . . ."

Jean stared at her.

"How do I smell?" he laughed.

"Good. So—so clean. There is a kind of soap you use that has a wonderful smell—and then there is your tobacco, mingled with the smell of the wool in your clothes. Your clothes are very fine, because only the best wool smells like that. Yet, you don't use perfumes. That's strange. Most other great gentlemen do. . . ."

"I'm not a great gentleman," Jean told her.

"Oh yes you are! Perhaps you are not of noble birth, because you talk French very plainly—no La! La's—and other such foolishness. But it's very beautiful the way you talk. Your voice is like music—very deep and rich, with no harshness in it at all. I think that you haven't any harshness in you at all. You help me because you are kind, really kind—not, as so many do, because it makes them feel powerful and important to aid a beggar. . . ."

"I help you because I like you," Jean said.

"And I like you. I wake up in the night dreading the day that you'll leave Paris. I—I shall be so lonely, then. I was always lonely, I guess; but I never thought about it much before now . . ." She sighed. "Strange, I dreamed of having a friend one day—a real friend, like you are to me. I thought it would make me so happy. . . ."

"Well, doesn't it?" Jean said.

"Yes, oh, yes! Wonderfully happy; but sad, too—at the same time. You see, it makes the other things worse: the being alone so much, and the thinking. . . ."

"What do you think about, little Fleurette?"

"You, mostly," she said, and it touched him, because he knew she was entirely without guile. "About you, and about the future, which was a thing I never permitted myself to think about before. Now I think about it all the time, and that's what makes me sad. What will happen to me when you go back to your own town?"

"I'm not going back, Fleurette," Jean said; "I'm going to stay here—"

He stopped without finishing what he had intended to say, for the radiance in her face startled him. He had to remind himself of her blindness, because she kept her great, dark eyes fixed upon his face the whole time they were talking, following, he guessed, the sound of his voice; but he remembered it now. The glow in her eyes was unfocused, and when he moved his head quickly aside, her gaze did not follow him. He often did things like that now, almost subconsciously; for the better he came to know Fleurette, the more intolerable he found her blindness.

There is absolutely no justice in the universe, he was thinking, when he saw that her face had become sad again.

"What's the matter?" he asked her.

"I just remembered that even if you do stay here, you'll probably get married. And no wife would put up with your spending so much time talking to a blind beggar. . . ."

"How do you know I'm not already married," Jean teased.

"Oh, I know you aren't. You don't talk or act anything like a married man. You're too calm and free and unworried. Married men are never like that. . . ."

"Mlle. Fleurette, la clairvoyante!" Jean laughed. "What makes you so sure that any woman would have me—even if I wanted to get married, which I don't. . . ."

"Women aren't all fools," Fleurette said seriously; "one of them will be sure to realize soon how lucky she'd be to have you . . ."

"Lucky?" Jean mocked.

"Yes. You are so kind, that's one thing. For another, you're tall—"

"How the devil do you know that?"

"I hear where your voice comes from—from above my head. And then, you're strong. I can tell that from the way you walk, and the way your hand grips my elbow when you help me across streets. Also, I think you're probably very handsome. . . ."

"Handsome!" Jean growled. He had remembered, suddenly, the streetwalker in Marseille, and the curious effect the sight of his broken face had had upon her. "Now, you're wrong," he laughed; "I'm as ugly as sin—no, uglier. . . ."

"Let me see," Fleurette whispered, and put up her delicate fingertips to touch his face.

"No!" Jean got out; "by God's love, no!"

"My—my hands are clean," Fleurette whispered; "it's the only way I can tell what people really are like. . . ."

"I'm sorry," Jean said gently; "but let that be one secret between us, Fleurette—how I look, I mean. I'd rather you didn't know. . . ."

"Why?" Fleurette said.

"Because I really am ugly—uglier than you can possibly imagine. It's better like this. If you knew, it might make a difference. . . ."

"It wouldn't," Fleurette said; "but if M'sieur prefers . . ."

"M'sieur prefers," Jean said. "Au 'voir, Fleurette."

"Au revoir, M'sieur Jean," Fleurette whispered. "You —you aren't angry at me?"

"No," Jean laughed; "I could never be angry with you, little Fleurette. . . ."

"I'm glad," she said gravely; "till tomorrow, then. . . ."

He was surprised at the force of the emotion that had prompted him to conceal his face from Fleurette. What difference did it make? he asked himself, what earthly difference if that poor blind waif knows I'm ugly or not? Yet, I didn't want her to know. I desperately didn't want her to. Is that why I cling to this curious friendship? I think perhaps it is. I have sunk so far as to gain warmth and comfort from the admiration of this child—basking in the fact that she cannot be repelled by this horror of a face. Still, it has gone too far to be ended now—besides, the poor child depends upon it, too. Not too much harm in that, I guess—two forlorn ones clinging together against the indifference of the world. . . .

He was so preoccupied with his thoughts, that he missed
a step at the top landing and almost plunged through the
broken railing. Have to fix that, he thought; now—been
putting it off too long. . . . Thereupon he gathered up a
few tools, and having bought wood from the shop on the
ground floor, he put up a new railing. When he had finished it, he had to laugh. It was, he had to admit, a miserable job. All it would serve for would be to warn a person in the darkness, in time to draw back from the danger, for it certainly would not support even the weight of
a child.

Strange, he mused, we bourgeois are the really helpless ones. The peasants have strength and skill gained
from their work. The nobles, come to think of it, are
usually powerful men because of their training in sports,
riding, warfare; only we bourgeois are wedded to the pen
and the ledger, growing up pale and thin and studious
with no manual dexterity at all. I'm strong—grace of the
Toulon *bagne*—but the only two things I know how to do
with my hands are breaking rocks and writing letters. . . .

He and Pierre were well along now with their newspaper. They called it the *Mercury of the Third Estate,* and
from the first it was popular. There were other papers
much more popular, however—all of them extremist
sheets, really nothing more than pamphlets, bearing such
grotesque titles as: *Le Gloria in Excelsis du Peuple, Le
De Profundis de la Noblesse et du Clergé, La Semaine
Sainte ou les Lamentations du Tiers État*—and written in
language so highflown as to be utterly ridiculous. But the
lackeys, unemployed hairdressers, fishwives, stonecutters,
vagabonds and criminals who swarmed the streets of
Paris those first weeks of April, 1789, literally devoured
them. They had only one thing in common: their blood-
thirstiness. For already, in the court of the Palais Royal,
under the protection of the treasonable Duc d'Orleans,
who hoped to profit by all the confusion that he permitted, and often even paid for, by making himself King,
men like Camille Desmoulins were making themselves
heard with both tongue and pen.

It was, strangely, the very moderation of Jean Paul
Marin's writings that gained him a solid audience. Real
moderates had practically no other sheet to read. Pierre

and Jean were making a handsome profit, for their clients came from the wealthy bourgeoisie without notable exception. And Pierre, canny peasant that he was, insisted upon instantly converting every franc they earned into gold.

Jean worked hard. He saw Fleurette every day. He sat every evening in one or another of the cafés and talked politics with M. Reveillon and his friends. The unvarying ritual of his life pleased him. Unvarying, that is, up to the twenty-seventh of April. For after that, he never saw M. Reveillon again.

He heard about it first on Saturday, the twenty-fifth. He came down into the Rue Saint-Antoine to find a mob of more than five hundred people collected before the paper works.

"Down with Reveillon!" they were roaring. "Kill the traitor! Burn the place down!"

Jean moved among the fringes of the crowd.

"What is it?" he asked of a man rather better dressed than the others.

" 'Tis said that Reveillon spoke badly of the people in Assembly yesterday," the man said.

Jean stared at him.

"Reveillon?" Jean said. "I don't believe that. Why, the people have no better friend. What, precisely, did he say?"

A bearded rough standing beside the man to whom Jean had spoken turned upon him.

"What's it to you, you dandy?" he snarled. "I'll tell you, if you want to know. That fat bloodsucker said that a workman with a family could live on fifteen sous a day!"

"That's a lie," Jean snapped; "Reveillon's a friend of mine. I happen to know he pays the man who sweeps up the cuttings twenty-five sous a day."

"A friend of yours, hein?" the bearded villain roared. "Look, boys! Here's one of the bloodsucker's friends! Regard his clothes—a damned aristocrat or I miss my guess!"

Twenty sticks were lifted before the echoes of his shout had died away.

Jean stood there, smiling his icy smile.

"You rat," he said quietly, "you ordure of scum and unspeakable vileness. Lay a finger on me and I'll break every bone in your unwashed body."

The rough hesitated.

Jean started walking toward him, straight toward him

and the twenty other scoundrels at his back. The sticks
wavered. They weren't prepared for this. Nothing in their
previous experience had prepared them to deal with a man
who wouldn't run when outnumbered twenty to one.

When he was close enough, Jean's left hand shot out
suddenly and caught the man by his shirt front. The
muscles of his arms bunched. Inch by inch he lifted the
man up with his left hand until only the toes of his ragged
boots were dragging in the dirt. Then Jean stiffened his
arm suddenly, straight out, and the man went flying backward to crash into the circle of his friends. The impact
knocked several of them to the earth. They came up,
roaring, only to stare straight into the muzzle of Jean
Paul's pistol.

"Don't follow me," he said pleasantly; "I haven't done
any rat-hunting lately, but 'tis a sport I always enjoy. . . ."

Then he spun on his heel and walked away from them,
moving quietly, but without haste. They didn't follow him.
He had known that they wouldn't. The one trait that all
mobs possess in common is cowardice.

All day Sunday the rioting grew worse. By Monday, the
twenty-seventh, the mobs were completely out of hand.
Jean put on workman's clothes and mingled with them. He
was troubled by the fact that neither Saturday nor Sunday had he seen Fleurette. He guessed that she must be
staying at home, out of fear of the ceaseless uproar. He
cursed the fact that he had never troubled to find out
where her room was.

The mob was screaming curses at every priest who
passed. They came pouring into the Place de Grève, bearing an effigy of M. Reveillon. They had decorated the
effigy with the ribbon of the order of St. Michael. There
with much howling and buffoonery, they proceeded to
have a mock trial. The effigy was condemned and burned
on the spot.

"His house!" they roared now. "Burn the scoundrel's
house!"

They boiled back into the Rue Saint-Antoine. But the
Guard was already there, drawn up before M. Reveillon's
dwelling. The mob, Jean saw at once, had no stomach for
gunfire. They recoiled from the leveled muskets of the
guards, muttering obscenities. But five minutes later, they
gave Jean a demonstration of how dangerous it had be-

come in Paris to be even known as a friend of anyone who had fallen out of favor.

Five houses down the street they stopped again. A man lived here, a manufacturer of saltpeter, whom Jean had often seen in Reveillon's company. This guilt by association was entirely enough for the mob. Within the hour they had stripped the house of Reveillon's friend, piling his effects and furniture up in the street before it. Then they made a bonfire of all the innocent man's possessions.

Jean left the crowd then, and went back to his printing shop. He sat there all night, with his loaded pistols close at hand. But the mob passed his establishment by. It came to him, finally, that all the time he had spent in M. Reveillon's company had been in one or another café away from the Faubourg of Saint-Antoine, and that most of the troublemakers came from other sections of Paris anyway. Except for his own mistake in identifying himself as one of Reveillon's friends, he was in little danger from the mob. Whatever danger existed lay in the chance of his scarred face being recognized by the small group of men he had fought. That was a serious enough danger if it happened, but the chances of it happening were not very great.

Tuesday was the same as Monday—only worse. The crowds in the *quartier* were thicker than ever. The rumors had spread, gaining new additions with every telling. What troubled Jean most of all was the fact that most of the new recruits were good, solid folk, grim in their belief that they were somehow fighting for the Third Estate. Looters, bandits, madmen, scum were actually less dangerous, he realized, than good, determined men fighting for an ideal, however mistaken.

"We shall be lost," a sturdy baker told Jean, "if we don't all stick together. . . ."

The organization was better now. Crowds of stern men moved off into the Faubourg Saint-Marceau. When they came back, their numbers had tripled. They, Jean learned, had been enrolling new recruits—willingly, for the most part, but under the threat of lifted clubs, if need be.

Reveillon was gone. He had fled Paris during the night. Jean was glad of that. The Paris mob was capable of killing him without giving him a chance to prove how absurd the charges against him were.

There was no point in trying to work. Pierre du Pain

kept to his flat, pistols ready, to defend Marianne. Jean
wandered with the mob, seeing it all, recording it all in his
mind, so that he could set it down when the city had
quieted.

At the Porte Saint-Antoine, he saw the Noblesse get
their first lesson in what their changed status was going
to be. With their usual arrogant indifference to the tumults of the people, hundreds of them, with many wealthy
bourgeois as well, had left the city that morning to go to
the races. When they returned that evening, the mob
stopped them at the Saint-Antoine Gate. Burly fellows
seized the reins of the horses, and around the doors of
each carriage knots of men and women gathered with
clubs and rude pikes ready.

"Down with you!" they growled.

There was nothing for the brilliantly clad gentlefolk to
do but to obey.

"Now shout 'Vive Necker!'" the ruffians commanded;
"Say, 'Long Live the Third Estate!' Louder, you aristocratic dogs! All right you noble whores—make a noise!
You shrilled better than that when your favorite was
running behind this afternoon!"

Jean felt a surge of pity, for these delicate, perfumed,
powdered creatures, forced to kneel in the dusty street.
Then he touched his own scarred face and all his pity
vanished.

Give it to them, he thought. They've had it coming a
long time. . . .

He tired of watching it after a while, and turned away.
Then his whole face slackened with relief, for he saw
Fleurette coming across the street, her cane tapping on
the stones.

Thank God she's all right, he thought, and waited.

That was his mistake. For one desperate madman of a
nobleman, braver, or drunker than his fellows, came hurtling through the throng, his coachman lashing the horses,
the yellow coach careening between all the halted vehicles so fast that now this pair of wheels, now that, were
lifted clear of the ground, the horses' hoofs making
sparks against the cobblestones, the sound of their coming
like thunder; and he, standing there, having no time, no
time at all, even to scream out, "Fleurette!" before the
maddened, lathered animals were upon her.

He dug in his heels and started running, at a diagonal,

seeing that some of her clothes, the good dress he had
bought her, being of stout stuff that would not tear like
the rags she formerly wore, had caught in a projection of
the yellow coach, and she was being dragged like a doll
beneath the coach, whose wheels miraculously had not
passed over her.

He ran faster than he had ever run before in his life.
The last three yards he covered in a gigantic leap, his
fingers closing around the reins of the lead horse, and he
swinging there, dragging the beast's head down with
a strength that was beyond strength, that was pure fury,
desperation, slowing them, catching with his other hand
the reins of the next horse, turning the outside pair aside,
so that all four horses were forced to turn, and the coach,
skidding, crashed into the walls of a house. He was under
it before it had stopped shaking from the impact, dragging her out.

She was unconscious, but alive. A thin trickle of blood
came out of both corners of her mouth. He lifted her up
and faced the coach door. Even before it opened, the coat
of arms on it seized his attention almost like a physical
blow, so that when Gervais la Moyte stepped down, he
was almost prepared for him.

"Behold your work!" he said, and for all its quiet, his
voice was like a suddenly unsheathed blade.

"My God!" Gervais exclaimed; "I didn't see, I didn't
know. . . ."

Jean opened his mouth to answer him, but he stopped
then, frozen, his blood congealed, his breath thickened
into solidity, a ball at the base of his throat. For a woman
had appeared in the door of the coach behind Gervais la
Moyte. A tall woman, bejeweled, painted, her tawny hair
unpowdered, her hazel eyes widening like those of a great
cat come suddenly from a lighted place into darkness.

"Lucienne!" Jean breathed.

She had been lovely before. But then it had been a
beauty without art. Paris had changed her. And, because
she was one of those women so basically perfect that even
artificiality heightened her, she had become something
more than lovely. Now, Jean thought weakly, now she is
glorious. . . .

He heard the thunder of running feet, hundreds of feet
pounding toward them.

"Ran over her!" they were roaring. "Fleurette—poor, blind Fleurette! Kill them! Kill the noble swine!"

Jean freed one arm from beneath his pitiful, broken little burden. He caught Gervais la Moyte by the shoulder, and spun him, hard in the direction of a narrow street.

"Run," he spat, "both of you! Damn you, run!"

They flew into the little street an instant before the first of the fishwives, stonecutters, brigands, workers, thieves hurtled around the corner and saw the coach, and Jean standing there, with Fleurette in his arms.

"Where are they?" they screamed at him. "Where? Is she dead?"

"Gone," Jean said. "No, she isn't dead—but she will be, if you don't let me get her to a doctor. . . ."

They cleared a way for him. Some of the women and a man or two went with him. But before he was ten yards away, he heard the sound of smashing wood, glass breaking; then hoarse-voiced, deep, terror-filled at first, then louder, shriller with the ragged note of pain getting into it, the first screams of the Comte de Gravereau's lackeys.

He didn't look back. There was nothing he could do, now. He heard a new sound, a scream, too; but not a scream, nothing that was human even, and it was this that forced him to look back. He saw what it was. They were even killing the horses.

Marianne worked wonders. It was she, actually, who saved Fleurette's life. She bathed the poor broken body, straightening the blind waif's limbs into a comfortable position, got the brandy down her throat without strangling her, so that when Pierre came back with the Surgeon of the Guard, a military doctor quite accustomed to broken bones, all he had to do was to set her three fractured ribs, and her broken left arm. He worked well, with rough skill. Toward nightfall, she regained consciousness, and was able to take a little hot soup. Then she sank into a deep sleep.

Jean was glad of that, because not even the incessant gunfire in the Rue Saint-Antoine disturbed her. When, finally, the guards were forced to bring up cannon to disperse the mob, she jumped and whimpered a little in her sleep, but the belly-deep, bass rumble of the artillery fire could not waken her.

The mob, during those hours that Fleurette lay unconscious, sacked the Reveillon house from top to bottom.

They burned everything that blameless man owned, even casting live chickens into the bonfire. They drank every drop of wine he had in his cellar, and when that was finished, they drank the casks of varnish he also had there, being by this time too drunk to know the difference. Five of them died in convulsions from drinking the varnish.

When the Watch, the Royal Croats Cavalry, the French Guards, and the Swiss Guards finally got there to rescue the thirty guards the mob had overwhelmed, they had the courage of M. Reveillon's good brandy. They charged the soldiers again and again. Two hundred rioters were killed. Three hundred more were wounded. The only thing that stopped them, finally, was the cannon.

The revolt had lasted four days. And everybody in Paris—except the higher Noblesse, who had long since forgotten how to use either their brains or their eyes—knew that the world had ended.

"To be born again," Jean Paul Marin whispered, as he sat beside his own bed looking at Fleurette's sleeping form; "but not the same—not ever the same again. . . ."

Then, moved by sudden impulse, he leaned over, and touched her fevered brow lightly with his lips.

7

"It is strange," Jean Paul Marin wrote to his brother, Bertrand, "how ill adapted the human animal is to any kind of change whatsoever. On Monday, the fourth day of May, the States-General begin their sessions at Versailles. . . ."

He paused, looking at his calendar.

"That historic day being now but two days off, I find myself in the midst of preparations. They are simple, as I have decided against moving to Versailles. The weather is mild, and the daily ride to that fair seat of Royalty cannot but be beneficial to my health. Besides, my business affairs in Paris require that I keep in constant touch. But to return to the matter of change:

"You and I, dear brother, have had many bitter quarrels over my radicalism. Honesty, at the moment, leaves me no other course but to humbly beg your pardon, and to admit that in many things you were right. This will astonish you, I know; but the things I have seen in and around Paris have brought me to the reluctant conclusion that the overthrow of an established order of society is not a thing to be undertaken lightly. . . .

"Ills there are in our realm; grave ills, intolerable ills. But now I wonder if in our pellmell rush toward reform, we may be merely substituting for them others graver, even more insufferable. The arrogance and folly of the nobles was for men of our class a perpetual insult; but contrasting it now with the beastly stupidity and the murderous fury of the *canaille,* I remind myself that it at least had the saving grace of the forms of courtesy. . . .

"In short, your fire-eating brother finds himself in the curious position of being spoken of in all quarters as a known moderate, in some, indeed, he is damned as a conservative. I have changed, Bertie—so much that it sometimes startles me. . . ."

He stretched out his hand to dip his pen in the inkwell. He had said all he needed to, but he must make the courteous inquiries after the health of Simone, and ask of some word of Thérèse, and even of Nicole, neither of whom, strangely, had written him. At that moment, he glanced toward Fleurette. She was lying very still on the bed with her eyes opened wide. From her very stillness he knew she was listening to something. He knew also that it would be several minutes before the same sound reached his ears.

"What is it?" he said.

"Someone is coming," she told him. "The *facteur,* I think. Ah, yes, it is the *facteur.* The poor man, his feet must hurt him so. I can tell by the way he limps. . . ."

Jean got up at once. He had never ceased to be amazed at this faculty of hers, but he knew better than to doubt her. Besides, it was actually his fault that she could hear the postman. In his great need to have some word from Nicole, Jean had begged the old man to bring all his mail directly up to his flat, instead of leaving it with the concierge below. Of course, he tipped the *facteur* liberally each time the old man had to climb the stairs; but he was conscious of the fact that it wasn't really necessary. He went up and down the stairs several times a day, and any letter that came for him, even one from Nicole, could easily wait the short time that elapsed before he passed the office of the concierge.

He went around the little cot he had bought for himself. Pierre and Marianne had offered to take Fleurette off his hands, but the doctor had stressed the inadvisability of moving her. So Jean had given up his good bed and bought the cot.

He met the postman at the *entresol,* thus saving that tired old man a climb of three more flights of stairs. There was only one letter for him. To his disappointment, he recognized Bertrand's bold hand. Still, Bertrand might conceivably mention Nicole, so he took the letter and went back upstairs to his flat. That he didn't open it at once, was not due to any restraint on his part, but to the fact that even in the daytime it was so dark in the hallways of the building that he couldn't have read it anyway.

Fleurette lay on the bed listening to his breathing. She heard the first rasping note get into it. Then it stopped altogether.

"What is it?" she cried out, forcing herself half up with her one good arm. "Tell me what it is, Jean?"

She realized at once that she had called him by his name without any title. It was the first time she had ever done that. She opened her lips to apologize, to say—but Jean's voice cut her off. She would not have recognized it, if she hadn't known it was he.

"Oh, my God!" he got out. "Oh, dear God!"

"Tell me what it is!" she screamed at him. "Please tell me!"

But he was beyond speech. He was sitting on the little cot without knowing how he got there, staring at the words in Bertrand's letter, his sight clear, unblurred, for this was a thing beyond tears, reading over and over again in pure naked anguish, the words:

". . . a major *Jacquerie*. Every château in this part of the province was burned to the ground. Prepare yourself, mon Jean, for this will be hard. Thérèse—is dead. Gervais defended his château with some courage, but when he saw that there was no chance, he fled, leaving our poor sister to her fate. 'Tis said that he is now in Paris. You may even see him, soon, because he will sit for the nobles of the province in the States. . . .

"I have no suggestion of how you should deal with him in such eventuality. I cannot make suggestions. You, and you alone, of us all opposed this match. Were you here, I'd ask your forgiveness upon my knees. . . ."

"Jean!" Fleurette wept. "You're ill! Speak to me, tell me. . . ."

"Lie down again, little one," Jean said; and his voice was curiously gentle. "You'll harm yourself. . . ."

He sat there, holding the letter. It had several pages, and he had read only part of the first. He must read it all, but he couldn't seem to. His fingers wouldn't work, somehow. He couldn't separate the pages. He sat there, holding it. Fleurette was crying, very softly. He could hear her. The sound came from a million leagues away, somewhere on the other side of the moon.

He had the second page now. The words leaped up at him, smashed into his consciousness like ax blows:

". . . complete   carbonization . . . recognized   her only by her jewelry . . . burial at once . . . held mob at bay with pistols while the Abbé Grégoire said the last rites. They stoned him while he was praying . . . never got back to the Abbey—murdered on the road. . . ."

Jean's lips moved forming words, but not even Fleurette's keen ears could catch them.

"I am myself in hiding; I must flee the country. Because of Simone and our connection with the nobility, Villa Marin also is no more. . . . Every noble family, and many of the richer bourgeois suffered the same fate. . . .

"Of Gervais' sister," he read and stopped; for those were the last words on the page. He sat there, staring at them. He had faced the guns of his enemies. He had walked into the clubs and knives of the most dangerous criminals of Paris. He had risked torture not once but a dozen times in his attempts to escape the *bagne* at Toulon. But he could not turn that page.

"Turn it, Jean," Fleurette whispered; "read what it says. It's better that you know. . . ."

He stared at her. But her face was not even turned in his direction. Then he too heard how loudly the stiff paper rattled in his shaking hands. He moved, convulsively. The letter fell from his stiffened fingers, and scattered over the floor. He bent over and began to pick them up. The forever precise Bertrand had numbered them. Jean held page three in his hand.

". . . I can tell you but little. The *petit château* of the Marquis de Saint Gravert was burned with the rest. This I know, beyond all doubt. From there on, the rumors contradict one another. Many hold that the entire family perished in the flames. I doubt this, because Julien Lamont has not been at home for some months. Then, at least one of their servants escaped. This one, I have seen, and he believes that it is possible for Madame la Marquise and the children to have escaped, for he himself helped them into a fast fiacre, and though they were pursued, none of their pursuers were mounted. Here, my knowledge of Nicole la Moyte and her children ends. . . .

"You will wonder why I single her out. The reason, *mon pauvre,* is simple: the last time I visited our poor, sainted sister, she was there. She inquired after you with such extravagant interest that Thérèse gave her a warning look. She said quite calmly: 'I don't care if he knows.' Then, turning to me, she looked me full in the face and told me, 'I love your brother. I have since the first night

I saw him. I intend to go on loving him till the day I die.'
Which astonished me, though it shouldn't have; you, *mon
frère,* have always had a way with women. What troubles
me more is the fact that Thérèse told me that you return
this mad love of hers. I pray God that some day you may
find her again, for, who knows?—after the world has
been completely turned upside down, there may no longer
be any barriers between you. . . .

"One word more, and I am done. It is my plan, as soon
as it is feasible, to flee to Austria, where so many of those
fortunate enough to escape have already gone. It may be
that I shall learn something of your lost Nicole there;
because, if she made good her escape, it will be there
that she will have gone. . . ."

There was more, but Jean didn't read it. He had to get
out of the flat, walk in the open, think. But then he saw
Fleurette, lying on the bed, her left arm in a sling, her
body under her nightgown bulky with bandages. He
couldn't leave her alone. Of course, it was almost time for
Marianne to come and see after her, but the short space
of time he would have to wait was intolerable to him.

"I'm going out," he told her, and his voice was strange,
even to his own ears; "I'll send Marianne to you. . . ."

"As you will, M'sieur Jean," she said. And somehow,
without moving from the bed she had withdrawn a distance of a thousand leagues.

"Fleurette—" he said. "What's the matter?"

"I—I am nothing to you!" she sobbed. "You push me
away. You always keep me outside your life. . . ."

"What do you want me to do?" he asked wonderingly.

"Share things with me. Your joys—your sorrows, as I
have shared with you. For instance, something in that
letter you got has troubled you, terribly. But you won't
tell me what it is. I asked you, but you wouldn't tell me."

Jean studied her face a long time.

"All right," he whispered, "I'll tell you. My little sister
is dead. She was murdered by the peasants in an uprising
near Marseille. They burned the house of her husband,
who is a noble. She was in the house, and they burned
her with it. Enough?"

"Too much!" she whispered. Then: "Come here, my
Jean. . . ."

He came over to where she lay.

"Sit down," she murmured.

He sat down on the edge of the bed, and she put up her good hand and stroked his hair. She was crying. She didn't say anything. She just lay there and stroked his hair and cried.

He stood up.

"I have to go," he said. "I'll send Marianne. . . ."

Then he went through the door and down the stairs.

Pierre came out of the printing shop as he passed. He took one look at Jean's face and fell into step beside him.

"Want to tell me about it?" he said.

"No," Jean Paul said. "I don't want to talk about it."

Pierre kept on walking beside him. They walked a long time until they came to the Café Victoire, in the Rue de Sèvres, already becoming known as the rendezvous of the moderates.

"Sit down," Pierre growled. "Have a drink."

"All right," Jean Paul said.

The waiter brought the two brandies. Jean downed his at a gulp. "Another," he said to the waiter.

"That bad?" Pierre said.

Jean didn't answer him.

"Damn you!" Pierre spat. "Talk! Get it out of your system. . . ."

"All right," Jean Paul said wearily. Then he told him.

Pierre sat there very quietly for a long moment. Then he began to swear. He swore very quietly and precisely and fluently with deep feeling and great art. Jean listened to him with awe. This was priestly swearing, masterly profanity, for Pierre du Pain did not descend to obscenities; he merely pronounced malediction upon Gervais la Moyte, calling down the wrath of heaven upon his head with an invention and variety that would have done credit to a Prince of the Church.

Jean put out his hand and caught his friend's wrist.

"Wait, Pierre," he said. "What of the men and women who actually killed her? La Moyte was guilty of selfishness and cowardice; but it was our people—the people whose representative I am, who killed her. I find myself confused. La Moyte left my sister, and she was murdered—by people whom I spent years in inciting to violence myself. If La Moyte is an accessory after the fact by reason of his cowardly desertion, what am I? Am I not guilty *a priori?*"

"You damned provincial lawyer!" Pierre roared. "Must you be forever splitting hairs?"

"If I meet La Moyte," Jean said quietly, "I shall kill him. But what judgment should be meted out upon my own head? Tell me that, Pierre!"

Pierre smiled at him.

"You, *mon vieux*, are an idealist—and therefore a fool. Would you engage in dialectics with one trained by the Jesuit Fathers? All right then. Go to England, where the yeomen as they call them are prosperous and happy—where one man considers himself as good as the next. Stand up in the marketplace and preach sedition—shout riot until you're blue in the face. What would happen? I'll tell you—exactly nothing. You and I and a thousand others like us played our part, a necessary part, Jean, at a certain juncture of history. You think we led the people? Nay, rather we followed them. If you want to find blame for these things, blame the winter of '88 which destroyed the grain, blame the hailstorm that smashed the crops—blame the idle, vicious triflers who for two hundred years had despoiled the people until they could bear it no longer. . . .

"For every riot incited, inspired—there were an hundred spontaneous ones, whose authors were not men but desperation, hunger and despair. The nobles would not give way; they will not give way. They must hold on to their ancient privileges, which once they earned by affording protection and security to their peasants against the brigands who infested the land in the Middle Ages. But the Dark Ages are gone—enlightenment creeps over the land. The nobles collect for services no longer rendered. Ask people to starve so that you may wear silk; ask them to watch their babies die so that you may keep courtesans and ride in fine carriages—tax away their bread and their salt, and they riot—it's as simple as that, my Jean. . . .

"Your sister died, in her sweet innocence, because she fell in love, and accidentally allied herself with a doomed system. You would not have blamed yourself if she had been run over by a carriage. Her death was as accidental as that. . . ."

He stopped, staring at Jean's face.

"What ails you?" he said.

"Run over by a carriage," Jean whispered; "run over by a carriage—like Fleurette. . . ."

His hand tightened around the brandy glass until his knuckles showed white. He threw back his head and laughed aloud. The men at the other tables turned at the sound of that laughter. It was mirthless, bitter as wormwood, wild.

"Jean!" Pierre gasped. "Have you gone mad?"

"No, good Pierre," Jean whispered, "I have not taken leave of my senses. I merely remembered something. A week after Gervais left my sister and perhaps even his own to be destroyed by the mob, he was in Paris out driving with his favorite daughter of joy. 'Twas he who ran down Fleurette. And I—I, God help me! I saved his life. . . ."

Pierre's lips formed a soundless whistle.

"Why, Jean?" he said. "Name of God, why?"

Jean Paul looked his friend in the face and his eyes were clear.

"Because," he said, "the girl with him was Lucienne, Pierre. I could not see her murdered. . . ."

"And now?" Pierre said.

"I am clear again," Jean said. "Ah, yes—I am very clear. La Moyte must be destroyed, and the system which produced him must be ended forever. The witless, tortured beasts who ran wild and smashed the objects of their hatred, them I can forgive, Pierre—but La Moyte, and his ilk—never!"

So, Pierre thought, again you besotted fools have driven away another who might have had pity enough to help you. I should not like to be a noble in France now. . . . You've lived grandly, you great ones; I wonder how you'll manage the dying?

However they, individually, all those who had not fled France by then, were to manage it, they had at least managed one last brave display. Walking in the procession, among the other deputies of the Third Estate, on that Monday, May fourth, 1789, Jean Paul Marin was keenly aware of that. He was, like all the men of his order, soberly and decently attired in black. But the nobles were peacocks, rainbows in the sun. Jean would not, even by choice, have dressed in silks and velvets, in scarlet and sky blue, with ostrich plumes blowing back from his tricorne;

but like every member of the Third Estate, he bitterly
resented the fact that royal order had prescribed the dress
of each of the three Estates, and by its very prescription
seemed bent upon emphasizing the quite artificial differences between them.

He held his irritation in check, however, by the reflection that he was taking part in history. Whatever this
new States-General did tomorrow, for good or ill, it was
sure to be forever remembered. Even the crowds in the
streets seemed aware of that. Every walk, every balcony,
every rooftop along that route between the Church of
Notre Dame—where the members of the Assembly had
gathered at seven o'clock that morning to wait in silence
until the King tardily appeared at ten, and the Church of
Saint Louis, where the Mass to bless the proceedings of
the States was to be held—was black with people.

Not only was all Versailles there, but seemingly half the
population of Paris had risen before dawn to march,
drive, and ride to the ancient seat of Kings.

Jean studied the crowd. He recognized some of them,
quite easily. Big, lion-like Georges Danton, with slender
Camille Desmoulins at his side, glared at the procession.
There was Doctor Marat—a doctor of horses, actually,
from Switzerland, his dark face betraying his Italian an-
cestry, already known to the crowds in the Palais Royal
almost as well as firebrand Desmoulins himself. Every one
of the two thousand *poules* from that vast garden en-
closure of the Duc d'Orleans seemed to be here at Versailles, watching the deputies file by behind the local
clergy. After the priests of Versailles, tendering the religious welcome to the whole States-General, came the
Deputies of the Third Estate; behind them marched
the nobles, so many and so brilliant in their court dress
that Jean was unable to pick out Gervais La Moyte among
the throng; behind the nobles, the representatives of the
clergy; after them, the King and Queen, surrounded by
the Prince and Princesses of the Blood Royal. . . .

From the crowds, they, nobles, and priests, and royal
family, might have read their future; for though the mul-
titudes screamed themselves hoarse in greeting the Third
Estate, they let the nobles and clergy pass in stony silence;
a spattering of applause for the King; none for the Princes
of the Blood, and for the Queen:

"Austrian! Foreign woman! We are French, remember! We want no stranger for our Queen!"

This, and other things, less kind, in hoarse mutters, designed to be heard. Actual obscenities, now; and she, proud, and beautiful, riding there not deigning to hear.

Jean looked at the men who marched with him. Of them all, he knew only one, Gabriel Honoré Requeti, Comte de Mirabeau, like himself a native of Provence. He studied Mirabeau with some care. Strange to find him here, a noble of ancient lineage, among the men of the Third! Stranger, in fact was Mirabeau himself: ugly to the point of a perverse attractiveness, pockmarked, scarred with scars and his own dissipations, a blackguard, scoundrel—yet a true man for all that. Jean could feel sympathy for a man who had spent a goodly part of his adult life in one jail or another upon *lettres de cachet* obtained by his father. Even his crimes were to Jean completely understandable. 'Tis plaguedly hard not to forgive a man, Jean thought with secret amusement, who has spent three years in the dungeon of Vincennes for the high crime of kidnaping the woman whom he loved.

. . .

Others among the deputies of the Third Estate had been pointed out to him. He glanced at them now, playing the interesting mental game of trying to guess their capabilities:

Mounier, Malouet, Barnave, Rabaut St. Étienne—silent men, these, wrapped in their own dignity. And behind that dignity, what? Jean had to admit he didn't know. Petion, marching with Bailly—birds of a feather, a little too self-consciously proud. Showy types—frothy mediocrities, Jean guessed. The Abbé Sieyès—a rapier blade of a man, like Mirabeau sitting in opposition to the order to which he rightfully belonged; a doubting priest obviously, that lean face all intelligence, the line of a mouth acid with sarcasm even in repose. And last, walking alone, that strange little lawyer from Arras, whom everybody sneered at: a bewigged head too large for his tiny body, white skinned with that whiteness that is without health . . . like, Jean mused, the belly of a toad. . . . The only color in that face a hint of greenishness.

This man turned now, perhaps sensing Jean's steady gaze, and his cold eyes, of some indistinguishable color behind his steel-rimmed spectacles, swept over Jean with a flick like—like a whiplash? No—rather like the tongue of a snake.

They are wrong, Jean Paul decided at that instant. This one could be deadly. Ah, yes—this Maximilien Robespierre is a man to be watched. . . .

They had almost reached the Church of Saint Louis, now. Jean, wearying of his bootless game of trying to catalogue his colleagues, turned his attention to the spectators.

A ripple of feminine laughter washed over him. He raised his eyes toward the low balcony on which five or six young women sat. They were all exquisitely dressed; but something in their manner told him at once that they were not of the Noblesse. A certain bold directness, perhaps; something, even about their sacques and habits, finer cut, more tastefully beautiful than even those of the noblewomen. Their faces, too, betrayed more art: for though rice powder, rouge, and red lipsalve were in common use among the ladies of the court, these stunning creatures had applied it with such skill, that had he not been so close to them, Jean Paul would have sworn these marvelous complexions were their own. An overprofusion of patches and artificial beauty spots, that he marked—a dizzy cloud of exciting perfumes. . . .

"A parade of crows!" one of them laughed scornfully, as the black-gowned Commons went by.

"Being watched," the Abbé Sieyès replied instantly, "by a roost of *poules!* Verily we have the kingdom of fowls in full session!"

Jean envied the Abbé his remark, and the readiness of wit that had brought it so aptly to his lips. I, he mused sadly, would have thought of that an hour too late. . . .

The laughter on the balcony stopped. Some of the women—actresses and dancers from the Opéra, Jean guessed, stood up to see who had tossed them back so bitter a jibe. Jean looked up once more, and met her eyes.

"Jean!" she whispered, saying the word so softly that he guessed it from the shape of her lips. Then she said it again aloud:

"Jean! You—here? I must see you! After the service, perhaps?"

"*D'accord,*" Jean murmured, miserably aware of the gaze of the other deputies.

"Ah, Marin," the Abbé Sieyès quipped, "I see you have your depths!"

Jean stared at him.

"So you know my name, M'sieur?" he said; "I am flattered."

"I know everyone's names," Sieyès answered, smiling his dry smile, "and most of their histories. Yours, I must confess, has eluded me. We must talk soon, you and I. Not today, however. I fear me that you have far more interesting plans. . . ."

"It may be," Jean smiled, "that you are right, M'sieur l'Abbé."

It was difficult, after that, to pay attention to the service. The Bishop exhausted his art in describing the misery of the people. Jean, to whom this was all too familiar, stopped listening. From where he sat, he could see the King and Queen clearly. Louis XVI appeared half asleep, his pudgy hands clasped across his brocaded, fat middle.

I have seldom seen a man, Jean thought, who looked less kingly! He studied the King with some care. Small, gray-blue eyes sunk in mounds of fat, a loose, weak mouth, under the great Capet nose. A face, Jean decided, that lacks evil, but not good; except that the good is overshadowed by the feebleness. God help France, to have at this juncture a dullard for a King!

The Queen was more rewarding. A stately woman, not without beauty. Young still, but already grayhaired, from worry, from care; for the Dauphin lay at that moment at the doors of death. More, the sea of unearned hatred with which the poor woman was surrounded was enough to madden a stouter soul. Jean glanced toward Count Fersen, the gallant Swede, already linked by the tongue of scandal to the Queen. Count Axel Fersen's gaze was warm, tender; his eyes never left Marie Antoinette's face. How much of it was true?

What difference does it make? Jean thought with Gallic clarity. She is young and fair. Such a one has need of love. When a marriage is an affair of State, an extension of foreign policy, what can one expect. Look at him, now, His Royal Majesty! Is he awake or asleep—or even entirely alive? I think I've never seen a forehead more aptly designed for horns. If you, my Queen are not guilty of this, you should be—and have my blessing. . . .

But the Bishop's words had caught him again. He was

telling the Third Estate that they should not expect too much, that the surrender of privilege must be a thing of grace, not ever of compulsion. . . .

Jean stiffened angrily, but when he gazed at his colleagues, his dark eyes widened in astonishment. Most of them were visibly moved. Several had tears in their eyes.

For what? Jean wondered; because you've been told that the people starve, that the taxes are intolerable, that privilege has become a burden, all of which you know, else you would not be here? Why do you weep, my friends? Because after all his windy mouthings, my lord, his Grace, the Bishop of Versailles, advises you to sit upon your haunches and wait until men like the Comte D'Artois, or even Gervais la Moyte voluntarily surrender their privileges? I tell you that you will see Hell frozen over from stem to shore and a legion of fiends disporting themselves on skates upon the ice before such a thing comes to pass.

The Abbé Sieyès caught his eye and smiled at him. Jean clenched his fist and pointed his thumb downward in the ancient gesture of the Romans. The Abbé's smile broadened. He nodded. We two, he seemed to be saying, are not fooled by all this. . . .

Then it was all over. The deputies gathered in little knots outside the church to discuss the sermon. Jean did not join any of the groups. What I think of it, he thought bitterly, is scarcely likely to be popular among you facile ones. . . .

He started to walk away, toward that balcony on which he had seen Lucienne. He had gone scarcely ten yards when he saw her coming toward him, her tawny hair unpowdered, piled high upon her head. She had always been graceful, but the way she walked now was poetry, music —her steps small, light, so that they seemed almost not to touch the stones of the street, her body willow-slender above the great bell of her brocaded skirts, swaying a little, as though she were impelled toward him by the lightest, gentlest of breezes. He felt something moving in the region of his heart. Something deep and harsh—like pain.

I don't love her, he told himself with bitter clarity. I don't think I ever have. What I feel for Lucienne is something more primitive than love—something ancient and terrible and—and ugly— But whatever it is, I am not free of it. Not yet—dear God, not yet!

She put out a bejeweled hand.

"Jean!" she breathed. "How fine you look!"

"With this face?" Jean snorted. "Spare me your lies, Lucienne."

"Oh," she laughed, "I didn't mean your face. You are a monster, aren't you? But such a monster as any woman should delight in keeping chained in the cellar for the pleasure of taming—if, indeed, you could be tamed. No matter, it might be even pleasanter to fail to tame you, is it not so?"

"And your mockery," Jean added bitterly.

"Oh, I mean it," Lucienne said. "Come let us go sit in the sun at a café—where we can talk. It has been such a long time, hasn't it? You must have a lot to tell me. . . ."

"I," Jean said flatly, "have nothing to tell you."

"Don't try to live up to your face, Jeannot!" Lucienne laughed. "You aren't like that, you know. . . ."

"And how am I," Jean growled.

"As soft as butter—in the proper hands. Oh, come along!"

Even her voice had changed. She no longer spoke with the accent of the Côte. Her speech was Parisian now, low, cultivated, exact. Listening to her was a pleasure. Almost as much of a pleasure, Jean thought, as looking at her. . . .

She sat facing him across the small table over the coffee cups and smiled at him. Her smile was enchanting. He felt ill at ease, like a boy.

"I haven't thanked you for saving my life," she said pleasantly. "That was gallant of you, Jean. . . ."

"I have regretted that gallantry since," Jean said.

Her hazel eyes widened.

"You want me dead then?" she breathed.

"No," Jean said truthfully, "I don't."

"Then why . . . ? Oh, I see—Gervais! Don't tell me you're still jealous! How childish of you, my Jeannot. . . ."

"Don't call me your Jeannot," Jean said; "I've long since ceased to be anything of yours. . . ."

"Have you? I doubt it. Anyone who has been mine, stays mine forever—if I want him. Even if I don't, he still remains mine in his heart. All I need do is beckon, Jean—not—true?"

"You witch!" Jean swore.

Lucienne threw back her head and laughed, merrily.

"How funny you are!" she laughed. "Even with that wonderful horror of a face you're still funny. . . ."

"You didn't think so once," Jean said.

"I was a child," Lucienne said. "I knew nothing of the world—or of men. . . ."

"And now you know?" Jean growled.

Lucienne sat back in her chair, smiling peacefully.

"Yes," she said, "now I know."

Jean sat there looking at her, thinking: You were always a real woman, weren't you, Lucienne? But now you're something more; you're complete now. When you were younger you were very complicated. You're still very complicated, but you've dominated your complications, so that now you're very clear. An awful thing, that clarity of yours—a dangerous thing, really. For you have to live in a world that's very muddled, and the only thing it knows to do with the clear ones like you is to kill them. . . .

He smiled at her a little, searching her face with his eyes.

I think you've found out that the only unforgivable sins are weakness and stupidity. I know that too, but I don't believe it. That's the difference between us, you believe it. And that disbelief of mine makes me unclear and a part of the world I live in, while your clarity and your force make you superior to it, so it must destroy you. And it will, my sweet—because the stupid and the weak always destroy the clear and the strong, by sheer weight of numbers.

"What are you thinking?" Lucienne said.

"That you've become very clear," Jean told her.

"Ah," Lucienne said. Then: "Clear, yes—but not transparent. For instance, you don't know what I'm thinking now."

Jean smiled at her. He was recovering his poise now.

"My indifference," he said, "is both complete—and profound."

"Liar!" Lucienne laughed.

Jean Paul shrugged.

"Have it your own way," he said.

"I always have my own way," Lucienne said; and Jean believed her.

"I'm going to see you again?" she said. It was more than half a statement.

Jean thought about that one. He started to say no, that she would never see him again; but he knew she'd smile at that and accept it as a kind of cowardice. Yet to say yes was to add fuel to that vanity of hers that wasn't vanity really but a part of her clarity. It isn't vanity, Jean thought wryly, to believe that you can wind most men around your little finger—when you know perfectly and from long experience that you actually can.

"If you like," he said, the note of indifference in his voice just right, not overdone, with no crudities or staginess. He stifled the impulse to cover a feigned yawn with the back of his hand. She, he decided, would see through that in an instant. She's clear—oh, yes, she's very clear. . . .

"I like," Lucienne smiled. "But not tonight. Gervais is calling tonight. Day after tomorrow, perhaps?"

Jean stood up. The scar blazed across his face. It came to him, that next to Gervais la Moyte, he hated this woman. She could do too many things to him, and he hated her. The inseparable twins, he thought bitterly, hatred—and love. . . .

"I," he said, damning himself for a sophomore as he said it, "shall be busy all this week. You're at l'Opéra, aren't you? I'll leave a note for you backstage. . . ."

But she wasn't listening to him. She was staring past him, and the warmest, most inviting of smiles lighted her face.

"Gervais!" she said laughingly. "I didn't expect you so soon!"

"Obviously," the Comte de Gravereau smiled. "Ah, Marin—my worthy political opponent. That's right, the two of you know each other—don't you?"

"Rather well," Lucienne said. "It's fortunate you came, Gervais. M. Marin was about to desolate me by leaving. . . ."

"Far be it from me to detain him," Gervais la Moyte laughed, "busy as he must be with the terribly weighty matters of state. . . ."

Jean had control of himself, now. He had even stopped trembling.

"Yet," he said frigidly, "I fear that I must detain M. le Comte for a moment. Not long though—just long enough to exchange cards. I believe this tiresome business of face-slapping is unnecessary between two such old acquaintances. . . ."

"Jean!" Lucienne said; "don't be an utter idiot. I won't have you getting yourself run through over me. You're a bourgeois—like me. What training have you had in sword-play?"

"None," Jean said grimly, "not that it matters. But at the risk of seeming unflattering, I must inform you, Mademoiselle—that I shan't be fighting over you. I can't think of any combination of circumstances that would make me risk nicking a fingertip in your behalf. M. le Comte de Gravereau knows well why I challenge him. . . ."

Gervais' face was filled with honest puzzlement.

"You'll forgive me, M. Marin," he said, "but I don't—truly I don't."

Jean stared at him. He shook his head as though to clear it.

"You mean to tell me," he said, "that when you rode away from Château Gravereau, leaving it surrounded by that peasant mob, you didn't know they'd burn it to the ground?"

Horror flared in La Moyte's eyes.

"They burned it?" he whispered; "they burned my château?"

"You didn't know?" Jean spat.

"Of course not! Why hasn't Thérèse written and told me? When I rode away, I did so only to save it. Those madmen love Thérèse—I was sure they wouldn't. . . ." He stopped, staring into Jean's eyes. "My God!" he got out. "You don't mean that they—that Thérèse . . ."

"Yes," Jean said. "Your château—and Thérèse. My brother, Bertrand, was able to recognize my sister's body only by that part of her jewelry that remained unmelted. Why else did you think I challenged you?"

"I didn't know," Gervais said weakly. "Oh, the beasts! The foul, unspeakable beasts!"

"They were men once," Jean said. "Your class is damnably expert in making beasts of men. . . ."

"I won't meet you," Gervais said quietly. "Not over

this—not ever over this. Please, a chair—I think I'd better sit down. . . ."

Jean pushed one forward. Lucienne was already beside Gervais, cradling his head upon her arm.

Jean sighed. I cannot finish this now, he thought; not now—if ever. He started to walk away, but two yards away he turned.

"You had best write, M. le Comte," he said drily, "and inquire after your own sister. When last seen she was fleeing for the woods, pursued by a horde of armed men. . . ."

"God!" Gervais got out. It was a cry of pure agony.

Lucienne's eyes flamed.

"You *are* a monster!" she said. "You haven't any heart!"

"On the contrary, Mademoiselle," Jean laughed, "I'm as soft as butter in the proper hands—remember?"

He made them both a deep bow.

"Au 'voir, M'sieur, M'amzelle," he said. Then he turned and went down the street, leaving the sound of his laughter trailing behind him.

But a minute or two later, when it came to him what he had done, he stopped still. Lucienne is right, he thought bitterly, I haven't a heart. I believe that Nicole escaped. I couldn't countenance a universe that would permit such a thing to happen to her. But that same fate, God, universe—call it what you will, permitted Thérèse to die in horrible agony. To believe a thing because it is pleasant to believe is the worst of stupidity. . . . Fool, fool—how long will it take you to accept the fact that life is pitiless, and between a man's deserts and what actually happens to him there is no connection whatsoever?

He moved on, his face brooding.

To have fought La Moyte was one thing; but to slash at him with words was another. And to use Nicole—poor, lost Nicole—as a weapon against him was quite the most despicable thing I've ever done in all my life. . . .

There was a tavern on the corner. He stopped before it, frowning. This, too, is a weakness, he thought. But he went in just the same.

Between a man's plans and his deeds lies a distance that sometimes must be measured in leagues. Jean Paul Marin found that out during the first weeks of the sittings of the States-General. He had planned to live in Paris, and ride each day to Versailles; but he soon found that this was impossible. Events were moving too fast.

Not that he regretted this thunderous onrush of history. It was exhilarating to be a part of it: To stand in the tennis court, and swear with uplifted hand Mounier's deathless oath: "We take our solemn oath not to separate until the Constitution of France be established . . ."; to listen to Mirabeau's roar on June twenty-third, after the King had enjoined each Order to repair to its separate chamber, and the Grand Master of Ceremonies had announced, pompously: "Gentlemen, you know the intentions of the King . . . ," and Mirabeau rising, ugly, magnificent, thundering:

"If, sir, you have been charged to make us quit this place, you must ask for orders to use force, for we will not stir from our places save at the point of the bayonet!"

And Louis, informed, shrugging his fat shoulders, saying:

"If the gentlemen of the Third Estate do not choose to leave the hall, why then, there is nothing to do but leave them there. . . ."

It did something to a man to measure skill with the best in debate. Of them all, only Sieyès could best him. Mirabeau commanded more admiration; but Deputy Marin's speeches made up in pristine clarity what they wanted in rhetoric. He was in the thick of it all, and he gloried in it.

He saw the battle won, finally, when debating the King's censure of their temerity in calling themselves the National Assembly, as though they, the Third Estate alone, constituted all France, he rose and said:

"But, Gentlemen, we are all France! If the representatives of twenty-four million people are not the deputies of the Nation, what then are those who sit for a mere two hundred thousand—one percent of the population, and that part consisting of the drones and parasites of society, the men who do nothing, produce nothing, who live like leeches upon the lifeblood of the people. . . ."

The applause from the gallery drowned his words. But even then he heard himself bested by the invincible Sieyès, who rose and pronounced one sentence and then sat down again. But that sentence, clear, incisive, perfect, would echo down the halls of time forever:

"Gentlemen," Sieyès said quietly; "you are today, what yesterday you were."

And the debate was over, ended in the stunned silence of the recognition of its perfection. The National Assembly they were, and would remain.

By July second, it was over. The last, most reluctant of the nobles had accepted defeat. The three Orders sat together, and the battle between them was joined.

On July twelfth, Jean was back in Paris, sent with twenty-four other deputies and all the Paris contingent, to investigate the disorders there. After a day spent in walking through a city torn from one end to the other by rioting, he came at nightfall to the little flat that Pierre and Marianne, at his orders, had furnished for Fleurette.

She opened the door at his knock, and hearing his voice, the joy in her face was almost too much to be borne.

"You're well now?" he asked, gruffly.

"Oh, yes, M'sieur Jean—entirely! My bones have all knit together, and I have no pain. I've even gained a little weight—see?"

Jean saw. The good food that Pierre and Marianne furnished her with, paid for by Jean, had had its effect. Her little figure was becoming fetchingly rounded.

"It's becoming," he said. "The dress is pretty, too. . . ."

"Marianne made it. It's so good to have friends—though—"

"What were you going to say, little one?" Jean said gently.

"I—I shouldn't say it. It's just that—that I miss you so! It's been so awful—Jean—" She stopped, her face flooded with color. "May I call you that? You are so young, and so good to me; so much my friend that it seems strange to say M'sieur. . . ."

"Of course, Fleurette," Jean said. "I'm pleased that you want to."

"Marianne calls you that. And I feel ever so much closer to you than she. . . ." She had gained confidence now, and she kept her sightless eyes upon him, her face smiling, happy. "I'm so glad that you came back. Are you going to stay?"

"Yes," Jean said, "as much as possible now—things have quieted down at Versailles."

She stood up then, and came toward him, her face radiant.

"Then take me back with you!" she breathed, "to your place I mean. Oh, Jean, Jean—I wouldn't be any trouble; I could keep it clean and cook for you—I can do those things, and wash too. Anything, so long as I am near you. . . ."

Jean stared at her.

"But, Fleurette," he got out, "you're a young woman —and a pretty one, too. Don't you know what people would say?"

"I don't care what they'd say—as long as it isn't true. And it wouldn't be. There could never be anything wrong between us—because you are good, and kind and feel only pity for me. If they said I was your mistress, they would be lying, and I don't care about lies. I—I couldn't be your mistress, Jean, because you don't love me. . . ."

"And if I did?" he asked, out of curiosity.

"I don't know. I—I'm so afraid. For you see—I do love you. I have for ever so long a time. . . ."

"This is a grave thing," Jean said sadly. "There would be days, even weeks, sometimes when I wouldn't be there. And when I came, there would always be this thing between us. I should be troubled, Fleurette, trying not to offend you. You are good and sweet and lovely, but—"

"My blindness?" she breathed.

"No. I don't think that bothers me any more. It is simpler than that, Fleurette. There is someone else— whom I love. . . ."

"I see." He could almost hear the joy fall from her voice. "She is here—in Paris, I mean?"

"No. I don't know where she is. She may even be— dead."

"Oh," Fleurette said.

"I'm waiting for news of her. When it comes, things may be different for me. But one thing—and this is the bad thing, little Fleurette—no matter how long it takes to come; if I should grow old and be lying upon my final bed, I shall be waiting still—for word of her. That's how it is, Fleurette; that's how it will always be. . . ."

She put out her hand to him.

"Forgive me," she said quietly; "I hope you find her— Jean."

He went from there down the streets flaming with burning barriers, which the mobs had forced and set afire. Overturned carriages blazed fiercely. Jean walked as close as he dared to these vehicles. He wanted to find out something. And not one coach that was not already too far gone for him to be able to determine it, bore a coat of arms upon its door.

So it goes, he thought bitterly. When we unleashed the hatred and envy that lies at the heart of every man, we thought only to destroy our enemies thereby. But unchain a beast, and he turns and rends you. . . . Fools that we were to think that they would draw fine distinctions between the upper bourgeoisie and the nobles. . . .

He heard, close at hand, a scattered burst of musket fire, then screams, curses, and the clatter of stones against walls, doors.

He turned toward the sound, for one of the tasks that he and all the other deputies had undertaken ever since they reached Paris was to save people from the mobs. It was for that reason that he wore his black uniform. In Paris, those first weeks of July, the black garb of a Deputy of the Third Estate was better protection for a man than a suit of armor.

In the street, some two hundred men, women and children were throwing stones at ten or twelve members of the *Garde Française*. The guards had their bayonets ready, but they weren't firing any more. They were trying to call out to the madmen bent upon murdering them, but the roars of the men, and the shrieks of the women drowned their voices.

Jean took a deep breath. Then he walked out into that shower of stones. He was struck three times before someone recognized his dress.

"A Deputy!" they cried out. "One of our Deputies!"

The stones ceased. The street became very still.

"Give a cheer for *M'sieur le Député!*" a burly fellow roared.

"*Vive le Député!*" they bellowed. The noise of their cheering reverberated between the walls of the houses.

"Citizens!" Jean cried out. "These soldiers are citizens, too! They have their orders to see that the peace is kept, and to put down disturbances. Yet, regard how nobly, they, your servants, have behaved. Not one of you is wounded. These men have fired above your heads—have refrained from slaughter. I beg of you, citizens—let them go!"

"We have something to say, *M. le Député!*" one of the *Garde* called out, taking advantage of the moment of silence.

"Hear the Sergeant, *mes amis,*" Jean pleaded.

"Let him speak!" the big fellow who was leading the mob called.

"Citizens," the Sergeant said: "As *M. le Député* has told you, we have our orders—from the King, from the nobles. Know ye what those orders were? We were to shoot at sight anyone suspected of rioting or pillage! Have we done so, citizens, friends? I ask you, have we?"

"No!" the mob roared out. "*Vive Messieurs les Cito-yens-Soldats!*"

"We," the Sergeant said proudly, "have taken our oath never to fire upon the people of Paris! You are our friends, we have married among you; think ye we'd shoot the brothers and sisters of our wives?"

"*Vive!*" the mob bellowed. Then they swarmed forward, and Jean found himself and the twelve soldiers lifted to their shoulders. They were borne with cheers and laughter to the nearest tavern. There, innumerable toasts were drunk to their health, and to liberty, equality, and fraternity.

It was a good two hours before Jean, pleading duties of state, could escape. His head was far from clear, and that was a dangerous thing. He had his work to do. He had to try to calm the people as much as possible. For that he needed all his wits about him. The toasts he had had to drink hadn't helped matters. He walked uncertainly in the direction where he judged the uproar to be greatest, though that decision was a hard one to make—all Paris was a surging sea of sound and fury—was, and had been, since noon, when the news that the King had dismissed M. Necker, had reached the Palais Royal.

M. Necker, the King's Minister of Finances, was Swiss, a banker, a Protestant, a pedant, and a fool. But the Queen hated him, which alone was enough to make the people love him. Besides, even his religion stood in his favor in the great wave of anti-clericalism sweeping over France. And now, poor weak Louis, under his wife's thumb as usual, had dismissed the man the people revered in the mistaken belief that he could ameliorate their hard lot.

Jean Paul saw men hurrying by, sprigs of green stuck in their hats—the green cockade proposed by Camille Desmoulins that same hour that the news had been brought to him.

"Morbleu!" Jean swore, thinking of the young orator. "He's got everything—youth, good looks, a telling rhetorical style—everything in the world save an ounce of brains in his head or the slightest sense of responsibility. . . ."

He remembered the fury of Desmoulins' speech, the young man, his auburn locks flying, mounted upon a table in the Palais Royal, swearing that the court planned a St. Bartholomew of patriots. That the court meditated no such thing, that even the King had given his *Gardes* orders to show the utmost forbearance in dealing with the people—for the Sergeant had lied when he said they had been commanded to shoot to kill; Jean, who had seen the orders himself, knew that—disturbed Desmoulins and others of his ilk not the least. They were bent upon revolt, and any pretext served.

A singing, dancing mob whirled into the street, bearing a bust of M. Necker.

Fools! Jean swore under his breath; if you knew how wanting in sense or talent your Swiss banker is, you'd smash that piece of plaster. . . .

But the horde lifted aloft their demigod, and forced all they encountered to pay homage. Jean saluted the bust with goodwill. For, he mused wryly to himself, M. Necker's not worth dying for in plaster or in the flesh. . . . Yet, after he had given the required salute, the mob, composed largely of fishwomen from the Faubourg Saint-Antoine, would not let him go.

"For," said a bedraggled slattern, "we'd be highly honored to have the Citizen Deputy accompany us. Lends a bit of swank to our company, eh, girls?"

The other toothless, ill-favored, vile-smelling hags shrilled their assent to her statement, lifting a forest of sticks to emphasize their words. There was nothing for Jean Paul to do but to go with them, so he went.

They wound through the crooked streets for what

seemed to him several hours, beating unmercifully all
those who would not salute the bust of Necker. Jean no
longer knew what section of the city he was in. He was
half dead of fatigue, but the fishwives and their few
male satellites seemed as fresh as ever.

Then he stopped short, and all the tiredness went out of
him. For Lucienne Talbot was coming toward them, walking a little unsteadily, her hair a trifle disarrayed, trailing
a cloak over one shoulder. He could see as she passed
under a street lamp, that her lipsalve was smeared, and
her eyes deep sunken.

"A lady," the fishwomen howled; "a great lady—a
Duchess. How now, my lady? M. Necker is lonely—all
he wants of your ladyship is a kiss."

Lucienne straightened up, staring at them. There was
fear in her eyes, mingled with a bottomless contempt.

"No," she got out; but they raised their clubs on high.
"All right, all right," Lucienne said; "I'll kiss M. Necker—
then by God's love, let me go, I'm dead for want of
sleep. . . ."

They lowered M. Necker's stony face for her to kiss.
Lucienne looked at it with acute distaste. Then she kissed
it, full upon the mouth, hard.

She drew back, staring at it in mock wonder.

"You, you stony bastard," she whispered, "are the first
man I ever kissed who didn't melt!"

It was only then that she became aware of the little
gamine of some ten years who stood beside her, close
enough to hear her words.

"Maw!" the indescribably filthy child screamed, "she
insulted M. Necker! She called him a bastard under her
breath! I heard her!"

The fishwomen split the sky apart with their screeches.
They fell over each other in their haste to get to her.

"Tear off her fine duds!" the slattern next to Jean
howled; "strip her mother-naked and let her run!"

This suggestion raised a fierce chorus of agreement.
Before Jean could move forward ten feet, it was done.

I thought, he reflected bitterly, that she could never
become more beautiful than she was. But she is—God in
glory, she is—and now they're going to ruin her. . . .

Lucienne took the first blows without crying out. But
they brought blood from her bare back before Jean

reached her side. She cursed at them, using words that no duchess of France could possibly have known. It stopped them for a moment—just long enough for Jean Paul to reach her side. But they were closing in now for the kill.

Jean took out his pistols.

"I have never shot a woman," he said. "But, by heaven and the memory of my mother, I'll burn the brains of the first of you that dares touch her again!"

They fell back, snarling. But they had no stomach for gunfire.

"Make way!" Jean cried, "and let us through!"

The women opened a way for the two of them. Jean pointed his big flintlocks right and left, and when they were entirely through the mob, he walked backwards, covering them all, until he came to a corner.

"Don't follow us!" he called out; "the first who tries it—dies!"

They ran, then, through the crooked streets, turning at each corner, doubling back, hearing the noise of the pursuit growing fainter, dying at last into silence.

"Here," Jean panted, "take my coat. . . ."

"Thank you," Lucienne mocked, "for your rather tardy respect for my modesty. I'll take it, all right; but because I'm beginning to get chilled after all the exercise. My body shouldn't disturb you, mon Jeannot—you've seen me like this often enough. . . ."

"Not," Jean said, "in years—and never running through the streets. Take it, quickly, damn you! 'Tis not your modesty I'm concerned with, but my own inclinations. . . ."

She slipped her soft arms into his sleeves, and gathered the long frockcoat about her. The effect was fetching; the more so, Jean realized, because she was being deliberately careless.

Lucienne groaned a bit when the coat touched her bruised back.

"Take me home with you," she said; "I'd never make it to my place alive. You can apply salve to my wounds—that should be amusing, shouldn't it?"

"Too blessed amusing," Jean said grimly. "Come along, then. And you might beguile the tedium of our promenade by telling me what the devil you were doing walking through that *quartier* at such an hour. . . ."

"That," Lucienne said coolly, "is none of your business. I'll tell you why I was walking at least—you saw what they did to every coach that tried to pass through the streets tonight?"

"You were wise to walk," Jean said; "but you should have kept your mouth shut after you'd kissed that bloody plaster. What difference did it make anyhow?"

"None, really. But I wish I'd been brave enough to refuse to kiss it at all. It's a thing I've lived by up until now. I've never before in all my life done anything I didn't want to. I have also never regretted for a second anything I've ever done—because you see, Jeannot, if I do a thing, it's because I really want to. . . ."

"This," Jean said, "has some connection with your ideas of right and wrong?"

"Of course not!" Lucienne laughed. "The wronger a thing is, by other people's standards, that is, the more I want to do it, usually. . . ."

Jean looked at her. He was beginning to understand her, now. After all these years, he was beginning to. *M. le Philosophe!* he mocked himself, thinking that it was no affair of his, that nothing Lucienne said or did should concern him now.

But it does, he admitted. With himself, Jean Paul was always honest.

"Other people's standards?" he said quietly; "I take it, then, that your own are different?"

"Quite. It's a habit I got from you, Jeannot—this business of thinking for myself. Only with you, it never went very deep. You used to say many things, but when it came to practicing them, your emotions always got in the way. I'm different—my head always dominates my heart. . . ."

"This explains Gervais la Moyte, perhaps?" Jean said grimly.

"Jealous?" Lucienne laughed. "Don't be. That's very unintelligent. That's thinking like everybody else—and unworthy of you, my Jeannot, because, oddly enough, you are or could become a person. Most people aren't, you know. They're puppets, controlled by those above them, by their own fears, by other people. . . ."

"Now you're being unclear," Jean mocked, "and on purpose, too."

"No, I'm not. You're jealous of Gervais. You always have been, and that's rather pitiful. You and men like you have turned a fairly good world upside down, because you were eaten up with envy. Gervais is taller, gayer, far better looking than you ever were. He has beautiful manners; he even understands women. Because he and men like him never bothered to hide their natural contempt for you industrious, grubbing bourgeois, you had to unleash the mob against them. The peasantry of France, with all its troubles, Gervais tells me, is far better off than any other peasantry in Europe. And Gervais doesn't lie—you know that. He's far too sure of himself to ever feel the slightest compulsion to. . . ."

"That's true," Jean sighed; "there are many things about La Moyte I admire. . . ."

"Good! Now you're on your way to becoming somebody. But to return to your jealousy—as far as I'm concerned. I, Jeannot, have always found the ideas that most men have about women faintly ridiculous, and a little insulting. You list us among your possessions, like your dogs and your horses. I used to sleep with you. Fine. I did so because I liked to; it was something I enjoyed. But you, who should have been intelligent enough to know better, figured you owned me. Nobody owns me—I own myself. . . ."

"Not even—Gervais?" Jean said.

"Not even God—if there is a God. Gervais, bless him, has never been too possessive. He knows, I think, that I have been unfaithful to him two dozen times—no, more. And he, likewise. But we manage it well. We never flaunt things in each other's face. And we never, never pry into each other's affairs. In all the years I've known Gervais he has yet to ask me, 'Where the devil were you last night?' Never. He doesn't, I think, because he knows I'd tell him. And because nobody can be that different from the common run of men, he wouldn't like it. So he doesn't ask. Good?"

"Mad!" Jean spat.

"Sane, I think. 'Tis the world that's mad, Jeannot. When do we get to that place of yours? I'm dead tired. . . ."

"Soon," Jean told her. "It's not very far, now. . . ."

She looked at him, smiling.

"Did you have an affair with Gervais' sister, Jean?" she said.

"You," Jean reminded her, "never ask questions."

"Then you did! How frightfully amusing! I rather thought so, but Gervais wouldn't tell me. That's one time you got to him, Jean."

"What ever," Jean growled, "made you think a thing like that?"

"Her letters. Gervais is very careless. He used to swear like a trooper every time he got one from her. But he never thought to destroy them. So I read them. She always asked about you, and in such a pitiful fashion. It amused me. Have you really become so good in that department, or was it just her inexperience?"

"Damn you, Lucienne!" Jean began; then he checked himself. "Wouldn't you like to find out?" he asked mockingly.

"Perhaps. That depends upon the mood I'm in. Those things are never really very important—except to men. Any woman who has escaped the deadening routine expected of us: home, husband, family, knows better. When one is hungry, one eats. When one is not, one doesn't. And not the same food all the time—not even caviar. Right, Jeannot?"

"You," Jean breathed, "are fantastic!"

"No—just tired, and awfully sore. I hope you have some decent wine in that place of yours."

"The best," Jean said.

But it took him longer than he expected. They had to detour around a half-dozen new tumults. Everywhere there were gunshots, screams. In every major street barricades had been erected by the soldiers; and three-quarters of them had been torn down or set afire by the people. This thing was out of hand now, completely out of hand.

When Lucienne gazed upward at that first flight of stairs, she swore feelingly.

"Take me up, Jean," she said; "you look strong enough, now."

Jean swept her up as though she were weightless.

"My God," she breathed, "you *are* strong! That prison did wonders for you. . . . This affair of the gentle Nicole, did it occur before or after the jail?"

"Questions again?" Jean said.

"Oh, I can ask you. You're a part of the past. Besides, it amuses me. It's rare. Nobles like Gervais think nothing of taking their pleasure among bourgeoise maids—or even among the peasants, if it pleases them. But being men, and a part of our rather primitive society, they don't relish the tables being turned. That's why it amuses me. I love seeing their arrogance deflated. . . ."

"That," Jean said flatly, "is none of your business, Lucienne. So I'm part of your past, eh?"

"Sorry. I didn't mean to hurt your pride, Jeannot. You are. Perhaps you could become a part of my future, too; but that depends. . . ."

Jean's leg touched the flimsy railing and he drew away from it, closer to the wall. He shifted Lucienne easily, and groped in his pocket for the key. He got the door open, and walked over to the bed.. He laid Lucienne down upon it, and took his firepistol out of his secretary.

Somebody, he swore, should invent a better way of making fire than this. But he kept on blowing on the little rags that caught the sparks from the barrel-less flintlock, until they stopped smoldering and made enough flame to light the candle. Then he turned back to her.

"What does it depend upon?" he said.

"What? *Mon Dieu*—what a persistent devil you are! That's the kind of question you shouldn't ask. But I'll answer it. It depends upon many things: whether I find you sufficiently amusing. That's the first thing, and the most important. . . ."

"And the second?" Jean growled.

"Whether you rise to a position of power and influence in the new state. I can't be bothered with nobodies. I'm very fond of Gervais, but I think he and his kind are doomed. Put it this way, Jeannot. I could never put up with hardships or poverty again. I could never love a poor man, no matter how charming I found him. On the other hand I couldn't live with the richest, most powerful man on earth, if I did not find him amusing and charming. There you have it—the *code personnel de* Lucienne Talbot. Now, for God's sake stop catechizing me and give me some wine!"

Jean got out the bottles and the glasses. She's very clear, he thought again, but for the life of me, I cannot like such clarity. . . .

Lucienne took the goblet from his hand and sipped the wine. A grimace of pain passed over her face.

"Now for God's love," she snapped, "stop standing there staring at me, and do something about my back—it's killing me!"

Jean walked into the bathroom-kitchen, with a second candle he had lighted from the first. He was taking the salves down when he heard the whisper of her bare feet upon the floor. Then she was beside him, staring at the slipper-shaped tub he had bought at great expense and put in the kitchen next to the stove so that he might always have his water hot for bathing. Jean had for his times what amounted to an obsession with personal cleanliness.

"A tub!" Lucienne said delightedly. "Oh, Jeannot, be an angel and heat some water—it would take all the soreness out of me. Besides, after that marathon, my aroma must be anything but pleasant; do be sweet and light a fire. . . ."

"All right," Jean said, and bent to his task.

After he had the fire going, he went all the way down to the street, and came back with two huge pails of water from the public fountain. He put them on the stove, and waited. Lucienne was stretched out on the bed again.

"Come help me out of your coat," she said. "It was hot enough in this cubbyhole of yours in the beginning; but with that fire going . . ."

"Lucienne, for God's sake," he began.

"Oh, don't be childish. Don't tell me that at your age, and after all the interesting experiences you've had with highborn ladies, the sight of a naked woman would trouble you!"

"Not a woman," Jean said, "you."

"How sweet! That's quite the nicest thing you've said to me in ever so long. Nevertheless, I'll just have to trouble you, that's all. It's too confounded hot, and this coat of yours is beginning to itch. Help me out of it like a good boy."

Jean helped her out of it.

She got up from the bed and walked over to the mirror, tall, lithe-limbed, graceful. She raised both arms, and pushed her hair, which had come loose during their flight, high on top of her head. Jean found the gesture charming. But her back had half a dozen great greenish-blue splotches, and one or two places where the skin was broken were dark with dried and clotted blood.

"Lend me your comb, darling," Lucienne drawled. "I think I have enough pins left to keep it up while I bathe. . . ."

Jean tested the water while she combed her hair. It was almost hot enough. He waited until it was a little short of scalding and poured it in, knowing that the iron of the tub would cool it enough.

"Ready," he called, and stepped aside to let her pass.

With a grateful sigh she sank into the tub, made so that the bather had to assume a sitting position, with his feet and legs far deeper than his trunk. Jean brought her a cloth and soap, then went back to his wine.

"Jeannot," she called, "come wash my back for me. I can't reach. But please be careful—I am so sore. . . ."

"May I ask," Jean asked mockingly, "who was your personal valet before I came to Paris?"

"Oh, I've had many," Lucienne said airily. "You really couldn't expect me to remember them all, could you? Now be a dear and dry me. You really are quite gentle for all your strength. . . ."

When she was dry, she stretched up her arms and yawned.

"I'm so sleepy," she said; "come put the salves on my back—so that I can sleep. I hope you're not an early riser. I mean to sleep until noon. . . ."

Jean sat down on the edge of the bed and rubbed the salve into her bruises.

"And where," he said, "am I expected to sleep?"

"Beside me, of course. That shouldn't bother you. You must be very tired after your day. . . ."

"And if I tell you I am not tired?"

She smiled at him. Her smile, Jean thought, is absolutely the wickedest thing in the world.

"You may lie awake and listen to the music of my gentle breathing. I don't snore, I've been told. Some other time, I may be more wakeful. But tonight, darling Jeannot, I'm as sore as a boil—besides you really haven't been very amusing today, now have you?"

And without another word, she burrowed deeper into the pillows and closed her eyes.

Jean sat there looking at her.

She was always too much for me, he thought bitterly. She defeats me utterly and without effort. She knows just how, and she does it with so much *éclat*. What superb technique! She has walled me off now behind the mountain of my own pride. She knows I'd never touch her unless she came to me willingly. Oh, damn your eyes, Lucienne—I—

The knocking on the door brought him upright. He opened it, and Fleurette stood there, smiling at him.

"May I come in, Jean?" she said. "Oh, I know it's late, far after midnight, really; but I'll only stay a minute. . . . I brought you something—a letter—I was here earlier, and the *facteur* gave it to me."

"Why were you here?" Jean asked, more to gain time than for any other reason.

"I—I wanted to apologize for the things I said today. But no matter. It can wait. I would have waited until tomorrow, anyway; but I thought the letter might be important. . . ."

Jean heard the creak of the bed as Lucienne stirred.

"Darling," she drawled, "have you forgotten I am here? Get rid of that *poule* and come to bed. . . ."

Fleurette stiffened. Jean saw death coming into her sightless eyes.

"Oh!" she breathed; then: "Take your letter, Jean!"

Jean took it, and stood there in dumb misery, listening to the clatter of her slippers upon the stairs. She went down very fast, and with complete recklessness.

Behind him, Lucienne was laughing softly.

"You witch!" Jean swore.

"Sorry," she laughed; "but I do find you interesting, Jeannot. And who knows how great and famous you might become? Better to cut off the competition at the beginning, *n'est-ce pas?*"

"You are absolutely impossible!" Jean said. Then he tore open the letter. It came from Bertrand, and had been written from Austria. Jean read it very quickly, his face growing darker, until the scar made it a white blaze against his skin. He folded it slowly and with great care, and put it into the pocket of his frockcoat. Then he bent down and picked up his pistols from the table.

"You're going out?" Lucienne said. "Now?"

Jean didn't answer her. He slipped on the coat. In the interval of silence, a musket shot sounded, heavy and close at hand. Somewhere, further off, a woman screamed.

"Yes," Jean said very quietly, "I'm going out."

Lucienne stared at him, her eyes questioning. Then, very slowly, she smiled.

"I," she murmured, "don't think I'm sleepy any more—Jeannot. . . ."

Jean looked at her, and what she saw in his eyes startled her.

He walked on to the door. In the doorway, he turned.

"The next time you see Gervais la Moyte," he said, "you might tell him that—his sister is—dead. . . ."

Then he went down the stairs and into the flameshot, terror-ridden night.

8

Never, in all the rest of his life, was Jean Paul Marin ever able to determine precisely where he went and what he did in those twelve hours between midnight July 12, and noon, July 13, 1789. It appeared to him afterwards, listening to Pierre du Pain's account of the things that happened in Paris during those hours, that he must have borne a charmed life. For he had wandered in a daze through streets echoing with musket fire, and blazing from one end to the other, without getting so much as a scratch.

"Life is a gamble," he said wryly to Pierre, "and every gambler knows you never win when you need the money. . . ."

"What the devil do you mean by that?" Pierre said.

"A musketball through the head would be a kindness," Jean whispered, "for which I'd thank the assassin who sped it home. . . ."

Pierre stared at him.

"Now what ails you?" he growled.

"Nicole—" Jean croaked, and passed Bertrand's letter to him.

Pierre read it with frowning concentration. Then he straightened up, his face a satyr's mask once more.

"And it is for this you court death?" he mocked. "Jean, Jean, how big a fool can a man be?"

"Big enough, I guess," Jean said. "But by God's love don't tell me there are other women in France as fair, or any other such nonsense. There was only one Nicole. . . ."

"I don't doubt it. The point I'm trying to make is a thing that should have been instantly apparent to your trained legal mind. According to the evidence in your brother's letter there is not one iota of proof that the Comtesse de Saint Gravert is dead. Where are your witnesses? Upon what does your brother base his belief—

which he plainly states is belief only—? That, to the best of his knowledge she has never reached Austria! What kind of evidence is that?"

"Read further," Jean whispered; "read the words of her own *maître d'hôtel.* . . ."

"I saw that. This man escaped the mob, fled to Villa Marin, because he knew of your friendship with the Lady Nicole, and believed that your influence among the peasants would make your house a safe refuge. . . ."

"He was wrong," Jean said drily. "They burned it too. . . ."

"I know. But, why, by all the lies in the Breviary of Saints, did he wait until after the Lady Simone had taken him along with them as a servant—all of yours having fled, it appears—to produce his curious evidence?"

"I don't know," Jean said.

"He found in the woods the bloodstained clothing of the children, and a part of the house sacque, also blood-stained, that the Lady Nicole was wearing. What manner of man was he to preserve his bloody trophies? To whom did he intend to show them?"

"To Gervais la Moyte, perhaps. Pierre, for the love of heaven—can't you see? This senile fool must have be-lieved that all the nobles of the Côte had fled abroad, and hoped to gain some credit with the Comte with his gruesome relics and the tale of his own devotion—there being none to gainsay him. . . ."

"There is," Jean pointed out, "a darker interpretation, which appears to have escaped you, Pierre. Augustin, my lady's coachman, was in league with the mobs. Why not then, others among her servants—perhaps Robert, the old *maître d'hôtel,* himself?"

"Doesn't stand up," Pierre replied promptly. "If he were in league with them, why, then, did he have to flee? He could have gone over to them like all the rest of the ser-vants seem to have done. It looks bad, I'll admit. But in the absence of any conclusive evidence to the contrary, why not believe that at worst they may have been hurt, and afterwards managed to escape?"

"That," Jean said, "is what I have been trying to believe." But there was no hope at all in his voice.

They were passing by this time the hotel of the Lazarists —or rather what was left of that refuge. The belongings of the monks—chairs, tables, pictures, religious objects, the clothes presses, curtains, dishes, drapes—were piled up in the street in a broken mound so big that the street was half choked by it. The mob was busily engaged in hauling off the grain that the Lazarists by law had been entitled to keep, since the chief function of that order was the care and feeding of the indigent sick.

"Fifty-one loads since this morning!" a bearded villain told Jean and Pierre triumphantly. "Come, Citizens! Have a drink of the shaven ones' good wine—there is plenty more where this came from!"

Jean and Pierre drank. They were but two against fifty; and they had long since learned when discretion must triumph over valor.

The smell of wine was everywhere. It ran down the gutters in a purple flood. Ragged, filthy men lay on their bellies, lapping it up like dogs.

Jean stared at these men. He was sure he had never seen their like in Paris by daylight. Their rags, visibly crawling with vermin, barely hid their nakedness. And their stench, even in that open street, was well-nigh overpowering. Most of them were bearded, many were hideously scarred, or wanting an eye or an ear.

"They look," he whispered to Pierre, "like fiends from hell."

"They are," Pierre said grimly.

While they waited for the wagonloads of grain to work their way past the debris piled up in the street, a great outcry burst from the cave, or cellar, of the hôtel. They turned toward the sound. A horde of the sewer rats of Paris, as bearded and filthy as the ones Jean and Pierre had seen in the street, came out of the hôtel, bearing on their shoulders sodden, shapeless burdens that had been men and women like themselves. The bodies were all stained deep purple, and their rags dripped wine.

"Drowned!" one of their pallbearers howled; "some fool stove in the casks in the cave, and they drowned in the wine! *Ma foi,* what a happy way to die!"

One of the women they carried, Jean saw, had been far gone with child.

"Dear God!" he whispered to Pierre, "let's get out of here!"

At the corner of the next street, an apelike brute was standing next to a pile of muskets, sabers, and pistols.

"Come, *Citoyens!*" he was bawling. "Arms! The best

—taken this morning from the *Garde Meuble* by patriots for the defense of our liberties! Come—buy! Muskets—three livres apiece! Pistols twelve sous! Sabers—likewise! Powder and ball, I leave up to the generosity of you good citizens!"

"Got any money?" Pierre said.

"Yes," Jean told him, "why?"

"I left my pistols with Marianne this morning when I came to look for you. She can use them, too; I taught her how. But a man's a fool to wander through Paris unarmed today. I'd like a brace of pistols and a musket, too—it'll carry a lot further, and discourage these madmen quicker. . . ."

"Here," Jean said, and gave him the money.

"You'd better buy a musket, too. That's why I was looking for you. Bailly has called upon all good citizens to enroll in the militia and put down disorder; Lafayette is heading it. . . ."

"Very well," Jean said, "buy me some powder and pistol shot. And a saber. I think that whatever fighting we'll see will be at close quarters. I'd rather have a blade in my hands. . . ."

"Aristocrat!" Pierre mocked; but he bought the arms just the same.

Half an hour later they were marching in a company of sober bourgeois, grim, determined men, bent upon their duty. By nightfall, the forty-eight thousand men that Bailly had called to arms had put down the rioting and pillage. Jean had acted as legal adviser to his company. As such, he sent three brigands, whose only interest in the tumult was the wonderful opportunities for thievery it presented, to impromptu gallows on the lampposts; but he had also saved by acquittal the lives of five sturdy citizens who had taken part in the rioting under the belief they had been fighting for the Third Estate.

They could not, of course, halt the revolt. But they could and did keep it largely political, instead of allowing it to degenerate into wholesale anarchy and brigandage, as it was rapidly threatening to do.

But by midnight of that terrible July thirteenth, the entire company was half dead of fatigue. The things they had been called upon to do would have taxed the strength of giants and demigods. They were quartered by then in the Hôtel de Ville, having lived through that hour when

LeGrand, their captain, and one of the Paris electors, had sent for three barrels of gunpowder, and stood beside them with a lighted taper, threatening to blow the building, his company, and himself to Kingdom Come for the privilege of taking a sizable portion of the mob along with them, if those howling madmen did not cease from attacking.

Things like that, Jean thought bitterly, age a man twenty years in as many minutes. . . . By the eyes of God, I've had enough!

But his relief, when it came, brought him no rest. He heard LeGrand calling his name, and got wearily to his feet.

"Here," he croaked.

"There's a lad, here, Marin," the Captain said, "with a note for you. Says it's important. . . ."

Jean stumbled forward. He recognized the boy at once. He was one of the printer's devils in the shop, which meant that Marianne had sent him. Jean glanced toward Pierre, half asleep with back leaning against one of the barrels of gunpowder. But, he reasoned, if there were anything wrong, she'd have addressed it to Pierre—not to me. . . .

"This came for you this evening," the boy said. "Madame du Pain said I was to bring it to you at once, but I couldn't find you sir, before now. . . ."

"You've done well," Jean said, and gave him a five-franc note.

The note was only one line. It read:

"They've got me in l'Abbaye; for God's sake come get me out!" It was signed "Lucienne."

Jean looked at LeGrand.

"A friend of mine," he said, "has been arrested by mistake. She's of the people—of peasant stock on both sides, but now she talks and dresses like a lady. . . ."

"Where is she?" LeGrand demanded.

"L'Abbaye," Jean told him.

"She'll be safe enough there. But you've done enough for one day. You look like hell, Marin. . . ."

"I know," Jean smiled.

"You're relieved from duty until tomorrow. What you do after you leave here is your affair. But I advise you to leave the wench in jail. There are any number of soft bedfellows in Paris; no point in arousing the ire of the people trying to befriend anyone who has fallen out of favor. . . ."

Jean grinned at him, a touch of his old *diablerie* showing in his crooked smile.

"I thank you for your advice, *M'sieur le Capitaine*," he said.

"But you don't intend to follow it," LeGrand said.

"No," Jean laughed, "I don't. Perhaps one day soon you'll see why. . . ."

"Perhaps," LeGrand sighed, staring out into a night sky shot through with flame and smoke, "if any of us lives that long."

Once more, at that grim prison called l'Abbaye, Jean's soiled and dusty uniform of a Deputy of the National Assembly served him well. He was admitted at once to see the prisoner.

Lucienne came forward to greet him. Her tawny hair hung loose about her shoulders. Her face was exceedingly dirty. A great bruise ran from her cheekbone to the point of her chin on the left side of her face. She was wearing one of Jean's suits. She was so tall that it didn't fit her badly in length, though it was much too big for her in all the other dimensions.

"Don't just stand there!" she snapped at him; "get me out of here!"

Jean stared at her. Then very softly, he started to laugh.

She put her hands on the bars and shook them furiously.

"Let me out, damn you!" she screamed.

Jean threw back his head and roared.

The Prefect of the prison stared at them both in wonder.

"Perhaps," he ventured, "there has been some mistake, Citizen Marin. . . ."

"Oh, no!" Jean laughed; "no mistake at all. This woman is a dangerous enemy of the people. I think you should put her in irons as well."

Lucienne was speechless with rage.

The Prefect looked at Jean. He had a suspicion that he was being put upon, but he didn't know quite how.

"But, M. Marin—" he began.

"When I do get out," Lucienne spat, "I'm going to scratch out both your eyes, Jean!"

"Jean is your first name, M'sieur?" the Prefect said.

"It is," Jean chuckled. "And the lady is my wife. She,

unfortunately, *M. le Préfet*, is one of your modern women—given to marked disrespect for husbandly authority. . . ."

"I begin to see," the Prefect smiled.

"I told her to stay at home—that the streets were dangerous. She disobeyed my commands not once, but twice. So I took away her clothes. The result, you see, I think you will even find my name sewed into the lining of that frockcoat. . . ."

"Oh your word is enough for me, Citizen!" the Prefect laughed. "We only had your wife here under protective custody, anyway. It seemed that the mob found her masculine dress highly suspicious, and were about to tear her to pieces as a disguised noblewoman. But I don't think you'll have any trouble with her after this—eh, Madame? Surely after all your experiences . . ."

"He'll have trouble enough, thank you!" Lucienne said. "Pretending to be out guarding the city while actually he's consorting with the wenches at the Palais Royal—a fine husband, I tell you, *M. le Préfet!* Thought I wouldn't find you out, eh, Jeannot? Just wait until I get you home!"

"Perhaps we should leave her locked up for a week—say," Jean suggested in mock alarm. "She's a dangerous woman when her temper's aroused. . . ."

The Prefect turned the key in the big lock.

"I think you have no cause for anxiety, Citizen Marin," he said; "for Madame surely cannot believe the things she is saying. Any man so fortunate as to be married to anyone as beautiful as Madame, would never in his life turn his head to look at another woman!"

"You are gallant, Citizen Prefect," Lucienne said as he bowed her out of the cell. "Perhaps if this husband of mine continues to be so negligent you might be willing to show me the sights of Paris?"

The Prefect reddened to the roots of his hair.

"You honor me too much, Madame," he said drily, "but your husband does not appear to be the type of man I'd risk making an enemy of. Au 'voir, Madame, M'sieur."

"Au 'voir," Jean said.

Lucienne smiled at him.

"Precisely when did I marry you, Citizen Marin?" she said; "I don't seem to be able to recall the circumstances. . . ."

"You wouldn't," Jean laughed; "you were far gone with

wine. But I'll show you the certificate—in the morning. . . ."

"Strange," Lucienne mused; "we are really much alike—you and I. We carried that off well, didn't we?"

"Rather," Jean said.

"And you're already becoming a power in the city. Keep it up, Jeannot. You may even interest me again—one of these years. . . ."

Jean looked at her. He stopped smiling. Of all the things he disliked about Lucienne, nothing annoyed him more than her superb vanity.

"I suppose we'll have to walk," she sighed. "Oh well, it's not too far. It seems that all I've done for the last few days is to walk endless leagues and never get anywhere. . . ."

Jean didn't answer her. His mind was off on another track. He was wondering how it was that the two women who were capable of stirring his deepest emotions could be so entirely different as were Nicole and Lucienne.

"Here we are," she said mockingly; "I'd ask you to come up, but for the fact that I know you'd accept. . . ."

"I'm not so sure of that," Jean said.

"I am. And I've had enough labor for one day. I don't mean to spend the next two hours warding off your attempts to exercise your husbandly prerogatives. . . ."

"You're sure of yourself, aren't you?" Jean said.

"Quite. I've never met a man I couldn't have—if I wanted him. But he has to make me want him. That, believe it or not, is a tall order. You'd better work at it, Jean. . . ."

"What the devil makes you think I want to?" Jean growled.

"This," Lucienne said; then going up on tiptoe, she kissed his mouth. Jean felt his toes curling inside his boots. In twenty seconds there were hammers at his temples; in thirty, his blood was one long drumroll in his veins; but she didn't let him go. She clung her mouth to his achingly, endlessly, the soft underflesh of lip and tonguetip keeping up their devilish play. Then, suddenly, startlingly, she stepped back from him, and her trained ballet-dancer's arms thrust him away with a strength that was almost that of a man.

She swayed there before him, laughing.

"*Bonne nuit, mon* Jeannot!" she whispered; "I trust that you'll sleep well!"

"*Sacre bleu!*" Jean roared.

She leaned back against the door, weak with laughter.

"I have no need of you this night, Jeannot," she laughed; "nor any night, for that matter. When you saved me from those hags, I had just come from Gervais. I wouldn't permit him to accompany me, at the risk of his life. . . ."

Jean stood there, staring at her. There was black murder in his eyes.

"But you shouldn't be too lonesome, *mon pauvre*," she murmured; "after all, you can always send for that little wench with the gentle voice—the one I frightened away, remember?"

"Fleurette!" Jean breathed; "dear God, I had forgotten her!"

Then he whirled on his heel and ran off, down the street.

Lucienne looked after him, a little thoughtful frown puckering the flesh above her eyes.

Fleurette, she mused; I shall have to remember that name. . . .

"No," the concierge said, "the poor child hasn't been here, M'sieur . . . not since two nights ago. I'm sick with worry. With all the rioting in the streets, there's no telling. . . ."

But Jean didn't let her finish her words. He was off again, moving with astonishing speed for a man whose head had not touched a pillow in more than forty-eight hours.

But it was no good. Fleurette was not in any of the places she usually went to sell her flowers—though she could hardly have been expected to be in the small hours of the morning. Nor was she at the du Pains', where she often came to visit Marianne. Jean even returned to his own flat, hoping to find her there. It was empty, the fire cold, the bed still unmade, just as Lucienne had left it.

He dashed cold water into his face, and wiped the dust away with a towel. Then he picked up his saber and the two pistols again, and went down into the street.

By ten o'clock of that morning, July 14, 1789, he had

to give it up. He was too tired to even move. He walked back toward his flat, dragging his feet like a man of seventy years, until he turned into the Rue Saint-Antoine once more.

It was choked with people from wall to wall. There were fine ladies among them, and well-dressed gentlemen. Everybody was staring toward the grim, gray towers of the Bastille.

He couldn't see the top of the prison. It was wreathed in smoke. Jean heard the rattle of musketry, saw the puffs of gun smoke rising from the rooftops, the windows of houses, from the esplanade itself.

Jean worked his way forward through the crowd, his fatigue forgotten. Before it had been rioting, street tumults; but to attack the Bastille was more: this was revolution, itself.

What we wanted to do, Jean thought, would have been done slowly; but we would have won in the end. But now they're going to do it all quickly, and what man can foresee whether the results will be good or ill?

The crowd was so thick that he had to use his shoulders, his elbows to force a passage. But when they saw the naked saber in his hand, they opened a way for him.

The first thing he saw when he gained the esplanade before the outworks of the four-hundred-year-old fortress turned prison, was Pierre du Pain kneeling beside an overturned cart, firing with the rest. Jean started to bend over to work his way toward his friend, but he realized suddenly that the gesture was utterly ridiculous. The eighty ancient Invalides atop the towers, and the thirty-two Swiss with them were not firing a shot. So he straightened up and sauntered over to his embattled comrade.

He stood beside Pierre for several minutes while the redhaired one was busily engaged in reloading his musket. Before Pierre could fire again, Jean had laid a hand on his shoulders.

"Just what the devil do you think you're doing?" he asked mockingly.

Pierre grinned at him.

"Shooting," he said gleefully; "here, have a shot on me!"

Jean took the musket from Pierre's hands.

"Would you mind informing me," he said, holding the

gun as though he had never before seen one in his life, "what one is supposed to do with this?"

"Why, fire it, of course!"

"At what?" Jean demanded with mock gravity.

"Espèce d'un idiot!" Pierre roared. "At the Bastille, thou creature of the elongated ears! Or do you mean to tell me you cannot see it?"

"Oh, I see it right enough," Jean laughed; "what I don't see is the advantage of firing a musket at walls eight feet thick, behind which are hidden men I cannot even see, and who, additionally, are not shooting back. . . ."

Pierre shook his head mournfully.

"Jean, Jean," he groaned; "I wonder sometimes if there really is aught between your ears. Of course we can't take the Bastille with musket fire. But it's going to fall just the same, from noise, from fear like the walls of Jericho. . . . So I'm going to go on shooting. It pleases me that I shan't be able to kill anybody. I don't want to. All I want, *pauvre bête*, is that enough people see me in the act of being lionhearted, courageous, etcetera, in the forefront of the heroes who pulled down the age-old symbol of tyranny. . . . Afterwards, it will mean something in France to be one of the heroes of the Fall—you understand?"

There was, Jean saw at once, much method in this madness. The Bastille, he knew, was all but empty of prisoners —and had been for some years. Its defenders were Invalides, old soldiers home from half-forgotten wars, but recently reinforced by a sparse garrison of young Swiss. But in the minds of the people, the Bastille remained the chief symbol of age-old tyranny. To storm it, to take it, even, was to accomplish little against the regime. The government did not need it; its maintenance was actually burdensome.

But when in history, he thought wryly, have facts won out over ideas? As a thing, as a prison, it's nothing; but as an idea. . . . Win or lose, today we'll set all France aflame. . . .

So thinking, he lifted the musket and fired it, taking care to hit nothing at all.

Up until noon it was all comic opera, typically French. The people had the delirious experience of standing in the open street firing volley after volley at a fortress that did not shoot back at all. It was only after the elector Thuriot de la Rosière and his deputation had been admitted to the prison to parley with Governor de Launay that Jean began to realize that the situation was beginning to deteriorate, to sink into tragedy.

"If it becomes a battle," he said to Pierre, "if they shoot back, even few as they are, do you realize what carnage there'll be among this mob? They have cannon up there, remember—even if de Launay has drawn them back a little. . . ."

"You have right, Citizen," a young giant of a man who was nearby said; "but I'm going to do something about that."

"And what do you propose to do, Citizen?" Pierre asked.

"I'm off to the Place de Grève," the big one said, "to have a word with the *Garde* there. I'm a half-pay, remember, a reserve. They'll listen to me. Then we'll have cannon, Citizens! And that monstrosity will come tumbling about their ears!"

"Your name, Citizen?" Jean said quietly. It might be good later, to know such things.

"Hulin, Citizen," the young man rumbled in his thick Swiss accent; "I think that after today the world will have cause to remember that name!"

Then he was off, striding like Hercules toward the Hôtel de Ville.

Jean looked around him. In the crowd were several men he knew, Paris electors who had remained banded together after having chosen the Deputies to the National Assembly, and who furnished now the only shadow of a government that the city had. Jean had hoped to see some of the Deputies who had come down from Versailles with him; they, above all, might be able to accomplish something by negotiation. But he saw none. The others, he guessed, had all gone back to their seats in the Hall de Menus Plaisirs.

The electors would have to do. He moved among them, saying a few words to each. They nodded grimly, and fell in behind him. Jean marched up to the drawbridge, waving his white cravat upward at the towers.

The firing spluttered, died. After a time that stretched out to the crack of doom, they heard the first creak of the winches, lowering the bridge.

A soldier conducted them to de Launay. The old man was ashen; but with despair, not terror.

"I can never surrender my post," he said, "except on orders from my King."

"Consider well, *M'sieur le Gouverneur,*" Jean Paul said; "if this thing comes to bloodshed, it will mean death to many. As a soldier, I know you don't hold your own life too dear, but consider your men—consider the innocents down below. . . ."

"Innocents!" de Launay roared. "Madmen! I'll give you my answer M. Marin! Come with me. . . ."

Jean and his delegation followed the Governor. That gallant old soldier led them far below into the cellar of the prison. An ancient soldier opened the door.

One glance and Jean Paul knew where he was. This was the powder magazine. There was a rude chair beside a table. On the table was a candlestick with a tall candle in it, already lighted.

"Look!" M. de Launay said, and pointed.

Jean followed the gesture. On the floor thick trains of black powder led directly to several barrels.

"I need only to lower that candle," M. de Launay said grimly. "Tell them that, M. Marin! Tell them that if they persist in this folly, I'll sacrifice myself, my garrison, and the prisoners they've come to save. But, by God, I'll take an escort of thousands with me on that march to hell!"

Jean stared at the old Governor. There was no doubt that M. de Launay meant it.

"You, M. de Launay," he said slowly, "are a soldier—and a man of honor. I have never been a soldier, but my word means as much to me as yours does to you. I give it now, that if you desist for a reasonable length of time, I will personally dispatch a messenger to M. de Lafayette asking him to request such orders of the King. . . ."

"You'll do nothing of the kind!" de Launay growled. "You may, if you will, send a message to His Majesty informing him of my plight; but nothing more, M. Marin. 'Tis neither your place nor mine to tell Louis of France what he should do!"

Half the troubles of today, Jean thought hotly, stem from the fact that no one has ever been able to tell the fat one anything at all. Oh, he'll ask advice, all right; even keep to it—for five minutes—no, not even five. Even those who know him best swear it is easier to keep together oiled ivory balls in one's hand than it is to force any decisiveness from the King. . . .

"As you will, M. de Launay," he said, and went back down the stairs.

He sent Pierre du Pain with a written message to the Marquis de Lafayette. He might have spared himself the trouble. De Lafayette had been receiving such messages all morning long, and sending them on to the King. But from Versailles—nothing. No one knew if Louis got the frantic notes that kept pouring in. Men said that he was out hunting, or making locks—the two chief diversions into which he always escaped when the pressure of events became too much for him.

The pressure of events, Jean Paul saw, was now too much for any man. Burly Louis Tournay, a cartwright of Marais, was busily engaged in hammering bayonets into the joints of the masonry. Others swarmed to his aid, and a few minutes later, he was as high as the top of the draw-bridge, mounted upon his stairway of flashing blades.

"Now, the ax!" he roared, and other agile fellows swarmed upward, passing the great ax up to him. He balanced himself there, his feet widespread—one upon one bayonet, and the other upon another blade. Jean saw his muscles bunch, the ax lift, come whistling down, to clang in a shower of sparks against one of the chains holding up the bridge.

Now, on the other side, Aubin Bonnemère had climbed to the roof of the guardhouse and was attacking the other chain from his much firmer position. They were madmen, demons, striking with a strength beyond strength. A link gave first on Bonnemère's side, the weight of the great bridge pulling it slowly apart. Then Tournay's ax bit through the links on his side, and the drawbridge shivered, creaked, hung in midair for long seconds, then started downward, slowly at first, but falling even faster until it crashed against the bank with a noise louder than all the thunder in the world.

The mob, roaring, swarmed over it. But halfway across, some of them reeled, fell, lay there clawing the splintered planking with bloody fingers.

Jean looked up toward the tops of the towers. The smoke was thicker now. But at last it had flashes in it, firetongues, stabbing through the smoke. De Launay was firing back. Jean counted the flashes. As nearly as he could judge, there were thirty of them. That meant that only the Swiss were firing. The Invalides were sticking to their pledge not to fire upon the people of Paris.

But the thirty Swiss were shooting with terrible effectiveness. Lines of men moved away, now, bearing the wounded into the Rue Cerisaie. There were men lying in the esplanade who were beyond all need of surgery. This mad, useless siege of the Bastille had claimed the first of its martyrs—and the blood of martyrs is like oil upon the fire of any great cause. . . .

You're dead now, Jean thought bitterly, looking at them; you who wanted only freedom and bread. I, who would gladly change places with any of you, am alive, and must remain so until—

Must remain so? By what token, and for what reason? Nicole is dead, slain by cowards. Lucienne has become a thing it sickens me to contemplate. And everything I dreamed of, a new world, liberty, order, peace is being perverted by fools and scoundrels. . . .

He looked up at the eight great towers and smiled. Pierre said you were a symbol—that men would remember you, O pile of stone and keep of broken hearts! I have in me yet the pride that would be forever remembered—'tis this that you grant me, that in surrendering, I will seem victorious in the eyes of men. . . .

So thinking, he lifted his saber, and ran straight for the drawbridge. Behind him, a mob formed itself, and came after him howling:

"That's it, Citizen Deputy! Lead on, we'll follow you!"

But the Swiss on the ramparts had the cannon going now. Halfway to the bridge Jean's cohorts had melted into the earth, shot-torn, a few of them, fear-crazed, the rest. But Jean Paul ran on through the hail of musket fire, and not a ball came near him.

He paused at the bridge, and looked back. Behind him were only the wounded and the dead. He stood there, resting on his saber, staring out at the sea of humanity snarling at the edges of the esplanade, and himself alone, standing so close to the walls that only by leaning far out and thus exposing himself could the Swiss shoot at him.

Fool, fool! he mocked himself, not even death wants you! Then he threw back his head and sent the eerie boom of his laughter soaring out over the crowd. It held them for a long moment, during which not a shot was fired.

Then with magnificent foolhardiness, Jean Paul strolled back in the direction whence he had come, not even looking up at the towers, walking easily, casually through the musket fire and crash of cannon. His very sangfroid disconcerted the Swiss, so that they too stopped shooting and gazed down at this madman; and when he gained the edge of the crowd again, even the men on the ramparts sent up a cheer.

Thereafter it began again. Cholat, the wine dealer from whom Jean and Pierre had often bought their daily bottle, was busy at the side of Georget, of the Marine Service, the two of them serving the ancient bronze cannon brought an hundred yards ago from Siam. The pitiful balls of the antique weapons bounced off the round towers making scarcely a dent, but at every shot the people cheered.

All the outbuildings were afire, now, filling the air with dense, stifling smoke. The guardrooms, the messrooms blazed fiercely, adding greatly to the excitement, but contributing nothing at all to the taking of the Bastille. A woman came screaming from the doorway of the arsenal, her clothing smoking.

"A madman!" she shrieked; "with torches, there amid the powder!"

Jean was off at her words. He dived into the open door of the arsenal, in time to see a small man bending over, gleefully igniting trains of saltpeter and powder. That the resulting explosion would have harmed the Bastille not at all, while killing hundreds of the attackers, seemed not to have occurred to this man.

Jean gave him the butt of Pierre's musket in the stomach, and dragged him out. Once outside, he saw who the small man was: this firebrand, incendiary, suicidal maker of explosions was none other than the hairdresser and perruque-maker of the Saint-Antoine section—a small man noted for his mildness.

But there was no time now for such reflections. Inside the powder was hissing across the floor, straight toward those barrels that would send hundreds to their deaths. Jean drew one deep breath and plunged in, amid the smoke, kicking the trains of powder apart so that the gaps were too wide for the flames to bridge, watching one splutter out, as another blazed up, dashing toward that one now, kicking, stamping, seeing them all out at last, but one barrel of saltpeter smoldering. He turned this barrel over on its side, and kicked it through the door. Outside, other members of the crowd, seeing it smoking, fled in terror. Jean caught up with it and kicked it apart, scattering the saltpeter, and stamping out the small blaze.

There were other fires now. The howling mob had caught a young woman coming out of the inner courts of the prison, over the fallen drawbridge. They had her bound to a *paillasse,* and were piling straw and broken wood about her.

"Burn her!" they shrieked; "burn the witch! 'Tis old de Launay's daughter! When he sees the smoke rise about her feet, he'll surrender!"

Jean Paul hurled himself forward at once, swinging the musket; the mob broke before him; but another man, clawing his way from the other side of the circle reached her first. Jean was beside him an instant later, and the two of them tore at her bonds. Jean recognized the man; he was Aubin Bonnemère, one of the heroes of the drawbridge.

"His daughter?" Jean panted, when they had her free.

"No," Bonnemère growled; "this a milliner's clerk; I know her well. Here, let me have her—I'll get her to safety. . . ."

So it was, Jean realized afterwards, throughout the day: the brave men, the fighters behaved with conspicuous gallantry and honor; the others, the skulkers, the cowards committed the acts of vileness and cruelty.

But there was no time for sanity now. The wild mob was pushing carts of burning straw, wet enough to make smoke through the drawbridge, and up to other vantage points to stifle the defenders. The wind changed, and the attackers themselves were being suffocated. Jean Paul, Elie, big Reoli, the haberdasher, dragged them back, getting scorched hands and clothing for their pains.

It was all noise now, confusion, madness. The firemen of the *quartier* were busy at their pumps, trying to wet the torch holes of the cannon atop the towers. That their streams, at best could not reach half the height of the Bastille deterred them not a whit; they kept on pumping, wetting half the crowd with flying spray.

Jean saw a young carpenter, mounted on the shoulders of friends, crying out for aid in building a catapult. Santerre, the brewer, was for burning the cold stones to ashes with a mixture of spikenard, poppyseed oil, and phosphorus. Everybody was shooting. A young woman nearby was being given instructions in musketry by her sweetheart; a Turk in turban and baggy pants banged away gleefully.

A new note in the crowd's roar caught Jean's attention. Hulin was back with the *Garde Française*. The mob had cannon now, real cannon. The reserves among the crowd: Maillard, Elie, Hulin took command at once, and the big guns began to jump and bellow, showering down splinters of rock from the towers.

It was over very soon after that. From the towers the white of napkins fluttered from raised musket butts. Jean joined a crowd of men, led by Maillard, carrying a long plank. They stretched it out over the moat, and Jean and the others balanced it there, using the weight of their bodies to hold it in place. Then Maillard walked out on the springy, limber plank, and received the terms of surrender:

Pardons for all, immunity for all those surrendering.

"Granted!" Maillard roared, "upon my faith as an officer!"

Hulin and Eli seconded him, and the second bridge was let down.

Instantly the horde of screaming, cursing madmen surged into the prison, shooting, stabbing everything in sight, the ones who came after firing into their comrades who had gone before.

Jean Paul fell in with Hulin, Elie and Maillard, showing his weapons to protect the prisoners.

It was useless. The mob cheered the Swiss, who had fired upon them, believing them to be prisoners because of their blue smocks. But they fell upon the Invalides, who had refused to a man to shoot into the mob, like savage beasts. The poor old one, who at the last had knocked the torch from M. de Launay's hand and prevented his blowing up the prison, was pierced three times through the body with a sword, and had his right hand, the same hand that had saved the lives of his tormentors, severed from his arm and placed on the end of a pike, to be paraded through the streets.

Despite the efforts of Jean and the others, five officers and three old soldiers were butchered on the spot. Jean and Hulin, drunk with fatigue, covered M. de Launay with their own bodies. But in the gateway, a tall villain reached past them and slashed open the Governor's shoulder. In the Rue Saint-Antoine, the mob swarmed over them, tearing out his hair, spitting into his face, kicking him.

Jean Paul laid about him wrathfully with the flat of his sword; Maillard and Hulin used their musket butts, and thus got the bleeding, tormented old man as far as the arcade of Saint-Jean.

But it was no good. The screaming, shrieking madmen and women knocked even big Hulin to the earth. Jean fought on alone, separated from Maillard. In his fury, he even widened the space about the Governor, when he saw the slender, well known form standing in the crowd, turning her sightless gaze this way and that, her lovely face mirroring complete bewilderment.

"Fleurette!" he called out.

She started toward the sound of his voice; and he paused a moment waiting, which was a mistake, for it diverted his attention just long enough for a bearded blackguard to lift his musket butt and bring it whistling down. Jean heard it, and jumped aside, a fraction of a second too late, so that it caught him a glancing blow. He went down, all the darkness in the world crashing about his head. He heard the roar of the mob growing dimmer until it died away altogether. He was conscious that a great weight had been lifted from him, and willingly he drifted away on a soft tide of blackness.

Later, not long after, a few minutes only, so far as he was able to judge, he was conscious of a soft, sweet voice calling his name. Great droplets splashed into his face. He heard her crying:

"Jean! Oh, they've killed him! Jean, Jean—now I cannot live! Jean, by God's love, do not leave me. . . ."

With great effort, Jean opened his eyes.

"Nor shall I, little Fleurette," he whispered; "not ever. . . ."

She bent down and covered his face with kisses, babbling meaningless words from pure joy. Jean put down one hand, and forced himself upright. Then he saw it:

In an agony of despair, M. de Launay had kicked out at his torturers, screaming: "Kill me! By God's mercy, kill me!" A dozen bayonets pierced him the same instant; the mob dragged his body into the gutter, and handed the saber to the man he had kicked, roaring:

"Cut off his head! The honor is yours, since 'twas you he kicked!"

Only a few days before Jean had given a handful of sous to the fat simpleton who held the saber. This man had been a cook, thrown out of work because the nobles he had worked for had fled. Now the idiot stood there, grinning, slashing at the poor, dead throat of a man who had been an officer and a gentleman in the best sense of both those words. The saber was too dull; it would not even break the skin. The idiot threw it down, and took a small, black-handled knife from his pocket.

"In my job as a cook," he announced proudly, "I learned how to cut meat!" Then he bent and sawed away, until de Launay's head fell free.

They lifted it, stuck it upon the tines of a pitchfork, and started to march away.

"What is it, Jean?" Fleurette whispered. "What are they doing?"

"Nothing," Jean asked; "just making a noise."

He got to his feet, and took her arm, thinking: In this new world we've made, 'tis a blessing to be blind.

Then he led her away, through the scattering crowd.

9

"I've had enough!" Jean Paul said angrily; "I'm going to hand in my resignation tomorrow!"

Pierre grinned at him. It was a very wry grin.

"At the risk of being a bore," he drawled, "I can only say—"

"That you told me so. All right, so you did. But not even you predicted what murderous beasts the people were going to become. . . ."

"Still," Fleurette put in, "they were cruelly oppressed, Jean . . ."

"I know. But they fought to end that oppression—not, I fondly believed, to become oppressors in their turn. I don't think that either Pierre or I, or anyone I know, risked our lives a thousand times to turn France over to the street rabble of Paris. . . ."

He got up and walked over to where Fleurette sat. In her lap she held an object that looked like a picture frame. It was backed with a thin sheet of wood, through which Jean had cut the letters of the alphabet with the point of a sharp knife. Now, by using this stencil, she could trace her letters, and thus learn to write. With her natural dexterity, her progress had been nothing short of marvelous.

"Put it down," he said. "Write without it."

Fleurette did so. She slowly wrote his name, then her own, and held them up for him to see. The letters were shaky and ran down hill, but were entirely legible.

Pierre gazed over Jean's shoulder.

"Why," he suggested, "don't you make her another frame with flat cross bars? She could write in the spaces between the bars, and the bars themselves would prevent her writing from slanting like that. . . ."

"Good idea," Jean said; "I'll do it. . . ."

"I think," Pierre said, gazing at his friend, "that you're in on this conspiracy."

"What conspiracy?" Jean mocked.

"Between Marianne and Fleurette. For the last month they've been plotting something. . . ."

"Oh, Jean!" Fleurette scolded, "you must have told him! I knew you couldn't keep a secret. Now isn't that just like a man!"

Pierre smiled at the possessive note that appeared so frequently in her voice nowadays. If it were me, he mused, pretty and gentle as she is, I wouldn't care that she's blind. . . .

"I didn't tell him," Jean laughed, "but I will now, with your permission. Shall I?"

"Of course, Jean. After all he's going to be a partner. . . ."

"I'm going to be a partner in what?" Pierre demanded.

"Our new business," Jean said. "I'm selling the press, Pierre."

"Enfer!" Pierre swore. "Why, Jean? We've done well so far, and . . ."

"I'll tell you why. But you mustn't interrupt. If, after I've finished, you don't agree, I'll listen to your arguments and try to answer them. But first, hear me out. . . ."

"All right," Pierre said.

"I find," Jean said ruefully, "that I am, after all, my father's son. I seem to have a nose for business. Strange —I spend most of my youth quarreling bitterly with the old man over the inequity of making profits, the vileness of trade, etcetera; but the Paris *canaille* have convinced me that any society not founded upon solid industry, and sober trade, is lost. . . ."

"Hear! Hear!" Pierre mocked.

"You promised not to interrupt!" Fleurette said severely.

"You are becoming quite a typical petite bourgeoise!" Jean laughed. "A real domestic tyrant, isn't she, Pierre?"

"Of course," Fleurette said firmly; "that's precisely what you men need. Where do you think Pierre would be now without Marianne?"

"Somewhere in a gutter, drunk and happy," Pierre grinned.

"This is getting us nowhere," Jean said. "Look, Pierre,

have you examined our balance sheets for the past several months?"

"Yes."

"And what do they show?"

"A slow, but steady decline. But not enough to warrant our giving up the paper. . . ."

"Not by itself. But there are other factors. For instance, the reason for the decline. The *Mercury* is the only remaining journal for moderates—for those who want to keep France a constitutional monarchy somewhat after the English fashion. We are losing ground steadily for two reasons: our clients are steadily fleeing France because their lives are in constant danger; and because many of those who remain are afraid to be seen reading our sheet even in the privacy of their homes. . . ."

"I don't understand that," Pierre said. "A café filled with idlers is one thing; but it seems to me that at home, a man ought to be able to read what he damned well pleases."

"Remember who our clients are. They are men like poor Reveillon—men of substance. They nearly all have servants. In fact they're the only class left in Paris who can afford to hire domestics. And who are the chief spies for the Palais Royal, the Jacobin Club, and the Cordeliers?"

"You have right," Pierre groaned.

"I'm coming now to the most important point of all," Jean said gravely. "You're a married man, Pierre. So far you and Marianne have not been blessed with children. But you're both young, so who can tell? I—I find myself growing weary of the loneliness of my own life. . . ."

Pierre looked instantly at Fleurette, and saw the sudden flare of joy in her sightless eyes. Do not grow too happy, little waif, he thought; he is a strange beast, our Jean. . . .

"I expect little of the future; but it is foolish to think we can fight the whole world, Pierre. How long has it been since we went to work without our pistols? How many times now has that infamous horse doctor, Marat, singled out our paper for attack in his own slimy rag? Even Desmoulins has granted us a passing mention from time to time. We are listed among the proscribed of the Jacobin

Club; more than one orator at the Palais Royal has damned us. . . .

"It is well to be brave and defy them. But you and I, neither of us can afford such bravery any longer. You have Marianne; I have pledged myself to Fleurette's protection. Besides—but I'll not speak of that now. Our lives, then, are not entirely our own to give up heroically. And fruitless heroism is the worst of folly. We must wait, I think, until the people are sated with blood and folly; until there is a resurgence of sanity, of moderation. Then there must be men like us on hand to save France. If they drive us all out, kill us all—what then? These monsters will destroy themselves; but shall we leave the nation to the idiots and simpletons who follow them?"

"*M. l'Orateur!*" Pierre laughed. "I salute you. A great preamble. Now, if you please, the point of all this?"

"The point, *mon vieux,* is very simple. We must get out of politics, abstain even from any activity that has a political tinge. Newspapers are nothing but politics. Hence —no paper. But we must gain our livelihood."

"We can last quite a time," Pierre pointed out. "I converted all the money we made into gold, remember. And you haven't even had to touch your inheritance. . . ."

"True. But they've paper money, now, Pierre, the assignats. Our gold becomes daily a danger to us. Use it too freely and we are called hoarders—and to the lamp-post with us! My father always told me not to put too much trust in currency, Pierre; in threatening times, convert it into real property. That's what I've been doing. I've bought five *hôtels particuliers*. They're being converted into flats. I can live, and well, from the rents. They're fine houses, homes of former nobles and rich bourgeois who have fled. I got them for a song; I could buy many more, but there's also a danger in too much expansion. The street orators have taught the people the word 'profiteer,' too. . . ."

"Aren't you going to tell him about us?" Fleurette put in.

"Yes. It was Marianne's idea, really, Pierre. She saw those three thousand or so journeymen-tailors who meet daily near the Colonnade to discuss their wrongs. You realize, of course, that all the luxury trades have been paralyzed by the emigration. And your very intelligent wife, Pierre, got the idea of giving some of those people work by opening a shop, or even a series of shops to make clothes for the people—to make them in great numbers, in average sizes, so that a man or a woman could buy them finished except for small alterations from the shelves. Have you ever noticed that most Parisians don't vary more than an inch in height; the members of all the mobs are small men. The Swiss and Germans are much bigger, ever noticed that? So you make all your clothes to fit people of the average size—with a few larger and smaller sizes to take care of people whose build differs. . . ."

"Excellent!" Pierre said; "and to think she never told me!"

"She wanted to surprise you. We'll have the business under way in a few weeks now, after all the excitement of the Fête of the Federation is finished. . . ."

"Strange," Fleurette whispered, "to think that it is already a year since the Bastille fell. . . ."

"Time goes quickly," Jean said, "when something is happening every minute. You, Pierre, are to head the concern. Marianne will manage the seamstresses; and Fleurette, who is wonderfully quick with figures, will keep books. That is the best part of the whole scheme, to me; that it will make it possible for Fleurette to earn her living without exposing herself to danger and inclement weather. . . ."

There is another way to protect her from those things, Pierre thought bitterly, if you only had sense enough to see it. . . . But he didn't say it. All he said was:

"And you?"

Jean laughed.

"I cannot fancy myself in the role of a manufacturer of clothing," he said; "I have other plans. I've protected myself already with my rents; but I must confess, as my father's son, my ideas are rather grandiose. I mean to revive Marin et Fils. As soon as I've resigned from the Assembly, I shall go south, and see what can be done. But I'm going to transfer the shipping to Calais, because I'd rather live in Paris. Then, since you need armed convoys to get anything into the city unpillaged, it will be much easier to bring goods in through the northern ports. . . ."

Pierre looked at one of his watches. He carried two, as was the custom. Then he pulled out the other and looked at it. They both agreed within a matter of minutes.

"I wonder what the devil's keeping Marianne?" he said worriedly. "She should have been back hours ago. . . ."

Jean glanced out of the window. It was rapidly growing dusk.

"We'd better have a look," he said. "You'll be all right, Fleurette?"

"Yes, Jean," Fleurette said; "I'll be all right." Even saying his name she made of it a caress.

The two men picked up their pistols and examined them. Then they went down the stairs together.

"Jean," Pierre said, as soon as they had reached the Rue Saint-Antoine; "I'm going to interfere in your private affairs. I've tried not to, but by God's name, I cannot help it! That's why I suggested coming to look for Marianne. I know where she is—standing in line before the baker's trying to get a piece of bread for us. That always takes hours, as you know. . . ."

Jean stared at him.

"Speak your piece," he said quietly.

"Fleurette," Pierre said. "That poor child loves you, Jean."

"I know," Jean said sadly.

"Look, I know she's blind. But name of a name, man! She's as pretty as a picture. On top of that, she's good; which, after that Talbot wench, should have some appeal to you. You're kind to her—all right. You rented rooms next to ours for her, so that Marianne could look in upon her—she really has no need for care; her self-sufficiency is astonishing. You treat her well—but like a child, a beloved adopted child. *Sacre bleu!* When are you going to see that she's a woman—a woman who needs you?"

"Are you suggesting," Jean said, "that I marry Fleurette?"

"Yes. Not suggesting—urging. There, I've said it. Now I feel better. Now you can tell me to go to hell."

Jean smiled at him.

"No, my old one," he said gently, "I won't tell you that. You see, I have almost every intention in the world of doing precisely what you suggest. . . ."

"I heard you," Pierre growled; "you said 'almost'. . . ."

"True. I know, from Bertrand's letters, that the Marquis de Saint Gravert's in Austria. My brother, Bertrand, has seen him. . . ."

"So?" Pierre said.

"Nicole isn't with him. Gervais thinks she's dead, too. He made some sort of investigation through agents. I—I also believe it, God help me! With my mind, Pierre. But only with my mind. In my heart I keep right on hoping. . . ."

"So poor Fleurette must wait," Pierre said grimly, "until you make up your mind that another man's wife, whom you couldn't marry anyhow, is dead or alive?"

"You're too damned logical!" Jean snapped. "I'm going down there and ferret out the facts myself. No agents like the ones her precious brother employed. If she's dead —I'll accept that, though I'll never forget her. If she's not, I'll find her. She married Lamont in the first place because she thought I had been killed. History repeats itself, but only if you let it. I mean to make sure. . . ."

"And if you find her alive?" Pierre said.

"There's already been discussion in the Assembly over the question of divorce. I'll see that the question's brought up again; I could even, by compromising on some matters that I've managed to put a stop to almost singlehanded, get a law of divorce established. . . ."

"Very fine!" Pierre mocked. "But if you'll pardon a further exercise of my logic: though any of these things singly are perhaps possible of attainment, all of them together are quite impossible."

"Why?" Jean said.

"You resign from the Assembly day after tomorrow. Hence no bills of divorcement introduced by you. Or, conversely, you don't resign. Therefore you cannot leave Paris to find out whether Nicole la Moyte, Marquise de Saint Gravert is alive or not. You have need of a little of my Jesuitical training, Jean."

"*Morbleu!*" Jean swore. "You're right! But I'll think of something. . . . By the way, here comes Marianne now. . . . See to her, Pierre; she looks positively ill!"

Pierre ran toward his wife. Marianne's plump, usually rosy face was now as white as a sheet. She leaned against her husband, half-fainting.

"I don't think I've ever seen anything quite so horrible in my life," she whispered.

Jean, who was only a step behind his friend, caught Marianne's other hand.

"What is it?" he said.

"Look!" Marianne got out, her voice shuddering with pure loathing, "behind me—look. . . ."

Jean's gaze followed her trembling finger. Down the street came a parade of children, street urchins, the gamins of Paris. They were beating a small keg for a drum, playing homemade flutes. And on the ends of improvised pikes, they bore the heads of three cats, still dripping blood.

"She's right," Pierre got out, "it is the most horrible . . ."

Jean stood there, looking at the filthy children. How many times now had he seen human heads paraded on the ends of pikes in the last year? De Launay's; Flessel's; Foulon's; Berthier's; those two poor devils of Swiss Guards who had tried to protect the Queen from the mob of Parisian women at Versailles, last October. He remembered then with an almost physical disgust, how, walking with the other members of the Assembly in that crowd, prisoners really, as much, in fact, as the royal family itself, being dragged, though they had had to make shameful protestations of willingness, back to Paris and that room in the Riding School of the Tuileries where the howling mob in the galleries could control their every action—he had witnessed things that had seemed to him the very nadir of degradation. The mob, bearing the heads of the heroic Swiss Guardsmen on pikes, had stopped at a hairdresser's. There, they had forced the barbers to curl and powder the hair of the warm and dripping heads. One barber's assistant had fainted. . . .

And I thought, Jean mused bitterly, that life could hold no worse horror than that. But it can—witness this. . . . He tried to analyze what it was about this blind, imitative cruelty of the children that sickened him so. It is, he guessed, that murder has become a daily commonplace. God in Glory! To what pass have we brought France that her children make of death a game?

Then he turned with Pierre and helped the sickened Marianne back toward their abode.

Fleurette made the supper. Marianne wasn't able to. Jean and Pierre helped as much as they could. But the evening was ruined. Constraint lay like a blight on every attempt at conversation. They couldn't discuss this thing before Fleurette. They did not want to talk about it anyway, but the silence in Pierre's dining room was oppressive.

"I think," Pierre said at last, "that you and I should go out and show ourselves at the Champs de Mars. Throw a few shovelfuls of dirt around the amphitheatre. Doesn't pay not to appear public spirited, these days. . . ."

Jean glared at him. He was about to say that he gave less than a damn whether he appeared public spirited or not, but he thought the better of it. Anything, after all, was better than sitting in this funereal silence, or returning to his own lonely rooms, and the blackness of his thoughts.

"All right," he said wearily, "I'll go. . . ."

It was no small journey, across the Bridge of Henry IV, and along the left bank of the Seine, past both the islands, the Île Saint Louis, and the Île de la Cité, seeing the soaring spires of Notre Dame and the grim round towers of the Conciergerie, winding through the small streets of the Saint Germain des Prés section, now choked with people, all bent upon the same errand, but during that long walk, neither of them spoke a word.

The Champs de Mars was black with people, all digging, hauling barrows of earth, working as though their lives depended upon the outcome of their labors. Tomorrow was to be the day. One full year since the Bastille had been taken by the heroic people of Paris. Delegations were expected from all over France; there would be no end of pageantry, and the grandiose earthen amphitheatre must be ready. Paid laborers had begun the work a month ago, but Desmoulins and other journalists had called to the attention of *la foule*, the mob, the people, that the work lagged, and a thrill of patriotic fervor had electrified all Paris.

"They are children," Jean said quietly to Pierre; "as excitable as children, and as thoughtlessly cruel. . . . Well, we'd best lend a hand. . . ."

They moved on toward the thick of the work! A gentleman of evident quality rushed past them, throwing off his coat as he came. He stood up rolling up his sleeves, taking off his waistcoat from which the fobs of his two watches showed.

"Your watches!" several workmen cried to him.

The man drew himself up proudly.

"Does one distrust his brothers?" he flung back at them, and marched off, leaving his fine clothing and gold watches where they lay.

"They'll be there when he comes back, I'll warrant you," Pierre declared. "You're right; they are children. Touch them at the right place and you can do wonders with them. . . ."

A brewer's cart drew up, loaded with wine casks. The brewer, a big man, stood up in the cart, crying:

"This wine is for the patriot-workers, given by me, free of all charge! But I beg you, Citizens, to drink it only as you have need—so that more may share of it, and that it may last longer!"

Then he and his helpers began to unload the cart. The hundreds of people within the sound of his voice could have emptied the barrels in less than ten minutes. Jean had seen them perform prodigies of drinking while pillaging the monasteries and the private hôtels of the Noblesse. But now, to his astonishment, they merely cheered the brewer at the echo, but not one of them broke ranks to touch the casks.

It was good, Jean found, to swing a pick again, to feel the prison-developed muscles of his arms bunch and release, the pick whistling down to bite deeply into the earth. In half an hour he had left Pierre far behind, feeling the good rivulets of sweat running down his back. It was dark now, but the whole Champs was illuminated with thousands of torches.

My God, Jean thought, all of Paris is here!

"Ah, Marin!" a light, dry voice called, a little breathless with exertion, " 'tis good to see you here!"

And Jean turned to see the Abbé Sieyès pulling a cart along with Beauharnais. The load was far too heavy for that wraithlike man, so Jean fell to with good will, pushing behind them. They passed the Marquis de Lafayette, digging alongside Bailly, Mayor of Paris. Sweat dripped out of the Marquis' red hair and ran down his long nose.

It was funny, ridiculous, but also curiously inspiring. Here, Jean realized, was the closest approach to real democracy the world had yet seen. Here a whole family worked, mother, father, and children, with the ancient grandsire holding the youngest infant in his arms.

Burly, gigantic Danton moved small mountains, assisted but badly by slender, too handsome, Camille Desmoulins.

Desmoulins, Jean noted, was rather busier with his note-book than his spade.

"A word with you, Citizen Marin," Danton rumbled. "A moment, only—I shan't detain you from your patriotic labors. . . ."

Jean stopped, overcome with astonishment. From the first day he had seen Georges Danton at the Café Charpentier there had been little friendship between him and the huge man. Desmoulins, Danton's satellite, had taken occasion several times to sneer at Jean Paul's moderation in his *Revolutions of France and Brabant*. But Danton's bass voice, now, was curiously mild, his big face bland and conciliatory.

"I am at your service, M. Danton," Jean said.

"Citizen Danton," the big man corrected. "None of your aristocratic airs. . . ." Yet even this rebuke was delivered mildly, and accompanied by a conspiratorial wink. Jean waited.

"I'd like to extend you an invitation to visit us at the Cordeliers' Club," Danton said. "Whether you know it or not, we Cordeliers have followed your career with interest. To us the strangest part about it has been your stubborn refusal to identify yourself with any faction. On some issues—the religious question, for instance, you've been as far to the Left as the wildest Jacobin; on certain others you seem almost a royalist. . . ."

"I am a royalist," Jean smiled. "A constitutional royalist—like most of my colleagues of the Left. I'd retain the kingship as a largely ceremonial and symbolic office, shorn of much of its powers. The people, Citizen Danton, need a visible symbol round which to rally. . . ."

"I don't agree," Danton rumbled, "but your argument has your usual force and clarity. That's why we want you in the Cordeliers. Once you've seen the light, politically, your unblemished reputation and incisive oratorical style could be valuable to us. Only Sieyès, and perhaps Robespierre can equal you for clarity, and Robespierre is a dullard, Sieyès a vain fool. All the rest of them are compromised, windy, and unclear. Come sit through one of our sessions—debate against us if you will; and I'll warrant we'll convince you!"

Despite himself, Jean Paul could not repress a chuckle.

"Yet," he laughed, "your friend here, Citizen Desmou-

lins has two or three times suggested that the nation
might profit if I were stretched from the nearest lamp-
post!"

Desmoulins smiled.

"But that, Citizen," he said, "was before I learned that
you were selling your press, and retiring from combating
me in the journalistic arena. Those things indicate to me
that you are beginning to think more clearly. Like Citizen
Danton, I've always respected your intelligence; and I am
too good a patriot to deprive the nation of it, if it can be
bent to useful ends. . . ."

"I thank you for your invitation," Jean said; " 'Tis very
flattering. Perhaps I shall accept—I'll send you word. . . ."

"Do!" Danton rumbled; and Jean walked on, after the
retreating cart of the Abbé Sieyès. He was aware as he
did so that several groups of workers stopped their work
to stare at him. In one of them horse-doctor Marat stood,
tearing with frantic fingers at his itching skin, which his
own skill could not cure, reason enough, men said, for
his venom; from another, Maximilien Robespierre watched
Jean with his icy, colorless eyes.

Strange, Jean thought, how little it takes to become a
marked man in Paris these days. A word from Georges
Danton, President of the Cordeliers—said to be the most
powerful man in Paris—and I am noted of those who
will presently come to ask favors; but also by those who
measure my neck for the hangman's noose. Dear God,
but what a juggler's act life has become!

He was close to the cart now before which the vain
little Abbé struggled. Sieyès who had said: "Politics is an
art I believe myself to have completed . . . ," believing
that all France would stand or fall upon his skill. Jean
smiled, thinking of it; then another curiosity caught his eye.

A group of nuns were laboring on a hillside, digging,
spading, pushing barrows. But it was not the Holy Sisters
who rooted Jean to the spot, his jaw sagging foolishly;
rather it was the group of young women who worked
with them, clad in garments as light as air, and almost as
transparent, their long hair in lovely dishevelment, tricolor sashes about their tiny waists, laughing and chattering as they worked.

Jean stood there a long moment; then he threw back
his head and roared. To see the dancers of the Opéra,

among the most notorious wantons of Paris, working side by side in perfect harmony with the chaste sisters of the church was too much. The sound of his laughter came over them, soaring and booming in curiously unearthly mirth. They stopped and stared at him. Then one of them broke away from the others and came skipping down the hill.

"Jean!" she laughed; "I thought I recognized that idiotic laughter of yours. . . ."

"Couldn't help it," Jean chuckled; "to see you, Lucienne, in such exalted company was vastly amusing. . . ."

Lucienne half turned toward the busy nuns.

"They are such dears," she smiled; "all evening I've been repressing a desire to shock them quite out of their robes; but they've been so sweet, I hadn't the heart. One of them has been questioning me all afternoon about my life. I'm sure she was inwardly panting for some really wicked details. In about ten more minutes I was going to oblige her, if you hadn't appeared. Poor thing, I'll wager she'd have to do penance for years for the thoughts I'd put in her head. . . ."

"You are incorrigible. . . ." Jean said.

"I know. And you love it. But really, Jeannot, darling— I came here chiefly because I was sure that sooner or later I'd see you. . . ."

"How flattering," Jean mocked. "Or rather it would be if every word of it weren't a pure, unmitigated lie. . . ."

"Why, Jeannot," Lucienne said, her tone of injury only a little exaggerated; "how distrustful you are! You know I told you long ago that I might find you interesting again —one of these years . . ."

"And that year has come?" Jean smiled.

"Why yes, darling," Lucienne whispered huskily, "I rather think it has. . . ."

"Now I am flattered," Jean laughed. "I thought that when Gervais la Moyte fled France with the rest of the émigrés last October you'd begin to cast about for a replacement. Fidelity, my dove, is not one of your virtues. But I hardly thought that an insignificant provincial deputy like me would merit your attentions. . . ."

"Hardly insignificant, Jeannot. They are saying that you will go far—that of all the men in the Assembly only you and Robespierre are absolutely incorruptible. That means something. Besides, it's a positively fascinating challenge;

how perfectly delightful, my Jeannot, to corrupt the incorruptible! By which I mean you, of course; I could scarcely fancy myself in bed with Robespierre—" She stared toward the little lawyer from Arras. "How utterly loathsome he is! I'd sooner touch a snake. . . ."

"And I," Jean mocked, "would rather wrestle with the lightnings, like the great American savant, Doctor Franklin, than risk getting singed another time by you. . . ."

"How sweet," Lucienne laughed. "Even when you're being both unfair and unkind, like now, you manage to flatter me. Are you really so frightened of me, Jeannot? After all, I am only a poor harmless girl. . . ."

"Du Barry and la Pompadour were harmless girls," Jean said drily, "but they managed, between them to wreck France. . . ."

Lucienne dropped him the prettiest curtsey imaginable.

"You don't know," she laughed, "how it helps my vanity to be compared to both my ideals at once! Come, take me away from here. You've been seen. A thousand idiots will boast tomorrow of having worked cheek by jowl with the Incorruptible Citizen Deputy Marin. And I'm perishing of thirst. . . ."

"All right," Jean said, and took her arm. But he had not gone ten feet before he was stopped again. This time it was the Comte de Mirabeau, that strange ex-noble who had deserted his class to sit for the Third Estate of Aix. Mirabeau dominated the whole Assembly, defied the gallery bullies, stood like a lion against all factions, working, Jean believed, truly for the good of France. But a lifelong, well-deserved reputation as a satyr and blackguard stood against him.

Two men in all France, Jean thought suddenly, could save the crown: Mirabeau and de Lafayette, and no one at court has sense enough to see them as anything but traitors to their class. . . .

"May I say, M. Marin," Mirabeau said in his deep oratorical voice, "that I vastly admire your taste?"

Jean frowned. He had often heard women complain of men who, in the feminine phrase, "undressed them with their eyes." But he had never seen a man accomplish that singular feat before. But this ugly, pockmarked old roué did precisely that, and with such thoroughness that Lucienne reddened to the roots of her hair.

"Thank you," Jean said stiffly. "But I think I'd rather

be admired for my wit and oratory, like *M. le Député* from Aix."

"The more fool you, then," Mirabeau smiled. "Anyone can have lungs of brass; but to be upon pleasant terms with beauty's self—that, M. Marin, is an accomplishment!"

"Thank you, M. le Comte," Lucienne said. She had recovered her poise now; but that this ugly old man had been able to disconcert her, rankled still.

"You are entirely welcome," Mirabeau chuckled, "though I can see it pains you to accept the compliments of the dirty old man I'm supposed to be. However, M. Marin, though you will scarcely credit this, I did not stop you to get a better view of your fair companion, though truth compels me to confess I'm heartily glad I did, because now I can perhaps combine pleasure with duty. There will be, you know, much social activity during the coming week. Next week, in fact, I'm entertaining a few guests at my house in the Chaussée d'Antin. I'd be honored to have you join me, M. Marin—the more so if you'll be so kind as to bring your lady. . . ."

Jean stared at him. Honoré-Gabriel Riqueti, Comte de Mirabeau, was a strange man. Yet, Jean thought quickly, *a just one, I truly believe. All his life he has been waiting for a role worthy of his talents—and the follies, and mistakes of his youth were born perhaps of resentment of a world unable to judge his worth. . . . But dare I accept the invitation of a man known to have been penniless upon his arrival in Paris, who has now no visible means of support save his paltry newspaper and his eighteen francs a day salary as a Deputy—yet, who, despite this owns today a magnificent home in Paris, an even greater country house at Argenteuil, gives parties that are the scandal of the whole city, spends money like a prince?*

'Tis folly perhaps to be proud of the bubble, reputation. Yet men call me honest, and respect me for it. Can any reputation, however great, stand such an association? Yet, if Mirabeau accepts money, as is reputed, from the Royalists—it is honest coin; for in his way he would preserve the King—all his speeches prove it. . . .

"Oh, for heaven's sake, Jean!" Lucienne said, "tell him we'll come! I, for one, would be delighted. . . ."

"You honor me, Madame," Mirabeau said, and made her a bow.

"Mademoiselle," Lucienne corrected. "M. Marin does not believe in haste. He has yet to honor me with a proposal. . . ."

"Would you accept him, Mademoiselle—" Mirabeau paused questioningly after the title.

"Talbot, Lucienne Talbot. Oh, yes! But I begin to despair of ever being asked. . . ."

"Ah, Mademoiselle Talbot, you desolate me! I find myself in need of M. Marin's judgment, and you shake my faith in it to the very foundations. . . ."

"Perhaps his reluctance to quit his bachelorhood," Lucienne laughed, "is a display of the very judgment you mention, M. le Comte. I fear me that I'm nobody's prize. . . ."

"Mademoiselle leaves me no other course open but to disagree with her—violently," Mirabeau laughed. "But come now, M. Marin—won't you honor me with your presence?"

"I gather," Jean said drily, "that your invitation involves more than mere sociability?"

"Yes—a chat afterwards, about matters important to France. I cannot speak of them now. But may I reassure you, M. Marin, that they involve no dishonesty? If you undertake what I shall ask of you, you will gain nothing in worldly goods; you will, in fact, risk much—even up to your life. But I think that as one of the rascals like myself who has brought France to this state, you should be willing to take a few risks to save your country. . . ."

"Now you interest me," Jean said. "Yes, M. Mirabeau, you can depend upon our presence. . . ."

Mirabeau bowed and kissed Lucienne's hand. For all his democracy, Gabriel Riqueti was every inch a lord. . . .

Walking into the amphitheatre that morning of July fourteenth, 1790, with Fleurette on his arm, and Pierre and Marianne following a few paces behind him, Jean could not repress a long, slow whistle of astonishment. Though he had worked upon the thing himself, though he had seen it done, the Champs de Mars had become something other than a parade ground, something more, an exemplification of the genius of the French nation perhaps, combining here the pride, the vainglory, the theatricality of a race essentially proud, vain, and theatrical, to whom the blood and terror of history were not enough,

needing always to intensify that which was already un-
bearably intense, to lift it into pageantry, into drama. . . .

"What is it, Jean?" Fleurette breathed. "Tell me about
it—what it's like, I mean. . . . Is it really so splendid?"

Splendid? Jean thought. I wonder. Cheap and gaudy,
and theatrical and a little obscene. But—splendid? Yes!
By God, it is splendid. Splendid and pitiful and funny and
awesome; because it adds up to that. With all our folly
and bloodlust and madness and cruelty we are still a
great people, the greatest, perhaps, that the world has
yet seen or ever will see. We overdo everything, from
sacking empty prisons, and parading with the heads of
harmless, honorable men dripping upon our pikes, to
standing magnificently in an Assembly and overturning
the wrongs of centuries in one day. . . . We build a Constitution not upon slow, sober experience like the English
have done, but upon logic, forgetting that nothing in life is
more foreign to the mind of man than logic, and yet this
very abstraction we have made is magnificent, too, a
tremendous parade of ideals which never in human history
have worked, and never will, because man is forever
greedy, grasping, vile, his heroism a comedy of errors,
his dying robbed even of tragedy by its uselessness, but it
was good to have written it, to have set it down, because
though it cannot be so, it ought to be. . . .

"Jean. . . ." Fleurette said, tugging at his sleeve.

"Yes, little dove," Jean said, "it's splendid. They've
made an artificial rock, about fifty feet high, so cunningly
that it looks real. It has steps cut into it, and a cavern,
which has a scroll over it labeling it the Temple of Con-
cord. On the top there's a Statute of Liberty, clad in a
red Phrygian cap, with a pike in her hand. . . ."

"A hell of a bad job, too," Pierre grumbled. "You can
see the cracks in the plaster from here. Besides I don't
fancy a pike as a symbol of liberty. What's that column
beside her for, Jean?"

"The Civic Column," Jean said. "And the altar at her
feet, is the Altar of the Country. Talleyrand, Bishop of
Autun, will say mass there today. . . ."

"Are there many people?" Fleurette asked; "I seem to
hear so many voices. And that music—I've never heard
anything like it before!"

"There are three hundred drummers," Jean said, "and
twelve hundred wind-musicians. Besides that there're

enough cannon here to win a major war. Every height is
covered with artillery, and there are still more mounted
on barges on the Seine. As for the people, Fleurette, any
Parisian not here today is either too old, paralyzed, or
dead. . . ."

Jean turned his head and looked about the Champs.
The whole top of the École Militaire had a new super-
structure built over it, galleries and canopies, painted by a
score of artists under the great David, showing scenes of
the past year, grandiose and allegorical, much improved
upon nature, the men whom Jean Paul knew well in all
their weakness and puny pride and cupidity become giants, demigods, larger than life, finer, now in their uni-
forms of state and again as antique Romans, toga-clad,
possessed of physiques that few, if any of them had in
reality.

And all of it, the paintings, the *arcs de triomphe* by the
gate and the river, the iron cranes with huge pans of incense swinging beneath them, perfuming the very air, the
boom of cannon, the martial music, the rooftops of every
high point in Paris black with men viewing the ceremony
through spyglasses, so that the sun glinted upon their
uplifted farseeing tubes making small lightnings, from
the cupolas of the Invalides to the Windmills, lazily turning upon Montmartre, Chaillot bright with silks and cot-
tons of fashionable women, was somehow splendid, now,
sublime; even the cracked plaster Liberty taking on the
aspect of grandeur. . . .

The music swelled to deafening harmonies, defying the
heavens. And through the gates, under the Arcs, the Fed-
erates came, banners flying, and after them Sieur Motier,
formerly Marquis de Lafayette, Generalissimo of France,
magnificent upon a white stallion, his red, unpowdered
hair glinting in the sun, and after him the nobles of the
Court, and the Royal family, and finally Talleyrand-Peri-
gord, Bishop of Autun with three hundred priests clad in
white with tricolor sashes, marching in to the boom of cannon echoing from all the heights of Paris, brazen voiced,
booming, to be picked up by other cannon on other
heights, some of them within Jean's hearing, so that gunroar by gunroar from one village to another lying within
the sound of gunfire the echoes of this day passed within
mere minutes all over France.

The cavalry was upon the field now, slow wheeling, its

precision matchless, every maneuver in the manuals done
perfectly, precisely, and new ones invented for the occasion.

Now de Lafayette mounted to the altar, and flourish-
ing his sword, swore eternal fealty "To King, To Law,
and To Nation," in his own name and in the name of the
armies of France. And after him, fat and bumbling as
usual, Louis mounted and swore in a firm voice to uphold
the Constitution, whereupon the people split open the
very skies with their cheering, and rising spontaneously,
swore the same oath in an hundred thousand hoarse
roaring voices, drowning for the moment, even the boom
of the cannon.

"It is too much," Jean said to Fleurette, "I cannot describe it. To me it seems almost blasphemy, as though
the people would make of themselves gods. . . ."

"It is a kind of blasphemy," Pierre whispered; "I—I
cannot believe, but what think you of this!"

Jean's gaze followed his pointing finger. Bishop Talleyrand was mounting his altar now to begin the solemn
mass, but above the altar itself, the scattered clouds had
gathered together suddenly, become black, faster than
the tricolored civil priests could mount the stairs and before the Bishop could even lift his hand for silence, the
rain came down in torrents.

The incense pots hissed out, the bravely painted scenes
began to run their colors, the finery of the Nymphs of
the Opéra, Lucienne among them, for Jean Paul had long
since found her among the throngs, clinging to their slender
limbs, drenched with the sullen torrents, and from everywhere umbrellas appearing, and frockcoats being drawn
over carefully coiffed heads.

Jean pulled off his own coat and wrapped Fleurette
in it, for none of them had thought to bring umbrellas;
but before he had her half covered, her light silk dress,
made for her by Marianne was soaked through. He stood
there holding her, feeling her shivering under the coat,
watching the dignitaries and nobles scurrying for cover,
and suddenly, irresistibly, the high comedy of this demonstration by Nature of the futility of mankind and all his
hopes, struck home to him. He loosed the soaring boom
of his laughter, peal after peal into the teeth of the rain,
all his old mockery caught up once more in that curiously

inhuman laughter of his, so that all those within sound of it, paused in their headlong flight for shelter and stared at the tall man with face of a scarred angel-fiend, who stood there laughing like a demented devil from hell itself; so that the very timbre of the sound raised the short hairs on the backs of their necks, making them go cold all over suddenly, and the goose-pimples rising upon their flesh.

"Stop it, Jean!" Fleurette screamed at him; "stop it this instant!"

Jean stared down at her, the sardonic smile upon his face fading slowly into tenderness.

"Forgive me, Love," he murmured; "I didn't mean to offend you."

"You—you didn't," she stammered, her voice shaking; "you frightened me, Jean. Sometimes when you laugh like that, I realize I don't know you really—that you are not one person, but two; and one side of you I don't know at all. . . ."

"And that side of me is—evil," Jean said.

"Yes— Oh, I don't know! All I do know is that it is not the man I love. . . ."

"Take her home, Jean," Marianne said, "can't you see she's blue with cold?"

"All right," Jean said.

"I'm coming with you," Marianne said, "that child's going to need some attention. You can stay if you like, Pierre. . . ."

"No," Pierre said; "I don't feel like getting soaked to hear a mass—especially one said by priests that bowed to civil authority, placing it above the Church. I'm an unbeliever, but if you're going to believe, why then, damn it, believe and don't compromise! Come along now. . . ."

Marianne was right. By the time they got Fleurette home, she was shaking in the grip of a hard chill. But Marianne was designed by nature for crises such as this. In ten minutes she had Fleurette in bed with hot stones wrapped in cloth at her feet, and was pouring steaming grog down her throat. Slowly the warmth crept back into the slender limbs, and the hot rum began to take hold of her, so that her lovely, ethereal face glowed once more with color. . . . Jean sat beside her bed until the great dark eyes drooped into slumber. Then he stood up.

"I'm going to change," he said; "she'll be all right, won't she, Marianne?"

"Perfectly. I'll stay with her, just in case she wakes up, which isn't likely. Run along and get dressed—both of you. Go on out to the Place de Bastille and dance with all the *poules* as I know you're going to. But if you, Pierre du Pain, are not in this house by midnight—I'll take a black iron skillet to you, by all the Saints!"

"By midnight," that rogue grinned, "I shall have pleasured myself with at least three of them!"

"*Le coq gaulois!*" Jean mocked. "Or is it a Riviera rabbit, which, *mon vieux?*"

"At least not a scarred-visaged monk of Satan and the black mass!" Pierre shot back at him.

"You are no good, neither of you," Marianne declared. "Now get out of here and let the poor child sleep. . . ."

At the place of the Bastille, for that grim prison was gone now, razed to its very foundations by the people of Paris, they had erected a Tree of Liberty, more than sixty feet high, with a huge red Phrygian cap, lately become the visible symbol of liberty, perched upon the top of it. Among the broken stones they had also put up artificial trees, festooned with lanterns, beneath which a mob of people were dancing.

Marianne was quite right, Jean said; at least half the *filles* of the Palais Royal were there. But there were also great ladies, some of them the remnants of the nobility, dancing not only with well-dressed bourgeois gentlemen, but with men clad in the jackets and long trousers of workers, the class called *sans culottes,* not because they wore no pantaloons, but because they did not wear the knee breeches of the upper classes. Here the whole of society had been leveled; to be built up again—into what?

There were numerous stalls of winesellers already set up, and from the noise and laughter they had been patronized freely. Jean stood there a long moment. His mood was strange, even to himself. When it came to both food and drink, Jean Paul was habitually frugal, even abstemious; he had, too, but little desire for the society of his fellows. But tonight, oddly, he found his usual loneliness intolerable. He had a strange desire to drink his fill of wine, to laugh with the others, to dance—to be for this once a human being like other humans, to desert his cynicism, his mockery, and to plunge into life; tomorrow he could come back again into the shadow, into loneliness—but tonight . . .

He walked over to the wineseller.

"A carafe!" he laughed; "and keep it full!"

Pierre grinned at him.

"See you later, my old one," he said; "I'm going to earn that coup de skillet!"

Jean watched him moving off into the crowd. He took a step toward Pierre, to call him back, for the last thing on earth he wanted, now, tonight, was to be alone; but already it was too late, the crowd of revelers had swallowed Pierre up as though he had never been.

Jean downed his wine in one steady draught, and put out his carafe again, feeling the wine curling hotly, meanly in his belly, the fumes of it rising black and sulphurous into his brain. He was not a good drinker and he knew it; he didn't even enjoy drinking; he hated intoxication as he hated all things that lessened his command of himself. But he had the need for it now. Any escape—even this cheap and tawdry one suited his mood. He was buried beneath the ruins of his private disasters: Thérèse dead in horror, four years stolen out of his life, his youth, his manly good looks irreparably smashed, Lucienne's betrayal, Nicole, lost—dead, too, perhaps, and if dead by what terrible means of dying? He had to get out from beneath the mountain of his sorrows; he had to see starlight, breathe air, laugh with good laughter, cleansed of mockery, of bitterness. . . .

Two hours later, he was wandering along the Champs Élysées without knowing precisely how he got there. It wasn't very late, but the lanterns in the trees danced wildly before his eyes, and the dancers had become for him dervishes, whirling at incredible speed, indistinguishable as people, mere swirls of light and color. He stared at them with vast benevolence, loving them all—all of them his brothers, his children, all the people of Paris, monsters and saints alike, nuns and prostitutes, all wonderfully beautiful and gay and happy, and he standing there like that, swaying a little on his feet, loving them, when he felt the air-light touch of her hand upon his shoulder.

"Jeannot," she whispered huskily, her face close to his,

so that her wine-perfumed breath stirred against his cheeks; "I've found you. But it took me ever so long. . . ." Then peering closer, the laughter getting into her hazel eyes: "You're drunk! How funny—I've never seen you like this before—it becomes you, I think; a man should be drunken once in a while. . . ."

He peered at her with owlish gravity. When he spoke, his voice was thick.

"Lucienne—" he croaked.

"I was going to ask you to dance the Carmagnole with me," she laughed, "but you can't. *Mon Dieu!* You can scarcely stand! Don't let it bother you, though, my Jeannot; neither can I, for that matter. . . . Come along with me, now. . . ."

"Where?" Jean got out.

"Never mind where. I must take care of you. You'll only be knocked down and robbed if you wander around like this. Come—where we can be alone, and talk, and—"

"And what?" Jean whispered thickly.

"You'll see," Lucienne said.

She took him by the arm, and they turned away from the Champs and wound through the Place de Louis Quinze across the bridge into the crooked little streets of the Left Bank. Jean never knew how many times they turned, the different streets were all of a pattern to him, a succession of bobbing lights, and utter darkness, rough cobbled under his feet, the lights dancing the shadows night deep, unfathomable, until she stopped at last, and drew from her bag a great key, turning it in a lock, and the two of them going upward, upward, treading spectrally up long flights of curving stairs, and Lucienne stopping once more, again turning a key, pushing open a door. . . .

"Here we are," she said.

The room, he could see by the candle she had left lighted, was richly furnished, silk hung, the bed ornate, canopied, the furniture gilded, carved, the firescreen hand painted, the rugs ankle deep, the whole of it having a smell of a subtle perfume, a slow, penetrating scent that got to him through all the wine-fog, making his breath come a little quicker, the whole of it exquisitely beautiful, even to the twenty-four-hour clock on the mantel which told not only the hours, but the days and months as well, with two fat, naked cupids perched atop it with brazen hammers in their hands, poised to strike the hour.

"Come," she said, "let me help you off with your boots. You must be tired. . . ."

"Tired?" Jean said, his voice coming from somewhere a thousand leagues outside of his body, "not tired, dead. I died in prison—of starvation, of torture at the hands of la Moyte's minions. I am a ghost, living on after all need or wish for living has left me. . . . You know that, Lucienne? It's strange to be dead— It takes such a long time to die. . . . I started dying the night you betrayed me; I only finished it when—" But he couldn't say it. He could not bring himself to mention Nicole's name, here, under such circumstances. "I'm only a ghost," he said.

"A most substantial ghost," she whispered, and he felt her hands, inside his shirt now, running soft and warm over his chest.

"Don't do that," he said; "I don't want . . ."

But her mouth was against his, soft and sweet, and tasting of wine, stopping his words, moving upon his with devilish expertness. She kept it there, holding him prisoner with an aching, anguished, age-long kiss, while her hands moved again, doing this, and again this, and he felt the coolness of the night upon his skin, and lying back against the chair, staring stupidly at his nakedness, while she swirled away from him in a ballet turn, sweeping her white arms up, so that the gossamer chiffon she was wearing floated upward like a cloud about her head, and drifted away and down to the floor. He stared at her.

"My God, but you're lovely!" he groaned.

"You think so?" she whispered. Then she caught at his arms and drew him upright, and went up on tiptoe and found his mouth, spinning the ceiling about his head in slow, concentric circles, until they weren't standing any more, but lying suddenly, miraculously beneath the silken canopy upon the great bed.

"Dear God!" Jean Paul murmured. "Dear, kind, merciful God. . . ."

Awakening to him was like resurrection, like being born again out of death. He struggled upward through layers of darkness, blinking his eyes against the light. His head was a ball, bigger than the earth, inhabited by a legion of tiny fiends with picks and hammers. His tongue was fur-coated, made from the pelt of the vilest animal upon earth; and his eyes. . . .

It took him a long time to get them focused; but when he did, he saw her lying there, her face soft with sleep, her eyes blue circled, her tawny hair a mesh, wild tangled, pillowing her head. Even by daylight she was lovely, even by the harsh glare of a noonday sun. One of her arms was flung out across him, her face was cradled in the hollow of his neck.

And he, lying there, remembering, hated himself suddenly with a hatred and contempt that were absolutely bottomless, himself, undeceived, knowing her for what she was, remembering Fleurette sick with colds and fever, waiting in fear and neglect in her eternal darkness for the sound of his step upon the stair.

He tried to move out and away from her without awakening her. But her eyes came open at once, utterly clear, filled with mockery, and laughter, and something else too, something he could not quite define, but which terrified him.

"And where do you think you're going?" she laughed.

"Home," he snapped.

"But, Jeannot, darling—this is home, now. Don't be a fool—it's ever so much more comfortable than that dreary rathole you live in. . . ." She came up on one elbow, and stared at him.

"You are strong," she whispered; "now I understand the pitiful letters of the poor Nicole. . . ."

"Don't mention her name!" he roared at her.

"I won't," she yawned; "the subject bores me. All subjects bore me—except you, my love. . . ."

He thrust himself up into a sitting position; but she came up beside him in a wild rush, encircling him with her soft arms, seeking his mouth.

"You," she whispered, "aren't going anywhere—at all. . . ."

Then her mouth was upon his, and he knew that he wasn't. Lost, he groaned inside his mind, while he could still think, which wasn't long.

For in a very few minutes, he stopped thinking altogether.

10

The house of the Citizen Riqueti, ci-devant Comte de Mirabeau, at number Forty-two, Chaussée d'Antin, was as luxurious as Jean Paul expected it to be. Even the anteroom in which they waited was hung with heavy silk, and the paneling was intricately carved. Jean looked briefly at the room, then back at Lucienne. As always, she looked enchanting.

She wore a gown of white cotton with vertical green stripes, because by the summer of 1790, silk was considered aristocratic, and hence unpatriotic, involving some danger to the wearer. But on Lucienne, it was lovely. She could wear discarded sacking, Jean thought, and look beautiful. . . . The gown was topped with a short jacket of the same material, over a tight bodice of the cotton cloth, so made that the stripes ran horizontally instead of vertically. A bow held her gauze fichu in place, the stiff gauze billowing out like a cloud, covering her slender throat almost to her chin; on her head there was a tiny bonnet of ribbon and ostrich plumes, perched at the jauntiest angle imaginable, above her dark tawny hair, done in a Cadogan, with dozens of little ringlets on each side, and a single great lock in the back, drawn down and looped up again, bag fashion, its ends done into an intricate series of curls pinned high on the back of her head.

She clung to Jean's arm and smiled at him. But he stood there, frowning morosely, hearing Mirabeau's great voice roaring from the salon:

"Utter nonsense! Half Europe has been trying to find out who this Citizen Riqueti they talk about is. Took my manservant aside, after the beggar had ventured to address me as 'Citizen,' and told him: Comte de Mirabeau to you, you bastard, and don't you ever dare forget it!"

A burst of laughter greeted this last remark. Lucienne turned to Jean.

"He's quite something, our Comte de Mirabeau, isn't he?" she said.

"Yes, quite," Jean agreed; but at this point the man-servant appeared, his face bright scarlet, leaving no doubt at all in their minds that he had been the subject of the discussion.

"M'sieur, Madame?" he murmured.

"M'sieur Marin, Mademoiselle Talbot," Jean told him.

Before the servant had gotten the announcement half out of his mouth, Mirabeau surged out into the anteroom, shaking his shaggy, lion-like mane.

"M. Marin!" he beamed, "and the fair enchantress, Mlle. Talbot! My house is too honored. Come, join the others. . . ."

Jean gazed at his host. How much more striking, he thought again, in this vigorous ugliness than good looks. Mirabeau's face, seamed, lined, bearing the marks of smallpox, and ancient dissipations, had yet an undeniable grandeur about it. The face of a man who has suffered, Jean mused, and largely because he has always broken the rules. . . . But the rules, I think, were not made for such a man. This has been always, this dilemma—that all beasts who run in packs must have laws set down for governing those who lack both force and wit; but when one has both, when one is truly a man, the rules, laws, call them what you will, become like a net or a snare, forever entrapping us. . . .

Mirabeau had already taken Lucienne's arm. Jean could not help noticing the perfect ease with which he conducted her into the salon. One might think him the hand-somest man alive, Jean smiled; because he acts with the perfect certainty that he is, and after a little time, one finds oneself believing it, too. . . .

"Gentlemen, Ladies," Mirabeau called; "Mlle. Talbot —whose face should decorate the emblems of France, for she is the fairest of the fair!"

A burst of bravos and Vives greeted his remark. Half a dozen gallants rose at once, and surrounded Lucienne. Jean frowned. What could you expect? he told himself; but a moment later his ironical sense of humor reasserted itself, and he smiled.

Chatter away, you perfumed monkeys! he thought gaily; old de Launay sitting above his powder kegs with his lighted torch was not in greater danger than any man who pursues too closely that beautiful witch. I call her mine, and perhaps she is—for the moment, until someone else catches her roving eye. She belongs to no one, because she is very complete, and very clear. No, *mes braves,* the danger is quite the reverse—that once burned by her, 'tis you who will learn the meaning of slavery. . . .

I like not being enslaved, and yet, I am. By her witchery —by mine own body's betrayal of my mind, my soul. I stand here, looking at her, and I am drunken; I take her and in the end, I know only exhaustion—never completion, fulfillment. Dear God, how this appetite grows upon excess of what it feeds upon! Will I never have done with wanting her? Yes, one day, perhaps—when she has destroyed me—entirely. . . .

"You shouldn't think such thoughts, young man," a woman's voice said.

Jean turned. As soon as he saw her face, he knew who she was. Madame le Jay, Mirabeau's current mistress— working with him under a pretext that fooled nobody, his business agent, he said, "my fair bookseller. . . ." Jean bowed over her hand, taking a long time about it, the better to give himself time to study this fascinating woman. It did him no good. In the end, she eluded his mind's grasp. For instance, how old was she? Thirty, he guessed, thirty-five. . . . But then she could equally have been twenty-eight—or even forty. And oddly enough, she wasn't beautiful, or even pretty. What she was—was, his mind groped for the word, striking. . . .

"Are you, perhaps, clairvoyant, Madame?" he said.

"Oh yes," Madame le Jay smiled; "but then all women are. Some more than others, of course; but the talent can be improved by practice. Besides, it really isn't much of a trick—you men are so pitifully transparent. . . ."

"And I?" Jean laughed; "am I also transparent?"

"Less than most men, I think. But in this one thing, more. It surprises me, I confess; it doesn't go with the rest of you. . . ."

"I," Jean said, "am not even clear, much less clairvoyant. Your meaning eludes me, Madame le Jay. . . ."

"Ah! So you know my name. There you have the advantage. . . ."

"Marin," Jean said; "Jean Paul Marin, late of Provence. . . ."

"The young orator. But, of course! Gabriel told me about your face—forgive me, M. Marin; I do babble, sometimes—like all women . . ."

"I am used to my face, Madame," Jean smiled. " 'Tis the rest of the world that it troubles. But we digress, don't we? You were reading my thoughts. . . ."

"Yes. And she isn't worth it!" Madame le Jay snapped. "That's what surprises me: you don't look like a fool."

"Yet, I'm afraid I am—about Lucienne, at least."

"Then don't be. From what I've heard of you, and what I see now, you don't have many weaknesses. And this one you cannot afford at the moment. France can't afford it. . . ."

"France?" Jean said in wonder.

"Yes. Gabriel has made a list of the men with whose help he could save France. De Lafayette heads the list. You are on it. And if you let that little minx destroy you . . ."

"I'm honored," Jean said.

"Don't be," Madame le Jay said; "there is no time now. There is only time for work, and a little time for tears, and all the time in the world for dying—if one can manage it usefully. Not heroically, M. Marin! The day has passed for your stupid male heroics! Now, one must manage the act of dying so that it benefits France—not one's vanity. . . ."

"Ah, Marin!" Mirabeau roared from the other side of the room; "I see you're being captured! Don't listen to her; she'll spoil you quite—she's much too intelligent; such women are dangerous!"

"All women are dangerous," Jean called back, "without notable exception!"

All the young gallants burst into laughter.

"You should know!" one of them said. "Come, join us, M. Marin, and describe the dangerous attributes of Mlle. Talbot. . . ."

Jean walked over to the group.

Lucienne turned toward him, and her eyes glowed with light and mockery and laughter.

"Am I dangerous, mon Jeannot?" she murmured. "You don't really believe such a thing, do you?"

"Believe it?" Jean smiled; "I know it. You are an enchantress. You are Circe, making swine of men; the Sirens, singing unheard melodies. And with the same result, my dear—men die, or go mad. . . ."

Lucienne puckered her forehead into an arch frown.

"You wrong me, I think," she said; "I have never made a pig of any man. Since when, my Jean, has that been necessary?"

"*Touché!*" the young blades chorused; and the room rocked with laughter. The manservant came, bearing goblets of wine. Everyone took his glass, and the party grew merrier.

Jean held his and sipped it, but did not really drink. It isn't, he thought, that one grows brighter as the evening wears on, but only that one thinks one does. 'Tis a delusion born of wine. Each man here thinks that his wit is brilliant, his quips terribly amusing; yet half the things they've laughed at in the last half-hour make scarcely any sense at all. But Mirabeau carries his wine well, I think; to look at him, you'd never guess he had touched a glass. . . .

At long last, now, some of the guests were beginning to leave. Jean glanced questioningly at Lucienne; but she was much too occupied with a trio of young elegants to notice his glance. But Mirabeau saw it, and shook his lion-like head.

"No, M. Marin," he whispered, "you and I have work, after the festivities are done. Amuse yourself for yet a while; afterwards we must think, and plan. . . ."

Jean nodded, and crossed the room toward Madame le Jay. But before he reached her, he stopped still, held there by pure surprise. For a tall, lean man had entered the room; a man, whose long, kindly face Jean had seen every day for weeks; who had done everything in his power to—

Jean rushed forward, his hand outstretched to greet M. Renoir Gerade, late Intendant of the King for Provence.

M. Gerade saw him coming and frowned warningly. Jean slowed his pace, his eyes a little puzzled.

Renoir Gerade put out his hand.

"*Bon soir, M'sieur,*" he said calmly, but rather too

loudly, Jean thought; then: "Whom have I the honor of addressing?"

Jean took a step backward, pure astonishment in his eyes. But M. Gerade kept his grip on Jean's hand tight, and even pulled him forward a little. Then, scarcely moving his lips at all, in the trained flat monotone of the expert conspirator which was ever so much more effective than a whisper, he said: "I haven't forgotten you, my learned footpad! But, by God's love, don't recognize me! You'll ruin everything. . . ."

Jean nodded.

"I am the Citizen Deputy Jean Paul Marin, from the district of Saint Jule. And you, Citizen?"

"Just plain Renoir Gerade," the tall man smiled. "Enchanted, Citizen Marin. . . . Ah, our good host!"

Mirabeau shook hands warmly with the newcomer. Then leaning forward, he whispered:

"The petit salon, Gerade, my friend. But not just now. Wander about a bit. Have wine. Then quietly disappear. You, Marin, can go there now. I will join you two as soon as I can. . . ."

Jean had to wait only a few minutes before Gerade appeared. This time his smile was open and frank, his brown eyes twinkling.

"Well, *mon vieux*," he said, "it has been a long time, eh?"

"Yes," Jean smiled; "too long. I have waited years for the chance to thank you, M. Gerade. . . ."

"Renoir, to you," Gerade said. "Sorry it didn't work. I heard the story. So the noble wench betrayed you, eh?"

"No!" Jean said. "You have not heard the truth, M. Gerade. . . ."

"And the truth is?" Renoir Gerade smiled.

Jean reddened to the roots of his hair.

"She—she merely delayed me a bit," he said; "nothing was further from her intent than . . ."

"Forget it, my old one!" Gerade laughed; "I made a pleasantry—and, I confess, indulged my curiosity a bit. 'Tis a failing of the old. . . ."

I, Jean thought suddenly, have never seen anyone who retained his youth like this one. He must be nearing sixty, and except for that white hair . . .

The door crashed open.

"Now to business!" the Comte de Mirabeau roared. "But first, a few questions, M. Marin. Gerade's ideas I know; yours, but imperfectly. In that madhouse of an assembly, who can gain a clear picture of what anybody thinks?"

"As you will, Citizen Riqueti," Jean mocked.

"Damn your eyes!" Mirabeau bellowed; "you must have your joke, eh, Marin?"

"Forgive me," Jean smiled; "what is it you want to know?"

"You want to retain the King—why?"

"Not the King," Jean corrected; "the office of kingship. I would gladly rid France of this bumbling incompetent who encumbers the throne at the moment, if I could do it without destroying the crown. Since we can't, we must suffer him."

"Good, but still—why the kingship?"

"Because of what I've seen of the people in action, I don't think they're ready for a Republic. I begin to wonder now, if people can ever be made ready to really govern themselves. Hence, a King—even a fairly strong King, but hedged about with such limitations as would eliminate any possibility of tyranny. A constitutional monarchy, M. Mirabeau. . . ."

"Sound, eh, Gerade?" Mirabeau mumbled.

"Quite," Renoir Gerade said.

"Wait," Jean said; "you'd better hear me out; because I disagree with you on one point that may make me useless to you. I am completely, unalterably opposed to a hereditary nobility."

"Why?" Mirabeau said.

"Because they corrupt men—as anything unearned always does. Titles and honors—fine; the King should have the power to give them for noteworthy services to the nation. But why should the idiotic son of a wise and just Comte be also a Comte, M. Mirabeau? If my son grows up intelligent and strong, it should be as easy for him to earn his patents of nobility, as it was for me; you catch my drift?"

"Very sound," Renoir Gerade said.

"Nonsense!" Mirabeau growled. "Any Riqueti whatsoever will be absolutely formidable. We always have been from the time the original Arrighettis—that was our true name—fled Florence with the Guelfs on their heels, we Riquetis have never produced a weakling! My grandfather, old Col d'Argent, silver stock, they called him, lived to beget my father after holding the bridge at Casono singlehanded, and taking twenty-seven wounds, any one of which would have killed an ordinary man. He married with his head held to his neck with a bar of silver, lived out a long life like that, got sons! I tell you two damned Jacobins—"

"A strange epithet," Jean smiled, "from one who frequents the Jacobin Club, and who has recently been suggested for the office of president of that organization. . . ."

"I," Mirabeau roared, "would frequent hell itself, and consort with the devil, if I thought by so doing, I could save France!"

"Well spoken," M. Gerade said quietly; "but the fact remains that the House of Bourbon, which produced many great and noble men, has lately produced mostly scoundrels and fools. We can suffer that of the Crown, because one house we can control; but a hereditary nobility, M. Mirabeau, has produced surprisingly few Riquetis—and all too many wastrels, coxcombs, and blackguards. I agree with M. Marin. . . ."

"All right, all right!" Mirabeau growled; "disagree if you will. The point is not important now. What is at issue at the moment is saving the Crown. I take it we are all agreed upon that?"

"We are," Jean Paul said.

"Good. You two will be my lieutenants in this enterprise. My plan is simple—and it is also the only feasible one: the King must leave Paris!"

"For where?" Jean said.

"Ah, but you are keen, Marin! That is precisely the point of points! The Queen, unfortunately, seems to want him to cross the border and depend upon foreign intervention—which is natural to her, since she is not French. But that would be—"

"Suicide," Renoir Gerade remarked drily.

"Exactly! They would never reach the border. And they would stand in the eyes of all Frenchmen as traitors to France. The Cordeliers want exactly that, to launch their filthy republic in which Danton, Desmoulins, Marat et al, would gain the power into their filthy hands. Part of the Jacobins want exactly the same thing—especially the faction that Robespierre dominates. I, on the other hand, being of no party, and committed to no one, can think clearly, you understand. The provinces are intensely loyal to the Crown. The King must flee to the Midi, you comprehend, and appeal publicly to all Frenchmen to flock to him to restore the monarchy, agreeing beforehand to stand by the limitations already imposed upon him. . . ."

"It would mean war," Jean sighed, "civil war, M. Mirabeau. . . ."

"And what have we now, *mon vieux?* Oh, la, la! A tea party? I prefer war which has at least organization and discipline, and out of which something might come, to this anarchy, in which *poules* and bullies and pimps in the gallery control the National Assembly of France at the behest of Philip of Orleans. Don't you?"

"And if her Majesty," Gerade said quietly, "refuses to permit the fat simpleton to stand by his word after he has given it—what then, M. le Comte?"

"Ah, therein lies the danger," Mirabeau groaned. "We want a strong throne; but what is to be done with a King who cannot even control his own wife? How in God's name can we ever expect him to truly rule his kingdom?"

I, Jean thought wryly, sympathize with him. I fear that the Queen is much like Lucienne. And neither of us, Louis of France, nor I, have sense enough to give up what we cannot manage. But he didn't say it. What he said was:

"Then we must appeal to the Queen."

"Excellent! But how? I finally succeeded in seeing both of them on the third of this month. The fat one had nothing to say; so I talked to her. At the time I thought I'd won her, surely; but every day I grow less certain. The point is I must have another interview with her—and her alone. But she now refuses to see me. She considers both me and that fool de Lafayette traitors, never dreaming that a man's loyalty should be to the nation, not his class. . . ."

He stopped and stared at Jean Paul.

"You!" he said. "You could do it! I'll wager you could get an interview with her. Look at the points in your favor: you have never been a noble, but you were brought up like one—nay, better. I'm told your manners are exquisite, when you want them to be. Gerade told me a wild story of your masquerading as an Italian prince once, and getting away with it. . . ."

"No," Jean Paul said flatly, "no more disguises, and other such folly. . . ."

"Hear me out. You'll go as you are, well but soberly dressed, and present yourself as a loyal subject who desires most of all to serve her Majesty. . . ."

"All of which is true enough," Jean said; "but what are you going to do about this face of mine? You want the Queen to have hysterics?"

"She's made of sterner stuff than that," Mirabeau said; "you can tell her you got the scar in one of the wars—Corsica perhaps! And—"

"No," Jean said; "I won't do it. In the first place, I won't lie. In the second—"

"But you must do it, Jeannot!" Lucienne's lovely voice sounded through the crack of the door; "for my sake. Then you can come back and—"

"Damn my eyes!" Mirabeau roared, "an eavesdropper! Come in, Mlle. Talbot—and let us decide whether we can permit you to leave this house alive. . . ."

Lucienne pushed the door half open and slipped in quickly, closing it behind her.

"How perfectly thrilling!" she breathed; "to be invited to a council of State. I'm sorry I eavesdropped; but I truly couldn't help it. You left me so long, Jeannot. Half those Muscadines in there were trying to take me home with them—and for quite improper purposes, you comprehend. And then you men were roaring so! Fine conspirators you are! Eavesdrop? Why, M'sieur le Comte, you could be heard fully ten yards away from the door. . . ."

"Enfer!" Mirabeau swore, then burst out laughing. "You have right, Mademoiselle, I am perhaps the most futile of conspirators. I would do many things, but nobody trusts me. They think me dishonest, because in my youth to live I did many things. But 'twas the world that rejected me—not I, the world. I have always been fully conscious of my powers. . . . But enough of this. You are an ally, I think, Mlle. Talbot. You must persuade him. This he must do—or perhaps France is lost. If someone, anyone could convince the Queen that she must not treat with

Austria, England, Russia, Spain—that she must depend upon the good people of France. . . ."

"How can she?" Lucienne observed, "when they spit at her, and call her Austrian—foreign woman, and things even worse?"

"True," Mirabeau groaned, "but Marie Antoinette is, *malheureusement,* King of France—we have no other! Fat Louis—what is he, *hein?* A good locksmith, I'm told —a fine hunter. But a King—pah! He obeys his Queen as though he were an infant and she his mother; he has no mind of his own, no force, no—*Sacre bleu!* They gave him an operation so that he could make children, heirs to the throne—and God alone knows, apart from *l'Autrichienne* herself and Count Fersen, whether or not fat Louis made them or not, or whether he had less royal assistance. I rave—forgive me. . . ."

He paused looking sternly at Jean Paul.

"You must convince her, *mon ami,* that if she does not cooperate with us in this matter—she will die at the hands of regicides. She, her husband, and her children— and France, God help her—will be lost. Come, M. Marin —what do you say?"

"He will, of course," Lucienne answered for him. "I will see to it. Of course it will take a bit of persuasion; but I've been told I am very good at changing people's minds. Why not leave him in my hands a day or two, M'sieur le Comte? I think I can guarantee results. . . ."

"Good!" Mirabeau laughed; "but only a day or two, my enchantress, time runs out—and grave issues are at stake. . . ."

"Why can't M. Gerade do these things?" Jean growled; "he's so much more presentable than I, and a seasoned diplomat to boot. . . ."

"I," Renoir Gerade smiled, "am but a rough soldier. I've heard you turn a phrase, Marin, to the last courtly hair. 'Tis that we need. No, you must allow yourself to be persuaded—which, if I may say so, should be a most pleasant occupation. . . ."

"Oh, I'll persuade him all right," Lucienne laughed. "Come, Jeannot—I am anxious to commence persuading you. . . ."

"*Bonne chance!*" Mirabeau roared; "how I envy you!"

"I think," Jean Paul said drily, when the fiacre had brought them once more to Lucienne's abode, "it is time I returned to my own flat. I have not slept there in five nights, and my friends will grow concerned. . . ."

Lucienne looked at him. Then she laughed, merrily.

"Tired of me?" she whispered, "or afraid of being persuaded—which?"

"Neither," Jean growled. "Afraid perhaps of losing my immortal soul!"

"Help me down," Lucienne said. "You need not fear that, I think—for strangely enough you are very like those maidens of the Mohammedan Paradise—you renew your virginity, your spiritual virginity, I mean, after each time with me. You really are pure at heart, Jeannot—and it maddens me. I wish I could really corrupt you; but then, with your talents, if I could, I should only lose you. So perhaps it's better like this. . . ."

Jean got down and lifted her to the earth.

She clung to him, whispering: "Come up with me, Jeannot—for a little time at least. You don't know what torture it was to chatter with those fools, and wait, and wait. . . . Come, my love, my old, old love—my first, and perhaps, my last. . . ."

"One does not count the ones in between, eh?" Jean mocked, "or the little extra ones at the same time on the side?"

"Of course not!" Lucienne laughed. "One should be permitted the condiments to give the main dish spice! Besides, all the little ways I have of diverting you so marvelously, how else could I have learned them, *mon pauvre?* You should be grateful for the others, for truly you have benefited thereby!"

"*Morbleu!*" Jean swore.

"Don't swear, my love. And think not of persuasions or my other loves, or of anything that will push us apart. For 'tis I who have need of you, now. Ah, Jeannot, I burn, I melt—'tis insupportable! You are kind; and to leave me now would be a fiendish cruelty. . . . Come with me, my great stallion, my fine, splendid wild beast— come with me, come!"

Lost, Jean groaned inside his heart, always and forever lost. . . .

But in the morning, before it was light, he rose and dressed very quietly in the darkness. He was tying his stock, when he became aware that she was watching him, her great eyes half luminous in the gloom.

"Where are you going?" she whispered.

"To the Salle à Manège," he said flatly, "to resign my post. I have had enough of politics—enough of all the things in life I cannot manage. I want quiet now, and peace. . . ."

"All the things you cannot manage," she mocked; "but that includes me, does it not? Are you leaving me, then?"

"Yes," Jean snapped, "yes, I am. . . ."

"You will come back," Lucienne laughed. "You will always come back to me. For no one else on earth can take my place—especially not that soft little brunette child I saw you with at the fête. . . . What's her name? Flower —ah, that's it, Fleurette, little flower. She seems very sweet and gentle. Such a one, mon Jeannot, is not for you. . . ."

"Why not?" Jean said.

"Oh, I don't know," Lucienne said airily; "perhaps because you would die of boredom the first week you spent with her. Or more likely because never in your life would you have done with comparing her with me—to her detriment. . . ."

Jean waited, staring at her.

"Run along to the Tuileries if you will. Resign your post—it matters not. What does matter, is this business of the Queen. That, too, you'll do—because you've never in your life failed to do your duty, *mon petit bourgeois!* And that is your duty. Besides, I want to sleep all day. Sleep is the most voluptuous thing in the world—especially after a night of love. . . ."

Jean did not answer her. There is never any answer I can give her, he thought bitterly; she is always too complete, and too clear for me. She knows me, I think, better than I know myself. . . .

"Adieu," he said, and started toward the door.

"Not adieu, Jeannot—au 'voir," she said lazily. "I'll see you tonight. . . ."

Jean pushed open the door and went down the stairs in a quiet kind of terror. I must escape her, he thought, I must! I'll go down to the Côte—pray God, they're wrong, and Nicole is alive. With her alone could I be free of this lovely witch. Fleurette, poor little thing, could scarcely prove enough of a diversion; still—who knows?

At the Riding School, it was the same as he remembered it, only worse. There was no order at all. At times, an hundred deputies were on their feet shouting at Mounier, the current President, trying each of them to be heard. In the galleries, gigantic Theroigne, the queen of the *poules* of Paris, was commanding her claque of fishwomen and prostitutes and their hangers-on, to drown out the speakers whose views proved unpopular to the mob, and to cheer to the echo any measure, however idiotic, that pleased them.

In such captivity did the National Assembly hold its daily meetings. No wonder then, Jean realized, that nothing of value could be accomplished. Of all the deputies, only he and Mirabeau refused to flatter the base passions of the *canaille*.

As he entered, the fishwives were shrieking:

"Who is that spouter? Silence the babbler—he doesn't know what he's gabbing about! Let Papa Mirabeau speak, we want to hear him! Bread at six sous the four pounds! Meat, six sous the pound! No more, you idiots! We aren't children to be played with! We are ready to strike! Do as you are told!"

Jean felt the fury beat about his ears. I fought, he raged, to free France of the tyranny of the Noblesse, but not, God help me, to turn her over to the worse tyranny of the *canaille!* Something must be done about this—and now!

He strode up to the rostrum, without signaling the President, or awaiting his turn, and stood up tall before them, his face dark mahogany with fury, the scar livid, and lifted his head to the gallery.

"Silence, you *claquedents!*" he roared at them, his voice thunderous, olympian. "Such behavior is obscene!"

Pure astonishment held them, all the *claquedents*, clatterteeth, all the whores, and their pimps, and army deserters, and the fishwives. For the first time in months, the silence was profound.

"We are here," Jean said slowly, evenly, "as representatives of the people of France—all the people! Not solely of one faction of them, and most certainly not of the scourings of the dungheaps of Paris!"

Mirabeau gazed at his young colleague, his big face slack with admiration.

"We will do what is best for France—after due consideration whether or not it really is best. It may please you—it may not! That makes nothing, and less than nothing, you comprehend. We threw off the yoke of slavery to the Noblesse, and ye scum and ordure of vileness presume now to dictate to us! Tyranny is tyranny whatever its source! And I, for one, do not propose to bow to it!"

"Nor I! Nor I!" half a hundred voices roared from the Right Center, and the Center. The Jacobins and the Cordeliers of the Left kept silent, watching him with furious eyes.

"I came here today," Jean went on, "to submit my resignation. . . ."

"Then resign, damn you!" Theroigne screamed. The others took up her cry: "Resign! Resign! Resign!"

Jean looked at them, the perpetual half smile on his face deepening into mockery, into an icy contempt that infuriated them all the more. Then staring straight at Theroigne, he started to laugh. The great boom of his laughter smashed their outcries into silence—its eerie quality drove them back upon themselves, recoiling physically, as from a rain of blows.

"Thou, Theroigne," he laughed, "would you become Queen of France? 'Tis a thing more difficult than reigning over the *poules* of Paris! As for the rest of you, keep still, and listen! I said I came to resign; but now I will not. I will not be cowed by cowards and whores, nor surrender my will, my judgment, my sense of what should be, what must be, done, to claques who applaud or hiss at the drift of Philip of Orleans' gold! I cannot be driven, *mes pauvres*—I can only do what I know to be right and just in the sight of God and mine own conscience—or die in the attempt. . . ."

He looked at them, his black eyes merciless.

"And before," he said quietly, "you count too hopefully upon that event—especially that son of stupidity who is now whispering my name for the list of the proscribed for the windy blood swillers of the Palais Royal—I propose to give you a demonstration of how expensive a proposition it would be to purchase my death. Ye odious scum can only pay for it with your own lives—many of them. *Alors, regardez!*"

He swung himself down from the rostrum in one great leap, and strode through the corridor to the foot of the gallery; then up the stairs four at a time, his black eyes filled with completely murderous glee, into their very midst. They broke before him, armed though they were, many of them with pikes, sabers, pistols, unable to stand before this, this absolutely incomprehensible thing—one man against them all, facing them not only without fear but with savage joy. And they opened before him until he came to the bully who had whispered his name, stopping there, throwing back his head and roaring with laughter.

"Augustin! As I live and breathe! What extraordinary good luck!"

"Don't touch me, Jean Marin!" Augustin whined, his face white with terror; "by God's love, don't—"

"The brotherhood of the broken faces, eh, Augustin?" Jean laughed; "on that, my friend, we are quits. But," and his voice sank to an icy whisper, more penetrating than a shout, "for my four years, lost from my life—for four years in hell, for that dear Augustin, we are not quits, are we, *hein?* No, Augustin—not quits—not ever quits—"

Then his two big hands shot out and caught the ex-coachman's shirtfront. He spread his legs apart, the muscles of his arms bunched, and Augustin, a big man, heavy as Jean himself, and almost as tall, came up from the floor, up until Jean shifted his left hand and held Augustin crosswise above his head, and turned, until he was standing close to the balustrade, and then once more he loosed his laughter.

"Citizen Deputies!" he laughed; "I give you a prize! Here, catch!"

Then with all his force, he hurled Augustin over the railing, while the deputies scurried for cover, the big man whirling downward turning over and over to crash into the chairs below, splintering three of them, and lying there stunned a moment while Jean Paul marched back through the thoroughly cowed claque until he reached the head of the stairs.

"As for the rest of you," he said, "I'd suggest you return

to your occupations of selling fish and other commodities of even less value, and leave us to our business, which is governing France. I suggest this very patiently—but as you have seen, my patience is remarkably short. . . ."

Then he turned and went quietly down the stairs. Three minutes later, the galleries of the Riding School were empty for the first time since the Assembly had met there. As for Augustin, hearing Jean's footsteps on the stairs, he rose in great haste, and fled the hall, dragging one leg behind him, making a quite remarkable speed for all that. . . .

Jean stood on the floor of the Assembly, and bowed to the President.

"I think, *M. le Président*," he said mockingly, "that we may resume our session, and rather more comfortably than before, *n'est-ce pas?*"

Then, quietly, he took his seat. There was a spattering of applause, but most of the Deputies turned eyes big with two things toward him. The two things, Jean saw, were: admiration—and terror. . . .

I have failed, he thought miserably; I have not freed them, and I have once more enslaved myself. I cannot leave Paris now, not even to search for my poor Nicole. And the longer I allow the business to remain dormant, the more difficult it will be to revive it. . . . All my theatrics of today went absolutely for nothing, except to endanger myself the more. . . .

He turned into the Rue de Sèvres, and took a seat in the Café de la Victoire, where the fast dwindling numbers of the moderates always met. He went there from pure habit, and because he was French to the very core. Like all Frenchmen, he thought mockingly, I'd sooner be found dead than in a café where uncongenial ideas are noised about. . . . Yet, this is folly, I think. I should frequent Café Charpentier with the Cordeliers, or even take a glass from time to time with the Jacobins. Then I would know what their next move will be—there's little to be gained by talking always with those who agree with you. . . . He turned in his chair.

"Garçon," he called, "a carafe of the best, if you please!"

But, this evening, even the solace of wine failed him. He

left the carafe half full, and engaged a fiacre to take him back to his lodgings in the Faubourg Saint-Antoine. But he did not go to his own flat.

I faced the mob, he thought; but this is more difficult. Why is it that a man can have so much of one kind of courage, and so little of another? Yet, this kind, this moral courage I seem to lack almost entirely. I'd rather die than face Pierre and Marianne, now. And Fleurette— dear God!

But it had to be done. He got down, paid the driver, and dismissed him. Then he mounted the stairs.

"Come in, Jean," Marianne said quietly.

He did not offer Pierre his hand. He had the feeling that Pierre would have refused to take it. Pierre sat there, looking at him, his eyes blue ice. Then he stood up.

"If," he said slowly, "I were not a practical man, and basically a peasant, I would show you my door, Jean Paul Marin. But I am both, and also a little of a coward, I think. The new business is already launched. We've flooded Paris with posters announcing it. And not one hour passes but a swarm of people descends upon us, demanding the clothes of which we have so far only samples to show them. Good. It will go well. What you do about your private life is your own business, of course. Under ordinary circumstances, I would laugh and forget it; I've been no saint myself, as you well know. . . ."

He paused, searching Jean's face.

"But now, knowing what you are doing, I find myself pitying you with all my heart, and hating you at the same time, for what you've done to Fleurette. . . ."

"She knows?" Jean breathed.

"She guesses. Jean, Jean, we—Marianne and I have come to love that poor, gentle child as though she were our own! She weeps her heart out every night over you; she eats less than nothing. . . . She is with us now, in that chamber; when I have finished with this, you must go to her, comfort her if you can. But this one thing I must say: From the fruits of this business, I will pay you every sou that you have advanced. Then you and I will be quits, our friendship at an end; for this is a kind of folly and cruelty I find insupportable. *Alors,* I have had my say. Perhaps I wrong you—perhaps there is some explanation. . . ."

Jean heard the pleading tone creep into Pierre's voice. His old friend, he knew, was searching for any basis upon which he could equate his sense of justice, his belief in right and wrong, with a friendship which was inexpressibly dear to him.

"No," Jean said flatly, "there is no explanation. May I see Fleurette now?"

Pierre stared at him.

"Very well," he said, "go ahead. . . ." And suddenly his voice was very tired, and very old.

Fleurette was lying face down on the little bed. But she turned at his step, and he saw the tear streaks on her face, trailing downward from her marvelous, sightless eyes.

"Jean?" she whispered.

"Yes, Fleurette," Jean said heavily; then: "Please don't weep over me. I am not worth it."

"It is because you are worth it that I weep," she said. "But don't trouble yourself, my Jean—I—I'll be all right. . . ."

"I'm a beast!" Jean said, his voice bitter with self-contempt. "Look, Fleurette, I'll never leave—"

But she came up from the bed and laid her fingers across his mouth.

"Don't say that, my love!" she whispered. "Go to her! Go, and have your fill of that woman, whose voice, even —is evil! Then come back to me. You will, I know; because you are good. One day you will sicken of her to the core of your being, one day the sight of her face will make you retch—then you will come back. I shall be waiting, my Jean. But now, I cannot permit you to stay against your will. I am a woman, Jean—entirely a woman, though you have never quite believed it. I am as capable of jealousy as any other. And when you are finally mine, you must be all mine. I would not share you with God or the Devil!"

"Fleurette!" Jean began.

"Hear me out! She has bewitched you, for in this one thing only are you weak. I know she must be lovely; and you, being a passionate man, have mistaken her corrupt passion of the body for something that is greater than it. One day, I shall show you what passion really is—what love is; for I have it all, guarded in my heart, in all my body, entirely for you. . . . I think I could burn you to a cinder; I know I could! Whatever she is, whatever she has will pale into insignificance beside what boils within my heart and runs scaldingly through all my veins each time you touch me. . . ."

She stood there, staring at him with her sightless eyes, the great tears penciling her cheeks.

"You have never kissed me," she whispered. "I want you to do that now. Yes, come here and kiss me—then go!"

Jean bent down gently, and took her in his arms. But her small hands swept up suddenly, convulsively, and locked themselves behind his neck, and going up on tiptoe, she found his mouth, and clung to it endlessly, cherishing it in terror, and anguish, and tenderness, and finally in pure, undisguised passion that was like the flame at the core of life itself, so wholeheartedly given, so unashamed, so complete that nothing he had ever experienced in all his life, not even Nicole's kiss had been at all like this, until he was forced at last to free himself and reel back away from her.

"My God!" he whispered.

"Go, Jean," she said softly; then: "Oh, damn you—go!"

He turned very quietly and went down the stairs.

There was a fiacre waiting before his door. Lucienne sat in it, waiting.

"Get in," she said; "I took the liberty of breaking the lock and packing your things. They're already in the carriage. . . ."

"You witch!" Jean swore.

"Oh, don't be tiresome!" Lucienne laughed; "up with you!" Jean Paul hesitated a long, long moment. Then he put up his hands and climbed up beside her. The driver cracked his whip, and the horses moved off, down the dim, lantern-lit street. The sound of the hoofs made a curious rhythm against the stones.

"Lost," they whispered against the stones, "lost, lost, lost. . . ."

And Jean Paul Marin, hearing them, echoed the sound in his heart.

11

"You're going to see her, really going to see her—at last?" Lucienne breathed.

"Yes," Jean smiled.

"Tonight? Oh, Jean! I think that's the most perfectly thrilling thing in the world!"

"Yes," Jean said slowly, "I'm going to see her Majesty tonight. And I'll admit quite freely, that I'm looking forward to the meeting with pleasure. . . ."

"I'm not so sure I like that remark," Lucienne said.

"Why?" Jean said.

"Because I'm a jealous woman, darling!" Lucienne laughed. "I hate every moment of your life that's spent away from me. Promise me you won't spend too much time with her, Jeannot—I've seen her many times, and she's lovely. Promise me, Jeannot!"

"Perhaps," Jean smiled. He looked at the calendar. February twenty-sixth, 1791. In a few more months it would be a year since he and Lucienne had been together again.

"Sometimes," he said drily, "I almost believe you, when you say things like that. . . ."

Lucienne danced over to him and kissed him, hard.

"I do mean it," she whispered. "I never thought I would fall in love again—truly in love. But then I didn't, really. I know now that I had never stopped loving you. Have I ever looked sidewise at another man in all this time?"

"Frequently," Jean mocked.

"Only looked, though. I don't want anyone else. Every other man bores me quite to tears. It's wonderful being with you, Jeannot. Everything about it is wonderful— having our coffee in bed together in the morning—the

223

long, long talks about all your grave problems of state—
Oh, it all makes me feel like a queen, myself!"

"You are," Jean said.

"Thank you darling—for that. Now run along like a
good boy to your dreadful Assembly. I'm going to lie in
bed another hour, then I must get up for rehearsals. Are
you coming to the performance tonight? Oh, but you
can't, can you? That's all right; this is one time I won't
mind. . . ."

Jean kissed her and went down the stairs. A servant
brought his horse. He rode off toward the Assembly, re-
flecting all the time on how groundless his fears about
Lucienne had proved. She had been faithful, kind, generous, amusing, apparently deeply interested in his work
from the intelligent questions she asked about it—and surprisingly frugal.

I was wrong on all counts, he mused; I thought she'd
make me miserable, and instead . . .

"*Bonjour*, Jean," Pierre du Pain said quietly.

"Ah, Pierre!" Jean said; "I'm glad to see you. Name of
a name, how prosperous you look! Come, ride with me
toward the Tuileries, and tell me about things. . . . Surely
you don't still bear a grudge against me. . . ."

"No," Pierre smiled sadly; "a man must do what he
must, I suppose. Yes, things go well with us. If the business
keeps up I shall become one of the richest men in Paris.
Marianne has an hundred dresses now, and has gone on a
regime in order to become fashionably slim. . . ."

"And Fleurette?" Jean murmured.

Pierre hesitated.

"She seems content," he said slowly; "she has become a
marvel with figures. And she is the heart and soul of the
business; all the workers, men and women alike adore
her. . . ."

"Is she happy?" Jean said.

"*Morbleu!*" Pierre roared; "what is it to you, you great
fool! Yes, yes, she is happy! So happy that she lives in a
dream—an idiotic dream that you will one day come back
to her! She believes you will, and lives in hope, and expec-
tancy for that day. But by heavens if that day ever comes,
and you should come back, I hope she has sense enough
to spit in your ugly face!"

"Sorry, Pierre," Jean said gently, "I didn't mean to anger you. . . ."

"No," Pierre said, shaking his head, " 'tis I who am sorry. I guess I can only truly become enraged with those I am fond of. And when I see the two people I love best on earth caught up in this ugly, hopeless mess . . ."

"The two people?" Jean said.

"Fleurette—and you, my old one. I would rather see you in prison again than in the hands of Lucienne Talbot. Ah—don't tell me! She is very lovely; she dances beautifully, better I'll wager, horizontally than vertically; and I dread seeing what you'll be like when she has finished with you! And when I reflect that you have the love of a veritable angel, I could weep. . . . Forgive me, Jean, but I was never good-at holding my tongue."

"It's all right," Jean said, "only our truest friends tell us the truth. May I come and see you some time?"

"No," Pierre said; "I'll meet you at one of the cafés, instead. Marianne and I are both agreed that it would be bad to upset Fleurette now that she has gained some measure of peace. . . ."

"Very well," Jean said; "I'm often at the Café de la Victoire. . . ."

"Good!" Pierre growled; "I'll meet you there. À bientôt, Jean."

"À bientôt, Pierre," Jean said, and gripped his outstretched hand. Then he turned his horse in the direction of the Tuileries, while Pierre rode back toward Saint-Antoine. And it came to Jean Paul then that unaccountably, by these few simple words, his whole day had been ruined.

He dressed with unusual care that night, conscious that the new clothes he had bought for his meeting with the Queen were very fine. They were almost à la mode muscadine, but Jean was too conservative by nature to descend to that ridiculous level of foppery. The new elegants of Paris were called muscadins because of their habit of carrying handkerchiefs perfumed with that scent; and everything about their dress was carried to the same extremes.

Yet, Jean mused, as he dressed himself, much of their innovations are really smart. The cut's good; 'tis in the colors that they go awry. . . .

His own frockcoat avoided this danger: it was fawn-colored, instead of crimson or pale blue, as a true *muscadin* would have had it. Though it was cut in the claw-hammer style they had introduced, it did not descend halfway below the knee the way the elegants liked theirs, but was sensibly knee-length in the back. The velvet collar was dark brown, above the three little redingotes or short capes. Jean had seen purple, green, or scarlet collars shrieking their contrasts to other violent colors in the dress of the more fashionable of his contemporaries. . . .

But he had to admit that he had gone a little to the extreme in the method of fastening the coat. The great, brown cloth buttons did not pass through buttonholes worked directly in the other side of the coat, but instead through straps of chamois sewed alternately to each side, so that the top buttoned on the left, the middle on the right, and so on. His skin-tight breeches were pale gray, tied below the knee with dark brown ribbons; and his dark tan jockey boots, turned down so their fawn colored inside showed, had been imported from England at the cost of a young fortune.

He gazed apprehensively at his scarred face in the mirror; but below his hair, carefully clubbed into a Cadogan, and powdered with a soft, mouse-gray powder, the face was not at all too bad. Lace spilled out over his hands at the wrist, and the stock wound around his throat was snowy. He had contented himself with only one watch, and absolutely no scent at all. . . .

Sighing, he picked up his brown felt hat, of the very newest mode, newer even than the bicorne, which had replaced the tricornered aristocratic hat at the beginning of the revolution. It had a round brim, entirely flat, and a tall, almost conical crown, which was cut off flat at the top. Jean spent some minutes adjusting the hat to the proper angle halfway between jauntiness and too stiff conservatism; but the results at the end pleased him.

He regretted that Lucienne was dancing, and was not home to see him. He had, he felt, achieved the minor miracle of being every inch the man of fashion without descending one iota into foppery. He picked up his gloves, and a short swagger stick, which, cunningly weighted with lead, was the only weapon he dared take with him.

He mounted and rode out of Paris, going toward the

house of Mirabeau's friend Clavière. He, Renoir Gerade, and Mirabeau had often met in that house to discuss their so far quite futile plans; but he had no intention of ever reaching that house.

There was need for haste now. Strange how the hand of God Himself seemed so often to intervene in the affairs of men! Mirabeau, the lion—scarce two and forty years—was visibly fading before their eyes. Since Christmas time he had been sick, but knowing his giant strength none of his friends had been much troubled by it. But the earth-shaker had not gotten better.

He's dying, Jean Paul thought, and the truth of the idea startled him. Mirabeau—dying! Impossible—but true. He spoke seldom now, and in a voice that was but a hollow echo of his former lion's roar. He dragged himself to the Salle à Manège; once, a week ago, he would have fallen, had not eager hands supported him. . . .

He seems a little better now, Jean mused; but I must prevail upon the Queen to see him. Everything depends upon that. Only Mirabeau can persuade her. . . .

She will not ask the King to cross the border, they say now. But she is for Metz; dear God! can't she see that in the eyes of Cordelier and Jacobin that is merely the same thing. A few short leagues from the army of Bouille in Austria—she might as well have Louis attempt the whole thing and cross over. What difference to Republicans if she is in Austria, or if she is two hours' march away from the aid of counter-revolutionary armies? The Midi, oh, my Queen—then no one can hold you disloyal to France!

He rode searching for the crossroad. It wouldn't be easy to find in the darkness. But neither a light nor an escort would have been feasible. They could ill afford to attract attention now.

I wonder, he thought, how Renoir fares in Austria? A man of parts, that Renoir! Strange that not even Mirabeau knew he spoke German like a native, grace of fifteen years spent in Alsace with his uncle's family, who were of that stiffnecked race. Useful man, Renoir Gerade—of enormous tact, and discretion. He has, I think, absolutely no need to confide in anyone, being, himself, entirely self-sufficient. I envy him that. I have lived so much in solitude that I have grown to have a horror of it; I need

human society—love; Renoir has little need of anyone—
I doubt that he confides in God in solitary prayer!

His hands tightened on the reins. It seemed to him
that the beat of hoofs on the road had doubled. He drew
his mount to a stop. Yes, there it was again. Another
rider coming toward him in the darkness, where there
should have been no other rider, and he almost entirely
unarmed, lacking for the first time in years, the comforting
weight of pistols in his pockets.

He gripped his weighted swagger stick hard. If the other
came close enough . . .

The other rider came on, broke around a curve ahead
at a brisk canter. In the moonlight, Jean could see the
white oval of his face. The other drew up his horse scant
yards from Jean Paul.

"M'sieur Marin?" he murmured.

"Yes," Jean growled.

"I am the Duc d'Aremberg," the man said without
offering him his hand; "I am here to conduct you to the
Queen. . . ."

Jean nodded. "Lead on," he said.

The young noble whirled his horse smartly about. Jean
clapped his spurs to his own mount and drew abreast. He
was aware that his silent companion was studying his
face in the moonlight, and clearly as upon a printed page
he could read the Duc's thoughts:

Dear God, to what pass has the world come when a
villainous blackguard with a face like this can have an
audience with the Queen!

Jean smiled. The thought amused him.

"Do you," he asked, "know aught of the Comte de
Gravereau? Is he still in Austria?"

The Duc d'Aremberg regarded him with grave eyes.

"Why?" he said.

"He," Jean said, "is my brother-in-law. Or at least he
was—up to my sister's tragic death. . . ."

"You jest," d'Aremberg said shortly.

"No," Jean smiled; "we Marins have a strange affinity
for the Noblesse. Simone de Beauvieux is my sister-in-
law."

He wasn't boasting, and d'Aremberg knew it. He was
simply putting the young noble's thoughts in order. The
danger existed that the young man might lead him astray,

prevent, in fact, his seeing the Queen. That had to be avoided. He had at all costs to remove the influence of his monstrous face. . . .

"Ah!" d'Aremberg said, and his tone was warmer, "those Marins! Sound people, your family; I understand you have suffered quite as much as we nobles. You lost your château, too, didn't you?"

"Yes," Jean said grimly, "and my sister lost her life at the hands of the peasantry of Provence. . . ."

"Murderous beasts!" d'Aremberg spat. "My sympathies, M. Marin!"

"Thank you," Jean said. "But you haven't answered my question."

"Yes," d'Aremberg replied, "Gervais is in Austria, where he has been performing notable services on behalf of their Majesties. Brave man, de Gravereau—and clever. 'Tis said he keeps the Emperor precisely informed of all events inside France. How he does it, no one knows; but my cousins there write that he often anticipates what action the National Assembly is going to take. . . ."

"Very clever," Jean said.

"Indeed it is. I realize now your reason for identifying yourself more precisely. You'll forgive my saying so, M. Marin, but as man to man, your face was scarcely calculated to inspire confidence. How came you by so formidable a wound?"

"An accident," Jean said smoothly. "I was lucky it was no worse. An inch or two in either direction, and I would have lost my sight. However, it has its advantages. On more than one occasion I have been able to outface the mob by merely frowning at them. If I could only manage to act as villainously as I look, I might one day become master of France!"

"You have a sense of humor," d'Aremberg laughed. "Had such a thing happened to me, I fear I should have grown quite morose. . . ."

"No point in that," Jean said.

He had, he found, as the guard opened the gate to the back entrance to Saint Cloud, gained his objective. D'Aremberg was at ease now; he would, he was certain, see the Queen.

But that event happened so quickly as to take him entirely by surprise. Two minutes after they had dismounted, d'Aremberg led him into her presence. She was seated on a bench atop a knoll. She was wrapped in furs against the cold, but she took her hand quickly from her enormous muff, and offered it to him.

Jean bowed deeply, and kissed it, confusion stopping his voice. He was aware first of all, that here was a rarely beautiful woman, still young, scarcely in her middle thirties; and secondly, that she was as regal as she was lovely.

He saw that her hair was not powdered, but naturally almost white, grown so from care, from sorrow; her first-born dead at a tender age, the same people who knelt before her in the streets, who raised statues of snow and ice in her honor because of her gifts to them of fuel and food during the winter of '88, spitting at her now in the streets, cursing her, calling her *l'Autrichienne!*, the Austrian, that foreign woman, holding her the cause of all the evils that had beset France.

But he saw, too, that all her misfortunes had stiffened her resolution. Her face was perfectly calm; her blue eyes, after one quick dilation at the sight of his scarred face, became instantly serene again, and remained so.

Whatever her faults, Jean thought quickly, this one is truly a Queen!

"Your most obedient servant, Madame," he murmured.

"Are you?" Marie Antoinette said crisply; "I doubt that, M. Marin. My most obedient servants don't sit in so-called National Assemblies and plot against the good of France!"

Jean took a half step backward; but the Duc d'Aremberg came instantly to his aid.

"You must confound M. Marin with some of the others, your Majesty," he said smoothly. "He is related by marriage to two of the noblest houses: de Gravereau, and de Beauvieux. Additionally, he has suffered tragic losses at the hands of the people, equal, in fact to those of any noble. His château near Marseille was burned; and his own sister perished. . . ."

The Queen's gaze softened.

"My condolences, M. Marin," she said. "Yet I find it most strange that you can sit among those directly responsible for your sister's murder. Perhaps you can explain this thing to me. . . ."

Jean smiled; he had recovered his poise now.

"Your Majesty, with your permission, I can only reply to that with another question. Is not the Royal Carriage equipped with brakes?"

"Yes—but I don't follow you, M. Marin. What have brakes and carriages to do with this?"

"I, your Majesty, and men like me—are the brakes of the nation. Without us, France would run pellmell downhill into anarchy. And we can only function within the Assembly. That is why I am here: to beg your Majesty to desist from your very natural and understandable resentment and make use of us!"

"I see," the Queen murmured; "a pretty simile, eh, d'Aremberg?"

"Indeed it is, my Queen!" the Duc smiled.

Jean pressed his advantage.

"Your Majesty spoke of our plotting against the good of France. It is my mission, and my most earnest desire to convince you that the contrary is our intent. At the risk of offending his grace, the Duc, I must point out to you, Madame, that it was the Noblesse who were the worst enemies of the Crown. Hear me out, my Queen! Not intentionally, not with malice—but from folly, and extravagance, they brought France to this pass. The people were not led into revolt, your Majesty—they were driven! At the moment, they are like horses who have broken their bridles, racing like mad toward anarchy, toward total destruction of all that we—my friends and I, as well as you and the Noblesse, my Queen, hold dear. . . ."

"You are eloquent," Marie Antoinette said.

"Thank you, your Majesty," Jean smiled. "I want your Majesty to see that you must make use of us. Since the fall of the Bastille, the nobles have increasingly fled France; lately even men of good will, and conservative temper have been so badgered, so threatened, that there is no longer in the National Assembly any Right—any good, honest conservatives; a small sprinkling of moderates alone hold out against the raging herd. . . .

"The Crown must have friends in the Assembly; I cannot emphasize that too strongly. And, unfortunately, the friends your Majesty does have, she has been constrained to reject. . . ."

"You mean, of course," the Queen said stiffly, "de Lafayette, and Mirabeau."

"Yes. You consider them both traitors because they turned against their class. But, my Queen, an hundred thousand nobles are not France! There is a higher loyalty —the loyalty to the nation—to your Majesty's twenty-four million subjects. Your Majesty must know that there is a movement afoot to dispense with the Crown entirely and form a republic; Mirabeau, whom you scorn, my Queen, has checked that movement almost singlehanded, with a little help from a few moderates like myself. Consider, your Majesty, the force of character of a man who, openly rejected by the Crown he wants to aid, yet continues to aid that Crown, despite rejection and scorn. . . ."

"You want me to see the Comte de Mirabeau, don't you?" the Queen said.

"Yes, your Majesty," Jean murmured; "that's why I'm here. . . ."

The Queen frowned thoughtfully. Then, very slowly, she smiled.

"Very well, M. Marin," she said gently, "tell the old ogre I'll see him. . . ."

She stood up, and Jean knew the interview was at an end. He bowed once more and kissed her hand, then backed away toward the gate.

"You may turn around and walk normally," the Queen said; "it is too dark for that sort of courtesy. But I thank you for it, M. Marin—so few people today bother to observe even the slightest forms of court etiquette. I have lost something, I think, from having had so few contacts with my better bourgeois families. Your manners and bearing, M. Marin, would do credit to a Duc. Right, d'Aremberg?"

"You are entirely correct, my Queen," the Duc said.

"My thanks for your patience, your Majesty; and to you, my lord, for your gracious aid. Adieu, then—your servitor, Madame!"

It came to Jean Paul as he rode away from Saint Cloud, that he had not observed the slightest detail of her dress, in order to satisfy Lucienne's hungry curiosity.

Oh, well, he thought, I can tell her enough. . . .

It was finished, finally, and the destiny of the whole

French nation was changed—was lost, by the intervention of Destiny into the affairs of men. True to her promise, the Queen saw Mirabeau, though the meeting was much delayed by a recurrence of the old lion's illness.

"She was," Mirabeau told Jean in a fading rumble, "charmed by me—now, now we'll accomplish it! We can save France. . . ."

But on April 4th, 1791, Honoré Gabriel Riqueti, Comte de Mirabeau, Deputy to the National Assembly, confounded all the world, and all the possible plans of royalty by the simple act of dying.

Jean was with him at the end, and wept; for Mirabeau's death was as thunderous, as olympian as his life. The noble lion of the Third Estate despaired utterly; and only he could save the Crown. He knew it, Jean Paul Marin knew it; all the world knew it. Handsome, vain, Generalissimo de Lafayette was not the man for the work. Brave enough, generous enough—but too wanting in depth, in true intelligence. This was Mirabeau's judgment, and Jean Paul could only agree with him.

Yet in his lucid intervals, Mirabeau charged his little group to carry on; despairing himself, he would not let them despair. A letter was dispatched to Austria, commanding Renoir Gerade to return. But, because of the circuitous route by which it had to be sent, and the precautions taken to prevent its falling into the wrong hands, Jean knew it would be some months before his old friend could return to France.

In those months, life went on as before: one tumult after another. It is strange, Jean Paul reflected, that the ennui born of constant excitements becomes as boring as any other. We yawn at bloodshed now; shots and screams at midnight no longer awaken us. . . .

"Nothing could awaken you, Jeannot," Lucienne laughed when he told her this, "not even I. What has happened to you, my poor darling? Have you suddenly grown old?"

"No," Jean smiled; "just tired with the kind of fatigue I could never support. 'Tis of the heart, the spirit. When Mirabeau died I lost hope, and this feeling descended upon me. I know my body is not tired, but my head and the thoughts inside it weigh tons. . . ."

"You—you're afraid about the Queen, aren't you?" Lucienne said.

"Yes. She doesn't see any of us now—no one in our group. We fear that she's listening to other counselors, who will work her ill. There's something afoot, too—we know that. Comings and goings—mysterious men admitted to the Royal chambers only by tickets. . . . A new yellow coach being tested in the streets. . . . Name of God! Do they mean finally to flee? They should have gone months ago, before Mirabeau died. And this magnificent yellow coach—surely they cannot be that stupid!"

"Oh, I think not!" Lucienne said airily. "Don't you see, Jeannot, that is merely to make a diversion? A magnificent yellow coach, with plumes and glass, and all the *canaille* riding like mad after it in wild pursuit in the wrong direction, while some shabby vehicle, old and black creaks away to safety unpursued—you see?"

Jean stared at her. "Damn my eyes, Lucienne!" he roared; "I believe you're right!"

"Of course I'm right, darling," she laughed; "now pass me the letter opener. I must read my mail. . . ."

"You've been getting many letters lately," Jean said sourly. "From what city do they come?"

"Why, Jeannot! How suspicious you have become. You never used to ask me things like that. . . ."

"From where do those letters come?" Jean said with grim quietness.

"If you must know, they're from Austria. But they are not from Gervais, my jealous one! Look—this is a feminine hand, you see?"

"I see," Jean said; "but how is it that you have letters from Austria at all. . . ?"

"Silly, they're from la Marquise de Forêtverte. She's a friend of mine. Many of the great ladies had become quite democratic before the Revolution. Poor Sophie envied and adored me. I do believe she would have changed places with me in an instant. Now lately, she has been dying for news of Paris, and writes me constantly; I keep her posted as best as I can—fashions, you comprehend, and other such female follies: who has a new lover, whether or not fashionable life can be renewed under such trying circumstances. . . ."

"But not a word about Gervais la Moyte, eh?" Jean said drily.

"Of course not! Sometimes you make me awfully tired,

Jeannot! Austria is a big country. She has never even seen him. . . ."

"Forgive me," Jean said gently; "jealousy is a pitiful emotion. Anyway I must go back to that miserable hall of sound and fury where nothing is ever accomplished. . . ."

But Lucienne looked up suddenly from the letter, her face drained of color. "Jean," she whispered, "when does Renoir Gerade return?"

At that moment, Jean was not looking at her; but something in her voice caused him to raise his eyes. He was too late, she already had had time to recover. She was very good at things like that.

"I don't know," Jean said; "it's impossible to communicate with him directly. But we expect him any day now. Why do you ask that?"

"Sophie—mentions him in her letter—that's all. It just —just seemed a little strange that she should. . . ."

"Strange," Jean said; "it's worse than that—rather a bad slip on Renoir's part to let himself become identified. She mentioned him by name?"

"Yes. She said that the police were becoming suspicious of him. You—you want to read her letter?"

"No," Jean said; "it would only bore me . . ." But this time he did not miss the quick relief that flared in her eyes.

Something's afoot here, he thought grimly; I'll wager she's writing la Moyte through this woman. No time to go into it now, though. Tonight will serve. . . .

But that night was June twentieth, 1791, and what it served for was quite other than he had expected.

He was sitting in his place in the Assembly when an usher brought him the note. It was already late, but the windy sessions of the National Assembly often dragged on for as long as twelve to eighteen hours at a stretch. He unfolded the note and read: "Waiting for you outside. Highest importance that I see you at once." It was signed, "R. Gerade."

Jean picked up his hat and his cane and went out at once.

Renoir Gerade had not even dismounted. He swayed there in the saddle, drunken with fatigue, even his face dust-covered, so that his teeth flashed brilliantly in contrast to his smile.

"You've a horse?" he croaked.

"Yes, but not here," Jean said; "I left him at home, and came by fiacre. However, it will only take a short time, to . . ."

"Then up behind me, man! For this night we must ride like hell!"

Jean stared at him.

"You're in no state to ride," he declared. "Tell me what's to be done, and I'll do it."

"No—both of us, and as many others as we can muster. We have to cover all the roads leading out of Paris like a fan." He leaned forward, his mouth almost brushing Jean's ear.

"The Royal family," he whispered, "has this night fled Paris!"

"My God!" Jean got out. "But, Renoir, isn't that precisely what we wanted them to do?"

"Not now—not in this fashion. Our royal idiots are for Metz, despite all our counseling! The émigrés have prevailed. They gained the ear of the Queen. From the day I learned of Mirabeau's death, I knew we hadn't a chance; I was playing for time; but they forestalled me. . . ."

Jean stepped out into the street and signaled a passing fiacre.

"Get in," he said; "we can tie your mount behind. Poor animal—completely blown. I have another to lend you and a draught of wine besides. And we can talk better as we ride. You said the émigrés got the better of you?"

"Not all of them," Gerade said grimly; "just one: your old friend Gervais la Moyte."

"De Gravereau!" Jean whispered; "but Name of God, Renoir—how?"

"He had some source of information here in Paris, I know not who, or how; but damn my infernal eyes, Jean —he knew what the Assembly was going to do before I did, and what was worse, he knew the plans of our group! That is what confounds me; a man might have a dozen ways of learning the political trends—the sessions are public, you know; but how in the name of everything unholy, did he know our plans?"

Jean sat very still, looking straight ahead. He did not move or speak. He simply sat there in a fiacre, riding through one of the splendid boulevards of Paris, and died inside his own heart of slow and fiendish torture.

Her lips against mine whispering nameless, terrible, glorious things. Her hands, her hands, the whole snowcovered, flamecored length of her, against me moving slow, softmoving sweetmoving gentle-tender, against me swiftmoving, wildmoving, terrible-wild, anguished exquisite, lava filled, scalding volcanic, surrounding me enveloping me destroying me into death into hell into agony of too great pleasure, into insupportable ecstasy, drawing the life from me the sense, the very soul, swift jetting, leaving me drunken, numb, between sleep and waking for what?

For those questions, so lightly, so airily asked; with what skillful feminine pretense at misunderstanding, drawing it all out of me, so easily, so damnably easily, laughing inside her insatiate body at this great and clumsy fool twice betrayed, once before in the flesh, and now worse, a million times worse, in the spirit. . . .

If she is there, he thought with terrible calm, I shall kill her. If I am hanged for it, it shall be no more than I deserve; for I am as guilty as she, nay more; for by lust and stupidity, by surrendering to my weakness, to the base animal within, I, Jean Paul Marin, have betrayed France!

"Why are you so still?" Renoir Gerade asked.

"I," Jean said, "am lost in thought. But don't worry, I shall arrange things. . . ."

She was not there. As soon as he entered the apartment, he saw that. She was gone—not merely to the Opéra, but fled, out of Paris by now—in two more days out of France. Several of her simpler frocks were gone from the closet. The armoire had been ravished: stockings, petticoats, had all vanished. Her valises, and his own. . . .

Then he saw the note on the mantel. He took it up and pocketed it without opening it. Then, in a voice flat, dead level, calm, he commanded the servant to heat water for Renoir Gerade, bring razors, and prepare a simple meal.

"There is no time," Renoir declared; "they—"

"Oh yes," Jean said, "there is time. They will not travel fast."

"You seem sure," Gerade sighed. "Very well, then I shall wash. . . ."

He went into the bathroom, and after he had gone, Jean opened the note.

"Mon Jeannot," it read, "whom I shall never cease to love, and of whom now I cannot even beg forgiveness, believe this: I love you. I betrayed you again, yes; but for reasons that match your own: I love France—the old France, the great France, that you, whom I love, have helped destroy. I hated what I was doing, but it had to be done. For I was fighting for something grander than us, something more important than any man's happiness, or even his life. Had I been ordered to, I would have killed you, or even myself. You, misguided as you are, are a true patriot, and will understand this, I think. . . .

"I weep as I write this, my tears blind me; they come from my heart, and seem almost of blood. Believe, as long as you live, this one thing: when I came to you, when I held you in my arms, took you inside my body, that was neither lies nor betrayals but me, myself, loving you, wanting you as I shall go on wanting you until I am dead and freed of all desire. Not even what I did afterwards—the questioning, the seeking for information, the hideous betrayal of your calm, manly trust in me, could truly profane that.

"You will never see me again, and knowing as I know that you can never, never forgive me this, I remain, your disconsolate,   Lucienne."

Jean stood there staring at the page. Then very slowly, he moved over to a candle, and held the edge of it to the flame. He watched it curl, turn brown, the yellow tongues of flame devouring it, and his eyes were steady, and very grave. He held it there in his hand until the flames licked around his fingertips, insensible to the pain; then at long last, he released it, watching it turn end over end in a slow spiral of smokewisp and tiny fire, until it drifted against the floor and crumbled into ash.

Half an hour later, he was in the saddle, riding toward the Flemish border, toward Brussels. In doing this, he followed Lucienne's idea that the great yellow coach was but a blind. Renoir, who had an unshakable faith in the invincible stupidity of all men, even Kings, did not believe this. He, taking another road, galloped straight for Va-rennes in the direction of Metz. So it was that the inde-fatigable ex-Intendant of Provence arrived in time to see the capture of the King and Queen. For Renoir Gerade was right; fat Louis and his proud Queen were as incapable of departing from their accustomed patterns of thought as he had deemed them: even in flight they had been unable to dispense with lackeys, livery, a fine coach, escorts awakening the whole countryside, thundering to meet them, all the pomp and trappings of majesty, become for them at last a noose and a snare. They had not even thought of taking a circuitous route; and their disguises were pitiful. Old Dragoon Drouet, Post Master of Varennes had only to search his pockets for a new assignat, and compare the portrait thereon with this fat, sleepy visage to recognize the King. And royalty from that moment was doomed in France.

But Jean Paul Marin, believing them cleverer than this, thundered northward. And at last, when not one but two shabby coaches of the kind he had expected creaked into a sleepy village, he recognized at once Monsieur le Comte de Provence, the King's brother, in one of them, and Madame, his wife, in the other; superbly disciplined, they gazed straight at each other, and gave not the slightest sign of recognition, as the horses were being changed.

Jean stared at them, but made no move. Whether or not the Comte de Provence and his wife escaped, had no bearing upon the fate of France. I, Jean thought, am glad to see them go. They are good people and nothing will be served by their dying. He mounted once more, and was about to turn back toward Paris, when Madame, plagued by thirst, sent her maidservant toward the pump with a crystal goblet. The girl came straight toward him.

Hell of a good-looking maid, Jean thought, seeing her walking toward him, tall, willow-slender, tawny-haired. . . .

Then he froze, staring straight at her, straight into those hazel eyes widening in pure terror, her footsteps, slowing, halting, until Madame, leaning out from the coach, called:

"Do hurry, my girl!"

"Ah, yes," Jean mocked, "do!"

Then he threw back his head, and loosed peal after peal of wild, demonic laughter, the sound of it washing over her in waves, bitter, mirthless, mocking—subhuman, and superhuman, so that she stood there trembling under the impact of it, her face ghost white, until Jean lifted his hat to her and said:

"Come, wench—you must not keep Madame la Comtesse de Provence waiting!"

Then he yanked at the reins so hard his mount reared, and whirled the beast southward, thundering away toward Paris, leaving only the echo of satanic laughter trailing behind him.

Lucienne stood there a long time after he was gone. Then she went to the pump and came back with the water. It was crystalline, limpid, clear.

But no clearer, and not half so bright—as her tears.

12

Jean Paul sat on the edge of the bed, and cradled his head between his hands. The silence in the apartment crawled like a million tiny feet along his nerves. Nothing had been changed: the curtains, the drapes, the clock on the mantel, the firescreen, any of two dozen other household furnishings reflected Lucienne's exquisite taste, and cried out to him through the stillness, whispering her name.

I should leave here, he thought. I should go back to my own place in Saint-Antoine, but that would mean seeing Pierre, Marianne, and Fleurette daily. . . . Dear God, what a thing of patchwork is man! I have been praised for my courage, because I care nothing for physical pain or even the danger of death. But this is a species of courage that I have not. Go back, say I'm sorry—I was wrong—that's an easy thing, or it should be. But I cannot. . . .

To have gone of mine own volition and humbly asked forgiveness would have been one thing, and in its way, very fine. . . .

But to crawl back now, defeated, betrayed, deserted—exactly as they predicted; to say in effect to my friends: "I left you proudly, willfully; but now I come back to you, my second choices, because I have nothing left, because I find my loneliness insupportable—what greater insult could I offer them? No—I must find another place that will not always remind me; build another, emptier life, which, lacking both great joys and great sorrows, will supply its measure of peace. . . .

He got up and walked to the window. Sunday, July 17, he mused; less than a month since Lucienne's flight, but centuries, ages of silence, loneliness to me. A man must have some measure of contentment in his life, I know that. But throughout my days 'tis one thing I've achieved only at the rarest intervals: an hour, a day, with Nicole —talking with poor little Fleurette, my months with Lucienne—and even that has proved counterfeit now, false, robbed of everything that gave it beauty or dignity or joy. . . .

My work? Ah! What a snare and a delusion that was: all those conspiratorial meetings with Pierre, those night-long rides, wild with the excitement of being a part of destiny, of history, of risking everything: wealth, liberty, even life itself for the cause; what headier wine has there ever been than that?

But, Name of a Pig! Look at it now! The tyranny of Kings ended, perhaps, only to have a worse raised in its stead. For with all his bumbling incompetence, fat Louis was a good man; but what of goodness lives in the heart of Danton, spouting Desmoulins, slimy Robespierre, tormented Marat? Better to have left things as they were; for every evil we had then, we have loosed ten thousand new ones. Then it took a bad harvest to make bread dear—now everything is dear, bad harvests or good, the country flooded with worthless assignats, the roads infested with patriotic brigands, so that the very necessities of life trickle into Paris under guard. . . . Now every man deems himself a statesman-king; and murder and violence are daily commonplaces. . . .

And for this, I, and men like me are responsible—nay even guilty. In our vanity, we loosed the hurricane, thinking ourselves gods, able to rebuke the winds. And in the end, the very forces we invoked will destroy us one by one, which is only just; but they will also destroy France, which is monstrous. . . .

He sighed, turned away from the window. All life's efforts were bent toward the end of resigning a man toward death.

Down below, the street was packed with people. He knew where they were going—to the Champs de Mars, where the Cordeliers and Jacobins had erected a rude wooden Altar of Federation. On it a huge scroll had been laid, upon which they hoped to gain thousands of signatures, and tens of thousands of crosses laboriously scrawled by those who could not write.

Before June twenty-first, such a scroll would have been

unthinkable: but now, after the monumental folly of the
King's attempted flight, Hébert, Danton, Marat, Robespierre and the rest could come out boldly with the dream
that had possessed them from the first. Depose the King!
Make France a republic!

A good idea in the abstract, Jean thought as he picked
up his hat, his cane, and his pistols; but wanting this, I
think: to have a republic, you must have republicans,
and neither these power-drunk madmen at the fore, nor
this screeching unwashed rabble fills that bill. Dignity,
calm, foresight, resolution—control of self and of emotions—where are those things in France today? Where
are real disinterest, and negation of self? Each of these
bloodthirsty ones, these rabid republicans care nothing
truly for republicanism, but only for the opportunities it
presents to clutch power, wealth, fame into their unsavory
paws. And this, too, damn my foolish soul, I have helped
to arrange!

He clapped his tall hat on his head and went down the
stairs. Once in the street, he was caught up in the surging
mob; his nose was assaulted by a thousand evil smells,
each worse than the last; he was buffeted, elbowed by
dirty, vermin-infested louts, cackling, toothless harridans,
most of them wearing the red cap, all of them decorated
with tricolor cockades hidden in various degrees by plain
dirt. He caught references to his fine clothes and aristocratic bearing; but he shoved back with such force of arm,
and turned upon them a visage so terrible that they shrank
from him and made way. This evil face of mine, he
thought, with wry self-mockery, is the best weapon that I
have. . . .

The mob poured into the Champs de Mars, roaring out
their terrible hymn, *Ça Ira:*

> "Ah, that will be, will be, will be,
> The aristocrats to the lantern!
> Ah, that will be, will be, will be,
> The aristocrats, we'll hang them!
> Ah—that will be!"

They surged up in long lines to sign the petition. The
chief authors of it, Robert, Chaumette, Hanriot, the infamous Hébert, Coffinhal, and Monmoro stood beside the

wooden altar watching. But Danton, Marat, and Robespierre, all of whom Jean Paul knew well, had profoundly influenced the form of the petition, were either not present or had hidden themselves in the crowd.

Sniff the wind, ye hounds of hell! Jean Paul mocked them in his mind; scent whither it drifts before you show your fangs. . . .

He stood a little aside, watching. A group of young women mounted the altar. They were young, lovely. With a pang Jean recognized them as former colleagues of Lucienne's from l'Opéra. They were about their usual business of letting themselves be seen, making a show of their patriotism, because, since their noble lovers had fled, it behooved them to make the public forget as quickly as possible their well-deserved reputations as the playthings of the Noblesse.

How many of you, Jean thought, are also spies and traitors? I wonder if—

But he never finished his thought. One of the girls shrieked suddenly, piercingly. She had, Jean saw, lifted her left foot and was hopping about on her right.

The crowd surged forward, roaring. In two minutes they had half-wrecked the altar, and dragged from beneath it two miserable individuals, one of whom still had the awl in his hand.

"Spies!" they bellowed; "spies of Sieur Motier! General de Lafayette's henchmen! Kill them!"

Fools! Jean thought, cannot they see that those stinking grubworms were possessed of no other intent than a desire to peek at fair feminine flesh—and 'twas for this they were boring holes? Poor devils—one half blind, and the other with a wooden leg—how else would they ever get a glimpse of a pair of shapely limbs? But what an imbecility to die for!

That they would die for it was now quite certain. The two filthy old men were not to be given a chance to even explain their impotent lechery. What had kept them alive even so long was the surplus of would-be executioners. The Parisian ruffians fought like beasts for the privilege of killing the two harmless old fools. They were snatched from group to group, their rags torn, bloodied by a hundred blows.

Finally half a hundred Saint-Antoine *Quartier* roughs

broiled through. In two minutes the two Peeping Toms were kicking their miserable lives out on the ends of ropes suspended from the same lantern-post. There was a macabre ridiculousness about their antics; they bumped against each other, twirled, their hairy jaws sagging, their dirty grayish faces turning slowly blue, because their murderers had not known how to tie the knot properly so that it would break the necks cleanly, and bring instant death. So the two men strangled to death slowly, while the mob hooted and roared with laughter.

Jean Paul turned away from the sight. He felt sick down to the bottom of his guts. Though he had seen mob violence many times in Paris, it still sickened him. He did not want to watch the rest of it, but remained there with his back turned until another shout told him that it was done, finished in the only way *la foule de Paris* knew how to finish anything; and when he looked again the mob was bearing the two heads away, dripping, upon the ends of their pikes.

The crowd opened to let the pike-bearers through with their gruesome trophies. Jean saw a man reach out and snatch a young woman aside who had remained squarely in their way. He wondered at her action for barely a moment, before he saw who she was.

"Fleurette," he murmured. "Pray God that neither Pierre nor Marianne sees me here. . . ."

The slow, far-off boom of a cannon cut through his words. He lifted his head and listened, frowning. As he expected, a few moments later, he heard the muffled roll of drums.

The Civil Guard, coming to put down the disturbance. The warning gun, sounding its brass-throated invocation of martial law. Jean glanced once more at Fleurette. There might be bloodshed here. Pierre must realize that. He should take the two women away at once. Jean started working his way toward them, but it was hard going. When he was close enough he waited. He didn't want to talk to them now; above all things he wanted to avoid that. But he had to stay near them. In case of an outbreak they would need him. He waited.

He had not long to wait. Bailly, Mayor of Paris, came riding behind a color guard bearing *le drapeau rouge*, the red flag by which a civic or national emergency was proclaimed. At Bailly's side rode de Lafayette, and behind the general, rank after rank of the National Guard.

Even the artillery. The crowd made way for them in sullen silence. Then a woman shrilled:

"Down with the red flag! Down with the bayonets!"

A hundred voices took it up at once, screaming it shouting it roaring: "*À bas le drapeau rouge! À bas les baïonnettes!*" until they were all splitting the very heavens open with their cries.

Bailly was mounting the tottering platform now, reading the proclamation. Jean could see his lips moving, but he couldn't hear the words; the mob did not cease its bull bellow long enough.

Someone picked up a stone, threw it. A shower of missiles followed, raining upon the Guard.

The soldiers lifted their muskets. Jean started toward Fleurette. Then the volley, crisp, crackling, the air smoke plumed, but not a man falling, because the Guard had aimed above their heads.

The mob fell back, then surged forward again, emboldened by the Guard's clemency. The rain of stones redoubled. Jean saw the soldiers bring their pieces down smartly and begin to reload. The crowd pressed forward furiously. There was a spattering of pistol shots; General de Lafayette's aide-de-camp reeled in the saddle, wounded through the shoulder. No one, neither Bailly nor de Lafayette gave the order to fire. When the troops loosed their next volley, they did so only in defense of their lives. A few of the mob went down, sprawling grotesquely upon the ground, the life pumping out of their torn bodies. The rest of them reeled back, recoiling from the gunfire, then, wheeling like a herd of sheep before the winding horns of a great coach, they stampeded.

Jean saw the artillerymen, their matches lit, running for the touchholes of the cannon. But de Lafayette, with beautifully precise horsemanship, danced his charger between the fleeing mob and the guns, pressing the flank of his mount against the muzzle of one of the cannon.

The mob plunged on, trampling women, children, the old, and the infirm underfoot in its terror. Jean fought his way toward Fleurette. Just before he reached her, he saw her torn away from Pierre's grasp, and knocked to the earth by the herd of beasts for whom all semblance of humanity had fled.

Jean lifted his heavy cane, swung it in a circle, battering his way forward. His blows cleared a path for him like magic, and in a moment he was at her side. He knelt down and picked her up. She was not hurt, he saw, only dazed, and breathless.

"My thanks, M'sieur," she whispered; "you can put me down now—I—I'm quite all right. . . ."

"No, Fleurette," Jean said gravely. "It's too dangerous. Come, I'll get you out of here. . . ."

He saw her great, sightless eyes widening endlessly in her tiny face. Then all the light in the world got into them, softglowing warm, unfocused.

"Jean!" she breathed, "oh, my dearest. . . ." Then she swept both her arms up about his neck, and hid her face against his collar.

Jean marched with her like that until they were out of the crowd. He lifted his cane to signal a fiacre, and saw to his astonishment that only a stump of it was left. He had broken it against the heads of the mob without even realizing it.

It took him a long time to get a fiacre. Everyone who could afford it was trying to engage one. So it was that Pierre and Marianne were able to make their way out of the diminishing mob and join them.

Marianne's face was tear-streaked. She hugged Fleurette fiercely, babbling:

"Thank God, you're safe! Oh, thank God! I thought they'd trampled you. . . ."

"They would have," Fleurette said proudly, her voice lilting, flutelike, warm, "but for Jean—"

Marianne turned her face toward Jean.

"As for you, Jean Marin," she snapped, "have you decided to behave yourself and come back to us?"

"I," Jean laughed, "have no choice in the matter. Yes, Marianne, I'm moving back to my old place tomorrow. . . ."

Pierre stared at his friend. Then suddenly he put out his hand. Jean gripped it hard.

"I'm glad, Jean," Pierre said gravely; "you don't know how glad I am."

Fleurette touched his arm, shyly.

"Jean," she whispered; "it's over then? The—the other, I mean? You're not with her any more?"

"No, little dove," Jean said, "she's no longer here—not in Paris any more; not even in France. . . ."

The joy that flared in Fleurette's dark eyes was almost blinding. Jean felt something inside his heart rise up and fly away. It had been there a long time, dark, and heavy and formless, but it was gone now. "You're not with her any more?" Fleurette had asked; and now at last, at long, long last he wasn't. He was free. He stood there very still, savoring the feeling. It was a good one, very deep and strong and quiet—and the name of it was—peace.

Riding home with them in the fiacre that Pierre finally stopped, Jean marveled at how easy it had all been. He had been dreading this meeting. He had expected tears, recriminations, laborious explanations, apologies. Only it wasn't going to be like that at all. He had given all the explanations he was ever going to have to give. Pierre's gaze was steady, warm; and Marianne seemed to be regarding them with something of that peculiar satisfaction with which an artist views the work of his own hands. . . .

But there were still things to be done, and for a time it seemed to Jean Paul that they could be accomplished. After the so-called Massacre of the Champs de Mars, the Assembly tardily showed courage: a measure of direct reprimand against the seditious journals was voted, and for the time being, Marat's *Friend of the People*, Freron's *Orator of the People*, and Camille Desmoulins' *Revolutions of France and Brabant* ceased to appear. More, as the tide of moderation rose, Desmoulins, Legendre, and Santerre went into hiding, while Danton fled to England. Robespierre, who had prudently concealed his part in the whole affair, contented himself with accepting the hospitality of the rich M. Duplay, and staying away from his old lodgings. . . .

Lafayette, Barnave, Lameth, Le Chapelier, Duport, Sieyès, Talleyrand founded a new club, which met in the Convent of the Feuillants, and came to bear that name. Many of these founders of the Feuillant Club had been Jacobins, but as the extremists moved to the fore, their influence there had vanished. Jean attended many of the meetings of the Feuillants, whose politics he found more or less congenial; but he refused to actually become a member.

"If the Assembly were wise," he said to Pierre, "it would close all the Clubs. A deputy should not be subjected to pressure from without. 'Tis the ruination of democracy. . . ."

But the Assembly was far from wise. On September 3, 1791, it voted a constitution armed with provisions to keep the power in the hands of the bourgeoisie; but on the thirtieth of the same month it brought itself to an end, voting almost unanimously for the most monumental piece of political stupidity ever born of the warped mind of a singularly warped man:

Maximilien Robespierre, out of a fantastic desire to display his famed "Incorruptibility," urged that members of the National Assembly vote themselves ineligible to sit in the new, or Legislative Assembly. Thus, by the stroke of a pen, was France robbed of all the dearly bought experience of two terrible years, and turned over to novices once more.

Jean Paul voted with the rest. 'Tis madness and worse, he thought; but I have done what I could. I think that the rest of them are tired, too—as tired, perhaps, as I am. They want to go back to homes they have not seen in years, to take up the threads of their lives once more and weave them into a more acceptable pattern. . . .

That night, he had already begun to pack his clothes when Fleurette came into the room, and stood there listening to the sounds he made.

"You—you're going away," she said. It was a statement, not a question.

"Yes, Fleurette," Jean said, forcing cheerfulness into his voice; "but I shall come back—as soon as possible. . . ."

"How long will you be away, Jean?" Fleurette whispered.

"Two months—perhaps three. I'm going to try to revive my father's old business. It's a good time, now—for such a thing. Since the revolt of the Negroes of Sainte-Dominique, sugar and coffee are plaguedly hard to come by; I think I can start shipping those commodities again—from Louisiana, perhaps, or Martinique. I have the ships —'twill be only a matter of refitting them, and finding crews. . . ."

He chattered on, desperately searching her face. It was blank, expressionless. He was aware after a time that she wasn't even listening.

She came close to him, her great, dark eyes so fixed upon his face that he had the momentary illusion that she could see him after all, that her gaze probed beyond the surface into his brain.

"Jean," she said simply, "don't tell me all those things. They are men's affairs, and no concern of mine. Tell me just one thing, my Jean—the truth. When you come back to Paris, are you coming back—to me?"

He stood there, staring at her. It's the one thing I cannot cope with, he thought—this simplicity of hers. Being blind has done this for her, I think. She has never had to concern herself with non-essentials. And this thing she has asked, what is the answer to it? What can I say? That I will come back, poor waif, sweet child, sweet, lovely child, if the woman I seek is dead. That is what it amounts to, but I cannot say that, can I? Dear God, what can I say?

He put out his big hand and touched her soft cheek, letting his hand rest there as lightly as a breath.

"If," he murmured, "I do not come back to you, Fleurette—I shall not come back at all. . . ."

She brought her own hand up slowly, and closed it over his fingers. She drew them down and away from her face, turning them over until she held his hand, palm up. She stood there, like that, holding it.

"I think that you're being kind," she said; "or that you love me a little, I don't know which. . . ." She smiled, and the tears were there, bright and sudden in her eyes. She lifted his big hand, and pressed a kiss against the palm; then she closed his fingers over it.

"This, keep—in remembrance of me," she said, and ran from the room.

Jean stood very still, looking after her. I have many things to keep in memory of you, little Fleurette, he thought, all the good, gentle things—all the flowers of quietness. . . . Then he bent once more to the task of packing.

It was difficult, damnably difficult. In the first place, the journey down to Marseille, which had been a matter of some five or six days by fast diligence under the Kings of France, took more than two dreary weeks, due to the disorder into which transportation, like all else in France, had fallen. In the second, the recruiting of crews wasn't easy. The seamen were as idle as Jean had expected them to be, but they were not really suffering from their idleness; too many opportunities for pillage, blackguardism, and plain thievery existed in the France of 1791. And even worse than the task of finding ordinary seamen was the labor of discovering anyone with experience who wanted to serve as an officer.

" 'Tis like this, Jean Marin, lad," one old salt after another explained to him, "I knew your father, sailed under his colors often enough, ye ken; but 'tis different nowadays. These fools don't comprehend that a vessel's no place for politics. When I give an order, I want my lads to jump to it and look alive! What's more, their lives and mine are in danger every time they don't; if I tell the helmsman to take a starboard tack, because I plainly see white water and reefs to port, I'm not going to argue the matter with him save with a marlinspike or a belaying pin! But these republican idiots want to put every matter to a vote—even up to electing their own officers aboard a merchantman. And seamanship and the ability to command don't make a man popular. . . ."

But if there was any one thing his political career had taught Jean Paul, it was the art of persuasion. By dint of a ready tongue and a lavish expenditure of money he got three of his father's vessels outfitted again: two great ships, and one smart brig, which made up for its lack of tonnage by its agility as a sailor.

He bribed, bullied, pleaded with, flattered, and shamed most of his father's old seamen to sign aboard; even so the ships sailed short handed because of his steadfast refusal to accept landlubbers and unruly louts among the crews. . . .

As he fully expected, the warehouses had been pillaged; what the thieves had been unable to take away, they had destroyed. But somehow, out of respect for his father, Jean guessed, they had refrained from burning them. Jean found artisans to equip the windows with stout iron bars, and had locksmiths change all the smashed and useless locks. Now, when his vessels returned with his goods, he would have a place to store them.

He hired one Joseph Cocteau, a stern and honest man, and put him in charge, with the power to employ and discharge men as he saw fit.

Now, he thought, 'tis all done, and there is nothing to do but to wait. It's a gamble, and any failure could ruin me—the loss of a ship, the failure to obtain the goods in the troubled Antilles—anything at all. But let me win this time, and I am made. The demand for coffee, sugar, rum is greater than at any time in history. From this one voyage, I will be able to open Marin et Fils in Calais as well, and spend my whole time between there and Paris. . . . For there is nothing left here—nothing at all. . . .

He was riding along the highroad that led toward Saint Jule and Villa Marin as he thought these things; a moment later, rounding a bend in the road, he saw his thoughts had been right.

He got down from his horse and walked toward the fire-blackened ruins. The walls still stood, but the windows opened upon nothing but the heavens; floors and roof had crashed into rubble, from which rank weeds grew; vines climbed the streaked and sooty walls, and at his footsteps a horde of bats flitted wildly into the starlit sky.

Jean clenched his fist. I could rebuild it, he thought grimly, I could make it like new. . . .

But he could not, and he knew it. Physically, it could be done; the house had been so well built as to resist fire and the weathering of two long years; but it could never be the same again. All the things it had held could be duplicated, perhaps, in outward form, but how again to give them that look of having been treasured, tenderly touched, beloved of his sainted mother, of his sister, of his father? And some could never be restored—the curios brought by sailors from far lands as gifts to Henri Marin, the pieces his mother had embroidered with her own delicate fingers—gone, all gone, become ghosts of the love and skill that had gone into their making.

'Tis well that they cannot, Jean mused; for were I to see these mementos of my youth again, I doubt me that I could bear them. . . . .

He turned away from the blackened walls, the piles of rubble, forcing his way through paths, dimtraced now, overgrown with bush and weed, and remounted; but he did not return to his inn at Marseille. He rode on, through the great port, until he came at dawn to another ruin—the little château that had been the home of Nicole and Julien Lamont.

It had fared worse than Villa Marin. Only the part of one wall stood, and the overgrowth was thicker. In the dawnstillness birds twittered, flying through the gaping windows, and the hand of death lay heavy upon Jean Paul's heart.

He got down stiffly, and approached it, but he knew as he came on that he would find nothing, because there was nothing left. He circled the one remaining half wall, and as he did so, a goat bleated, shattering the silence.

Someone had built a lean-to against the wall, and at the sound of the goat's bleat, a woman pushed aside the curtain and gazed at him with ancient, rheumy eyes. She seemed older than death itself, than even life. Wisps of white hair straggled down to her thin shoulders, her face was a map of age and sorrow.

"Who be ye?" she croaked; then, in the same breath, "off with ye, now, afore I loose the dogs!"

"Wait," Jean said pleasantly; "I want only some tidings of the people who lived in this house. . . ."

He could see her expression soften.

"Were they friends of yours?" she demanded.

"The lady, yes—I did not know his lordship," Jean answered, truthfully.

"Then I'll tell ye," the ancient hag whispered, "because my lady were an angel. . . ."

"You have right," Jean murmured; "tell me of her. . . ."

"She lies over there," the old woman said, and pointed. "Would ye see her grave?"

Jean's lips moved, but nothing came out of them. Grimly he nodded his head.

"Come with me, young man," the old woman said.

He stood with her beside the three little mounds, leveled almost by the rains, one a little longer than the other two, without headstones, markers, anything—three mounds of grassy earth, hiding his dreams, his hopes, all, in fact that was left of his life.

But he could not accept it. Something deep, insistent, mounted within his heart and cried out against it.

"Did you see them buried?" he demanded harshly.

"Nay, not I. I was hiding—or else I would know aught of my poor Marie. . . ."

Jean probed into his memory and came up with a picture. Plump Marie, Nicole's maidservant, with her rosy, cheerful face, and hair of the same shade as the la Moytes; there had been rumors that a closer relationship existed between them than mistress and maid.

"Your daughter?" he said; "she was never found?"

"Why else do ye think I tarry in that haunted ruin," the old woman quavered, "save in hope that one day she may come back to me? Ah, but she is fled . . . far fled, from fear of those devils!"

"You did not see them buried," Jean said softly. "My thanks, good woman. . . ." He pressed a gold coin into her hand and went back to his horse.

An hour later, he was back again with three stout fellows armed with picks, and spades. He stood there and watched, his whole soul crying out against this desecration; but he had to know. He had lived too long with uncertainty; he had to know.

Then, finally, he looked down upon horror. The skeleton was that of a small woman, dressed in a dress of silk whose pattern he recognized instantly, remembering it with sickening clarity, as he remembered everything about Nicole. The skull had been crushed with a blunt instrument—a spade, perhaps, but a few wisps of pale gold clung to it and gleamed with persistent life in the sunlight. . . .

He knew now. There was no mistake, and no hope.

He commanded the gravediggers to take away the three pitiful heaps of bones back to his warehouse, wrapped tenderly in soft cloths. And he did not leave the Côte until a magnificent tomb of marble had been built, and the three, the woman and the two children had been laid to rest once more in lead-lined coffins against the cold and the wet.

When, at long last, he rode away northward toward Paris, it seemed to Jean Paul Marin that he had left the major portion of his heart entombed with them, lying there. . . .

13

As he looked in the mirror that morning of March 24, 1792, Jean Paul Marin looked into the face of a stranger. The hair above his temples was white now, and a snowy lock waved backward across the crown of his head, startling against the inky blackness of the rest of his hair. His face was thinner, and imperceptibly the great scar had softened so that in repose his face had grown strangely gentle.

But the greatest change of all was in his eyes. They were as great and dark and somber as always, but some of the bitterness, some of the mockery had gone out of them, and what was left was—peace. . . .

Life does this to a man, he thought, as he picked up his razor and tested the water that the innkeeper's lackey had brought him. Life never brings a man what he wants, and seldom what he expects, but in the flux of time all things run together finally, and one learns acceptance. . . .

I tormented myself for months with the knowledge that Nicole is really dead; but 'tis a good thing—the certainty of that knowledge. . . . She is dead and at peace, fled from a world too gross for angels . . . and I am left alone to put together the pieces of my life again. But no longer a rebel. They called me a philosopher when I was young, but I was not. I was one of God's angry men, big with a sense of justice, mad to right all wrongs—how strange that seems now. For if there is any one apparent fact in the universe, it is that we are but playthings of the cosmos, and God, if there is a God, concerned with us little—if at all. . . .

He picked up the razor and began to scrape the pepper and salt stubble from his lean jaw.

Vanity of vanities, he mocked laughingly, to think there should be such a thing as justice. When another two-legged insect dies, what boots it if he deserved or merited not his fate? And the strangest thing of all is I can think these things now without bitterness, with a kind of tenderness that embraces all the other pitiful victims of chance and circumstance who crawl like me over the surface of this world. Truly, my brothers, whom I can only love and pity—and never hate, nor appoint myself judge or executioner, since certainly I am not God. . . .

I have betrayed, and been betrayed, and of the two it was better to be the victim, for to suffer a thing takes less from man's dignity than to do it. And Lucienne's flight robbed me of what I was better without, of what would have destroyed me, finally. What remains then? Peace, I think—acceptance. Those, and Jean Paul Marin, a person, finally, a man living, breathing, enduring, surviving, undefeated finally, because what one accepts can never truly degrade one. Believe that men are thieves, liars, cheats, monsters of hatred, deceit and vanity, and you are half right, believe that the same men, at the same time are good, or would be if they could, and love them if one can, pity them if one cannot love, and hate them never, and one has won, I think, his battle. . . .

He looked out of the window at the fine lemon-yellow coach that awaited him. Is it, he mused, because I have never truly lacked this world's goods that I set so little store by them? Six ships now, plying between here and the Antilles, *facteurs* in New Orleans, and Fort de France, more money made in one month than even my father gained in a year. He would be proud of me, I think; but 'twas your doing, my father. Such an empire could not have been built in half a year without the foundation of thirty years' labor that you laid for me. Your name is the magic that opens all doors to me. . . .

He finished his dressing and the manservant came with the coffee and *brioche*. He drank the scalding black liquid slowly, leaving the *brioche* untouched as usual. Then, a few deft touches again to his hair and clothing, and down the stairs, following the sweating servant who bore his bags to the coach.

Paris again after so many long months. What would it be like now? The same really. My friends, the Feuillants, gone from power. A new group rising, the Girondist—a splinter faction of the Jacobin Club, led by a pastry-cook's son named Brissot, opposed to Robespierre et al—a fine falling-out of thieves. . . .

Clavière, at whose home Mirabeau and I used to meet, Clavière who invented assignats and wrecked the economy of France thereby, in the ministry, along with this new man Roland, of whom Pierre writes nothing but that he has a stunning wife. Everyone seems taken with this young Madame Roland—Pierre frequents her salon, as does practically everyone else, no matter what his politics. . . .

Danton, *Procureur Substitut* of Paris! A dangerous thing, I think, what with Petion, Mayor, and Manuel, *Procureur Général*—neither of them strong enough to stand against Danton. . . . The more it changes— Yet life goes on, civil strife and domiciliary visits, murder and pillage, but it goes, just the same. . . .

And Fleurette there, waiting. That's the crux of the matter, the point I've been avoiding so long? Do I love her? I don't know; that is not perhaps the question. Am I capable of love any more? Is any man of my age, having had my experiences, capable of it? Her blindness—nothing, and less than nothing, an advantage really, since my ugliness cannot disturb her. But herein lies the doubt that I can bring her the goodness and the patience that she needs, the gentleness and the understanding. . . .

He looked out of the window of his coach, at poplars spinning backward along the road. Soon, now, soon. What is love, anyway? That madness, that delirium, I had with Lucienne? That searing of the flesh, body-fusion, life-destroying annihilation of ecstasy? That thing of the flesh, too much of the flesh, good, perfect, a fine art, a death struggle, but lacking always something. . . . What? Tenderness, faith, mutual respect. . . .

Because betrayal had gotten into it; because the tears I shed over her were less tears of loss, than of sorrow at the destruction of love's own integrity. I wept, I think, less over Lucienne than over the loss of the last, the most dearly cherished illusion—that love is true and will not betray the beloved no matter what the provocation. But love is but one attribute of man, and man is never true— he merely longs to be. . . .

Strange. I love Lucienne more than I love Fleurette, and less. I want to keep and cherish Fleurette, I think; I wanted merely to possess Lucienne. . . .

And with Nicole, it was perfect, largely I know now, because it had no time to become less than perfect. But it would have. Life dulls all things, destroys all things finally, batters down our youth into age, our strength into fatigue, our hope into hopelessness, until we finally come to accept death—nay to welcome it. . . .

So wait my love, my little lost love in your eternal darkness, for I shall come to you, now. I shall smile and be tender, and pray God you never find out how little there is of me left alive to feel love or joy. But what I have left is yours, all yours; and by this kindness, for it is that, too, and more than that, I shall atone a little for evils I have brought upon my country and my fellows. . . .

He rode into Paris early in the afternoon, and stopped at once at a jeweler's. There he bought the two rings, one with a great diamond, to plight the troth, and the other a circle of heavy gold for the wedding. Then he drove at once to her lodgings.

She was not there, but across the hall, visiting, as usual, with Marianne. The two of them went less frequently now to the business, it had grown so that they had been forced to delegate their duties, and having trained competent help, all of them, including Pierre, had more leisure.

Marianne had no need to announce him. Fleurette stood up at his step, and flew toward him, her face radiant with joy.

"Come walk with me, Fleurette," Jean said; "there's a thing I would say to you. . . ."

"Can't you say it here?" Fleurette breathed; "I have no secrets from Marianne. . . ."

"It doesn't need words, really," Jean smiled. "Give me your hand. . . ."

Wonderingly, Fleurette stretched it out to him.

"Not that one," Jean said; "the other. . . ."

She gave him her left hand, and he slipped the ring on her finger, closing his hand over it, so that it took her a moment or two to free it, and touch the stone with her fingertips.

She turned slowly toward Marianne, stretching her hand out. The light caught the great stone, so that it blazed. Marianne stared at it, choked, and two big tears squeezed out of the corners of her eyes.

"What on earth?" Jean began in pure astonishment.

"Oh, kiss her, you great fool!" Marianne snapped at him; "what the devil are you waiting for?"

Fleurette went up on tiptoe and brushed his mouth, so lightly and so quickly that he was scarcely aware of it before it was gone; but the next instant she had fallen into Marianne's arms, and the two of them clung together, sobbing as though their hearts were entirely broken.

"What did I do?" Jean asked wonderingly; "I'm sure I had no intention of—"

"Oh, shut up, Jean Marin!" Marianne sobbed; "don't you know that all women cry when they're happy?"

"Well, I'll be blessed!" Jean said, and took a step toward the door; but at that moment, Pierre came out of the inner room. He took his pipe out of his mouth and stared at his wife and Fleurette.

"Now, what have you done to them?" he growled at Jean.

"Oh I've insulted them terribly," Jean grinned; "I merely asked Fleurette to marry me."

"*Sacre bleu!*" Pierre roared, and gathered Jean to him in a bear hug; "this calls for wine—lots of wine, all the blessed wine in the whole blessed world!"

He disappeared but came back instantly on the run, decanters and glasses filling his arms.

"Drink up, my doves!" he bellowed. "*Morbleu*, how long have I waited for this day!"

"When is it to be, Jean?" Marianne asked.

"As soon as possible—tomorrow if I can arrange it. . . ."

"Oh no you don't!" Marianne cried; "how on earth do you think I could make a wedding dress by tomorrow? It's got to be of the finest, heaviest white silk you ever saw—I've got just the material at the shop—and with little seed pearls all over it. As for the veil—tomorrow, hah! You can get married in two weeks, Jean Marin—no, three. Now, as I was saying about the veil . . ."

Jean stood there, staring at the two women with an expression of near-stupefaction on his face. Pierre came up to him and took his arm.

"Let's go for a walk," he laughed. "You and I are entirely superfluous here now, and we will be for quite some time. Come. . . ."

Jean went over to Fleurette and kissed her, quickly.

"Fleurette—" he began.

"Oh, go with Pierre, my dearest," she laughed. "Marianne and I have a thousand things to do, now. . . ."

"Regard," Pierre chuckled, as they were going down the stairs, "you are a man of experience, but you know nothing of women, really—of good women, anyhow, the kind men marry. . . ."

"I am beginning to believe you're right," Jean said ruefully.

"I am right. Let's go over to Charpentier's for a glass, and we can talk in the meantime. Your experience has been one-sided—all of it with mistresses, and none of it with wives."

"There is a difference?" Jean said. "Apart from the legality of the thing, I don't see . . ."

"There is a difference. A wife and a mistress are two different breeds entirely. Being a wife is a state of mind. And I'll anticipate your next point by admitting that a woman can be one man's wife, and another's mistress, and still the same thing holds true. . . ."

"I don't see . . ."

"You never see! Shut up and listen. I should charge you money for this lesson. To begin with, a husband is always a mere accessory after the fact, no matter how dearly his wife loves him; he makes possible the tremendous dramas of which his bride is the heroine: the beautiful, beautiful ceremony of marriage in which she can wear a gown like moonlight and mist, become for an hour, a day, a queen, and afterwards he also makes possible the even more stupendous drama of birth, and maternity. . . .

"Believe me, *mon vieux*, if the women could manage either of those things without the troublesome presence of the man, they would! We are, my friend, but means to an end, never the end itself."

"And afterwards?" Jean smiled.

"We are the ones who bring the necessary money to support the home, making it possible for our child-brides to go on playing house with living dolls made in their own images, wonderful sops to their vanity, allowing them to say: Behold what I have made! Behold, for this I knew agony, descended almost unto death itself; and you, thou great lout? An hour's pleasure—and no suffering! Verily, my Jean, I believe God made wives to teach a man a proper sense of humility!"

Jean laughed aloud.

"This table?" he said. "Good! Then how do mistresses differ?"

"Greatly," Pierre said, signaling to the garçon to bring wine; "in the first place, a mistress is stupid. . . ."

"Hardly," Jean objected, thinking of Lucienne.

"Yes, yes!" Pierre insisted; "even when her lover is a rich man who gives her many gifts. She can be left high and dry any time his fancy changes; her children, being bastards, cannot inherit; she must fawn and flatter to keep her slender hold upon him. Imagine Marianne flattering me! She'd use the black end of a skillet, dealt with a heavy hand! And yet, she loves me, I think. It's just that she knows, compared with the age-old wisdom of women —a wisdom that has nothing to do with logic, or reason, or sense—men are but backward children, not ever to be trusted. And she's right. . . ."

"You," Jean smiled, sipping his glass, "don't have a very high opinion of our sex, do you?"

"Oh, yes, I do. It's just that men and women complement each other—or should. Women are more primitive, depending more upon their instincts, and thereby getting closer to the truth of things. Men are, or think they are, logical, reasonable, objective—therefore, they try to build a state upon those things, and make one ungodly mess! The human race, Jean Paul, has never worked upon intelligence or logic, but upon emotion and prejudice. In any large group of people, anything that is simple, clear, logical, objective is certain not to work. You've got to get in mumbo-jumbo, witchcraft, pageantry, singing, fireworks, drama! Even when you're convinced that a measure is good and wise, you've got to get those things in to carry it over with the people. Even your politicians have learned that. Regard your Fêtes of Federation, fêtes of this and that—with lanterns, red caps, statues of liberty, trees of liberty, until Jacques Bonhomme is convinced that he is free, while actually his freedom consists in merely the liberty to riot, to pillage, to get drunk, and to starve!"

"You old cynic!" Jean chuckled.

"No, not cynicism, Jean—realism, which is the true foundation of happiness, since it eliminates disappointment. . . ."

They sat there a long time, talking, Pierre covered the political situation for Jean, bringing him up to date. He described the terrorism by which the Jacobins had gained a power out of all proportion to their numbers. "Were it not for the schisms among them, they, God help us, would now rule France. But they do split. Now the more moderate men among them, called Brissotins after their leader, at first, but more and more frequently now Girondins because their greatest orators, Vergniaud, Gaudet, and Gensonne are all from Gironde, have come to the fore. Isnard, Condorcet, Fauchet, and Valaze, sit with them; but they are directed from without. . . ."

"From without?" Jean said.

"Yes. Jean, today a woman rules France. Madame Roland, whose ancient, pedantic husband is Minister of the Interior, has but to lift an eyebrow and the world revolves! You must meet her; she's incredibly charming. Your old friend Sieyès thinks he influences and controls her; but the reverse is true. Dumouriez is in love with her, Barbaroux is in love with her, Buzot, too—and this last is returned, I think. After you're married, I'll introduce you—you'll meet everyone at her salon—from men as far Left as Robespierre to those as far Right as Barnave and Dupont de Nemours. . . ."

"And her influence is for good, or ill?"

"For ill, I fear. She hates the Queen with an intensity that only a woman is capable of. It seems that the Queen denied some paltry honor or title to Roland before the Revolution, and Manon Roland has never forgiven her. The whole Gironde is bent upon war—as a means to overthrow the Crown. And they'll succeed; I know it. With Madame Roland using her charms and wiles, the throne is doomed!"

"But war!" Jean whispered; "they really think we could fight all Europe? Unprepared as we are—all our trained officers fled, discipline gone . . . they think that?"

Pierre looked at his friend, sadly.

"They do," he said; "but then they are madmen, remember. . . ."

When it came to even such a private matter as marriage, Jean Paul learned how complicated life had become since the Revolution. In the first place, marriage was now a civil contract, though the law had not yet been fully codified. He had, therefore, to obtain a license from the municipal authorities. These insisted, not without reason, that one of their number perform the ceremony.

"You never know, Marin, what effect a slight mistake can have on a man's life in these times. Be a good fellow and have the civil ceremony. Afterwards, you can go quietly to a priest if you like. . . ."

Pierre sanctioned this as a part of the wisdom that was the better part of valor; but Fleurette, devoutly religious, stormed at Jean, with tears in her eyes. It took Marianne to convince her.

"You love Jean?" Marianne demanded; "well then, are you going to risk his life over a scruple? Men have been branded traitors for less than this. It's the law, so obey it. Then afterwards have a priest make it right. . . ."

So it was done, but after the ceremony, during which Fleurette stubbornly refused to wear her wedding dress, she went back to her own rooms.

"I'm not married to you, Jean," she said flatly. "When our vows have been said before a priest, I'll be your wife, but not before!"

Jean sighed. He was in trouble and he knew it. In his youthful rebelliousness, he had conducted the warfare on the Church which had stripped her in France of all her possessions, split her priesthood into two factions, those who had abnegated the authority of the Pope, and sworn loyalty to the nation as an authority even above the Church, and those who had refused to do so. To all devout Catholics, any priest who had taken this oath was a schismatic, and automatically excommunicated. Even the King had risked his life rather than compromise on this point; he had steadfastly vetoed all measures against the non-juring priests, as those loyal to orthodox concepts were called.

"And his now," Jean sighed to Pierre, "is the fruit of my own folly! Where am I to find a non-juring priest? And if I find one, will not this marriage itself put me beyond the pale, politically, jeopardizing our future, and that of any children we might have?"

"Fleurette won't consider it legal if you don't," Pierre grinned. "Don't worry, my old one—I'll fix something. . . ."

Pierre worked wonders. Early on the morning of April 14, Jean's yellow coach slipped out of Paris. None of them wore wedding clothes. These had been carefully packed in the valises above the carriage. They would change for the ceremony, and change once more afterwards, to come back to Paris.

On the way to Fontainebleau, Pierre explained how he had done it. By incredible maneuvering, he had gotten an audience with the King and Queen, prisoners now, still confined under guard in the ancient palace of the Tuileries ever since their pitiful attempt to flee France. The story he told their Majesties was well calculated to win their sympathies. Louis was instantly prepared to aid any man who wanted to be married by a non-juring priest; and when Pierre reminded the Queen of her interview with Jean Paul, she smiled and said:

"Of course I remember your friend—that charming man, with the incredibly scarred face; to be sure, 'twill be our pleasure to aid him. . . ."

And going to her secretary, Marie Antoinette had written a note in her own hand to her father-confessor at Fontainebleau, and sealed it with the royal seal. Everything was in readiness now, the priest awaited them in the Queen's own small chapel.

When Fleurette appeared, bearing a huge spray of lilies in her hand, walking with Pierre, all the radiance in the world seemed to have gathered itself into her small face. Jean drew in a deep, incense-laden breath.

Nothing, or no one, he thought, in all this world has ever been so lovely!

Her soft hair was a mist of midnight, under the dawn-mist of her veil; her gown was creamy, yellow white, and the tiny pearls glowed like droplets of milk upon it. But it was her smile that was the loveliest thing in all the world; it was so filled with peace, contentment, quiet joy. . . .

Jean felt something like terror moving through his heart.

Dear God, he prayed, make me deserve this! Make of me what I must be to bring her the joy, the happiness, the peace she was meant for. And thank Thee, Our Father, for this miracle which Thou hast given me. . . .

Marianne cried all through the ceremony, her sobs punctuating the stately Latin periods of the old priest. When it was done at last, and Jean Paul had kissed his bride, holding her as though she were something infinitely fragile and precious, touching her lips as if any more fleshly contact would bruise them, the priest stepped forward with a small box in his hand.

"From her Majesty," he smiled; "she made it for the bride with her own hands. . . ."

It was a handkerchief of lace, exquisitely embroidered. The card read:

"Every happiness, my dear. S. R. M. Marie Antoinette, R."

When Fleurette was told of the Queen's gift, tears stole slowly down her face; while Marianne sobbed so loudly she had to be led from the chapel.

The dinner that Pierre had ordered at the best inn in Fontainebleau was magnificent; but he alone ate it; Jean sat there very quietly, holding Fleurette's hand; while Marianne beamed at the two of them like a mother hen and picked at her own food as little as they.

"Now," Jean said, when they had finished, "I have a surprise for all of you."

He led them back to the coach, and the coachman wheeled the horses back toward Paris. They reached it at dusk, while there was still light enough to see. The coachman guided the big coach across the Pont Neuf into the Saint Germain des Prés Quartier, and they wound through crooked streets for what seemed hours, to draw up at last before a house.

A servant opened a small gate in the high wall, and they came into a garden choked with flowers, whose scent lay heavy upon the warm April air. The house was a true *hôtel particulier,* the former residence of a duc; tall and splendid, with high windows catching the last rays of the evening sun.

While other servants bowed them into the foyer, a manservant took their hats, gloves, canes.

"Magnificent!" Pierre breathed. But Jean felt Fleurette's small hand tugging at his arm.

"Tell me about it, Jean," she whispered, "what is it like, our new home?"

And Jean Paul stood there, wordless before the realization of how little all this splendor could mean to eyes that could not see.

He was awakened early in the morning, before it was light, by the soft touch of her fingers straying over his face. He came awake at once, and gripped her wrist, hard.

"Let me go, Jean," she whispered; "this preoccupation with your face is a great foolishness. You are my husband now—I have the right to know how you look. . . ."

Slowly he released her, and lay quite still, while she traced the outlines of his face, whispering:

" 'Tis but a scar, my Jean! It is this that you concealed from me so long? Scars are not ugliness—ugliness comes from within, from the heart; I think you are handsome—as handsome as a god—so tall and strong. . . ."

Her fingers strayed downward over his body, lightly as a breath, without provocation, or passion, with simple childlike curiosity.

"This is what a man is like," she murmured, to herself, "this is what my man is like—so fine and strong, so beautifully made. . . . Oh, Jean, Jean, how I wish I could see you!"

He did not move, or speak. He lay there with his breath caught somewhere deep inside of him, afraid to break the magic of the moment.

She moved close to him.

"Kiss me, Jean," she whispered; "kiss me as you love me—as a woman, Jean, not a fragile doll! I will not break, nothing of me will break, except my heart—if you keep me at arms' length any longer. . . . I know why. You think me delicate and ignorant of life, and you are right, but only partly. I am ignorant, but with my love I cannot remain so—Jean, Jean I married you to become your wife—not a blind and helpless doll to be taken care of!"

She was crying now, and he drew her to him, kissing the salt tears from her cheeks. Slowly she calmed.

"Teach me, Jean," she said.

14

"They told me I would find you here," Renoir Gerade said; "but I confess I wasn't prepared for such magnificence. I rather think it makes my visit pointless. . . ."

"Nevertheless," Jean smiled, "I'm indebted to whatever reasons you had that made you honor me with a visit. And, speaking of magnificence, that uniform you're wearing is not to be sneered at. . . . Some coffee, perhaps?"

"Gladly. I've been up since before dawn, and a cup or two would help matters; I'm not as young as I once was, you know. . . ."

Jean pulled the the bell-cord.

"There is," he said, "a connection between your uniform and this visit?"

"Right. I won't waste time, Jean. After all our plans collapsed, I cast about for something to do. My life has been all soldiering—either in military intelligence, or in active service. That penal command I had when you met me was the lowest depths to which I'd ever sunk. . . ."

"Coffee, Jeanne," Jean said to the maidservant; "and you might inquire if Madame is awake. If so, take her a up a cup—*au lait,* of course; but black for M'sieur and myself. You were saying, Renoir?"

"Only that I tried to find something to do along lines in which I had some knowledge. Fortunately, I had some money saved; and General de Lafayette offered me a command in the National Guard. . . ."

"That's not the Guard's uniform you're wearing," Jean pointed out.

"I know it isn't. This is the uniform of the new National Army. A number of respectable bourgeois have organized a company of volunteers. When they offered me the command, I snatched at the chance. That's why I'm here; I need a second in command. . . ."

"But I know nothing of military tactics," Jean protested.

"Which is good. You have nothing to unlearn. To beat the Austrians, we're going to have to fight a new kind of war—a war of lightning-like movement, hard blows dealt here today—tomorrow miles away in a new, unexpected sector. I don't want to be burdened with a lieutenant who'll argue mass frontal attacks and classic military movements with me. What you'll need to know, I'll teach you. . . ."

"War," Jean sighed. "Who would have ever thought those madmen were truly mad enough to declare war? Let's see—today is April twenty-fifth; we've been at war five days now. I'll confess I expect to see the Austrians marching into Paris any day now. . . ."

Gerade brought his fist down against his palm, hard.

"Don't be a fool!" he exploded. "We'll beat them. The Germanic mentality is the world's most rigid. We have the intelligence, we're natural improviseurs; and God knows we don't lack courage. . . .

"Still," Jean sighed, "as much as your offer intrigues me, there are other factors. . . ."

"Your business? How much business will you have left if we lose this war, Jean Marin? Think, man! You won't be fighting for the Jacobin Club, but for France; that should make a difference to you."

"It does," Jean said; "still . . ."

But at that moment, they both heard the whisper of Fleurette's slippers on the stairs.

She came straight over to Jean's chair, and put her arms about his neck. Jean marveled again at how quickly she had learned to move about the house with perfect surety, never bumping into the furniture or the walls.

"Forgive me, love," she said; "but my feminine curiosity got the better of me. I heard so much excited talk. . . ."

Renoir Gerade was already on his feet.

"Captain Gerade," Jean said, "may I present my wife? Fleurette, my old, old friend, Captain Renoir Gerade. . . ."

Gerade took a step forward, and put out his hand.

"You'll have to speak, M'sieur le Capitaine," Fleurette

said with perfect dignity, "for me to find you. You see, I am totally blind. . . ."

Jean saw the quick expression of pity flare in Gerade's eyes.

"I," he said in his old soldier's deep voice, "am enchanted to make your acquaintance, Madame. . . ." Then he bent and kissed her small hand.

"Please sit down, Captain Gerade," Fleurette said; "our house is honored. . . ."

"My felicitations, Jean," Renoir Gerade said. "This, I think, is the wisest thing you've ever done. As for the matters we were discussing, consider it closed. I have just met the most convincing of all reasons why you shouldn't even think of it. . . ."

He turned once more to Fleurette, and took her hand.

"Forgive me, Madame Marin," he said, "if I seem abrupt. But a soldier's time is not his own, especially now, you comprehend. Perhaps a day will come when I can give myself the great pleasure of an extended visit with my friends; but that will only be when the enemies of our country have been defeated. . . ."

"Those without—or within, Captain Gerade?" Fleurette said.

"Both, I hope," Renoir Gerade said, and smiled. "You have a ready wit, Madame. Au 'voir—I am honored to have met you. Au 'voir, Jean. . . ."

"Come, I'll walk you to the door," Jean said. "Fleurette will excuse us—won't you, dear?"

"Only if you're not too long, my Jean. I'm a terribly jealous woman, Captain Gerade. . . ."

"You have absolutely nothing to fear. . . ." Gerade said.

"I must see you again, Renoir," Jean said; "before you leave Paris. There are many things I want to talk over with you. . . ."

"That won't be difficult. Unless the enemy shows more force than he has so far, I shall scarcely leave Paris before the mobilization is complete—which will probably take until the middle of July. Speaking of seeing me, why don't you come along with me this afternoon and see the execution? I'm tremendously interested. . . ."

"I," Jean said flatly, "hate killing in any form whatsoever. What difference does it make to the victim whether they use the sword, an ax, or this infernal new invention of Doctor Guillotin's? The poor devil still loses his head. . . ."

"But this time absolutely without pain—so says the good Doctor. That appeals to me. If it works, this will be an historic day: April twenty-fifth, 1792; the first time in mankind's history that punishment was divorced from cruelty. . . ."

"If it works," Jean said drily; "they've never tried it before, remember. Besides, all pain is not physical. I should think that just the knowing that a certain exact second you were going to die—the business of being led from the cell, marching up to the platform of this new kind of fiendishness, seeing everything in readiness to stop forever your dreams, your hopes, even your simplest enjoyments like sitting in the sun—what are these things but a refinement of cruelty, Renoir? No thanks, they can test the infernal machine of the so very humane Doctor Guillotin without me!"

"*Alors,* you have much right, as usual," Gerade sighed; "but I just remembered something: Madame Roland, the wife of the Minister of the Interior, charged me with the task of bringing you to their next grand *soirée*, the first Friday in May. At the time, I didn't know you had a wife; but I'm sure that Manon Roland would be charmed with your Fleurette. I'll be the ·, of course; I never miss Manon's *soirées*. . . ."

"So," Jean smiled; "that fair Madame Roland has captured even you, Renoir? How does it feel to rub shoulders with Robespierre, Danton, Desmoulins, Petion—even Marat, I'm told?"

"They are but noises in the crowd," Gerade said. "All shades of political opinion meet at the Rolands', and Manon, by God, makes them keep peace with one another. She, I think, favors the far Left; but she's so infernally clever, one can never be sure. But I, too, have a reason for begging you to accept this invitation: Manon Roland's influence is far too great upon the young politicians who love her, even upon the old ones like Sieyès, who respect her. And her intelligence, great as it is, has one dangerous female flaw; she hates the Queen with a passion that is absolutely bottomless—which would be unimportant if Manon Roland were unimportant; but she is not. . . ."

"I'm told," Jean said, "that she's the most powerful figure in France. . . ."

"That, *mon vieux*, is scarcely an understatement. The men around her are but puppets dancing upon the wires that she pulls and how she knows to make them dance! Her ancient, pedantic fool of a husband adores her, and is consumed with jealousy of the younger men around her—particularly of Barbaroux, in which idea he is mistaken, for 'tis Leonard Buzot, who truly catches her eye. . . . *Ma foi!* What an old gossip I've become! Where was I?"

"You want me, I think," Jean said, "to dissuade this Madame Roland from continually attacking the Crown through her political henchmen. 'Tis for this, I think, that you got me an invitation to her famous *soirée*. . . ."

"Not I," Gerade swore; "I merely thought of taking advantage of matters after she had asked me. You're not unknown in Paris, Jean Marin; and even if you were, your clothes, your manners, your obvious wealth, and that romantic scar of yours would not let you remain so, long. . . ."

"Thank you," Jean laughed. "Tell Madame Roland that I accept with pleasure—but only if the invitation includes my bride. Find out about that and let me know. . . ."

"I shall," Gerade said, and put out his hand. "Au 'voir, Jean. . . ."

Fleurette was still in the *petit salon* when Jean came back. She was frowning. My little angel, Jean thought with secret amusement, has quite a temper. . . .

"What kept you so long, Jean Marin!" she snapped at him. "I don't think I like that man, for all his gruff, honest-sounding voice. I think he's a faker—and that he's arranging some scheme to take you away from me!"

"How you've changed," Jean laughed; "before we were married you scarcely ever spoke above a whisper; now listen to you! How long is it going to take you to start throwing things—like Marianne?"

"Not very long," Fleurette said, "if all the raffish characters out of your past life continue to turn up; I tell you, Jean Marin. . . ."

"That," Jean said with mock severity, "is the second time you've called me Jean Marin, and in precisely the same tone of voice. For that I claim a forfeit—" And without another word he gathered Fleurette into his arms and kissed her, hard.

For a moment she remained rigid in his arms, then the stiffness went out of her limbs, and her mouth clung softly to his. She brought her small hands up and wound her fingers into his coarse black hair.

"Forgive me, love," she whispered; "it's just that I become so afraid sometimes. . . . I remember the beggar waif I was when you found me, and when I remember, it seems so impossible that you should love me. You must be patient with me, Jean—I have so very much to learn. . . ."

"And so have I," Jean sighed; "but we'll learn together. As for Renoir, he risked his life to let me escape from a prison camp that he commanded, has remained my faithful friend up to this hour, and admires you deeply. He has gotten us an invitation to visit the famous Madame Roland. . . ."

"Oh, Jean—I couldn't!" Fleurette wailed; "I wouldn't know what to say, or how to act, or anything! I'm not even sure of my grammar, and I might fall over things, and. . . ."

"You," Jean said gravely, "will enter upon my arm. I shan't lead you into tables and vases, I assure you. You speak beautifully—and you're extravagantly lovely—more now than ever before, for which I claim full credit. . . ."

"Braggart!" Fleurette laughed, and kissed him once more. "But it's true, I guess. If happiness makes one beautiful, why then I am the most beautiful woman in all the world!"

"You are," Jean said.

These are the times, Jean Paul thought, a few days later that first week in May, when the news of the disasters of April 29 reached Paris, when no man can count his life his own. The choices I have should be simple, but no choices are simple any more. Paris is intolerable—even to remain in it is to give silent consent to abominations. . . . And now that Renoir has offered me an honorable avenue of escape, I cannot take it, because of Fleurette. To go to war, to fight in defense of one's country takes courage, but that kind of courage, I have. . . .

'Tis this other thing that I cannot bear: to know that they plot new murders, new riots, new assaults upon that poor, harmless idiot who wears the crown, that they will never desist until they gain their heart's desire—his death, and more especially that of the Queen. . . . Dear God, no drunkenness is worse than that which comes from the wine of power! Nothing touches them, nothing stops them. They hurl us into war, unprepared, bankrupt, our most skilled officers fled, our soldiery a *canaille* in arms, willing to sacrifice the country itself to their mad dreams, and madder ambitions. . . .

Fleurette came up behind his chair and let her arms rest lightly upon his shoulders, listening to the newsvenders crying in the streeet below.

"What are they shouting about, Jean?" she said.

"Dillon and Brion," Jean said, "two of Rochambeau's lieutenants, met the Austrians a few days ago near Tournai and Mons. Their troops threw down their arms and baggage, and ran like sheep. Dillon tried to stop his men. They killed him. The Austrians have crossed the frontier and taken Quiévrain. . . ."

"This is grave," Fleurette said. "Jean—"

"Yes, love?"

"That's what the captain was here to see you about, wasn't it? To get you to join the army, I mean?"

"Yes, Fleurette," Jean said.

"Why didn't you, Jean? Because of me?"

"Yes, Fleurette," Jean said.

She came slowly around in front of the chair and faced him.

"Tell me a few things, my husband," she said; "as your wife, I have a right to know. What effect will this war have upon your business?"

"If England comes in—as nearly everyone is sure she will, my business will be finished. Bad as the morale in the army is, it's worse in the fleet. We can't hope to cope with the British Navy. French merchant shipping will be swept from the seas within six months. But don't trouble yourself about that. We can live, and well, from the rents from my houses. I've bought more—at Marseille, Calais, Toulon, Bordeaux—largely because I didn't want to concentrate my capital in any one place where it would be vulnerable to mad politicians and rioters. . . ."

"Then, it's not the business, but me alone that keeps you from the fighting?"

"Yes, love," Jean smiled; "I consider you the best of all possible reasons. . . ."

"You are not afraid, I know that," Fleurette said slowly; "you're braver than a lion. Listen, my heart—you know how stubborn and bad I was about the priests and the marriage? Well, I have another faith, almost as strong —and that faith is France. I should die almost of terror and loneliness if you left me, but I should hate you, I think, and myself, if you would not go. . . ."

"Fleurette!" Jean said.

"Hear me out. Not now—the country is not truly in any great danger, despite all their shouting. These men were but lieutenants, therefore they commanded at best a few hundred men. A small battle, Jean, that these news-venders exaggerate, as they puff up everything. But if it becomes serious—if France is truly in danger, I should despise a man who put his business, his personal safety, even his love for his wife above his country. . . .

"We've done bad things in France, but the ideas that you fought for, my Jean, were good; 'twas not you and your friends who corrupted them. It's only here that the common man has a chance, now—here and perhaps in America. The Austrians and the Prussians want to turn back the clock; the world grows too old now for Kings. . . ."

Jean stared at her. That she was intelligent, he had always known; but he was astonished at her penetration.

"You're amazing!" he whispered; "I think this Madame Roland has found her match in you. . . ."

"We go there tonight, don't we?" Fleurette said. "I'm glad—I'm not afraid any more. No one will dare despise your wife, even if she is blind. . . ."

"No one would ever dream of it, Fleurette," Jean said; "that is the worst of your blindness, that you cannot realize how utterly lovely you are. . . ."

"Thank you, M'sieur my husband!" Fleurette laughed, and kissed him. "But please, Jean—if ever you feel you must go, do it! The God who blessed me with your love will never be so unkind as to take you away from me. You will come back again, covered with honor, and we will live in a new France where all men will appreciate your greatness, and respect you—as I do. . . ."

"If the need arises," Jean said slowly, "I will go, love.

I'm glad you told me this—it has lifted a burden from my mind. But I am less hopeful than you; I think we will be old, and perhaps even die before France is peaceful again. I'll tell you what I thought of: Once when I was a stripling, my father took me on a voyage to the Antilles. You have no idea how beautiful Martinique and Guadeloupe are. Haiti—Sainte-Dominique, are finished; the Negroes have burned every plantation to the ground. . . ."

"I cannot blame them," Fleurette said; "if any man tried to buy and sell me like a horse. . . ."

"Nor I," Jean sighed; "but the point is this: my father owned land on both islands. By his will, it was divided among Bertrand, Thérèse and me. When the worst of this is over, we can go there and live out our lives in peace. I would go now, but I would not forgive myself if France needed all her sons to defend her, and I had fled. . . ."

"Anywhere on earth, or under it, my Jean," Fleurette whispered; "as long as it is with you. . . ."

The salon of the Rolands, in the great house formerly occupied by Necker, was magnificent. Great mirrors glittered everywhere, so that the number of guests seemed doubled or trebled by the reflection. Manon Roland, clad in the white she nearly always wore, greeted them herself. Jean found her disappointing: in the first place, she was too plump to suit his taste; in the second, while she was indisputably pretty, her beauty had a certain coarseness about it that repelled him. It was not until she began to talk that he realized the depth of her charm. Her voice was low, beautifully modulated; and her French was a joy to hear. She used speech like a rapier, flashingly brilliant, so that Jean almost expected to see the flash of a phrase hanging blindingly in mid-air. But she detached herself quickly from young Barbaroux, late town clerk at Marseille, now becoming in his early twenties a power in France, and returned at once to Fleurette.

"Sit down, my dear," she said, "you don't know what a pleasure it is to have a lovely creature like you as my guest. My parties overflow with men who seldom bring their wives. . . ."

"I think it is because," Fleurette said clearly, "their

wives would make jealous scenes over you once they were home again. . . ."

"You little flatterer!" Manon Roland laughed. "But you, I think, have nothing to fear in that department; any man who does not adore you to the exclusion of all else is simply a fool. . . ."

"But then," Fleurette countered, "men are often fools, are they not, Madame?"

"She has wit, too!" Madame Roland said; "my felicitations, Citizen Marin, upon your choice. . . ."

"Thank you, Madame," Jean said. "I hope I caused no derangement by bringing my wife. I seem to be the only man here who did; but you understand, Madame Roland, that I have not yet grown so tired of her that I would leave her willingly for any great length of time. . . ."

Fleurette groped for his hand until she found it, and pressed it softly against her cheek.

"A pretty speech, Citizen," Manon Roland said; "and an even more charming tableau! You are fortunate—such true love is rare in our day. But don't be troubled, there are three or four other wives here. They're upstairs repairing their beauty. And there's another couple here you must meet . . . the Bethunes. . . . He's a provincial businessman, cultured, and rather handsome, too; but she! She's a doll of Dresden china, quite as lovely as your wife, but a complementary opposite, you understand. I'm sure you'll adore her. . . ."

"I have no doubt I shall," Fleurette smiled; "that is, as long as Jean doesn't too much. Then I might be tempted to pull out some of her hair. . . ."

"They're somewhere about," Manon said. "Wait here, and I'll find them. . . ."

"There'll be time," Jean said. "We'll meet your friends; but I'd like to wander about a bit, with your and Fleurette's permission, and catch the drift of the political wind. . . . You'll excuse me?"

He moved off, joining first one group then another, listening to the fierce debates being waged for or against the war. Big Georges Danton thrust a thumb in his ribs.

"Damn my soul, Marin!" he rumbled; "but that wife of yours is a pretty wench! Convenient, too—I have no doubt; at least you can pinch the maid's bottom without causing a scene. My wife raises hell!"

Jean smiled. He had long since become accustomed to Danton's healthy vulgarity.

He started to frame a jesting reply, but it never came out. Danton stared at him curiously, seeing his face drained of color, his lips moving, shaping words, but no sound coming out of them, no sound at all. . . .

"Now what the devil ails you, Marin?" Danton roared.

"I," Jean whispered, "have just seen a ghost . . . you'll excuse me, Citizen Danton?"

Then he marched away, straight toward the small girl with the silvery blonde hair who had just entered the room on the arm of a tall, distinguished man in his late fifties.

When he was close, he stopped before her, his face dark and terrible.

"Nicole!" he croaked.

She stared at him, her blue eyss widening in amazement.

"That is my name, M'sieur," she said quietly; "but how did you know it, pray? To the best of my knowledge, I've never seen you before in my life. . . ."

Jean hung there, staring from her small, well known, achingly beloved face to the dark countenance of the tall man. The man's brown eyes were troubled.

"My wife is telling the truth, Citizen," the man said drily; "you must be aware of that."

"I am," Jean said slowly; "and I confess it frightens me, M'sieur—?"

"Bethune—Claude Bethune of Marseille. Why should it frighten you, Citizen? It is, after all, a simple mistake— people often do resemble one another, you know. . . ."

"Because, Citizen," Jean said, "it makes me doubt my own sanity. This is not a resemblance, but a miracle. Unless your—your wife has a twin sister, born the same instant of the same mother—and then there is that matter of the name. . . ."

"Darling," Nicole whispered to Bethune; "perhaps he *did* know me! Perhaps he could tell us. . . ."

"Hush, child!" Bethune said. "Perhaps, Citizen, you would be so kind as to conduct us to our hostess; we have yet to pay our respects. . . ."

"Gladly," Jean said; "but permit me to introduce myself: I am Jean Paul Marin, late of Marseille, and Saint Jule. . . ."

"Marin, eh?" Claude Bethune smiled, and put out his hand; "I knew your late father well, Citizen Marin. I've even done business with him, in a small way. I am honored. . . ."

Jean shook Bethune's hand. Nicole stared at him, and clutched at her new husband's sleeve.

"Claude—" she begged.

"Later, my love," Bethune said firmly. "First we must mind our manners. . . ."

Jean led them over to Manon Roland.

"So you've met," she said; "I'm glad, I did so want you to. Citizen Marin and his wife are ideally designed for a friendship with you two. You're from the same part of France, have much the same ideals, and I do believe that you two men have captured the two loveliest women in all France. . . ."

At the mention of the word "wife," Jean could see a look of relief come into Claude Bethune's eyes.

"We should be delighted to meet the Citizeness Marin," Nicole smiled; "is she here, Citizen?"

"Come," Jean said, "I'll present you. But I must warn you of one thing: my wife is completely—blind. . . ."

He saw the quick stab of pity show in Nicole's eyes. She has not changed, he thought; she is still good and kind and lovely. But why this denial of me? And a new husband—dear God! A fine man so far as I can judge, devoted to her, as any man would be. I must write Bertrand. It has been a year or more since he mentioned Julien Lamont; but if Lamont was alive a year ago, there shouldn't be any reason for his having died since. Lamont is my age, no—younger; and as long as he remains in Austria he cannot be in any physical danger. . . .

But they had come up to the group around Fleurette now. Several of the younger men had already joined it. Buzot and Barbaroux were vying with each other to render her homage, trying to outdo each other in their gallantries. Roland de la Platière himself, Minister of the Interior, and Manon's "wife" as all the world jestingly called him, stood at Fleurette's side. He was a tall man, thin as a reed, dry, pedantic, dull. Manon had married him because in her intellectual youth, one of the co-authors of the Encyclopedia had seemed a demigod to her. But the feet of clay—that indeed the whole man was clay—had soon become apparent.

"Fleurette. . . ." Jean said.

Again that quick, vivacious lift of her small head, those darkly beautiful eyes staring straight at his face as though she could see him.

"My God!" Nicole whispered, "how incredibly lovely!"

"I want to present two new friends," Jean said slowly, "who will become old friends, I hope. Citizen and Citizeness Bethune—my wife. . . ."

Claude Bethune took Fleurette's hand and kissed it. But moved by some obscure impulse, Nicole bent forward and kissed her cheek. As she did so, Fleurette felt her tears.

"Why do you cry, *Citoyenne*?" Fleurette said.

"Forgive me," Nicole whispered, "but I am horribly impulsive. My husband says it's because I've been so ill. I wept, my dear, at the thought that eyes so beautiful could—not see. . . ."

"Nicole!" Bethune growled.

"Do not rebuke her, M'sieur," Fleurette said. "Her voice is kind, and I am quite used to pity. It is very tiresome sometimes, but only when the person pitying me does so out of a feeling of superiority. When it is sincere, when it shows real kindness, I don't mind it much. Come, *Citoyenne* Bethune, and sit by me. . . ."

Nicole came over, and the two handsome Barbaroux made a place for her.

"Look at them!" Manon Roland exclaimed; "Venus—and Diana—the opposites of perfect beauty!"

"I," Claude Bethune murmured, "would have said day —and night. But they do set each other off, don't they? Come, *Citoyen* Marin, a glass and a word with you. . . ."

Jean nodded and moved off with the provincial businessman. Glancing back, he could see Nicole and Fleurette already deep in conversation, both of them now perfectly at ease as though they had known each other all their lives.

Standing by the buffet, Claude Bethune looked at Jean with somber eyes.

"I, Citizen Marin," he said slowly, "have been dreading this day. . . ."

Jean stood there, waiting.

"I knew it would come, some time, in spite of all my hopes. I removed my residence and my business to Paris to avoid it. And here, ironically, I find it almost at once. . . ."

"I think I follow your drift," Jean Paul said. "You know nothing of your wife's past, do you?"

"No. Nor do I want to! You, Citizen Marin, are of a distinguished family. Besides you, yourself, are a man of parts and attainments. . . ."

"The flattery," Jean said drily, "is unnecessary, M. Bethune. . . ."

"I do not flatter. I have heard of you, as has anyone who has lived in Paris for any length of time. You are known as a just and honorable man; it is said that you are not wanting in mercy. 'Tis upon that I must rely. . . ."

"Mercy?" Jean said. "Why?"

"Look, I am not young. Put yourself in my place. Now late in life, I have found perfect happiness. Naturally I want to keep it."

"Naturally," Jean said.

"I have told you that I have no desire to learn of my wife's past. What is more important, I don't want her to. She has forgotten it—because, I think, it was so terrible that her mind cannot bear to contemplate it. . . ."

"It was," Jean said grimly.

"Don't tell me! This much I know. When I found Nicole, whose last name I do not yet know, she was mad. She wept day and night and could not eat. She was terribly, terribly ill—from exposure, from starvation, from—brutality. . . ."

"She had been ravished," Jean said with blunt cruelty. "that was it, Citizen Bethune?"

Naked anguish showed in Bethune's eyes, and instantly Jean was sorry. I have been hating this man, he thought, and my hatred is petty and worse. He is a man, and nowise is this his fault. . . .

"Yes—" Bethune whispered, "repeatedly. . . ."

Jean put his hand on Bethune's shoulder.

"My friend," he said gravely, and his eyes held Bethune's, "this I must tell you, because it will be good for you to know. Your wife was the finest, sweetest, and most decent of women. I knew her well. I do not lie. I will not tell you more, because there are things in her past dangerous to her present safety. But nothing in her past reflects any discredit upon her. She was, and is—an angel. . . ."

Bethune gazed at him, shrewdly.

"She was an aristocrat?" he whispered.

"A noblewoman," Jean murmured, scarcely moving his lips, "of one of the greatest families in France."

"I knew it! Her manners, her grace . . ."

"Quiet!" Jean warned. "Let one of these howling Jacobins discover that, and . . ."

"Thank you, Marin," Bethune said quietly. "You don't know what a weight you've lifted from my heart. I've tortured myself with formless jealousy—that she could have been a courtesan, for instance—they too, often have lovely manners. . . ."

"I know. That's why I told you."

"But what I fear most is the fact that my wife's mental health is still—delicate. You've seen how easily she cries. If she were reminded, if the past were brought back to her, she might easily slip back into the madness I labored so long to bring her out of. . . ."

Jean thought suddenly, bitterly, of the two little mounds of earth, of the pitiful bones of Nicole's children, brutally slain.

"You are right," he said. "I know better than you how right you are. You have my most solemn oath, *Citoyen*, that never in this life will I, do anything, say anything either to your wife, or mine, or anyone upon the face of God's earth that would cause her to be confronted with her tragic past. . . ."

Claude Bethune put out his hand. Jean took it.

"You, Marin," he said, "have my undying gratitude and my lifelong friendship. At long last I have met a man who is all that people say of him. . . ."

"Thank you," Jean smiled; "but we'd better go back now. The ladies will be getting suspicious. . . ."

"Right," Claude Bethune said.

"Jean," Fleurette said, in the carriage on their way home, "I just love that Nicole Bethune! She is the sweetest thing; I've invited her to visit me—often. . . ."

"No!" Jean got out.

"Why not?" Fleurette asked.

"I—I cannot tell you that. But take my word for it, love, we must see as little of them as possible. The connection is politically dangerous. . . ."

"Oh," Fleurette said.

The carriage moved along in silence. Just before it turned into their street, Fleurette spoke again.

"Jean," she said, "why did you lie to me?"

"I?" Jean gasped; "whatever on earth made you say that?"

"Because I know. This has nothing to do with politics. I gathered from the way the young men spoke of her that Madame Bethune is terribly beautiful. You knew her before, didn't you? Were you in love with her?"

Jean Paul stared at his wife.

"Yes," he said quietly; "to both questions—yes."

More silence. The carriage moved on, stopped before their gate.

"For God's love, Fleurette," Jean shouted; "say something!"

"Why?" Fleurette said. "What is there to say? She remembers nothing of her life before her illness. She told me that you recognized her, that she was hoping you'd tell her husband what you knew. I know now you didn't tell him, because you couldn't. I like her. That she was once in love with you is unimportant; it simply shows she has good taste. . . ."

"Thank you," Jean said drily.

"I know you're disturbed by seeing her again, but you'll get over it. I'll see to that. I'm not going to ask you how you feel about her now, because I don't think you know. You men are so terribly stupid. And that, too, is unimportant; because she's married to a man whom she loves. You, my great bear of a husband, have a wonderful sense of honor. However much you may be confused at the moment, you won't do anything about it. First because you don't even know how to play dirty tricks; and secondly because I won't let you. . . ."

Jean stared at her, wondering: Whence came this wonderful sense of security? It is, I think, because life has done all it could to her, and now she knows her strength. . . .

"I am listening, Madame General!" he mocked.

Fleurette turned to him, and took both his big hands between her own.

"I love you, Jean," she said simply, "far, far more than you'll ever love me. I know that. But I don't care. After a life of sorrow, I have finally found happiness. More than I ever dreamed possible. The whole point is I am not going to give it up. I'll fight for my happiness, fight for you—in any way I have to. I don't think this poor, half-demented woman is any threat. Even if she later becomes one, I can handle her—and I have already proved to my own satisfaction that I can manage you, without you ever knowing you're being managed. *Alors,* what are we waiting for? Help me down, my great, handsome husband of the ten thousand mysterious loves!"

Jean stared at her a long moment. Then, very slowly, he started to laugh. But it was very good laughter, lacking even mockery. Fleurette stopped it finally, by closing his laughing mouth with a kiss.

"Come," she whispered, "and I'll convince you once and for all you have no need to look at other women. For what, mon Jean, could you find abroad that you have not already—at home?"

But the Bethunes did pay them a call, and seeing Fleurette's unfeigned delight in Nicole's company, Jean knew that he was powerless to interfere. The two women struck up a sisterly camaraderie as close as that which existed between Fleurette and Marianne.

"It's a good thing," Claude Bethune pointed out; "beware of a woman who has no true feminine friends, Jean. There is sure to be a predatory streak in her character. Besides this friendship seems good for Nicole, and apparently your Fleurette enjoys it. You—you've told her nothing, I hope?"

"No," Jean smiled. "I know that much about women. They could never keep such a secret for an instant. . . ."

But he was not prepared for their becoming literally inseparable. Nicole was in his house morning, noon, and night. Seeing her laughing, gay, filled with happiness, he suffered. Seeing her, as he often did, sad, brooding, he suffered more. Often he found her blue eyes following him with accusing speculation. He had told her the first time she requested information about her past that he would not give it, simply because it was not good for her to know. She seemed to accept this, but he was more and more aware of the angry puzzlement in her eyes.

He had finally an answer to the letter he had written Bertrand:

"Of course," it read in part, "Lamont is alive. I see him frequently, poor devil. Why do you ask this? La Moyte is here, and your red-haired minx, Mlle. Talbot; she is making his life a hell—they have the most disgraceful scenes, and in public, too. . . .

"Everyone is alarmed over the war. I have finally gotten passports for Simone and myself to go to England. You've been very good about sending me monies; but now I have, I think, a wonderful scheme! Send me, if you can, all that is left of my inheritance. I will open Marin et Fils in London. You've mentioned your fear that a war with England would ruin you; here, dear brother, will be your preservation. I shall become a British citizen as soon as possible. You invest as heavily as you can in my company. Then, when the war is over—join me! You may depend upon it that an English Marin and Sons will never be swept from the seas. . . ."

There was more. But the chief things had been established. Nicole's marriage to Bethune had not a shadow of legality, honest mistake that it doubtless was. And Bertrand's scheme for salvaging the family fortunes against the wreckage of war was perfectly feasible.

But, Jean mused, is it patriotic? In the event of war, will I not be arming the sinews of the enemy? Will not even my brother become the enemy? God, it makes a man's head spin. . . .

And this other thing. It is bootless to tell Bethune that he has merely a mistress, not a wife, since it can only cause him pain and arrange nothing. . . . *Sacre bleu!* Is there nothing simple in life . . . ?

But nothing was. Already in the Legislative Assembly, the mere possession of wealth was beginning to make a man the target of unbridled attacks. It was this that beat down at last Jean's scruples against investing in Bertrand's company. If my country denies me the right to keep the money I've earned by my honest efforts, I must limit my defense of her to the bearing of arms; for in this she is not right, and I am entitled to protect myself. . . .

But it was Pierre who pointed out how alarming things had become.

"Look, my old one," he said, "I took the liberty of buying that old tenement in the Faubourg Saint-Antoine where you used to live. If they keep up their legal attacks, you're going to need it. You'd best sell that magnificent castle of yours. . . ."

"Never!" Jean growled.

"Listen, and don't be a stubborn fool! Today France is ruled by men who were failures in everything they attempted, misfits, madmen—and their politics is merely envy elevated to a religion. Tomorrow your glaring wealth may cost you your life and Fleurette's too! Pack away your fine clothes—come back to the apartment, live simply, but comfortably, loudly complain of reverses in public, and you'll be let alone. . . ."

"The day," Jean said flatly, "that I crawl into a hole because of the sewer rats of Paris, I would rather be dead. As for the vermin that currently infest the Assembly, I would not waste my spittle upon their dirty faces. In most things, *mon ami,* I have always been a man. The day they make of me a whimpering thing, dependent upon their sufferance—that day I die!"

Pierre shrugged.

"As you will, my old one," he said.

On the morning of June 20, Jean was alone in the house except for the servants. Fleurette had gone shopping with Marianne to buy certain rare silks, lately smuggled into Paris. Jean had a small office on the second floor, where he often worked alone. In truth, he had a secret set of books there which alone showed the true state of his business, kept there under lock and key far from the prying eyes of the bureaucracy. The manservant knocked on the door.

"Madame Bethune is below," he said.

Jean groaned inside his heart. How can I see her, he thought, like this—alone? Every time I look at her my whole body tingles with memory. I think that sometimes she almost remembers too—I have surprised upon her face certain expressions like—like tenderness. My imagination, perhaps. . . .

He got up from his chair, patted a glossy lock of hair back into place, and went down the stairs.

Nicole put out her small hand to him.

"Fleurette is not here?" she said.

Slowly Jean shook his head.

"Then I must go," Nicole said nervously.

"Why?" Jean said mockingly; "are you afraid of me?"

Nicole studied his dark, scarred face.

"Yes," she whispered.

"Why?" Jean Paul said. "My face?"

"No. I—I don't know. Ring for some coffee, M. Marin, and I'll try to explain. . . ."

Jean opened the door to the *petit salon.*

"Entrez, Madame," he said.

Nicole sat on the edge of her chair staring at him. Jean didn't say anything until after the servant brought the coffee. Then, very sadly, he smiled.

"You were going to tell me why you feared me," he said.

"Must I?" Nicole whispered; "it is, I think, a shameful thing. . . ."

"As you like," Jean said gravely; "I would never press you. . . ."

Nicole stiffened, and her eyes flashed blue fire.

"I'll tell you," she said. "Perhaps I'm wrong. At any rate, I sicken of it—the way I feel, I mean. I love my husband. He is the kindest, the best of men. But my past is a blank. I must ask you one thing: was I ever, in my past life—married to you, perhaps?"

"No," Jean said.

"Then I am mad!" Nicole whispered in pure horror.

"Why do you think that?" Jean said.

"Because, because—oh, Jean, I cannot say it!"

"You called me Jean," he pointed out, "you've never done that before. . . ."

"Never before to you. But how many million times to myself when I am alone! I have had to stop myself on the brink of calling my husband 'Jean.' You ask me why I fear you; the answer is that I don't—'tis myself I fear! I look at you and my hands yearn to stroke your face, in some old, old way—as though they have done it—how many times before?—as though they were accustomed to the feel. I see your mouth, your wild, terrible mouth, forever smiling as though it mocked God and Satan, and I know, I know precisely how your kisses feel. . . ."

She bent her head and gave way to wild and soundless weeping.

Jean sat there frozen, not daring to move.

She straightened up, looking at him, her eyes twin sapphires, her cheeks diamond-streaked.

"I love my husband. I have loved him with my body, dutifully, as a good wife should. But Jean, tell me, have you a scar from an old wound—a pistol shot, I think, on your back, to the left, just below your ribs?"

"Yes," Jean said grimly, "I have."

"How did I know that? Tell me how? How could I know your body as I know my own? I am a decent woman; but I know your skin is bronzed and silken smooth with but the lightest down of hair upon your chest. I know your arms are like bands of steel, and your mouth, your mouth. . . ."

She stood up wildly.

"Let me go!" she screamed, "let me out of here!"

Jean stood up and moved aside.

"I have not detained you," he said; but the next instant she was in his arms.

He tasted her mouth, sweet and tearsalt at the same time, wild, swiftmoving, terrible, tender, whispering muffled words against his own:

"Jean, my Jean, mine! How and when and where I do not know—but mine! I am a beast, a she-thing beast, unworthy to touch poor Fleur's finger tips, but, Jean, Jean, Jean . . ."

The door opened quietly.

"You'll forgive the intrusion," Renoir Gerade said quietly; "but this is truly important, Jean. . . ."

They sprang apart. The slow red started at the line of Jean Paul's jaw and crawled upward into the roots of his hair.

"Oh come now, Jean!" Renoir laughed; "I'm not the public censor; besides there is no time. Mademoiselle will excuse us, I know. . . ."

Nicole snatched her hat from the little table, and fled wildly through the door.

"You certainly have good taste," Renoir said with tolerant amusement.

"Look Renoir," Jean Paul spluttered; "I didn't, I wouldn't . . ."

"I would," Renoir mocked. "Besides you were both fully clothed in the *petit salon,* so what's the odds? Of course, in your own house with a chance that your wife might return any moment—I'm afraid I must condemn your folly; your morals I haven't any right to—mine are far worse!"

"What did you come to see me about?" Jean growled.

"The mob has invaded the Tuileries. They're holding both the King and Queen prisoners, trying to provoke them into doing something, I think, that will give those fiends from hell an excuse to assassinate them. The guards are unreliable—except the Swiss; so some of us are going there to try to talk them out of it and foil the Jacobins, and Girondins; if not, we can die, if need be, in their defense. . . ."

Jean walked out of the salon and mounted the stairs. When he came down, two minutes later, he had his hat, his pistols, and his cane.

"I'm ready," he said.

He was one of the small group who assigned themselves to the apartment of the Queen. By so doing he missed Louis' quiet heroism in refusing to revoke his vetoes, in accepting the sword and waving it above his head, shouting *"Vive la Nation!"* with perfect dignity, wearing even the red cap without seeming a fool, until he melted them finally, sending them away after Petion's base and cowardly speech, without having budged an inch from his principles.

But Jean saw Marie Antoinette demonstrate what greatness was; a prostitute, one of the worst *poules* of the Palais Royal, stopped before her and screamed at her:

"Autrichienne! Étrangère! Sale putaine, ordure de toutes les choses sales; bête et fille de sottise, vieille poule!"

The Queen looked at her steadily.

"Have I ever done you any harm?" she said.

"No, but it is you who do so much harm to the nation!" the *poule* shrieked.

"You have been deceived," the Queen said quietly. "I married the King of France. I am the mother of the Dauphin. I am a Frenchwoman. I shall never again see my own country. I shall never be happy or miserable anywhere but in France. When you loved me, I was happy then."

To Jean's vast astonishment, the *poule* burst into great tears.

"Ah, Madame," she sobbed; "forgive me! I did not know you. I see you've been very good. . . ."

Santerre, the revolutionary brewer of Saint-Antoine section, seized her roughly by the arm.

"The girl's drunk!" he growled, and shoved her away from the Queen with all his force.

Jean Paul stepped over to him.

"Santerre," he murmured, through half-closed lips; "I know why you did that. You don't want them swayed, do you?"

"Hell no!" the brewer spat.

"I do. Open those flabby lips of yours again, and I'll put a double ounce of lead through your guts. And don't tell me your friends will tear me to pieces; I don't care about that. I came here prepared to die. . . ."

Santerre stared at him.

"And whatever they do," Jean measured out the words, flat, calm, expressionless; "will aid you not at all. For by then, my friend, you will be dead."

Santerre moved away from him quickly. The last Jean saw of him, he was moving through the doorway.

Jean came back to the Queen's side.

"Thank you, M. Marin," Marie Antoinette said.

When the ordeal was over at last, after endless hours, Jean Paul sought out Renoir Gerade.

"Renoir," he said tiredly, "enroll me in your company. I'll report for drill tomorrow. . . ."

"Good!" Renoir smiled. Then: "I'd wager that half the army is made of men who are running away from something. . . ."

"What the devil do you mean?" Jean said.

"You know as well as I do," Renoir mocked, "so why should I bother to tell you?"

By the time they left Paris finally, marching away northward toward death and glory, Jean Paul had become truly a soldier. They marched down the Champs Élysées that thirtieth day of July, and behind them, entering the

city came the formidable Marseillaise, brigands all, roaring
Rouget de Lisle's new "Song of War for the Army of
the Rhine."

Jean heard the sound of it like a trumpet call, roaring
through his blood:

> "Aux armes, citoyens!"
> Formez vos bataillons!
> Marchons, marchons. . . ."

It was great, stirring, sublime. He could just make out
Fleurette's dark head, with Nicole's fair one resting
against her shoulder.

But he was already too far away to see their tears.

15

Jean Paul Marin lay on his filthy bed in the military hospital atop Montmartre, staring out of his window at the windmills. He had arrived in Paris two days ago on October first, 1793, a year and two months after he had marched away toward death or glory. He stared at the windmills, paying no attention to the shrieks and groans and curses of the wounded men around him. The windmills reminded him of the heroic defense of Valmy, for there had been a windmill on top of that historic hill. Valmy was the only battle which he remembered well, because it was his first. After that, all the others ran together in the flux of time, so that he could never remember whether he had done a thing at Jemappes, or Neerwinden, or Mainz, or Verdun or even Hondeschoote. It didn't matter really; the mind had a way of insulating itself away from horror.

Like Nicole, he mused. She saw her children killed—and Marie, her maid. Strange that I didn't remember that the girl was blonde, too; a wisp of hair, and immediately I accepted, despaired. I never really looked at Marie. I knew she was fair, fat; but that one cannot tell from a skeleton. Poor Marie—there was devotion in that—sacrifice. Why was she wearing Nicole's clothes? Why else indeed except to lead those hounds of hell astray and give her mistress a chance to escape. God bless you, poor Marie; if there is a God who appreciates devotion, and rewards sacrifice. . . .

No one will ever know, I guess, what happened to her between the time the château was burned, and the morning that Claude Bethune found her sleeping in his stable, a pitiful wreck of a woman who knew not even her name. . . .

Fleurette will come for me, as soon as she gets my

letter. The orderly posted it yesterday—she should have it
by now. I wonder if she's changed—everything else has.
. . . Strange to have left a kingdom, and return to a
republic. A republic of regicides. Poor Louis! 'Tis said he
died bravely—after all those terrible months with his family at the Tower of the Temple Prison, he could still
manage it. I wonder if it's true that they've taken the
Queen away from her children at the Temple and lodged
her at La Conciergerie? If so—it's the end for her,
too. . . .

God, God, how changed everything is! The King guillotined, Dumouriez a traitor, fled to Austria, Marat murdered in his bath by a chit of a girl—bless her, whoever
she is! And Robespierre master of France, with even
Danton unable to stand against him. . . .

And I, coming back to it all, not because of my twenty-
three honorable scars—I walked off the field at Hondeschoote with those scratches, but from wound fever, and
this persistent sickness—la grippe, they call it.

He took the medal that General Houchard had given
him on the field for conspicuous gallantry in action, and
looked at it. Then he drew back his arm and tossed it
weakly through the window. He hadn't been gallant, but
merely foolhardy, leading a wild charge of skirmishers
against the enemy's flank because he thought he recognized the officer opposing him as Gervais la Moyte. He
turned the flank, but he never reached la Moyte or his
double, because one of the Austrian batteries laid a barrage dead center on his company, and only five of them
came out alive, and of that five, he was the only one who
hadn't been badly hurt.

He had gotten twenty-three small pieces of shrapnel in
his body. He had been quite impressively bloody; but the
wounds actually were only surface wounds, because he
had been further away from the blast than anyone else.
It had been the infections and the chill afterwards that
had gotten him—not the wounds themselves. Once the
sickness had gone, he would be as good as new. He
couldn't quite forgive himself that, for although his charge
had turned the flank against the Austrians and the English
(who had come into the war in February, 1793, along
with the Spanish and the Dutch, making the ring of fire
around France complete, and ruining Jean's shipping busi-

ness in the bargain with their blockades) and contributed to winning the notable victory at Hondeschoote, he had lost almost his entire company. . . .

"Murderer," he snarled at himself, and turned away from the window. The military hospital atop Montmartre was like any military hospital in the 1790's; if a man survived it, he was obviously born to be guillotined. The food, what there was of it, would have disgraced a pigsty. The bed they had put Jean Paul into had still on its tattered sheets the rusty stains of the blood of the last poor devil who had coughed out his life there. But the worst thing of all was the stench. It was compounded of the smell of gangrene, the foulness of human excreta, and the fetid odors of sick, unwashed bodies. All day and all night there was a ceaseless parade of corpsmen removing the bodies of the men who had died to make room for the wounded being brought home from the front.

In three days, Jean Paul got rapidly worse; on the fourth, Fleurette appeared, with Pierre and Marianne, having only that morning received the letter that Jean had sent her the day after he arrived. The hospital authorities were only too glad to release a wounded man into the custody of his wife; they needed every available bed.

Fleurette was superb. She didn't even cry. She sat in the hired carriage, and cradled his filthy, vermin-infested head against her shoulder, and stroked his bearded face with an almost maternal joy. She talked to him with her soft, sweet voice, but he did not hear her; he had slipped into a state somewhere between sleep and unconsciousness, coming out of it long enough to mutter a few unintelligible words, as he was lifted from the carriage and carried up the stairs.

When he did awake, finally, it was the afternoon of the next day, and the sunlight was pouring in through his window. Fleurette was sitting beside his bed, but he came awake so quietly that she was not aware of it. He lay very still and looked at her, seeing her changed a little by sorrow, by loneliness; but seeing too that it was merely a change, not a diminution of beauty. She has gained in dignity, he thought; but there is something strange about her. . . .

After a time, he saw what it was: the clothes she was wearing were of poor quality, such as any Parisian housewife of the lower classes would wear; and looking quickly away from the clothes, he saw that it was not to the magnificent *hôtel particulier* he had bought for Fleurette that they had brought him, but to his old, dingy flat.

He shifted his weight a little to ease the dull ache in his body. Small as the motion was the sound of it came over to Fleurette.

"Jean?" she whispered.

"Yes, love," he said gently.

"Jean," she whispered, "my Jean—you're back now, really back—and I'll never let you go again!"

She groped across the coverlet until she found his face, and bending across him kissed him slowly, lingeringly, tenderly, as if all of life were to be found upon his mouth. He brought up his arms and drew her to him, holding her against him, like that, stroking her head with one hand and smiled at her as though she could see him.

"You're stronger," she said. "You were so weak last night that I quite despaired. But Pierre insisted that you'd be all right. I held your head while Pierre shaved off that horrible beard; but it took all four of us to bathe you. Pierre did most of the work; he turned you this way and that, while we women scrubbed you as gently as we could. . . ."

"Four of you?" Jean gasped; "women?"

"Of course, silly! Marianne, and Nicole Bethune and I. Three women, and Pierre. That makes four, doesn't it?"

"Nicole!" Jean whispered; "Name of God!"

"Oh don't be so modest," Fleurette laughed. "We're all old married women, remember. And you really aren't anything so much to look at any more, my Jean. You're just skin and bones—and not too much skin either, from what they tell me. Marianne says you're as full of holes as a sieve. . . ."

"What did Nicole say?" Jean growled.

"Nothing much. She just cried. She's very tender-hearted; and besides I don't think she's ever really gotten over being in love with you. I can understand that. 'Tis a fatal sickness from which one rarely recovers. . . ."

"And you," Jean muttered; "have you recovered from it?"

She put her mouth so close to his that he could feel the stirring of her breath.

"No," she whispered; "it is the disease that I shall die of. . . ."

She lay there very quietly against him. They didn't talk any more. They just lay there very quietly and watched the sunlight pour through the window, and heard the noises from the Rue Saint-Antoine, far off and faint as though they came from another world.

"I hope," Fleurette said gently, "that I shall never learn to hate Nicole Bethune. . . ."

"Could you?" Jean said.

"No—not now. That is, nothing she could ever do would ever make me hate her. Only you could make me do that. . . ."

"I?" Jean said; "how, Fleurette?"

"By forgetting a vow you made. The best, the most beautiful vow on earth—'Forsaking all others. . . .'"

"I have not forgotten it," Jean said. He looked at her gravely, tenderly. "Fleurette, why are we here?" he said.

"Because of those terrible men: Robespierre, but more than he, Chaumette and Hébert. It has become dangerous in France to have a nice house, and pretty dresses, and money. I—I closed our house, Jean. Pierre advised me to. When they want to get rid of a man, nowadays, all they have to do is to accuse him of 'incivisme'—a term that includes everything from dressing neatly to owning a carriage and hiring servants. The ideal now is to be slovenly, dress like a dock hand like the Montagnards, and use foul language to prove you're of the people. A person can be attacked in the streets for dressing too well. So I packed away our things, and gave up the house. Besides, we can't really afford it, now. . . ."

"And the business?" Jean whispered.

"Gone. The English blockade ended it months ago. We have only your rents to live upon now, Jean—and only a few of those; because it has become common practice to denounce one's landlord as a monopolist, a capitalist, or for the all-embracing crime of *incivisme* when one doesn't want to pay one's rent. It doesn't matter, really—with money, or without it, one starves. There is no bread to be bought; business of all kinds is at a standstill; Paris has become a hell. . . .

"Pierre manages to keep a few men working; but Claude Bethune has lost everything; were it not for Pierre's charity, and mine, he and Nicole would have starved long ago. *Alors*—enough of sadness; everything is going to be all right, now that you're home again. . . ."

"I hope so," Jean Paul whispered. "God knows I hope so. . . ."

But everything was not going to be all right. On October 14, in spite of every argument that his friends could advance to dissuade him, Jean Paul forced them to take him in a wheelchair to the gallery of the Revolutionary Tribunal to witness the beginning of the trial of the Queen. Still too weak to walk, he was pushed up the gallery steps by Pierre du Pain and Claude Bethune. The three women walked behind their husbands, their faces white and set. Fleurette walked in the middle, with Nicole and Marianne holding her arms. None of them spoke— there was no need for words. For they all were breathing the same silent prayer:

"Dear God, let him control himself! Please God, don't let him say anything!"

The prayer was futile and they knew it. From the moment that Hébert rose and made his monstrous accusations to which the Queen refused with regal contempt to even reply, Nicole and Marianne could see that nothing on earth or from the bowels of hell itself was going to restrain Jean Paul from speaking out in defense of this great lady he had come to venerate. But Marie Antoinette needed not even Jean's help.

The indictment read, she answered it regally, calmly, making ridiculous every charge that besotted satyr made. But to that one hideous charge she made no reply. Fleurette could hear the quickening of Jean Paul's breathing. A juryman stood, snarling:

"Widow Capet, why have you not answered this charge, too?"

The Queen stared at him.

"I have not replied," she said slowly, "because Nature itself refuses to answer to such a charge brought against a mother." Then turning toward the women seated in the galleries, she threw up her arms and cried out: "I appeal to every woman here who has ever borne a child!"

And the whole gallery was loud with the sobbing of the women seated there.

At once Herman, President of the Tribunal, shouted for silence; and began to roar out the charges in his coarse, brutal voice.

Before he was half done, they heard the creak of Jean Paul's wheelchair as he pushed it back. He stood up, tottering, his face white as death with rage and weakness; but before he could open his mouth to get a word out, Nicole hurled herself upon him, hurling him back into his chair, clamping both her small hands over his mouth, crying:

"Don't Jeannot, for God's love don't speak! They will only kill you, too, and I could not bear that! Please, Jeannot, please, please, please!"

He brought his hands up to unclamp her fierce fingers, but he could not tear them away from his mouth. And suddenly it was all too much, the realization of his own weakness, the sight of that sublime woman below, guilty at worst of a certain amount of normal folly, being hounded to death by the worst pack of scoundrels who ever disgraced the name of humanity, so that the great knot of sickness and disgust and shame, the feeling of shared guilt inside his heart burst like a torn wound, and the great tears splashed over Nicole's hands.

She released him, and stepped back; but he didn't make an outcry, or say anything, but sat there, a great, broken hulk of a man weeping quietly with an anguish that was real and terrible and absolutely impossible to bear.

Pierre nodded to Claude Bethune. The two of them caught hold of the wheelchair and pushed him out of the gallery, bumping him down the long flight of stairs, so that each of the twenty-three red, freshly healed scars stabbed him anew, and he, loose against the chair, his head lolling upon his neck, the unashamed tears penciling his scarred face, took again the indignity of his helplessness without a murmur of complaint, knowing these things to be nothing, and less than nothing compared with the big, the terrible, the insufferable pain inside his heart.

He was home again, and in bed, with Fleurette bathing his face before a vagrant oddity of the morning came to his attention.

Jeannot, he thought, Nicole called me Jeannot. I wonder if she's beginning to remember?

It was two weeks before he was able to leave his bed again. And it was good that this was so. Of October 16, he heard only the noise and shouting in the streets. Fleurette and Marianne stayed with him, but Pierre went, drawn by the subtle fascination of horror to the former Place Louis XV, become now the Place de la Révolution, the statue of Louis XV pulled down, and a huge plaster figure of Liberty set up in its place, through the thirty thousand foot and horse drawn up in double rows to prevent insurrection, waiting there in the dense-packed crowds, seeing and hearing all the elements of tragedy, of drama become commonplaces, the high, two-wheeled cart creaking through the crowd, the tricoteuses, the knitting women, sitting about the scaffold, counting the fall of heads without dropping a stitch, the drumrolls, great Samson waiting by the infernal machine of the merciful Doctor Guillotin, and the cart finally appearing across the bridge from the Île de la Cité and the grim Conciergerie, and she sitting there, dressed in white, her hands tied behind her like a common criminal.

She looked very tired and very old, her hair snow-white now, despite her mere thirty-eight years; but enwrapped all the same in majesty, in dignity so complete, so serene, that it cut off from her the rabble, the screaming, the shouting, the obscenities roared at her, as though they had never been. They knew, after a time, that they could not reach her, which enraged them so that they redoubled their efforts. Beside her, on the cart, the constitutional priest in lay clothes, stood, mumbling Latin, but she ignored him with a contempt that was absolute, holding him schismatic, traitor to her faith, dirt, and less.

She mounted the scaffold with a firm step. Samson bound her to the plank. Pierre saw only part of the rest of it, for at the roar of *Vive la République!* he glanced once quickly at the dripping thing that Samson was holding high so that the mob might see, and moved away through the crowd, his whole body shaking with loathing and disgust.

So died Marie Antoinette, Queen of France. For with all their Widow Capets, and Austrian Tigress, and other less printable epithets, they could not take that away from her. Queen she was, and remained; and never was she more queenly than upon the day of her dying.

By the first week in November, Jean was up and about, walking with the aid of a stout stick. He was well now. A certain weakness lingered; but that, time and care would cure. What nothing would cure was his horror of idleness.

He walked through the streets at all hours, taking upon himself the endless, daylong search for bread, going from one *quartier* to another—sometimes accompanied by Claude Bethune, who, like Jean, had had his business cut from under him by the Revolution—but usually alone, which he preferred, in the hope of finding enough loaves for Pierre, Marianne, Fleurette and himself. For it was not the lack of money that troubled them chiefly, but the dearth of supplies; assignats, or even gold, when there was no bread to be had, made a most insubstantial diet. . . .

He took his place, that morning at the end of the long line standing before the baker's shop. He was aware that probably long before he reached the door, all the bread would be sold. Still, one had to chance things like that, and it was much better for him to do it than to send Fleurette to suffer the shoving and buffeting of the hungry crowd.

He didn't have to wait long. The baker appeared before half the crowd had reached his door.

"No more, *mes enfants!*" he said pleadingly, "believe me, there is no more!"

An angry mutter ran through the crowd. Jean Paul caught the words "Hoarder! Aristocrat!" "All the bakers have become aristocrats!" a woman said.

"My children!" the baker half wept, "come, see for yourselves! The store is empty. Search my house if you will! My own wife and children weep from hunger! I would bake more loaves if I had the wheat!" His face was red with anger, suddenly.

"Go there and search for your hoarders!" he cried. "Lantern those who let the grain come into Paris in trickles, and that of bad quality! Hang them, not your neighbor and your friend who has lived among you all these years!"

"He has right," a man said. "*Alors*, good François, try to have some bread for us tomorrow."

"That I will," the baker said; "but come early, *mes pauvres*—I cannot promise to supply you all—only the first ones here can get the bread. . . ."

The crowd melted away, muttering. Jean turned to continue his endless search for one baker in Paris who might have a moldy loaf to sell him, when he saw Nicole coming toward him, clutching a precious flute, as the long loaves were called, to her bosom.

"Come, Jean," she said, "walk me home, and you can have half, no, three-quarters for your family—as you have the greater need. With you along they won't dare snatch it away from me. I've been robbed of bread twice already this week. . . ."

Jean fell into step beside her, putting much of his weight upon his stick. Nicole stepped lightly along, glancing at him out of the corner of her blue eyes. When they reached the miserable tenement in which she and her husband lived, she turned to him, smiling.

"Come up with me, Jean," she said.

"Is Claude at home?" Jean demanded.

"No. He has left Paris—to try his luck elsewhere. He has gone back to Provence—to Marseille to see if he cannot begin again far from the eye of these monsters here in Paris. . . ."

Jean shuddered, thinking of the news from the Midi and Provence. The Republican armies were putting down the good people of the Vendée and the Côte (both of which had revolted against the Government), with every refinement of cruelty. In Marseille, even the guillotine had proved too slow; there, and in Lyon, the Republicans were using massed fusillades to slaughter two hundred people at a volley.

"No, Nicole," he said, "I will not come up."

"Is it," she whispered, "because I called you—Jeannot, that time before the Tribunal? I don't know why I said that, but once I did, I knew I had said it before—a thousand, thousand times before. . . . 'Tis that I used to call you, is it not?"

"Yes," Jean growled.

"Jean—Jeannot—please come up for just a little while. I shall be good. It—It's just that I'm so lonely; besides, today, I'm afraid as well. . . ."

"Afraid?"

"I've had all day the strange feeling that I've been followed. I know I'm subject to fancies; but this time I'm almost sure. Twice I caught a glimpse of this man, but each time he hung back, or dashed out of sight around a corner. I know—I can see from your face that you think I'm imagining things. I swear I am not; and the oddest part about it all, my Jean, is that there was something oddly familiar about this man. . . ."

"Familiar?" Jean growled.

"Yes, yes! I know him—I have known him well! He is someone out of my past life, the past I don't remember; someone I knew longer, and even better than I knew you; you see, Jeannot, I did not recognize you at first, but this man I recognized instantly. That's why I want you to stay with me a while, Jean. I'm so terribly afraid!"

Jean studied her small, oval face. Whether or not she had imagined this man from her past, her fear at least was real.

"All right," he growled, and the two of them mounted the stairs.

The stark poverty of the little room tore at his heart. It was very clean, but it lacked almost every kind of comfort. Nicole moved about, setting before him bread, cheese, even a scrap of meat, and a tall bottle of wine. Jean drank some of the wine, knowing that it at least was plentiful; but the other things he would not touch, rightly guessing that they had been saved for her supper.

She sat there gazing at him, devouring him with her eyes.

"Jean," she whispered, "when are you going to tell me —about me, I mean—about us?"

"Never," Jean said quietly. "Perhaps one day you will remember it yourself. I pray God you never do. Not that it was wickedness, but that it was very sad, and terrible. You're better not knowing—little Nicole. . . ."

She got up and came over to where he sat.

"But I do know so many things," she said slowly; "my —my body remembers, not my mind. Let me come near you—like this, and I tingle all over. . . ."

"Then don't come near me," Jean Paul said.

She stared at him, pain clouding her clear blue eyes.

"Why do you hate me?" she whispered. "Was it something I did—before?"

"I don't hate you," Jean said gravely. "I was in love with you once. Perhaps I still am. But I have a wife who is one of God's own angels. You are married to a fine and upright man. What was, is dead and buried. Let's leave it that way, please. . . ."

"No," Nicole said. "I—I cannot. God help me, Jean, I cannot! I am a woman, and morality to a woman is always something she accepts as long as it does not interfere with the way her heart feels. Let it interfere, and she tosses it out the window without a qualm. I love your Fleurette; I—I respect Claude. But I would betray them both this instant if you were to stretch out your hand to me. . . ."

Jean sat quite still, looking at her.

"Even though you won't stretch it out," she breathed, and sought his mouth blindly, in a kiss so savage, so pain-filled, hungry, that all his evasions were nothing, and less, his big hands coming up against his will, despite his will, and she clinging to him, crying, thrusting her hand inside the rough cloth of his shirt, and letting her fingers trail achingly, lingeringly, over his body, caressing each ridge of scar tissue, until he stood up, and moved by something close to pure terror, thrust her aside, and ran from the room and down the stairs.

But he could not go home. The confusion inside his mind and heart drove him on through the dark and twisting streets of Paris under the pitiless stars. He had to be alone. He did not want to consider the matter, or think about his relationship to Fleurette, or his own position in the ghastly travesty that life had become. He did not want to think at all; he wanted merely to be alone, because then, at that moment, the presence of any other person upon earth, loved or hated, or simply not cared about, was intolerable to him. What he needed was the silence and the dim streets and the far stars. Some dim, monastic impulse drove him, and blindly he obeyed it.

He came back to his own flat late the next morning to find a visitor awaiting him. He stared at the man with dull curiosity, conscious that this face was familiar, but not knowing where in his past to place it until the man spoke.

"You're Marin, aren't you?" the man said. "You shouldn't leave your flat unlocked. Deuced careless of you. . . ."

"You waited," Jean said, "so obviously you're not a thief."

"No," the man said evenly, "but perhaps a murderer. My name is Julien Lamont, Marquis de Saint Gravert, and I have come to kill you." Then very quietly he produced a long pistol already cocked, and pointed it straight at Jean Paul's heart.

Jean stared at his visitor for a long moment; then, leaning upon his stick, he eased himself down into a chair. Julien Lamont remained still, the pistol steady in his hand.

Jean let a slow chuckle escape his lips, then he began to laugh, the sound of it mocking, terrible, demonic, and Lamont, hearing it stared at him in astonishment and dismay, letting the muzzle of the pistol droop a little.

"Are you mad?" he whispered; but his words came too late, for Jean lashed out suddenly with terrible accuracy, and smashed his heavy stick across Lamont's wrist, sending the pistol spinning across the room.

"Now," he said easily, pleasantly, "we can discuss the matter. But first, some wine. I must tender you the hospitality of my house. . . ."

He got up, walked across the room and retrieved the pistol. He eased the hammer down out of cock, and lifting the striking plate, dug the priming powder out. Then he gave the weapon back to Lamont.

"I don't think you'll want to kill me after we've talked," he said quietly, "but God knows you'll need that pistol in Paris. . . ." Then he got the bottle and the glasses down from the cupboard.

"Why did you laugh?" Lamont demanded.

"Because your face was familiar," Jean smiled; "but I didn't recognize the familiarity until after you introduced yourself. Your face is my own, before this scar. . . ."

Lamont stared at him, seeing that what he said was true. He took the goblet Jean offered him.

"Now," Jean said, "why did you want to kill me?"

"Because of Nicole. Almost a year ago, Lucienne Talbot told me I was a fool to believe that she had remained faithful to me. I—I thought her dead, but a little before that time, a scoundrelly rascal, fallen out of favor here, crossed the border, and gave me evidence that she was still alive. When I told Gervais about it, Lucienne laughed and said: "Seek her in Paris—for that's where Jean Paul Marin is. . . ."

"So you came," Jean said.

"As soon as I could. It was hellishly difficult. Took me four months to get the necessary forged papers. Another month to get here. The rest of the time I spent searching Paris street by street. I didn't dare ask questions—my speech, my tone of voice alone would have betrayed me. . . ."

"But you found her."

"Yes. I met her in the street, but she pretended not to recognize me. It was then that I began to believe Lucienne. So I followed her—for days. And yesterday evening, I saw her go up with you into her place—and remained. . . ."

Jean could have heard, had he been less intent upon his visitor, the sound that Fleurette made outside on the landing, where she stood, listening to their voices. It would have been familiar to him. He had heard it many times upon the battlefield. All death rattles—even this soft one in a woman's throat, sound curiously alike.

"Why didn't you come up?" Jean said.

"I was afraid of what I might find. I knew in my rage I would kill both of you. And I don't want to kill Nicole. I only want to forgive her, and take her back. . . ."

"Noble of you," Jean mocked, "but you haven't actually anything to forgive her for. Had you waited ten minutes, you would have seen me come down again. . . ."

Why do you lie, oh my husband? Fleurette cried inside her heart. You're not afraid of him, so why do you lie? All night long—with her—with her! Oh, dear God—

Then she turned, and fled wildly down the stairs, heedless of the fact she could not see.

"You came down?" Julien breathed, hope in his voice. "Now really, Marin . . ."

"Look!" Jean roared at him; "I've had enough of this nonsense! Your wife is a sick woman, Lamont. She is not feigning loss of memory—she is today more than half mad. Had you remained at home and protected her and your children like a husband should, she would not be in this state today. For it was seeing your infants murdered that did this thing to her—"

"Infant Jesus!" Julien wept. "Marin, for God's love . . ."

Jean put out his hand and touched his shoulder.

"I'm sorry," he said. "That was cruel of me. Your wife is my wife's best friend. I've tried to do all I could to protect, and help her—that's all. I loved her once, long before you married her; but what I feel for her today is— pity. . . ."

"Forgive me," Julien Lamont said, "I didn't know. . . ."

"But now you do. One word of advice, M. Lamont. Leave Paris at once. The life of a noble is not worth a candle here."

"I knew that," Lamont whispered, "and I risked it! But now more than ever I cannot go until I can take Nicole with me."

"Your affair," Jean shrugged; "but for God's sake be careful. If you must be guillotined, don't drag her along with you. We're very fond of Nicole, my wife and I. . . ."

"Thank you," Julien Lamont said, and took Jean's outstretched hand.

When, after a sleepless night of waiting, it was dawn finally, Jean got up and went to Pierre's flat. Marianne opened the door, the barest crack, and looked at him, contempt written all over her broad face.

"You," she spat, "go away from here, Jean Marin! She doesn't want to see you!"

"Would you," Jean said angrily, "have the decency to tell me why?"

"As if you didn't know! What some women won't do to steal another's husband! And the poor thing blind, at that. Nobility certainly doesn't help a woman's morals, does it, Jean Marin? Well, I hope you enjoyed yourself, because it has cost you your wife!"

Then she slammed the door in his face, and shot the bolts home. Nor would she open it, not even to his thunderous barrage of knocking.

"God in heaven!" Jean swore. "Who on earth would have ever thought of this!"

Then he turned and went out of the building, walking like a man very tired, and very old.

16

He knew where to find her; that was not the difficult part. The clothing business that she and Marianne and Pierre had founded could weather the storm produced by the absurd measures introduced by the Hébertists and the Montagnards, so Fleurette was not faced with the drastic necessity of becoming once more a flower-seller in the streets. Her wants were few; and even with the reduced earnings of the firm that fall of 1793 and winter of 1794, Fleurette was adequately provided for. That she would take refuge with the du Pains, he had known at once; what he had not known was that no protestations on his part, no pleas would change her icy resolve.

And this I gave her, he thought bitterly, this iron pride in herself. Yet I would not have it otherwise. I transformed her from a beggarmaid into a woman, nay, more, into a princess; and though this transformation now defeats me utterly, it is still a fine thing, and a true one. . . .

It came to him, finally, as he walked back toward his lonely flat after his fifth or sixth attempt to see her, that this situation had its value: there was nothing like depriving a man of a thing to make him appreciate it. He knew now with absolute certainty that he loved Fleurette, that this love had nothing to do with pity or his desire to protect her or her blindness or any of a half-dozen irrelevancies. She is a woman now, he thought; she has mastered her blindness; more than that, she has mastered life. For what one refuses to submit to is the measure of one's conquest of living, and Fleurette from the beginning with simple firmness has refused to bow to anything that she holds wrong. . . . She is braver than I. She would have given me up or died before saying her vows before a constitutional priest. She loves me still, I think; but she will give me up rather than submit to the profanation of our love, or take another woman's leavings. . . . I could go to Nicole, and have her tell Fleurette the truth; but what good would that do? Fleurette would believe her, I think, even less than she believes me. 'Tis a thing too difficult to explain, and I am caught up in a truth that nobody, not even Pierre will believe—that I walked the streets all night, because I was confused and troubled and wanted to be alone. . . .

He gave vent to a burst of bitter laughter, thinking how much better a facile lie would have served. But about this thing he would not lie; he had seen too often how a noble end had been dirtied by the means used to attain it. He could live; he had his few rents, and hidden still a large part of the money his father had left him, though that he could not use since the coinage had been changed. To melt the gold down was likewise impossible; in a world of teeming suspicions the mere possession of gold was enough to condemn a man. But he was prepared to keep his peace, and live quietly, abstaining from all politics until the day that he and his kind could strike. In all things, then, his life consisted of waiting. . . .

He even grew accustomed to it finally, and took a dark pleasure in his loneliness, knowing that he could end it any time he wished by paying a simple call upon Nicole. That he did not pay this call was a source of pride to him. When there is nothing else to be done, he told himself, man endures. He beguiled the tedium of his waiting by attending the daily executions, for the Terror was in full swing by now. They horrified him, but the dualism of his nature took hold of him, and the endless creaking parade of death had its fascination. There was, he told himself, a certain connection between what a man was, and the way he died. Only those with a certain residue of honor, he saw, were able to quit life honorably. On the morning of November 10, 1793, Manon Roland proved that to him beyond all doubting.

She came to the foot of the guillotine holding the hand of ancient Larmarche, the old man quaking with fear, but she, proud, serene, comforting him in the tumbril, asking the authorities for pen and paper to write down the strange thoughts arising in her, having her request refused, making one more, that the old man be permitted to die first, that the sight of her blood should not unnerve him. Then, still proud and beautiful, she mounted with firm step, condemned for nonsense, upon trumped-up charges, for, in reality, being the heart and soul of the dead Girondists, for being her husband's wife, and standing there, facing the ugly, crumbling plaster monster that they called Liberty, she said in a clear, firm voice that carried over the Place de la Révolution:

"Oh Liberty, what crimes are committed in thy name!"

Thus, after Marie Antoinette, the second woman of all France died; for the revolution had commenced the natural diet of revolutions everywhere in all times and all places, its own children. . . .

Coming away from the Place, turning it over in his mind, Jean saw a surging crowd of mummers, dressed in cope and miter, in priestly vestments, all drunk as lords, laughing and singing, leading along the members of the Convention captive in their train.

"There is this about idleness," he mocked himself, "it encourages meddling in other people's affairs; but this is a rare sight, and a curious one, and what better thing have I to do?"

He fell in with the throng. They surged across the bridge to the Île Saint Louis, and Jean saw that it was to Notre Dame that they were going. To Notre Dame, a church no longer, bearing over the doorway the curious inscription: "The Temple of Reason." Inside, the ancient church was even more changed, the hoary saints tumbled from their niches, busts of Marat and other revolutionary "heroes" set up in their places, the crucifixes torn down, removed, the host destroyed, and high upon the altar itself Demoiselle Candeille of the Opéra, swathed in wisps of transparent material presiding as the Goddess of Reason. At her side were other members of the troupe, in even more complete demi-nudity; their ballet skirts covering their bodies from mid-thigh to waist, and above that, nothing but whatever charms with which nature had endowed them.

Jean studied them with cool mockery, thinking to himself that the invention of clothing was one of civilization's real advances, for among all the rarities of life, nothing is more rare than a body sufficiently lovely to be paraded naked before the eyes of men.

His mocking gaze was arrested finally, by the sole form

which could bear such scrutiny, a willow-slim, tall girl whose breasts were perfect, high, conical, upthrusting, and his natural curiosity caused him to lift his eyes to her face to see if it matched the perfection of the rest of her. It did—and more. It froze him there like one transfixed, his breath stopping in his throat from pure astonishment, his lips, moving, shaping her name.

"Lucienne!" he breathed. Then, very quietly he began to laugh. He was careful not to laugh too loudly, so she could not have heard him. But something about the very intensity of his gaze caught her, and her hazel eyes met his, their pupils dilating in pure terror. He stood there, staring at her, his face distorted with that unholy laughter of his, which was all the more terrible because she could not hear him.

They were singing now, the hymn that Marie-Joseph Chenier had written to music by Gossec:

Descend, O Liberty, daughter of Nature
The people have reconquered their immortal power;
Upon the pompous debris of ancient imposture,
Their hands raise your holy bower. . . .

After that, the chief Hébertists rose one after another and gave their harangues announcing the closing of the churches, the necessity for atheism, the splendor of the new return to pure reason. Jean did not listen to the puerile nonsense they spouted; he kept his gaze fixed upon Lucienne Talbot, torturing her with his eyes.

The ceremony grew wilder—the holy chalices were passed back and forth in profane mockery of the Holy Eucharist, drunken howls burst from the spectators. From the side aisles, curtained off from the rest of the cathedral, other sounds came over to Jean; Hébert, Chaumette and their fellows had seen no incongruity in introducing a form of worship more ancient than the worship of reason, that dated back to the devotées of Astarte of Nineveh, and beyond.

Temple prostitutes; Jean laughed silently, but his laughter was bitter with contempt. *Morbleu!* Is there no obscenity beyond these filthy pigs?

Half an hour later even his rhetorical question was answered; nothing was beyond the degeneracy of the Hé-

bertists—absolutely nothing at all. High priests and god-
desses of the new religion joined the worshipers in dancing
the Carmagnole, there within the sacred walls of Notre
Dame de Paris, the half-nude dancers from the Opéra
rapidly became wholly so under the clutching fingers of
the male rabble of Paris, and what had begun as a dance
became something else, too, degenerating into an orgy of
such complete bestiality that even Jean's mockery deserted
him. He wanted to vomit, to spew up the bottomless disgust churning at the bottom of his stomach.

He turned, stepping over the writhing, close-coupled
bodies upon the floor, closing his ears against the animal
moans, the muttered obscenities, but before he reached
the door, a slim hand gripped his arm, hard. He half
turned, raising his heavy stick to strike, holding it there,
lifted, then bringing it down again, staring into those
hazel eyes in mockery, in contempt, the half smile upon
his broken mouth, deepening, becoming crueler than
death itself.

"Jean," she breathed, "please, Jeannot—take me out of
here!"

"Why?" he laughed; "I should think you'd find your
surroundings most congenial. . . ."

"Oh, Jean, Jean—I didn't know! Believe me, I didn't!
They told me it was only a fête. . . ."

"And for this mere fête," he mocked, lifting his iron-
shod cane so that its point grazed lightly across her bare
breasts, "you attired yourself—thus!"

"I didn't know!" she wept. "We were to be an—an ar-
tistic spectacle; for God's love, Jeannot—get me out of
here!"

Jean smiled into her eyes, and made no effort to help
her into the cloak she had brought with her. Then he
took her arm, and started toward the doors; but the
saturnalia within had boiled over into the streets, mobs of
half-naked savages danced the Farandole, and Carmagnole, singing verses composed wholly of words which
could not be printed in any language upon the earth, and
repeating in full daylight all those acts which mankind
has always cloaked in the utmost privacy. . . .

Jean did not bother to look for a fiacre; since the revolt
of the devoutly religious people of the Vendée, and the
rebellions at Marseille and Lyon, so many horses had

been requisitioned for the army, fighting now foes both within and without, that any form of public transportation had ceased to exist. He walked along, and Lucienne, clinging to his arm, studied him with concern. He had grown older, she could see that; there was more white in his hair than black now. But it became him. His lean face was but little more lined than before; still almost a year short of his thirtieth birthday, he looked much older; but his hair and face were marked by care and sorrow, not by age. His body was still splendid; and he had something new about him, an air of calm, of dignity, serene and olympian and complete—an appearance of quiet mastery that she found oddly exciting. . . .

"You've been hurt," she whispered.

"Yes," he said shortly. "The war. There is a war, you know."

"I know," Lucienne said. "Is it—bad?"

He turned his great black eyes upon her.

"Nothing—a fleabite. I was born to be guillotined," he said.

At the word, guillotined, her smile froze. He had only to say a word, and she, too, would "sneeze into the sack" or be "shortened" as they put it in the irreverent slang of the day. I, she thought, am become his prisoner—his slave. He can do what he likes with me, and I have no means of escape. Thank God I've kept my figure; I intoxicated him once—and I can again. I know his weakness in that regard. 'Tis fortunate that nature made men such sensual beasts, or else we women could never control them. . . .

But, when they had reached her small, poor room, she was subtle. She made supper for him and gave him wine, and only after he had eaten and drunk, did she sit on the arm of his chair and begin to stroke his coarse hair, running her slim fingers through it, whispering:

"Jeannot—you do not know how good it is to be home again. . . ."

"Is it?" he said coolly.

"I know—you think me false; and I was. It wasn't until I reached Austria that I saw how wrong I was. Those silly, posturing idiots; there is not a man among them! No one at all like you, my Jeannot. . . ."

"Thank you," he said quietly.

"After all, I did no real harm. All the things I told them about have been undone here in France; and they know not now what to do. There is nothing they can do —they are lost. All the Kings are lost; tomorrow belongs to the common man. . . ."

"You bore me," Jean said; "I've heard enough false rhetoric to last me a lifetime. . . ."

He reached for his stick, and terror flared in her eyes.

"Don't go!" she begged; "stay here with me tonight, Jeannot—tonight, and all the other nights. I—I'm so lonely. . . ."

Jean looked at her, and smiled.

"Liar," he said.

She came close to him, veiling her hazel eyes with her marvelous lashes, putting her mouth inches from his own.

"I want you," she crooned; "I've never known another man like you. You make my whole body sing with desire, and afterward I purr with contentment. . . . Come, Jeannot, forget the past. Love me like you used to. I shall never leave you again—never, never, never!"

Jean pushed his weight down upon his stick and stood up.

"You," he said, "are fantastic—really fantastic, Lucienne."

"Jean," she screamed at him, her voice hoarse with terror; "don't go! Please don't go!"

"Rest tranquil," he said gently; "I shan't betray you to the authorities. It is a matter of indifference to me whether you live or die; but I shall not betray you. Not for your sake, Lucienne, but for mine. You see, my dear, there are some things that are beneath me."

Then he put his hat on his head and went very quietly through the door.

But within the next two weeks, the lonely peace of his life was twice broken. The first time it was Nicole, her blue eyes big with terror, who flew into his room where he sat huddled before his fire.

"Jean!" she cried; "you must save me! This man, this madman is giving me no peace! He swears I am married to him, not to Claude. He says we had children! Oh, Jean, Jean make him leave me alone—make him go away. . . ."

Jean looked at her.

"I'll do my best," he said tiredly; "but it would be better,

I think, if you went away. If you were to rejoin Claude in Marseille. . . ."

Firepoints showed in her eyes.

"You think me mad," she whispered, "don't you? You want to be rid of me. . . ."

"I know you're ill," Jean said gently. "Look, Nicole—I bear the scars of my wounds upon my body, where they can be seen; yours are deeper than that; they're upon your soul. What happened to you, your mind refuses to remember; if that be madness, why then I approve of it. I agree with whatever there is within you that refuses to recall these things. They are better not recalled. . . ."

A look of cunning stole across her lovely, childlike face. Had he been better versed in such things, he would have recognized it for what it was, the cunning of near-madness.

"I—I have no money," she said; "else I would go. . . ."

"I'll give you the money," Jean said, and rose.

"Thank you," Nicole said; then: "Jean—where is Fleurette?"

"Visiting Marianne for the afternoon," he lied. This, too, he thought, my poor sick one, is a thing you're better off not knowing. . . .

He crossed the room and got her the money. She took it and hugged it to her bosom.

"Thank you, Jean," she said, "you're very kind. . . ."

He thought it odd that she did not mention their last meeting; but he was relieved that she did not. It was better like this. And when she was gone, he could resume his lonely vigil. One day, perhaps, Fleurette would come back again. One day there would be love between them again, and joy.

After Nicole had gone, he questioned in his mind the ethics of sending her to join a man she was not married to, rather than the man to whom she was. But nothing in life was as simple as it appeared; to send her to Julien was to join her life to that of a man she did not remember, drive her back into a terrible past. That way lay madness. Worse, it was to link her with a man proscribed, to deliver her surely to the whistling blade of the guillotine, in all her mad innocence, condemn her in fact to die for a way of life she had never truly sanctioned or been a part of, and which she did not, could not remember. . . .

Goodness, justice, virtue, truth, he mused bitterly, are all poor creatures of circumstance. I am myself a murderer an hundred times over, and men count it a virtue because I killed not for myself, but in defense of my country. At least this way, she lives, and I have done what I could. . . .

But he was conscious several times in the next weeks of being followed; light, dainty footsteps would sound behind him for a space, but no matter how quickly he looked, there was no one there. He dismissed the idea finally, putting it down to nerves. The climate of Paris today, he mused, is enough to drive any man mad. . . .

Life went on. On November 24, the Convention closed every church in Paris; within twenty days, 2,446 churches throughout France were converted into profane "Temples of Reason." Roland de la Platière stabbed himself to death upon learning of his wife's execution. Clavière took poison. The death carts creaked endlessly through the streets of Paris. Danton was in Paris once more, having returned November 21 from his month-long self-exile at Arcis. The lion had mellowed, Jean knew; how much, he was to learn. . . .

On December 1, he learned firsthand of the astonishing change in Danton; for on that day, he had a visitor. Opening upon slim, wonderfully handsome Camille Desmoulins, Jean Paul could not conceal his astonishment.

"Come in," he said. "Sit down, Citizen Desmoulins; I confess I hardly expected . . ."

"Ah, yes," the young journalist smiled; "I knew you'd be astonished. Yet in a way, you should not be: the mountain comes at last to the prophet. . . ."

"You speak riddles," Jean Paul said.

"Yes, I know. It is simply this, painful as it is for me to confess it; time and experience have brought us around to seeing that you were right all the time; the only workable, worth-while government is a moderate one. . . ."

"Us?" Jean Paul was astonished.

"Danton—and I. Even Robespierre approves. But it was Danton who sent me to you: 'Go to Marin,' he said, 'he's your man. . . .'"

"I?" Jean gasped.

"Yes. We are beginning a new paper to be called the

Vieux Cordelier. I have brought some samples with me.
I ask you only to read them. . . ."

Jean took the papers, written in Desmoulins' own flowing script, from his outstretched hand. There were three
complete issues, ready to be set up in print. The first two
were innocuous enough, though they both contained hints
of greater things to come. But the third boldly attacked
the Hébertists, and cried out with stinging eloquence for
a policy of mercy.

Jean raised his eyes, stared at Desmoulins.

"The ideas are Danton's," the young man said; "only
the style is mine. . . ."

"Then Danton is prepared to die," Jean said flatly; "as
one of the authors of the Terror, he will be caught up in
the retribution its cessation is sure to bring; if on the
other hand, this new policy fails, it will involve its advo-
cates in its own ruin. . . ."

"He realizes this," Desmoulins said tensely; "but then
Georges Danton is an authentically great man. 'Tis only
little men, Citizen Marin, who are unwilling to undo and
atone for their own errors. . . ."

"*Morbleu!*" Jean swore, "I cannot believe it!"

"Nevertheless, it's true. Danton believes his personal
magnetism will ride him over the tumult; but, at bottom,
he is prepared to die. He is a patriot, Citizen, which is
why I respect him. . . ."

Jean sat very still, staring at his visitor. Of all the facts
of human nature difficult to accept, the hardest was the
basic inconsistency of human nature. Big, roaring, infinitely
complex Danton. Danton of the September massacres;
but Danton who killed always in the belief it was for
France, Danton who would abandon killing if mercy
served his country better. Big, bluff, growling, vulgar; but
healthily vulgar—never puerile and obscene like Hébert.
Danton who had been sickened as much as Jean himself
at the Hébertist degeneracy; Danton who could change,
who was big enough to. . . .

"You say Robespierre has seen this?" Jean said.

"And approves. The corrections on the manuscripts are
in his hand."

"What is it you want me to do, Citizen Desmoulins?"

"Work with us—openly or secretly, we care not. We
need your experience, your ideas. . . ."

Jean smiled.

"Secretly," he said, "as long as Robespierre has any connection with it at all. . . ."

Desmoulins' smile was half a sneer.

"Afraid?" he mocked.

"No," Jean smiled. "But I consider it my duty to preserve my life, and the lives of as many moderates as possible until the time comes when we may strike. Any man who trusts Maximilien Robespierre is a fool. He would turn upon his own mother if circumstances demanded it. I will work with you and Danton, because I understand you; but that feline little monster, I neither trust nor understand. He is not to know I'm with you. . . ."

"Very well," Camille Desmoulins said.

As he opened the door to let Desmoulins out, they both heard the clatter of feminine footsteps on the stairs. Desmoulins took Jean's hand, and started down, bowing on the next landing to Lucienne Talbot as he passed.

"Jean," Lucienne said breathlessly, "who on earth was that beautiful young man?"

"Why?" Jean demanded.

"Oh, don't be so prickly!" She smiled at him mockingly. "Is he the reason that you spurned me? La! I never dreamed that your fancies would turn in the direction of pretty boys!"

Jean recognized her attempt to provoke him for what it was.

"That," he said evenly, "was Camille Desmoulins. He came on business. . . ."

"Ah, politics again. So you've become a Dantonist! You're a surprising person, Jeannot. . . ."

"What I am, and what I have become, are none of your affair, Lucienne," Jean said. "Now, what do you want to see me about?"

"Oh, nothing—just a social call. Perhaps I wanted to see if you'd changed your mind. I'm a persistent female, Jean. . . ."

"You may take yourself, and your persistence straight to the devil, as far as I am concerned," Jean said. "Now, get out of here—I have work to do. . . ."

To his surprise, she went.

He would have been more surprised if he could have known what was going on inside her lovely head as she descended the stairs. There was in her mind the first faint stirring of an idea. It was vague now, and almost unformed; but it was there, and it would grow.

Jean—in politics again, she thought. But politics today nearly always ends in a one-way cart ride to the Place de la Révolution. He's a fool to take the risk. Ah, yes—he's a fool; and he holds my life in the hollow of his hand. 'Tis not good to be at the mercy of a fool. . . . If I could win him over—but he persists in spurning me. . . . People make such a fuss about what a woman does with her body; my body is my own. Besides, with Jean, it's exceedingly pleasant. . . . That way I could bind him, and I would be safe. But he's a fool, an honorable fool and I am not safe. I shall never be safe as long as he rejects me, and he's stubborn enough to reject me as long as he lives. . . .

She stopped still, one foot poised to take the next downward step.

"As long as he lives. . . ." she whispered, "as long as he lives!"

Then she started down again, running as though all the hounds of hell pursued her. They did. But only inside her own mind.

This, Jean Paul told himself, has gone on quite long enough! I have tried pleas, entreaties, reason, and to none of them will my poor Fleurette listen. But there is another language she will understand, because she is a woman. Nicole's mind is blank, but her body remembers. That is a thing not easily forgotten, especially when it has been so tender, and so fine as it was between Fleurette and me. . . .

He dressed with great care, and went down the stairs. Mounting to Pierre's apartment, a matter of some minutes only, because the two houses were not separated by any great distance, he knocked on the door.

Fleurette, herself, answered his knocking.

"Yes?" she said.

"I've come to take you home," Jean said.

"No!" she shrieked at him; "I will not go! If you, Jean Marin, think that I—"

She got no further. His big hands came down, and clutched her shoulders. He drew her to him, imprisoning her wildly moving head with one hand, holding it there like that, finding her mouth, cherishing it with his own, slowly, tenderly, longingly, until he could feel the wetness of her tears against his own cheeks, taste their salt, until finally her small hands stole up and locked themselves into his coarse hair, the fingers working, and he, stooping a little, swept her up bodily into his arms.

"Jean," she said oddly, "you've dropped your cane. . . ."

"I don't need it any more, love," Jean said; "I haven't for weeks, now. . . . Don't concern yourself about it—we're going home."

But when he reached his own building, she whispered:

"Put me down, Jean—I'll walk. You've carried me over the doorsill once—and there're five flights of stairs."

He smiled, hearing the almost maternal tenderness in her voice. But he did not put her down.

Inside the flat, he put her down, and she turned to him at once, going up on tiptoes, kissing his mouth, his face, his throat, crying:

"Oh Jean, Jean, you great fool! How long it took you to learn what to do! You came to me with arguments, reasons, excuses; O my love, I am a woman and a woman doesn't want to be reasoned with, cannot be convinced intellectually, because she knows what one thinks is never important but what one feels, what one feels!"

He kissed her slowly.

"You great bear!" she wept; "how much time you've wasted! I sat there day after day, waiting for you to say only, 'I love you,' longing to be taken in your arms, and you preferred to reason with me! Jean, Jean, don't you know that there is only one place a man can successfully reason with a woman?"

"And where is that?" Jean asked her.

"In bed, thou fool!" Fleurette whispered; "and that's where I would be now!"

But seeing her there, slim, long-limbed, perfect, he waited, caressing her body with his eyes; but she came up on both elbows with mock fierceness, seizing both his ears like handles, rocking his head back and forth laughing:

"Pretend I am your mistress, Jean! You have no wife; I am thy mistress and a terrible wanton! Pretend that . . ."

"Why?" Jean chuckled.

"Because men are fools! Say 'my wife' and dull legality

and respect enter in. I don't want to be respected, I want to be loved! Look, thou great grandfather of stupidity! My eyes are dead but all the rest of me lives; I am neither sick, nor weak, nor delicate. You've always been so gentle with me that you've made me want to scream! So today I am Mlle. Candeille of the Opéra, or the worst *fille* of the Palais Royal, and I won't be gentled! You hear me, I won't be! Try it and I shall run away again!"

Jean stared at her, wicked laughter in his eyes. Then he hurled himself forward and caught her to him, entrapping her small body in a grip so fierce that all the air left her lungs in an explosive rush. He slackened his grip slightly so that she could breathe again.

"Ah!" she said, "that's better—ah yes, much better, Jean. . . ."

"And this?" Jean said cruelly.

She did not answer him. Her black brows had flown together, her whole face twisted in a grimace of pure pain. Then very quickly, the grimace was gone.

"Why do you stop, my husband?" Fleurette said.

Because Jean Paul would not go to his new colleagues, it was necessary for them to come to him. And this, keeping a constant vigil outside in the street, Lucienne Talbot saw. It was very easy for her to slip up the stairs behind them; she did not even need to station herself outside Jean's door, for Danton's whisper rocked windows; his full bellow could be heard a half-mile or more from where he stood. It was not important to her to hear what Camille or Jean Paul said; from Danton's roars she could supply the rest of the conversation.

She did not know what use she could make of the information she gained. She attended whenever she could the sessions of the Convention; but even to her inexperienced eyes, the deadlock there was apparent: Robespierre was twisting like a snake between the Hébertists and the Dantonists, seeming now to favor one party, then the other. If only he were to turn against the party of Danton, Lucienne's plans could crystallize; but up until now, no one knew where the fastidious little lawyer stood.

On the landing below, Danton's bull-like laughter came over to her:

"Thibaudau told me the same thing! You know what I told him, Marin? If Robespierre dares to turn against me, I'll eat him alive, guts and all!"

Lucienne moved closer. Now she could hear the others.

"You understand," Jean Paul was saying, "my reluctance to associate myself with a man held responsible for the September massacres. . . ."

"I was responsible," Danton rumbled. "I thought then that they were necessary to save France. But even then I saved as many men of worth as I could. I was unable to save the Girondists; but believe me, Marin, I was ill of grief; I wept like a child. You say you don't trust Robespierre. Neither do I, but I do trust his cowardice. He and his hounds would never dare lay hands upon me—I am the Ark. So we must force this policy of clemency upon him —let Robespierre and Saint-Just alone and there will soon be nothing left in France but a Thebaid of political Trappists. . . ."

"You risk your life," Jean Paul said.

"I know; but I prefer in the end to be guillotined than to guillotine. . . ."

Hearing some stirring above, Lucienne turned and fled down stairs. At the street entrance she almost collided with a small woman. She stopped, staring at the new-comer, seeing that she was pale, with enormous blue eyes, and silvery blonde hair; she was, or had been pretty, Lucienne saw, but there was something in her face that all but destroyed her beauty.

Mad, Lucienne guessed; but then the small woman spoke.

"M'sieur Jean Marin? Is he above?"

"Yes," Lucienne said calmly; "but I wouldn't go up now, if I were you. He's terribly busy. . . ."

"Oh," the small one said; then: "Thank you very much, Madame. . . ."

"*Je vous en prie*," Lucienne said, and walked away thinking: You have your depths, don't you, Jeannot? Is there no end to your conquests?

The *Vieux Cordelier* was out at last, printed by men summoned by Pierre du Pain at Jean's request, for Desenne, Desmoulins' old printer, was too terrified to touch it, and the party of mercy, *Le Faction des Indulgents*, was launched, sending a thrill of hope through the prostrate body of France.

But not for long. Lucienne Talbot, watching every move from the galleries, waiting her own hour, saw it all. On December 25, with incredible meanness, Robespierre recanted, cowed by Collot, the bloody monster of the Lyon massacres. Standing before the Convention, Robespierre deserted Danton and Desmoulins just as Jean had predicted he would, swearing his eternal allegiance to the Terror; on February 2, the Hébertists, whom Robespierre, a convinced Deist, had hated for their atheism, had himself had arrested, were released.

Now, Lucienne thought, now!

But she could not bring herself to do it. Seeing Jean Paul hunched over in another seat in the gallery like a wounded colossus, something like pity moved her. Pity and memory. A spark of the wild and sensual love that had been between them held her still.

Throughout February, the deadlock held. The Hébertists screamed and mouthed their empty threats. Danton thundered like Jove. But the tortuous Robespierre kept silent.

Then Saint-Just returned to Paris. Young, handsome, immensely brave, he was Robespierre's right arm, supplying the force the "leader" lacked.

"You hesitate?" he said to Robespierre. "It is not a matter of choice between Hébertist and Dantonist—they both must go! Both are a danger to the state. . . ."

First the Hébertists, for they were the easier prey. March 17 they were dragged before the Tribunal; on the twenty-fourth, they went to the guillotine, weeping and begging for mercy, displaying a cowardice as disgusting as their former arrogance, and Lucienne Talbot, seeing it, wept:

"I'm lost! I must win him back now, I must!"

But Jean Paul was not to be won. He told her flatly, "Leave me alone, Lucienne. We are finished, you and I—cannot you understand that?"

She understood that now—and more. She understood that the only way left to buy her own safety was with his life.

So it was that leaving the Tribunal that fourth day of April, 1794, the day that the rats who ruled France dared pull down a lion, condemning Georges Danton to death, and with him Desmoulins and many more, leaving Robespierre, feline, incredible Robespierre master of the country, sick with a disgust that filled up the whole world, Jean Paul Marin saw one more thing:

Lucienne Talbot clutching the sleeve of Fouquier-Tinville, the Public Prosecutor, and whispering in his ear.

Jean looked at the pair of them, thinking: I wonder what she's saying? But he didn't really care. He perhaps would not have cared if he could have heard her words:

"Send your men to my place, Rue de Sèvres 16—and I will deliver unto you yet another conspirator!"

This, to her, involved a lingering kindness; she could not send the police to arrest Jean Paul in the presence of his poor, blind wife; she would play Delilah to the hilt and deliver him in person.

Jean went once more to the executions, that next day, and saw Georges-Jacques Danton die, drawing himself up like the lion he was, rumbling to himself: "Come, Danton —no weakness!" Then turning to Samson: "Show my head to the people! It is worth showing!"

But when Jean reached home again, worn out and sick, he found Fleurette in tears.

"There was a woman here," she wept, "a horrible, horrible woman! She called me *Chérie!* Jean, Jean—how long must I be tormented with your past?"

"Be calm, my dove," Jean said tiredly. "Who was she? What did she say?"

"She said to tell you to come to her this afternoon! A matter of highest importance—even of life and death! Then it was that she called me '*Chérie!*' 'Don't worry, *Chérie*,' she said; 'I'm not trying to steal your husband. This is strictly business. . . .'"

Jean got heavily to his feet.

"You're not going?" Fleurette said in horror.

"Yes," Jean said grimly; "but I'm taking my pistols, and my cane. Which of them I shall use depends upon the circumstances. . . ."

"But Jean, that horrible woman . . ."

"You're right," Jean said grimly, "she is a horror; and in the service of my worst enemies. But I shall deal with her. . . ."

"But Jean," Fleurette wailed; "I have something to tell you!"

"It can wait," Jean Paul said, and went down the stairs.

In her room, Lucienne heard the knocking as he threw open the door. Then she fell back, her eyes dilated, her mouth frozen into a crimson "O," taking one step back, then another, all the color draining from her face. And Gervais la Moyte stepped into the room, closing the door behind him.

"You thought to escape me?" he murmured; "you thought that, Lucienne? You thought I would not enter France again at the risk of my life—nor would I have to take you back, you painted piece of garbage! But to kill you—yes. To hear you scream, to watch you go down on your knees, you lying, treacherous bitch and beg—for this I am willing to die—and gladly!"

He caught her wrist cruelly and twisted it, forcing her to the floor.

"You've betrayed every man you've ever known, haven't you?" he whispered. "Me—a thousand times—that poor beggar Marin. You betrayed the revolutionists to me, and the royalists to the Revolution! You sold your body for prices you thought high, but that were cheaper, actually than the sous a *poule* would accept. . . . But now to make an end of you; but slowly, my sweet, so that I can listen to your screams a long time. You're very vain, but when I have done with you, people will vomit at the sight of what's left of your face. . . ."

"That," Jean Paul said quietly, "is quite enough, M. la Moyte. Release her."

Gervais turned, and stared into the muzzle of Jean's pistol.

"Still enchanted, eh, Marin?" he mocked. "If you knew the truth . . ."

"I do," Jean began, but his words were silenced by the thunder of booted feet upon the stairs.

"Ah, Marin!" Fouquier-Tinville said; "I see you've exceeded us in your zeal! A citizenly arrest, eh? Who is this man?"

"Not him!" Lucienne screamed; "Marin, himself! He is your royalist-Dantonist conspirator!"

"Don't lie!" la Moyte said sharply; then turning to the

others: "Permit me to introduce myself, Messieurs. I am Gervais Hugue Robert Roget Marie la Moyte, Comte de Gravereau, late officer in the army of his Majesty of Austria, a loyal subject of the late murdered King of France, and this woman is my mistress and a paid spy in the employ of Austria."

Jean stared at him in pure astonishment.

Gervais put his hand on his shoulder.

"Now we are quits, my brother," he said gently; "I have nothing left but mine honor; and I am tired of life. 'Tis good to go thus, as long as I can take her with me. . . ."

"Brother?" Fouquier-Tinville said suspiciously.

"All men are brothers, are they not, M'sieur?" Gervais smiled; " 'tis one of your credos, is it not?"

"You'll testify against this precious pair, Citizen Marin?" Tinville growled.

"No!" Jean snapped; "I want no part in any further deaths!"

"But, Citizen," Fouquier-Tinville said ominously, "your duty—"

"M. Marin has done his duty and more by capturing us," Gervais said; "his testimony is unnecessary, as he is in possession of few of the facts. This woman was attempting to dupe him because he spurned her love. I shall freely give you a full confession that covers everything; you have no need of him. . . ."

"Very well, then, Marin," Tinville growled; "you can go."

But his murderous little eyes followed Jean as he left the room.

Mounting the stairs to his own flat was pure agony to Jean. When Fleurette opened the door for him, he collapsed in a heap in his chair.

She came over to him, and stroked his head.

"You came back quickly," she whispered. "Are you rid of her for good?"

"Yes," Jean groaned.

His tone caught her attention; she ran her fingers over his face.

"My God!" she murmured, "your face is a death mask!"

"I know," Jean said; "I have seen too much of death this day."

"Rest, my love," Fleurette said tenderly. "Here, let me help you off with your shoes. . . ."

A vagrant memory stirred in the tired recesses of his mind.

"You were going to tell me something," he said; "what was it, *ma petite?*"

She looked up from where she knelt before him, tugging at the buckles of his shoes. The last rays of the setting sun came in the window, pouring all the illumination in the world into her face.

"Only—that I am with child, Jean," she said.

17

The whole world is drowning in blood, Jean Paul thought, and I shall never sleep again. . . .

"You are so still," Fleurette said; "what was in that letter that so disturbed you?"

"Nothing," Jean lied; "'tis from a friend in Marseille, telling of conditions there. Things, there, are very grave. It did, I confess, make me a little sad. . . ."

"Don't be sad, my love," Fleurette said; "we have each other, and soon we'll have our son or our daughter—Jean, do you care which it is? A boy or a girl, I mean?"

"No," Jean said; "I don't care. . . ."

"Nor I. It's yours so it will be very fine. There is only one thing that worries me. . . ."

"What is that, Fleur?" Jean said. He had caught the edge of hysteria in her voice.

"Its eyes, Jean," she whispered. "I was born like this. Jean, do you think—"

Jean put an arm about her shoulder and drew her to him.

"No, sweet," he said; "I don't think that. He is going to be perfect, our son. . . ."

"Ah, so!" Fleurette laughed; "you do want a boy! I'll have to concentrate on masculine things like strength and courage and wisdom. I shan't disappoint you, love. . . ."

"Thank you," Jean said.

The letter had fallen to the floor when he put his arms around her. Now it caught his attention again:

"I was arrested for *incivisme* the moment I entered Marseille. You know what trials are today. I defended myself as best I could; but I was condemned from the moment they laid hands on me. My crime was I think that of having been successful, of having lived well—which is treason to the spirit of the mob. At any rate, Marin, by the time this reaches you, I shall be dead. I only hope I can manage it well and with dignity. . . .

"Take care of my poor Nicole. As long as you can, keep the news of my death from her. Another such shock would, I believe, destroy her reason. But, if ever she comes to know, tell her I died with her name on my lips, thanking God for the happiness I had with her. I shall be waiting for her wherever God provides a place for the souls of the harmless and the just, knowing that she must come to me one day, never again to leave my side.

"Adieu, dear friend; I pray you to accept my most tender farewells for both yourself, and your angel of a wife. . . ."

It was signed, "Claude Bethune."

Dear God, Jean whispered inside his heart, dear, kind, sweet merciful God!

"Now you've become too still again," Fleurette complained; "what ails you today, my Jean?"

"Nothing. Fleurette, love, I have to visit a man now. He is in prison awaiting trial. He was my brother-in-law, and ever since I've known him I've hated him. . . ."

"Then why must you visit him?" Fleurette said.

"Because I was wrong. My poor, dear sister adored him. I could never understand that; but now I do. For at the end he proved himself as gallant a gentlemen as ever drew the breath of life. People are strange, Fleur, love; they're hellishly complicated, and always we make the mistake of trying to reduce them to some one noticeable element in their characters. In September, '92, Danton was merciless; but Danton died because in December, '93, he wanted with all his heart to show mercy. Only madmen are all of a piece. Marat and Hébert were always perfectly consistent; because the pair of them belonged in a home for lunatics. . . ."

"And your brother-in-law?"

"Was gay, careless, a little heartless—your typical noble. He was frequently unfaithful to my sister; but he always loved her, I think. He was sick with grief the day I told him of her death. The day he was arrested, he could possibly have escaped by denouncing me as a Dantonist—which I was. But he would not. The many wrongs he had done me compelled him not to. He accepted his fate like the real gentleman he is, going so far as to deny any relationship to me—which again could have dragged me in with him. You see why I must go?"

"Oh yes!" Fleurette breathed; "go by all means! And tell him that I thank him with all my heart. . . ."

The stench inside the Conciergerie was indescribable. The prisoners were huddled together in a huge common cell, waiting for the guillotine to clear enough of the smaller cells for them to be separated. Gervais la Moyte came forward to greet Jean, a wan smile upon his face. His clothes were disarranged, through a rent in his fine shirt his lean, athletic body showed, his blond hair had not been combed, and hung loose about his shoulders.

But in this miserable state he was magnificent; robbed of the trappings of nobility, the man showed. And the man, Jean thought, freed of his wasted life, of the mis-education given his class, is quite something. . . .

"Behold your republic!" Gervais laughed, waving an airy hand. "You should be proud of yourself, Jean. For here, at least you have really succeeded in leveling the classes!"

"I am not proud," Jean said; "this was never what I wanted. I was too young, and too much a fool to realize that revolution is never a justifiable instrument of policy. Only those changes made gradually last—to overturn the world is to place the bottommost scum on the top, and scum remains scum no matter where it is placed!"

"Bravo!" Gervais said; "now you're talking sense. But aren't you being a bit foolhardy to visit me? Men have been condemned for less. . . ."

"I know. But I was honor-bound to come. To come and take your hand and ask your pardon. Not that you were right, for you were not. Oppression is never right, even when it is elegant. But then I, too, was wrong. In trying to end oppression I played into the hands of worse oppressors, so that the blood of ten thousand innocents is upon my soul. I want to say this while you still live, and while I live; I have no doubt that I shall follow you, and soon; unless by some miracle I can escape France. My friends are dead; my life hangs under the blade because at any moment they can discover that I was a Danton-ist. . . ."

"I shall not betray you," Gervais said.

"I know; but Lucienne will; not that it matters—except to my unborn child."

"I think you wrong her. She has changed. Go see her when you leave. You'll find her walking in the women's yard. . . ."

"Have I your pardon?" Jean said.

"Freely, gladly given," Gervais said. "And, I yours?"

"Yes," Jean murmured and embraced him through the bars.

He found her as Gervais had predicted, walking in the tiny paved courtyard where the women prisoners were allowed to exercise. She came up to him very quietly and thrust her hands through the bars.

"I'm glad you've come," she said.

"Lucienne—" Jean muttered; but something got in the way of his speech. A knot formed at the base of his throat, shutting off his words. And leaning forward, Lucienne saw the tears in his eyes.

"You weep for me?" she whispered. "How strange!"

Jean found his voice again.

"Strange?" he got out; "no, Lucienne—not strange. You will die—and I will follow you. The dying is nothing, for all men come to that. . . ."

She brought her hands up and gently stroked his face.

"Then what do you weep for, my Jean?" she said.

"For what we had together. For the real tragedy of living that comes long before the blessed relief of dying. . . ." He caught her hands in his own, and held them so hard that he hurt her. "I weep for the miracle we had and lost: each other, together, believing, hoping, loving under the sun— It was good then, wasn't it? In the days of youth, of—of our innocence even. . . ."

"Innocence?" Lucienne smiled.

"Yes, yes—innocence! Before our eyes were opened and we saw our nakedness! Before we were cast out of our enchanted garden into a world of lies, disenchantment, poverty of spirit, where not even love can keep its dignity. . . ."

He released her quite suddenly, and brought his knuckles up, dashing the hot tears from his eyes.

"Yes," he husked, "I weep for you, too. For you, and all the lost souls upon earth—for myself, for what we might have had together if your ambitions, and my revo-

lutionary folly, and life itself had not gotten in the
way. . . ."

"Life itself, more than anything else," Lucienne said.
"Don't blame yourself, my darling—here, give me your
hand again. . . ."

Jean thrust his hand through the bars, and she took it,
fondling it, her face strange, her voice far away—sad.

"Yes, life itself," she whispered; "and my overwhelming
belief in mine own cleverness. With all the examples I had
had set before me, I could not see that treachery never
works. The betrayer always betrays himself, doesn't he,
Jeannot?"

"Yes," Jean growled, "and by the very act of betrayal. . . ."

"I was always a cheat," Lucienne sighed, "but one cannot cheat life, can one? My monstrous vanity prompted
me to think I could. You, poor Jeannot, were the first
victim of my infidelity; but I am myself the chief one. I
die because vows, honor, my pledged word meant nothing to me—dust to be flicked aside, while I followed the
will-of-the-wisps of my desires. . . ."

"You are eloquent," Jean said.

"I have become so, listening to you, my Jean," Lucienne
smiled. "How many things I have learned too late! I had a
hunger, a lust for life. I knew it would pour its treasures
into my lap: fame, riches, great love . . . while I, the
queen, would smile and accept them as my due, and less,
never asking myself what I'd done to deserve them. . . ."

"You had those things," Jean said, his eyes brooding
over her face. "Dear God, Lucienne—why weren't you
ever content?"

"A great love," she whispered; "I had that from you.
But I had to have the other things as well. You became
an obstacle—I betrayed you. Riches and fame—Gervais
supplied them. Then he became tiresome and poor—so I
betrayed him. . . . The others—they were nothing—designed by nature to have a heel ground into their
faces. . . ."

"Nobody," Jean smiled flatly, "is designed for that."

"I know that now," she said, her voice so low that he
had to strain his ears to hear her. Then she came up hard
against the bars, thrusting herself close to him, crying:

"Jean, Jean—I don't want to die! I can't die, I can't, I, can't—"

He pulled her to him, embracing her through the bars. Slowly she quieted.

"That was unworthy of me," she whispered. "It's a hard thing, Jean—I know now that I will die without ever really knowing what happiness was. What is it, Jean? How does one find it?"

Jean looked across the barred courtyard, his eyes above the bright, sun-touched halo of her hair, and his voice, when he spoke, was endlessly deep.

"By not looking for it," he said. "By always giving, never trying to get. . . ." His fingers moved, toying with the auburn hair. He looked down at her gravely.

"Go on," she murmured.

"By loving, Lucienne—which is the thing you never understood. By loving every man and woman under God's heaven as brothers and more, so that death itself becomes easier than betrayal—so that one cannot violate what a man is, so that one respects him so, living, breathing, suffering, that not only can one not harm a hair on his head, but one cannot sneer at the most pitiful of his dreams, knowing them dear to him. . . ."

She looked up at him, and the tears caught in her lashes like jewels.

"Jean," she said slowly, "you never would have turned me in, would you?"

"I," Jean said flatly, "would have died first."

"I know. And because I couldn't believe that anyone given a chance to take vengeance, to betray—would refrain, I lived for months in terror of you. I tried to seduce you, not because your love mattered much to me—I have, truly, no heart—and a man's love to me was no more than the natural idolatry to which I was entitled for merely being me—I have always been the goddess of mine own idolatry. When you would not be faithless to your wife—you've always been true to her, haven't you?"

"Yes," Jean said.

"I thought so. But when you spurned me, I knew I had to kill you that I might live. It never even entered my head that in the scale of things your life is ever so much more important than mine; that you will one day make things better for all the people of France, while I can be nothing but a gilded parasite. But nothing existed for me outside myself, my precious, precious, beautiful self that I have loved as no man ever could!"

"A man might see the flaws," Jean said drily. "One does not stay blind forever, Lucienne. . . ."

"You're better than Gervais, nobler, really. You have never needed to revenge yourself upon me. . . ."

"Revenge is God's business," Jean said, "not man's. When one takes upon one's self the right to be judge, jury, executioner, one has exceeded one's functions, I think. I could not play God, Lucienne. I could only leave you, in sorrow, truly—and I did."

"Thank you for that. Jeannot—"

"Yes, Lucienne?"

"People cannot change—not entirely. I hate my vanity; but I have it still. I'm not afraid of death. It would come some day; better now, like this, before I grow old, and men no longer run their desiring gaze over my body. But this I do hate—that this head of mine, be dropped into that smelly, bloody basket! That I be mutilated in death. I—I want to look as though I were asleep, so that people seeing me will shake their heads and whisper: 'What a pity that so much loveliness had to die!' "

"What is it you want?" Jean said, catching her drift.

"There is a chemist's shop near the Place de Grève. Go there and buy a small vial for me. Tell him it's for rats; he'll know the truth; he has delivered many another from the tender mercies of Samson's knife. . . . Bring it to me here. Then I shall look as though I were asleep, and the *tricoteuses* shall not count my head, nor the *canaille* spit at me as I pass in that dreadful cart, and call me all the dreadful things I perhaps was, but which I never considered myself. . . ."

"Nor were you," Jean said; "tomorrow, then?"

"Yes, Jeannot—tomorrow. I won't ask your forgiveness; I have it, I know, without the asking. Au 'voir, mon Jeannot—till tomorrow. . . ."

Going home, it seemed to Jean Paul that his tired limbs could no longer support the weight of his heart.

The moment he saw Fleurette's face, he knew something was wrong.

"Jean!" she whispered; "men were here—horrible, rough men. They—they were kind enough to me after they had found out I was blind; but they left something for you. Here it is—some document or another. Oh, Jean—tell me what it is!"

Jean took the heavy paper, much decorated with official seals, and read it. One glance, and he knew what it was. Of all the devices by which the Revolution deprived a man of his liberty, and ultimately his life, this was the cruelest: the paper he held in his hand was an *ajournement* or a suspended order of arrest. In effect, he was already doomed; he could come and go as he pleased, as long as he remained in Paris; but each minute was menaced; as soon as Fouquier-Tinville got around to it, as soon as he had enough evidence, or it merely suited his whims or convenience, Jean would be clapped into l'Ab-baye, the Temple, La Conciergerie, Luxembourg or any of fifty other prisons, to emerge finally only in that creaking cart of death. It was, Jean knew, designed to break the prospective prisoner's spirit; by the time he was finally jailed, his nerves would be so shattered by the terrible ordeal of waiting, which could go on for weeks or even months, that his will to resist would be gone.

"What is it, Jean?" Fleurette said.

"Nothing," Jean said; "something to do with an as-sembly of ex-soldiers. I shan't go—'tis of no impor-tance. . . ."

"Oh, Jean," she whispered; "I'm so glad. . . ."

They do not know me, Jean thought, as he made his way to the chemist's shop to purchase the boon of merci-ful death for Lucienne; I shall not break. This means that their case against me is weak—they want to reduce me to gibbering terror before pressing it. . . . But they shall never press it. I shall arrange to get Fleurette out of Paris and then—

But even as he shaped the thought, he knew it was almost impossible. The Convention had multiplied the papers necessary to leave the country until it took weeks to procure them. He had no passport, and the authorities who issued these necessary documents were furnished with a list of suspects. Unless he could buy a forged document, he had no way to flee. . . .

But Pierre could go; in fact, he had to. Jean realized that if his small part in the printing of the *Vieux Cordelier* were ever discovered, his friend, too, would die. Pierre

had still the advantage of not being upon any list of suspects—he had never been in politics, his name had not
even appeared upon the pages of either Jean's papers, or
Desmoulins'. But it must be done quickly. . . . Out of
Paris, now—tonight—and then, in some provincial sea-
port, papers for going abroad could be procured. . . .

Jean raced to Pierre's shop, told him the news. Pierre
saw the necessity of flight at once; but at the next
breath, he proved how great was his loyalty.

"I cannot tell Marianne—she might let something slip
to Fleur. . . . Besides, there's no time. . . . When I'm
safe abroad, I'll send for her. . . ."

Leaving the shop, Jean turned at once toward the chemist's. He pushed the matter of his own escape out of his
mind, depending, as men in desperate straits often do,
upon inspiration, upon unforeseen developments. During
the whole of the night, after coming home with Lucienne's
vial, and another for himself if all else failed, he lay
awake, trying to puzzle the matter out, falling asleep at
dawn from weariness, without having the ghost of a plan
in his mind.

The next day, he clasped Lucienne's hands through the
bars, pressing the vial into her palm, and she, smiling into
his eyes, whispered:

"Thank you, mon Jeannot . . ." Then: "Would—would
you please kiss me good-bye?"

He put his two hands through the bars and drew her to
him. Her lips were ice; but they warmed slowly, became
unbelievably tender. She clung her mouth to his a long,
long time, until both their faces were wet with their com-
bined tears.

"Thank you, my Jeannot," she whispered; "and know
this—upon the oath of one about to die—that even if it
were never wholly true before, I shall quit this world
tonight, loving you with all my heart. . . ."

So it was that Gervais la Moyte rode to his death alone,
preceded by Lucille Desmoulins, and the widow of Hébert,
and a host of other people whose crime consisted of having
known, or married, or befriended the wrong people. He
died, as he had lived, with elegance.

Jean's slow, nerve-corroding ordeal went on until the
first of Thermidor, July 19 of the old calendar; and it
would have continued longer, but for Nicole.

She came flying into the flat crying his name. Jean looked up from the big chair and smiled at her, mockingly.

"You," he said, "are supposed to be in Marseille, remember?"

There was no surprise in his voice. He had known for a long time that she had never left Paris; but he had had too many other things to think about. As long as she did not trouble him, he was content. He realized this with a mild feeling of surprise. Life, he thought tiredly, takes the edges off everything—fades all colors; once I would have died for this woman, but now . . .

"Jean," Nicole gasped; "you really must help him! He is truly a nice man and . . ."

"Who is truly a nice man, Nicole?" Fleurette demanded from the doorway. Her voice was ice.

"Julien—you know, the one who says he is my husband. . . ."

"Can't you," Fleurette said acidly, "keep even your husbands straight?"

Nicole stared at her. The edge in Fleurette's voice had gotten through to her finally.

"Fleur," she breathed; "you—you're angry at me! Why, Fleur? What did I do to annoy you?"

"Nothing," Fleurette said; "at least to you it was nothing. I imagine you're quite accustomed to taking other women's husbands up to your flat and keeping them there all night!"

"Oh!" Nicole said; "but I didn't, Fleur! Jean was at my place barely ten minutes. It isn't my fault if he didn't come home. . . ."

All her life, in her world of darkness, Fleurette had been listening to the tones of human voices, and judging them. She knew the truth when she heard it. Very quietly she came over to where Jean sat and touched her lips to his cheek.

"Forgive me, my love," she said. "And you, too, Nicole. I misjudged you, and I'm sorry. . . ."

"So?" Nicole said in her odd, vacant way; "it doesn't matter, Fleur. Jean, you must help him! They've arrested him and he's going to be tried. You're a lawyer, and—"

"No!" Fleurette got out; "no, Jean, no!"

"Why not, Fleur?" Nicole said; "they'll guillotine him if he doesn't have help. . . ."

"And even if he does," Fleurette snapped; "and afterwards they'll kill Jean for trying to help him! Listen, Nicole—try to understand. They killed Manuel merely because he refused to testify against the Queen; they've murdered people because they were seen talking to Danton; they killed Lucille Desmoulins and poor Madame Hébert merely because they were their husbands' wives—your friend Madame Roland, because she was married to a Girondist. All the people we used to meet at her house are dead, guillotined, or hounded to death: Roland killed himself, Clavière killed himself, Condorcet took poison, and Petion and Buzot shot themselves to death and their poor bodies were eaten by wolves! And these are among the people we know alone. Do you know what you're asking? That my Jean go out and give his life for a man he scarcely knows! You want that, Nicole? I ask you —is that what you want?"

Nicole's voice shuddered up from the depths of an unutterable horror. "No," she whispered; "dear God—no!"

"Where is he imprisoned?" Jean said.

"Luxembourg. But Jean, you can't . . ."

"Jean!" Fleurette cried; "you cannot! I can't let you, I can't. . . ."

Jean stood up, slowly.

"Listen, my dove," he said gently; "I was going to have to tell you this sometime; now I cannot hide it longer: I am already proscribed. . . ."

"Jean!" Fleurette screamed; "oh no, Jean—no!"

Jean came over to her, and drew her gently into his arms.

"That document those men brought," he said slowly, "was an adjourned order for my arrest. That's a technicality; it means that they are not yet ready to strike. But it means also that I cannot leave Paris. I have not the papers, and every gate is watched. So—under the circumstances, love—I prefer to defend M. Lamont. I'd rather defy them, and go down fighting. I have already procured passports for you and Nicole; you will go to Switzerland, from there to England. My brother Bertrand is there. . . ."

"No!" Fleurette wept; "I will not leave you!"

"You have no choice, my love," Jean said. "You have two lives to guard, remember. . . ."

"No," Fleurette said flatly, "my child is better dead than having to grow up in a world of murderers!"

And nothing he said would move her from her stand.

The trial of Julien Lamont was a foregone conclusion: an émigré, a noble, was automatically an enemy of the state. But unlike Gervais la Moyte, he had not taken up arms against France, and Jean made this the basis of his defense.

"You quote the law to me," he said, glaring into the face of the public prosecutor, Fouquier-Tinville; "and I say to you that this law is itself a crime! Of what is this man guilty? I tell you simply—of fleeing for his life! He was a neighbor of mine on the Côte d'Azur; he oppressed no one, his people loved him; and because he preferred to go rather than stay and die—by officially permitted butchery like the Princess Lamballe's, you condemn him. . . ."

"The law is not on trial here, Citizen," the President remarked acidly, ringing his little bell.

"Ah, but it is!" Jean cried; "the law and all the men who made it. I am trained to the law, Citizen President; but the law I learned was designed to safeguard the innocent against oppressors; not to be twisted into an instrument of oppression itself! This man fled, he has never borne arms against France, or plotted against her! Would you condemn him then for the crime of failing to choose his parents among the peasantry? Sever his innocent head indeed, for the crime of being born!"

A ripple of applause came from the galleries. The people of Paris were sick to death of the Terror; in the Convention itself, the Montagnards and the Moderates were closing ranks against Robespierre; he had united all his foes by removing the immunity of the members of the Convention themselves. Knowing themselves at the mercy of the arch-terrorist, men who had bowed with craven servility to Robespierre's will gained the desperate courage of cornered rats. Tallien, Barras, and Legendre, Sieyès, and Fouché, were plotting against him. Knowing these things, Jean Paul had hope.

Time, time, time! he thought; if they strike quickly, Lamont can be saved. If they can hold together long enough—if they hit him now while he sulks away from the Convention; since the arrest of his maniac priestess Cath-

erine Théot, he has not been seen. Ah, Robespierre—mark
well the words that Danton left you! For truly if they are
brave, you'll follow him, and France will know peace
again. . . .

But time was running out while they delayed. Fouquier-
Tinville was on his feet screaming:

"This speech of yours, Citizen, is dangerously close to
incivisme!"

In the gallery, Fleurette caught her breath. Nicole caught
her hand and held it, hard.

"Incivisme!" Jean spat, "always *incivisme!* Where were
you, Citizen Prosecutor, when the Prussians crossed the
border? I ask you, where? I ask you further to define this
incivisme of yours: a lack of civic spirit is it not—in
short a want of love for France? Answer me! Is it not so
defined?"

"Yes," Fouquier sneered, "that definition is as good as
any other. . . ."

"And I am *incivique?*" Jean thundered, his voice as big as
Danton's now, as thunderous; "I?" His hands came up,
ripping at his coat, his shirt. In a moment he stood before
the Tribunal, naked to the waist; the whole of his upper
trunk covered with the red, semicircular scars the shrapnel
had made, his back crisscrossed with the scars of the whip.

"Look, Citizens!" he boomed, "upon the marks of my
incivisme! Count them if you will—twenty-three wounds
through which my blood poured at Hondeschoote in
defense of France! I beg you, Citizen President, Citizen
Procurator, Citizens Jurymen, to pay special attention to
my left forearm, and my back! Those marks you see
there are the stripes laid upon me in the *bagne* at Toulon;
this brand which marks me a *forçat*, a convict, is a tender
memento of Royalist gentility! For I was arrested, as Citizen Fouquier-Tinville well knows, for my revolutionary
activities at a time when it was dangerous to be a revolu-
tionist; at a time when the rats who now gnaw upon the
prostrate body of France were still skulking in their
holes!"

The galleries were loud now, with cheering.

"Enough of my *incivisme,*" Jean smiled. "It means nothing to the men who hounded Danton to death, who murdered that same Camille Desmoulins who launched the
attack upon the Bastille. Their memories are short, their

eyes blinded by the blood of women, children, the ancient and the helpless. . . .

"I defend this man because he is just, and pursued by an unjust law. I say, free him! End this law! End the government of France by murder. You must, you know, Citizen President, Citizen Procurator, for not even you can go home night after night to your beds pursued by the gibbering ghosts of the legions of the innocents you have so foully slain. I have done. Do what you will with this just man there. Do what you will with me!"

The President was on his feet ringing his bell, trying to still the uproar.

"The court stands adjourned until tomorrow!" he bellowed. "Bailiff, clear the court!"

And that next morning, after a sleepless night, spent holding his weeping wife in his arms, Jean looked up to see the galleries empty, closed to the spectators, turned to find himself cited for contempt, for inciting the spectators, listened to Fouquier-Tinville's weary tissue of lies in hopeless disgust. The jury was out in ten minutes; the verdict: death.

Lamont had time to embrace his defender before he was led away.

"You will die for this," he whispered in awe. "Now I know God still makes gallantry in man!"

They guillotined Julien Lamont, ci-devant Marquis de Saint Gravert, at nine o'clock the next morning. Jean did not go to see it. He waited quietly at home, for the sound of booted steps upon the stairs.

But Nicole la Moyte went, and saw an execution for the first time. She did not flinch or turn away from it. She heard it all, saw it all. There was something in Julien's face that stirred her; something about the color of blood. . . .

There was a veil before her eyes. She heard the hoarse voices of the *canaille,* double, once now, here, at this moment, and again far off at another place, another time; they shoved her cruelly, and at their touch, her flesh crawled, not from this touch, living, now, actual, but from another touch, blows, curses, long ago but again living superimposed upon the now. She wandered through the crowd, dazed, hearing them screaming, cursing, and a voice kept calling out: "Jean! Marmot! Where are you? My children, where are you?"

He was standing on the scaffold now, waiting to be bound. He looked toward her, and she heard someone crying: "Julien! Why it's Julien! Why are you not in Austria? Oh, Julien! Julien—the children—they're killing the children!"

And then, in that dead center of silence as Samson bound him to the plank, she knew the voice was her own.

"It's Julien," she whispered. "Julien, my husband—my good, brave, gallant husband whom I never loved. They're killing him. They killed my children. They killed Marie, thinking she was I, because we had changed dresses. And I—I forgot. Because they did things to me, I forgot. So many of them—so many things—horrible!"

The blade smashed down. She watched it, dry-eyed.

Blood. The color of blood. So much blood—who would have ever thought that such little bodies could hold so much? Dead. Little Jean dead—little Jean whom I named after the only man I ever truly loved. Marmot dead—my little blue-eyed doll. And Jean—Jeannot, is he dead, too?

She moved through the crowd slowly. The veil was clearing now, lifting inch by inch, and the brightness dazzled her. There was a man named Claude—gone now. I married him, though I should not have, for Julien was still alive. Forgive me, God—for that. This—this is Paris. I've been here a long time. I've seen Jean again. I've tried to make him love me again, with his body—as we did that lovely, lovely night of the snows. . . .

But he would not. Why? That—that girl! The girl who cannot see, Fleur—his wife. He loves her—not me . . . oh God, oh kind God, oh sacred, tender, loving, forgiving Mother of God! I'm alone—all alone, in a city of murderers! I have been dead, but now I am alive again and that is the cruelest thing of all, because now I would not live. . . .

Jean! Jeannot—you stood up in the Tribunal and defended Julien; yesterday—or years ago, when was it, love? You bared your body, your strong, beautiful body, and showed them your scars. So many, many scars—oh, my Jeannot, how they must have tortured you! Did you cry, my love, did you cry? No—you are too brave for that; but are you brave enough? Can you die like Julien died when they come for you? When they come for you! Dear God—for me you did this thing! To save my husband, your life is forfeited!

She was running now, wildly, through the crowd. She reached the house three minutes before the police of the Committee came to arrest him. She was on the landing panting from lack of breath, when they thundered up the stairs.

"Jean!" she screamed; her voice high, formlessly, deadly shrill; "Jean! They're coming—run!"

He threw open the door, and saw it. They had reached the landing, their pikes leveled. And Nicole la Moyte without hesitation hurled herself upon the points of those pikes, gathering death into her arms like a tender lover, and fell sidewise, crashing through the weak balustrade, to the *rez-de-chaussée,* five flights below.

But she took three of them with her, dragging them over by their pikeshafts.

Jean stood there, looking down at the broken heap at the bottom of the stairwell. Then he called over his shoulder:

"Stay inside, Fleurette!" And very quietly put out his wrists to be bound.

18

It was dark in the Conciergerie, and it stank. The ordinary prisoners, blackguards, footpads, men who made the mistake of having done murder for private ends instead of political ones, were unbelievably filthy. They dropped their excreta upon the straw upon which they slept, then wallowed in it during their rest. All visages of decency, of humanity had vanished from them. They tormented the better-class political prisoners, standing by to watch while the guards stripped gently-bred women naked, supposedly to search them for weapons, or felt their bodies under their clothing, for the same official reason. Jean saw women faint under the brutality dealt them.

It must end, he thought, it must. If they arrest Fleurette as they did Madame Desmoulins, I pray God to visit his wrath upon their heads! Was Lucienne subjected to this? At least at the end she escaped them; she had her wish—when they laid her out she was beautiful and serene. . . .

And I—how will I manage the act of dying? Bravely I hope; for I cannot claim I have not merited it. I helped to make this thing, and it matters not that it took this monstrous form so different from all I ever planned. I made it of envy, hating la Moyte because he was gay and fair. . . . Out of my sense of justice, never realizing that justice is ever a stranger to the affairs of men. Better to have died with honor at Valmy, Jemappes, Hondeschoote than this. . . .

But I've done what I could. I tried to save the crown; I labored always on the side of mercy; I've killed no one save my country's enemies.

Little Fleur, my love, how will you fare? And this child of ours that swells your tender body now, and kicks beneath thy heart? I can only pray that God will take care of you and this lovely fruit of our love; for I must leave you now, my sweet, going into deeper darkness than that in which you live. . . .

He turned to another prisoner, a small man, sitting there, his head sunk upon his breast, lost in pure despair.

"What day is this?" Jean said.

"Eh—the ninth of Thermidor," the small man said.

The ninth of Thermidor, Jean counted; that would be July 27; and I have been here five days—since the fourth of Thermidor, July 22. What has delayed them so long? So many before, I suppose—that not even Fouquier and Samson can keep abreast. Five days since Nicole died, trying to save me. . . . I was ever her evil genius; till I entered her life, she had known only peace; when I helped throw down the system that sustained her, I had doomed her already; the only difference being that I knew her as a person, living, breathing—that I loved her. And it was as a person that she died, with wild courage sacrificing her life for mine, not as an abstraction, a symbol called noble or aristocrat. Men are never abstractions, though we so label them; though we condemn them under the meaningless titles, they still die as Gervais la Moyte died, as men, going down to the ultimate loneliness.

I will die as a Dantonist-traitor; but it will not be those empty words whose heads fall into Samson's basket. It will be a creature unique upon the earth, taking with me dreams, beliefs, hopes, despairs and follies differing from those of any other man, and no sun shall ever rise again upon my like, which has no importance save alone to me.

Five days, and Fleurette has never once visited me in all that time. She is ill, there is no other explanation. There is not an ounce of cowardice in that tiny body. Of course she's ill; in her condition, any shock is likely to do her harm. . . . God keep her safe; her, and our child. . . .

But Jean was wrong. Fleurette was not ill. She was simply busy. One hour after they had dragged Jean Paul away, she dried the last hysterical tear from her eyes and sat up, saying to Marianne:

"Come, help me dress; I have things to do!"

"What things?" Marianne said.

Fleurette raised her sightless eyes, and her mouth was a line drawn hard across her face.

"I have to save my husband," she said. "What else?"

"But how?" Marianne said, terror rustling through her voice.

"I shall go to Robespierre himself, and beg for mercy. Tell me, Marianne, am I very big?"

"No—not very," Marianne said truthfully; "but it shows—"

"Good! They say that Robespierre is without pity; but I don't believe it. Jean says he once defended Desmoulins against the Committee. I think he is weak, and lets himself be driven into those positions. . . ."

"Weak!" Marianne snorted; "then how did he get where he is?"

"Because he is one of those curious people who act a part until they begin to believe it themselves. Jean says he's horribly stupid; but he believes himself a genius. What's more, he believes it so firmly, and acts the part so well that he has been able to convince the rest. There. I'm ready—come. . . ."

As Marianne led her through the streets to the house of the wealthy Citizen Duplay in the Rue Saint Honoré, where Robespierre lived, Fleurette could feel her trembling.

"Don't fear, love," Fleurette smiled; "he's only a man, remember; and we are women—hence infinitely superior! Come. . . ."

But when the domestic of Duplay mounted to Maximilien's chamber and announced that the pregnant wife of a jailed man was below seeking an audience, Robespierre snarled:

"I won't see her! You know I abhor women—and particularly pregnant ones! Send her away. . . ."

He did not sense the courage of the woman who waited below. The next day she was back again, and the next. Twice he escaped her by plunging headlong into his carriage; but he could not escape her forever.

Fleurette caught up with him finally while he was walking on the Champs Élysées with Eleonore Duplay, rich Duplay's daughter, the two of them accompanied by Robespierre's giant Great Dane, Brount.

"Citizen Robespierre," she said, clutching his arm; "you must save my husband!"

"And who, pray, is your husband?" Robespierre said in his dry voice.

"Jean Paul Marin," Fleurette blurted; "he has never done you harm and . . ."

"Marin!" Robespierre shrieked, his voice shrill, woman-ish; "*Citoyenne*, your husband was one of the most relent-less of my enemies! Save him, pah! A Dantonist, and a traitor! Why should I save him?"

But the gentle Eleonore, clutching his arm, whispered:

"Max—can't you see she's both pregnant—and blind?"

"So?" Maximilien screeched, "what is that to me? I am responsible for neither state! Come, Eleonore. . . ."

He started to walk away. But Fleurette, standing there trembling, had the last word:

"I charge you to remember, Citizen," she said, "there was once a man called Marat—and a woman named Charlotte Corday!"

Maximilien Robespierre turned, looking at her thought-fully through the thick lenses of his spectacles. He opened his mouth to reply, but no sound came out of it—no sound at all. And had not Fleurette Marin been blind, she would have seen that his face was as white as death.

There was something afoot. Jean Paul knew it. That whole night of Thermidor ninth, the streets had echoed with marching, and countermarching. From the rooftops, men waved lanterns at the prisoners, and held them up to their own faces so that the prisoners could see their smiles.

Rumors flew from cell to cell as bearded faces thrust themselves against the bars:

" 'Tis said Robespierre's been arrested! They've got him at last—" The words themselves being drowned in a wild burst of cheering. But the joy didn't last long. Close to midnight, a wild-voiced citizen appeared at the gates of the Conciergerie, crying: "All is lost! He's free! Robes-pierre is free—and they plan a new massacre of prisoners!"

Jean Paul got up from his pallet of straw. A vein stood at his temple, and beat with his blood. He bent and rubbed his stiffened limbs thinking:

When, in all this time, Jean Marin, have you played the man? Nicole died like a heroine, but you went with them —a sheep to the slaughter! Have they truly broken you then, that you accept assassination at the hands of cow-ards without a struggle?

He straightened up, and a low chuckle escaped his lips. One of the other prisoners, hearing it, went cold all over.

At Valmy I was a man, at Jemappes, more. I have cowed the mob two dozen times, but I let my spirit flag, I grew weary, and accepted too much. But nothing measures to the last inch the spirit of a man better than what he refuses to accept. . . . *Alors,* you bastards! My head may decorate your pikes; but, by my faith, it shall cost you dear!

He was moving, then, toward the iron gate that separated the huge common cell from the hallway and the outer gates.

"Guard!" he called, his voice dark thunder.

The guard came running up, fury in his face.

"Closer," Jean smiled; "I have valuable information to give thee!"

"What is it?" the guard said suspiciously.

"They plan a prison break," Jean whispered; "I tell you to gain some clemency for myself. Come closer, man; they'll kill me if they hear!"

The guard moved in, too close. Jean's big hands were about his neck, squeezing until the tint of blue appeared in the man's face.

"Your keys!" he laughed; "or by Max Robespierre's Supreme Being, you die!"

The guard had scant reason to play the hero. He passed over the keys. Jean kept his left hand about his throat, it alone having strength enough to kill him, and unlocked the door. Then, still holding the guard with his left, he smashed his right fist into the man's face with force enough to fell an ox. When he released him, the guard sank to the stones without a sound.

Jean bent over and picked him up. Weaponless, he had need of the guard, living, to persuade the others not to shoot, to let him through. Then, turning, he called to the others:

"Who is with me! Who'll make a break for it?"

They hunched in their corners and stared at him, abject terror in their eyes.

Jean stared back, then soaring, merciless, mocking, he loosed his terrible laughter.

"*Alors!*" he boomed, "die then, like the rats you are!"

He marched straight for the door, carrying the guard.

From the little hut beside the main gate another turnkey came flying out, crying:

"What ails him, is he sick?"

"Yes," Jean said; "I think he's dying. . . ."

The turnkey came close. Then:

"You're a prisoner!" he shrilled; "how on earth—"

It was the last sound he made. Jean dropped the unconscious guard with one motion, and came up from the floor, hooking the turnkey's head right and left and right again, smashing the blows home, and the turnkey, hanging there, taking it, unconscious on his feet, so that when Jean Paul dropped his hands and stood back, the man fell forward on his face.

In the little booth, there was a brace of pistols. Jean took them, sticking one in his belt, then, picking up the turnkey, because he was smaller and lighter than the guard he had intended originally to use as hostage, he cradled him in his arms, with the muzzle of the cocked pistol jammed into his throat just below his chin.

He marched on then to the outer gates. The guards sprang toward him, pikes and pistols leveled.

"*Alors,* ye dogs!" Jean laughed; "drop your pretty toys! One shot from you and your master dies!"

They fell back and let him pass, and at the street gates it was the same.

"Do not follow me!" Jean roared at them, satanic laughter bubbling through his voice; "your friend and I will make a long promenade! If you want him back again, by God's love do not follow me!"

The night's events had unnerved them; they had no stomach for such work. Jean walked along across the bridge to the Right Bank, laughing softly to himself; never in years had he found life so amusing. At the intersection of the Avenue Henri IV, and the Rue Saint-Antoine; he dropped his burden, and ran, making quite remarkable speed through the dark street.

The Rue Saint-Antoine was alive with people, though it was now one o'clock in the morning of Thermidor tenth. From them, Jean had the story:

"Yes, he was freed! The jailers at Luxembourg were afraid to receive him. They took him to the *Marie,* but the officials there are his friends . . ."

"Wait, Citizen! He's no longer at the *Marie!*" a newcomer cried; "he's broken his arrest and gone to the Hôtel de Ville!"

"Then," Jean roared exultantly, "he's *hors de loi*—he's an outlaw, now, Citizens! And he can now be shot like the whining dog he is! Let me through, *mes amis*—this, this is work for my hands!"

He bounded up the stairs toward his flat, taking them three at a time. He threw the door open, without thinking about it, until he heard Fleurette's and Marianne's double scream.

"Jean!" Marianne gasped; "Name of God! How on earth. . . ."

"Jean," Fleurette cried; "Jean, my darling, how—oh, Jean tell me how. . . ?"

"There's no time, love," Jean laughed. "I broke out of jail, but that's not important now. But know this, love—by morning I shall be a free man, or I shall be dead; but you can tell my son I died with my hands unbound and a brace of pistols in them!"

"Jean, Jean you're mad!" Fleurette whispered.

"No—sane for the first time in a long while. Fighting is my *métier*, not tame submission! Love, give me my coat, my cane, and my pistols. Marianne—powder and ball—you know where I keep them. Wrap them in something, because it's starting to rain. . . ."

He kissed Fleurette hard.

"Robespierre's at the Hôtel de Ville," he said. "This night good men must end his tyranny once and for all. We'll win, I think, my love; but if we do not. . . ."

"I can tell our son," Fleurette whispered, "that his father was a brave man, and a gallant gentleman—who died like one, not bound to a plank stained with the blood of cowards!"

"Fleur!" Marianne gasped; "how can you say such a thing?"

"Because it's true," Fleurette exulted; "only because it's true!"

Then Jean was gone thundering down the stairs.

She sat there, the remainder of the night, ignoring the discomfort of her swollen body, listening at the window until the dawn was so far advanced that she felt the sun's heat upon her sightless face, and she sitting there, still not moving, waiting, hearing far off the first rows of exulta-

tion, growing louder, louder until they rolled in to the
street below, borne on a wild rush of feet, and people
shouting:

"He's dead! He's dead! The Tyrant is slain, and the
Terror is over!"

She got up then, and went slowly down the stairs and
mingled with the crowd. She had it all from them—how
Robespierre had died screaming, how the Convention had
already decreed a general release of prisoners jailed under
the Terror.

So all he had to do was to wait, she thought, and he
would have been freed anyway. But waiting is for cowards—and my Jean is too much a man! I'm glad he didn't
wait—that he fought his way out, took his place in this,
that with his own big hands he turned the world upside
down! Such good hands, my Jean's—so strong—so gentle—

Then she heard his great laughter booming above the
roar of the crowd, and his big voice calling: "Fleurette!"
and she was off, running wildly toward the sound.

Frank Yerby's

magnificent historical novels have enthralled millions around the world . . .

Dell Bestsellers